P9-DTS-486

Serendipity

Serendipity

a novel

LOUISE SHAFFER

BALLANTINE BOOKS

NEW YORK

A Ballantine Books Trade Paperback Original

Copyright © 2009 by Louise Shaffer
Reading group guide copyright © 2009 by Random House, Inc.

Published in the United States by Ballantine Books,
an imprint of The Random House Publishing Group,
a division of Random House, Inc., New York.

BALLANTINE and colophon are registered
trademarks of Random House, Inc.
RANDOM HOUSE READER'S CIRCLE and colophon
is a trademark of Random House, Inc.

Library of Congress Cataloging-in-Publication Data

Shaffer, Louise.
Serendipity : a novel / Louise Shaffer.
p. cm.
ISBN 978-0-345-50209-4 (pbk.)
1. Mothers and daughters—Fiction. 2. Intergenerational relations—
Fiction. 3. Domestic fiction. I. Title.
PS3569.H3112S47 2009b
813'.54—dc22   2009000665

Printed in the United States of America

www.randomhousereaderscircle.com

4 6 8 9 7 5 3

Book design by Cassandra J. Pappas

For Mom and Roger, no fancy words—
just "I love you"

Serendipity ·

CHAPTER 1

New York City

2008

"I JUST PUT hairspray on my armpits," Carrie said. She told herself the shrill note in her voice was not hysteria. She was not losing it; she had merely chosen to call her ex-fiancé to tell him a funny story. He was one of her very best friends, and you shared the good stuff with your pals. "I was going for the deodorant. I kept thinking, 'Wow, this deodorant is sticky.' Then I looked at the can. The thing is, I don't know why I had hairspray—I never use it. It makes my hair look like a Brillo pad."

"Carrie? You okay?" Howie's voice came at her over the phone. And suddenly she was going to lose it after all. *How the hell do you think I am, Howie? My mother died ten days ago.*

Carrie drew in a deep breath. "I'm fine," she said.

"You sure?" Howie sounded worried—and not quite awake. What time was it, anyway? "Why are you up at four-thirty in the morning?" he added, answering the question.

"Oh God, I'm sorry. I didn't know . . ." Explanations raced through her head. *See, Howie, I've been waking up a little early . . . No, the truth is, Howie, I can't sleep. I can't eat either—nothing except potato chips. I got into them when I was hanging around the hospital . . .* She stopped herself. Because she was rambling. True, it was an internal ramble, but anytime she started wandering mentally it was a sure sign that she had lost control. And dwelling on the hospital and her mother's last days there was definitely a bad idea. Carrie had gotten through the funeral Mass a week ago, and the memorial service the day before, by not dwelling. Not dwelling had gotten her out of bed that morning and it had gotten her dressed—except for the hairspray/deodorant mishap—and now she was on her way to clean out her mother's apartment. Although possibly not right at this moment. Not at four-thirty AM. "Go back to sleep, Howie. I'm sorry I bothered you."

I am fine. I am Carrie Manning. I am thirty-seven years old. And, okay, I'm a little tense this morning because my mother's . . . not alive anymore. But I'm not going to dwell on that. Not now. Now, I'm going to think about how I got through the memorial service yesterday without crying once. I was great at that service. I didn't even tear up when they sang the Panis Angelicus.

"Carrie?" Howie's voice on the phone brought her back to reality. "Honey, you're not still freaking out about the flowers, are you?"

Okay, so I didn't get through the memorial service quite as well as I might have.

"I didn't freak out. I was upset."

"However you want to say it, Carrie . . ."

"I put it in the obituary—'No flowers'—that's what it said. It was right there in the *New York Times*. I listed all of Mother's charities so people could make donations."

"Yes, I saw that."

"I did it exactly the way she wanted it. The woman was once voted Humanitarian of the Year by *Living Life* magazine. That's what the plaque said: *Rose Manning, Humanitarian of the Year, 1986* . . ."

"I know, Carrie—"

"Her wishes for her own funeral should have been obeyed. And I got it right. I got it goddamned right!"

"Absolutely."

"Everyone knows how Mother feels about flowers. Especially roses. Why would anyone send her a basket of white roses?"

"I guess there was someone who didn't know . . ."

"After the article she wrote about Guatemalan children? The one about the five-year-old kids who pick roses and wind up with respiratory diseases and blisters full of insecticides?"

"Sweetheart, calm down."

"You know what Mother says every time she sees those cheap roses in the delis on the street. She carries her pamphlets in her purse so she can show the owners—"

"She *carried* them."

"That's what I said."

"No, you said she *carries* them. Wrong tense, Carrie."

And suddenly it was real—in a way that it hadn't been at the memorial service, or at the funeral Mass, or at the mausoleum. Now there was no way not to think about it. Her mother was gone. And Carrie was an orphan. The room went cold. There was a lingering scent of hairspray in the air.

"Carrie? Would you like me to come into the city and stay with you until my first appointment?"

"No. Thank you."

"I could bring you some coffee—from the diner on the corner, all black and bitter. None of that Starbucks-wannabe stuff."

"You're the best ex on the planet—but I really am okay. And

you need to get your sleep. You probably have a gazillion root canals today."

"Only one."

"Go back to sleep. You'll need steady hands."

And I need to get through this without dramatics.

That was what her mother had called it when Carrie was a kid and her mother thought she was getting too worked up about something. "You're being dramatic, dear," Rose would say. "Are you sure you're not trying to draw attention to yourself? That's ego, Carrie, and you must never indulge in ego. The nuns tried to teach me that when I was your age, and I wish I had listened. Just remember, you and I are just ordinary people."

That had been a lie. Carrie's mother hadn't had an ordinary bone in her body. If you looked up "not ordinary" in the dictionary you'd find a picture of Rose Manning. And she never had to try to draw attention to herself—it came to her automatically. For years it was her looks that did it. When she was young, Rose Manning's beauty was almost unnerving. Carrie closed her eyes and pictured her mother: the tall, slender body made for fashion—although by the time Carrie knew her, Rose was no longer wearing couture—the huge, green almond-shaped eyes, the high, sculpted cheekbones, and the creamy skin. Rose's thick red-gold hair was always piled in a shiny mass at the back of her head, her mouth was delicate but somehow still full, and her nose was aquiline perfection. When you put the whole package together you got a mix of ethereal and elegant that stopped conversations. And the magic had lasted for decades. When Rose died she was sixty-four, and until her last year when the cancer finally took over, she could still silence a room just by entering it.

But Carrie's mother had always been more than just a breathtakingly pretty face. She had possessed an internal power her daughter could never define or understand. Wearing one of her interchangeable skirt-and-blouse ensembles—she never spent time on wardrobe—and exhausted from a night spent volunteering at her homeless shelter, Rose could glide into a board meeting packed with Wall Street sharks and dominate. Carrie opened her eyes.

"Is it pretty out there in Katonah?" she asked Howie. She and Howie were both city people, but after Carrie had canceled the wedding, he'd relocated to the suburbs, saying he'd needed to move on. Carrie couldn't imagine anyone voluntarily not living in Manhattan, but since he was her friend—thank you, God, because she wasn't quite sure she could handle it if he weren't—she tried to be supportive. "I bet it's pretty out there," she repeated.

"It's hard to tell; it's still a little dark outside."

"Was it pretty last night before you went to bed?"

"I guess," Howie said. "There's a big bush on my front yard that was there when I bought the place, and it's starting to get all these yellow flowers on it. The guy across the street says it's a forsythia."

"I'm glad you're happy, Howie." And she was. Truly. Even though it ached a little to think that he could be happy without her. But that was only natural—right? The real point, the thing to focus on here, was that he was still her friend, that he had understood that she backed out of marrying him for his own good, because emotionally speaking she was a disaster on two feet and she didn't want to inflict the train wreck that was her life on him. Howie, bless him forever, had understood the backing-out thing for the act of love that it was. "I mean that—about me being happy you're happy, Howie," she added.

"Thanks." He paused for a second, then chose his words carefully, "Listen . . . sweetheart, why don't you hold off on clearing out your mother's apartment for a few weeks? Give yourself a break."

Because if I don't do it right now, I'll never be able to.

"I'm cool. Really."

"Of course you are!" he said, way too heartily. "I know that!"

"Thanks. Night, Howie . . . well . . . good morning." She started to hang up, but his voice stopped her.

"Carrie?" he said. "You did get it right, yesterday. You got the memorial service right."

"Thank you," she said as she put down the phone. But Howie was wrong. Carrie's eyes shifted over to the doorway, where the basket of white roses sat on the floor.

"Would you like these?" the priest had asked her after the service was over. What she should have done was to tell him, vehemently, to toss the basket into the garbage. But the flowers were lovely, a soft off-white with just a touch of pinkish blush at the heart. In the days since Rose had died, there had been many speeches given about her. Her memorial service had been packed with people who had admired and respected her. But, per her instructions, there had not been one personal touch, not one moment in which anyone acknowledged that Rose Manning had been more than an icon, that she'd also been a widow, a daughter, and a mother. No one had thought to say good-bye with something extravagant and beautiful—except the clueless sender of the white roses.

"Yes, I want them," Carrie had said to the priest, and she had taken the basket out of his hands and brought the roses home.

I failed you, Mother. I'm sorry.

CARRIE STUMBLED THROUGH the obstacle course that was her bedroom. When she'd finally left her mother's apartment in her late twenties, she'd been determined to create a cozy space for herself, and she'd splurged on several large, cushy pieces of furniture. Unfortunately, she had not measured the size of the rooms in her small home. The monster bed ate up almost all of the floor space in her bedroom, so opening the bottom drawer of the bureau was impossible unless she was squatting in the closet. For bedding, Carrie had purchased eight white pillows and a white down-filled comforter. She'd been going for Sensuous Luxury; her best friend, Zoe, said she'd achieved Marshmallow Blob.

In the living room were more puffy oversize chairs, ottomans, and a sofa. Someone had told Carrie that putting a mirror on the wall above the sofa would make the room look bigger, and she had dutifully done so. The bottom of the mirror frame jutted out from the wall, so when guests sat on the couch they had to slouch or risk losing a piece of scalp.

Carrie carefully threaded her way to the bathroom. She looked at herself in the tiny mirror. She was not the beauty her mother had been, but that was not something she obsessed about. As Zoe once said, who the hell was as beautiful as Rose? Even in a time when any woman with enough cash could buy the nose and boobs of her dreams, Rose had been in a class by herself. On the other hand, Zoe had continued kindly, Carrie wasn't exactly a disaster. At five-four, she was cute rather than regal, but she was endowed with fairly impressive cleavage, and her legs were truly fine. Her nose might have been a little too long, her dark brown eyes were probably too deep set, and her curly hair—also dark brown—was always a mess by three in the afternoon. But her smile was fabulous. When she unleashed it. "Which you don't do often enough," Zoe had said, wrapping up her assessment. "You can't get away with your mom's ice princess act. And it wouldn't hurt if you used a little makeup."

Carrie searched around in her medicine chest and finally unearthed some seldom used blush and mascara. She found her lip gloss in her purse, managed to stall another minute or two with it, then went into her kitchen and dawdled over her breakfast quotient of sour-cream-and-onion-flavored chips. But it still wasn't six o'clock yet. For some reason she didn't want to go to her mother's apartment before six o'clock. On the other hand, staying in her own apartment was out of the question. There was only one person Carrie knew—except for poor Howie—who'd be awake at this hour. Carrie put on her coat and headed out the door.

ZOE WAS ALREADY up and working when Carrie rang her buzzer. Carrie knew this because when Zoe answered the door she was wearing her work clothes—flannel pajamas with red roses on them and an apron liberally smeared with chocolate—and her blond hair was bundled up under a net. Since Zoe was six feet tall and skinny, the look was distinctive. She stood in her doorway peeling off a pair of surgical gloves and eyeing Carrie with the look of sympathy and concern that everyone had been giving her for the last year.

"Hey, Carrie. Are you—"

"New rule," Carrie broke in hastily. "Don't ask me how I am, okay?" Zoe started to speak, then thought better of it. "And we're not talking about memorial services, or funerals." *Or mothers.*

Zoe nodded. "Can I ask why you're here?"

"Not really."

"Okay. Come into the kitchen."

Actually, Zoe's entire apartment was a kitchen. She'd stashed a cot in one corner of it, and there was a closet where she kept her wardrobe, but the rest of her small studio had been gutted and fitted out with two industrial-size refrigerators, a restaurant stove, a large table at which two people could work comfortably, and several huge storage bins full of sugar and cocoa. Stacked against one wall were shipping supplies, rolls of gold tissue paper, and cases of hand-painted candy boxes. Zoe was a candy maker who sold herb-flavored chocolate truffles to the hippest gourmet groceries and restaurants in Manhattan. Since five that morning she'd been taking baking sheets covered with little frozen balls of the chocolate-

and-cream mixture known as ganache out of the fridge and dipping them into melted bittersweet chocolate—the best Belgium had to offer—before dusting them with cocoa. The ganache had been infused with a variety of flavors such as lavender and rosewater, and in the case of one client—a Mexican restaurant—hot chili peppers.

Carrie knew all of this because for two years she too had stumbled out of bed at the crack of dawn to dip and dust truffles. That was when she had been Zoe's partner in the business—a business they had started together and worked on happily, until one day Carrie felt the walls start to close in. She'd begged Zoe to please understand that she still loved her but there had to be more meaning to life than candy. Zoe had argued that they were on the verge of landing their first big account with a chain of trendy Manhattan grocery stores, which they had both busted their buns for, and Carrie would be ripping herself off if she sold out. Carrie couldn't explain why she had to dump the business which had been her idea in the first place. She just knew if she had to wrap one more truffle in one more piece of gold tissue she was going to start throwing pots of chocolate around Zoe's apartment. She'd left the business, and six weeks later, Zoe, as sole owner, had landed the coveted account. Now Zoe could afford to hire people to help with the wrapping, although she was still doing the dipping and the dusting herself. And soon she'd be reclaiming her living space because she'd be renting a professional kitchen in Brooklyn.

As Zoe swirled the first of the truffles in the coating, the hot chocolate released a whisper of a scent from the frozen ganache. Carrie sniffed the air. "Basil?" she asked.

Intent on her candy, Zoe didn't look up. "It's still the most popular flavor," she said. "Bean and Brown can't keep it in stock." She placed the coated truffles on a piece of parchment paper and prepared to start rolling them in the cocoa.

"Hang on," Carrie said. She opened the cabinet under the sink where the hairnets and gloves were kept, and suited up. "It'll go faster if we work together."

Zoe threw her a funny look, but mercifully she didn't say anything. They worked side by side in silence, falling into the familiar rhythm they'd established over so many mornings, until five cookie sheets covered with finished truffles were back in the fridge. "You still have the feel for it," Zoe said as they stripped off their rubber gloves. "You know how many people I've hired and fired over the last four months because they didn't have the touch?" She hesitated, then said, "You know . . . if you wanted to, Carrie . . . you could buy back in."

There were a lot of people who would have been pissed about the way Carrie had split right before their big contract came through. But Zoe had known Carrie since they were in grammar school and she understood Carrie's problem with follow-through. She'd watched Carrie start and abandon a dog walking service, a vintage clothing store—this was with another, less understanding partner—and a brief, horrific career as a personal assistant. Now Zoe eased herself onto one of the stools that flanked the work-table. "I'm serious," she said. "Would you like to come back?"

For a moment it sounded wonderful. For the last year, most of Carrie's time, to say nothing of her available brain space, had been spent caring for her mother. Rose's doctors had admitted early on that there wasn't anything they could do for her, and faced with that reality, Carrie had set out to make sure her mother's death was a "good" one—even though she wasn't sure she believed there was such a thing. Rose had stayed in her own apartment for as long as the medical professionals would allow it, because that was what she had wanted. Only her last two weeks were spent in the hospital. The ordeal had been so absorbing that once it was over, Carrie had found herself with endless hours she couldn't fill. And she'd

never felt so lost in her life. If she went back into partnership with
Zoe, she'd have work, and a place to go every day, and . . . And
after two weeks she knew she'd be begging to get out again.

Something ragged and painful started growing in Carrie's
chest. "The business is big now. It would be too expensive for me
to get back in," she said.

"You'd pay what I did when I bought you out."

The ragged something moved up into her throat. "You're being
too nice to me," Carrie mumbled. And she wanted Zoe to please,
please stop. Because she couldn't take nice right now. Nasty she
could handle, but nice was going to make her lose it.

"Why the hell would you want to work with me again?" she
demanded belligerently. "I've messed up everything I've ever
tried. I washed out of college; I didn't make it through six months
of culinary school."

"But you came up with a great recipe for basil truffles—"

"I've had God knows how many jobs and I've quit every one of
them. This candy thing is the third business I've tried and dumped.
I couldn't even hang in with Howie and he's got to be the sweetest
man in the world. I am a complete and total screwup, and . . ." she
stopped herself. "And why aren't you all over me right now?"

"Why would I do that?"

"I'm whining and wallowing. Why aren't you busting me for
having a pity party? That's what girlfriends do—we bust each
other. Why aren't you telling me that I made those choices and I
need to take responsibility and grow up, like you always do?"

"Old rule," Zoe said softly. "A girlfriend doesn't bust a friend
whose mother has just died."

So Carrie finally lost it. She cried loudly for a long time. After
she finally finished, Zoe pointed out that was probably the reason
why she'd come over. "And you had mommy issues even before
Rose died," she added.

"Not anymore," Carrie said.

"They're probably worse now that she's gone. You never got it all cleared up with her, and you need to do that. You know?"

Carrie did know. But she didn't want to start sobbing again. "Unfortunately it's going to be hard to have a nice long talk."

"You need closure, Carrie."

"You really should stop Tivo-ing *Dr. Phil*. And for your information, I'm getting closure. I'm going to the apartment today to clean it out."

"Alone? Don't do that."

"Why does everyone keep saying that? I can handle it." Zoe looked at her. "I'm okay. Okay?"

After a second, Zoe nodded and pulled another tray of basil truffles out of the freezer. They dipped and dusted until it was nine o'clock and there was no way Carrie could tell herself that it was too early to go to Rose's apartment.

"CAN I ASK one question about the memorial service?" Zoe said as she walked Carrie to the elevator.

"Can I stop you?" Carrie braced herself for another *Dr. Phil* moment.

"Did you invite your grandmother?"

The question was a little worse than Carrie had expected. "I couldn't," she said after a moment. "Mother wouldn't have wanted it."

"Do you think your grandmother would have come anyway?"

"Why?"

"I thought I saw someone in the back . . . she looked a little like some of the pictures I've seen . . . from the end of your grandmother's career."

"The way I understand it, if she had shown up we would have

known it. At the very least there would have been an entire brass section."

"That sounds a little hostile."

"It's just a fact. Everyone says no one could milk an entrance like Lu Lawson."

CHAPTER 2

New York City

2008

CARRIE HAILED A cab to take her to her mother's apartment on Eighty-second Street—the home where Carrie had lived for the formative years of her life—and settled back in the seat. The idea that her formidable mother's formidable mother had attended the memorial service was almost as bad as the basket of white flowers showing up. For most of Carrie's life, her mother and her grandmother had been estranged, as they said in old movies. How it had happened or why, Carrie didn't know. As far as she could figure out, the break had occurred sometime around her father's death.

Carrie let her mind drift back to Bobby Manning, the mystery daddy she'd fantasized about until she was old enough to understand how much her mother wished she wouldn't.

"He loved you" was Rose's standard answer when Carrie asked about him. But one time Rose had slipped and said, "Bobby and my mother were two of a kind." Since they'd both been show business legends, there was nothing particularly startling about the statement—it was the bitterness in her mother's sweet voice that had made a lasting impression on little Carrie.

One of the many factors that made Carrie's life so confusing—dysfunctional, if you listened to Zoe—was that she came from theatrical royalty. On both sides. Carrie's grandmother—Rose's mother—was Lu Lawson, one of the biggest stars of Broadway musical comedies in the fifties and the sixties. Carrie's father, the fabulous Bobby Manning, had written six blockbuster musicals in the sixties and early seventies without having a single flop. But it wasn't just his incredible track record that had made him such a phenomenon. Most musicals of that day were written by a team of two: one person writing the book—the actual play—and the lyrics, and the other composing the music. Bobby didn't have a partner; he wrote the entire show, music and words, himself. In interviews he said he did it that way because it cut down on the arguments. Most people in the profession said he did it that way because he was a genius. One of those who had sung his praises the loudest back in those glory years was the woman who had given him his start, his mother-in-law, Lu Lawson. But then, she'd had reason to praise Bobby. She'd starred in Bobby's first show, called *The Lady*, and she'd won a Tony for her work. Bobby had won that year too.

Playbill, the program given out at theaters before a performance, had run twin articles about Bobby and Lu when *The Lady* swept the awards. In his article Bobby admitted that he'd created the musical for Lu before he'd ever met her, when he was a nobody who had no right to even dream that the greatest woman on the American stage would take a chance on him. He'd added—charmingly—that he still couldn't believe his luck. In the picture accompanying the story he'd been clutching his Tony, wide-eyed with amazement, which made his humility even more endearing.

In her companion article, Lu said she was the lucky one. This expression of mutual admiration had taken place two months after Bobby had married Lu's daughter, Rose. That event hadn't gotten any play in the press because the bride had insisted on keeping it low-profile. And besides, the big news was the team of Bobby Manning and Lu Lawson. The world of show business had its priorities.

Rose hadn't shared any of this touching history with her daughter. There were no framed copies of Bobby's theater posters hanging on the walls of their apartment. Both of his Tonys seemed to be missing—Carrie had looked for them once—and of course there were no pictures of Lu Lawson. In fact, there were no pictures of any family members anywhere in the apartment. For years Carrie had wondered why, but that was another subject her mother didn't like to talk about, and Carrie had learned to keep her questions to herself. She'd had a few vague memories of the father who had died when she was three and the grandmother who had dropped out of her life at the same time, but if asked, she couldn't have described either one of them. And when she was growing up, she thought she was okay with it. At least, she hadn't thought about it much.

Then when she was thirteen, a gala revival of *The Lady* was planned in London. This was nothing new; her father's shows were always being revived, but this time the producers had invited Carrie and Rose to be the guests of honor at the opening night party. Rose had sent her regrets immediately. And Carrie had suddenly realized that she was not okay with that.

"Why can't we go?" Carrie demanded. She waited for her mother to start listing the meetings that could not be missed, the volunteer programs that must be supervised, the fund-raisers that must be attended, the speeches that must be given. But Rose surprised her. Instead of going on about her obligations and promises, her mother said, "That opening night won't be what you think. You're not missing a thing."

"But they're reviving *The Lady*. Zoe's mother says it was a big hit."

"Back in its day." Her mother dismissed the show with a shrug.

Carrie found herself springing to the defense of the father she had never known. "It won a lot of awards."

A tiny frown creased Rose's perfect forehead. "Theater people like to give each other awards," she said. "That's how they know next time *they'll* get one. It really doesn't mean much." She paused, then she added, "It's all about ego." Ego was the vice the nuns had warned Rose about when she was a child, and in Carrie's life it was a four-letter word. But even in the light of this damning pronouncement, Carrie didn't back down.

"But the shows must have been good if they won."

Rose sighed. "Your father wrote musicals, honey," she said gently. "People thought they were entertaining in their day, but from what I've heard, they haven't aged very well. It's not surprising— most musical comedies back then were pretty silly. They still are. It's not exactly a profound medium."

"But they do my father's shows at City Opera. They do them in London and Japan and all over the world. That's not silly."

Her mother finally seemed to realize that this argument wasn't going to go away. "Where did you hear about that?"

"People tell me things. Everyone knows who my father was."

"I see," her mother said. "Well, from now on, if anyone asks you about him, just say he was a very gifted man. That's honest— he was."

Rose turned away to indicate that the conversation was over, but Carrie couldn't let it go. "People say my grandmother was gifted too," she said defiantly. "I know you don't talk to her or see her or anything, but everyone says Lu Lawson was a real big star."

Carrie saw her mother's back stiffen. "My mother had a following," Rose said in a flat tone. "So, yes, you could say she was a star." She started toward the door.

But once again Carrie couldn't let it go. She'd wondered for too many years why there weren't any pictures of Bobby and Lu in their apartment. "Were you ever proud of them, Mother?" she heard herself blurt out.

The huge green eyes that turned back to her were full of a pain so raw, it made Carrie look away. "That part of my life is over," Rose said. "I don't believe in looking back." Then she walked out of the room.

THE FOLLOWING SATURDAY, Carrie told her mother a lie. "Mrs. Forester invited me to come hang out at Zoe's apartment," she said. Mrs. Forester was Zoe's mother and she hadn't done anything of the kind, but Carrie knew Rose wouldn't check. Her mother gave her much more freedom than other kids had because she said Carrie was responsible and mature. Carrie knew she really wasn't, but since she wanted Rose to keep her illusions, she usually wound up doing the responsible, mature thing. Which probably proved her mother was right—most of the time. Not today, but Rose didn't know that. She had a busy day planned, and she was already late for her first appointment. So, after frowning about the idea of "hanging out"—a waste of valuable time—she told Carrie to come home by four so they could get to the shelter in time to help with dinner, and hurried out the door.

Carrie waited until her mother was out of sight before she took off herself. Instead of walking north from Eighty-third Street toward the Forester apartment on Eighty-eighth Street, she headed downtown to the Library for the Performing Arts at Lincoln Center. She'd decided to do some research and find out, once and for all, about Bobby Manning and Lu Lawson.

Carrie was familiar with libraries; she'd used the one at her school to look up information for all kinds of projects. But she wasn't sure exactly how an adult one would work, or even if they'd let a kid her age in, so she'd come prepared with a story about a school project and a letter—she'd written it herself—from a nonexistent English teacher requesting that Carrie Manning be allowed to use the research facilities. She was also prepared to cry if anyone gave her a hard time.

It turned out that neither the tears nor the fake letter were necessary. A smiling woman at the main desk sent Carrie to the Billy Rose Theater Collection on the third floor, where a kindly young male librarian listened to her requests and disappeared. He reappeared a few minutes later and placed three thick theater anthologies, a pile of theatrical yearbooks dating back to 1948, and two fat folders full of loose press clippings on the desk in front of her, one folder was devoted to Bobby and the other to Lu. The clippings—mostly theatrical reviews and articles written for magazines and newspapers—weren't organized in any order, so Carrie decided to start with the books, which seemed easier to follow. Heart racing, she opened the thickest of the anthologies and started to read.

She was stunned. She'd known her father and her grandmother were big deals, but she hadn't had any idea how big. The chapter covering Lu Lawson was twenty-two pages long. At the beginning of her career, phrases like "breath of fresh air" and "adorable" had been used to describe her. The theater historian who had written the anthology said that in her early days she had "epitomized the best of the feisty female musical comedy ingénues," and, he added, later on she had "reinvented herself as a queen of her genre." Carrie noticed with satisfaction that the historian didn't seem to think that musicals were silly. "America's greatest contribution to the magical, incomparable world of live theater" was what he said about them.

There was a section of photographs of Lu Lawson in the book.

Excited, Carrie turned to it, looked at the first picture of Lu Lawson—and gasped. Her grandmother's features were as familiar as her own. Because they *were* her own. That was her mouth, and her nose, and those were her eyes looking up at her from Lu Lawson's smiling publicity photo. She started turning the pages fast. There were several full-length pictures of Lu revealing that she wasn't tall but she did have a nice bust and great legs—which thirteen-year-old Carrie hoped she'd inherit too.

All of the photos in the book were black-and-white, and most of them were posed shots taken of scenes from the various plays Lu had appeared in. But as Carrie flipped through them she was aware of a growing feeling of disappointment. The book couldn't give her the help she really wanted. *What did my grandmother's voice sound like back then?* Carrie wanted to demand. *How did she look when she wasn't dressed up for a photograph? Who was she?* And most important of all, what was so special about being an actress who worked in the live theater? What made the live theater so magical and incomparable? Frustrated, Carrie moved on to the chapter about her father.

Bobby Manning's career hadn't been as long as Lu's because he'd died when he was still quite young. But according to the anthology, he had been a man ahead of his time who had pushed musical comedy forward more than anyone since Richard Rodgers and Oscar Hammerstein. "The loss of Bobby Manning was incalculable," said the anthology writer. "There is no way of knowing where the theater would be today if he had lived longer."

I wonder where I'd be if he had lived longer, Carrie thought. Her memories of her father were misty, and she was never sure if they were actually memories or just something she'd made up because she couldn't talk about him to her mother. When she was little she'd imagined that he looked like Dan Rather—the evening news being the only television show her mother would watch.

There were many pictures of Bobby in the anthology too, and Carrie studied them with the same intensity she'd given her grandmother's. Her father had had thick, dark hair, a thin face, a long nose, and a full, wide mouth. In the photos, it looked like he'd worn a tuxedo most of the time and spent a lot of time in restaurants and going to parties. Carrie had a quick flashback of a man dressed in black and white calling out, "Good night, princess," over his shoulder as he got into the backseat of a long black car. After the car—a limo?—pulled away, the scent of a citrusy cologne lingered in the air. But the limo she thought she remembered could have been in a scene in a movie. And lots of men wore that kind of cologne. Carrie sighed. Looking at her father's pictures was as useless as looking at the ones of Lu Lawson. Once again, she didn't have any sense of what her father had really been like—or what he had done that made him so famous. Or why her mother's eyes got big with pain when she talked about him. Or why she refused to attend any of his revivals.

Carrie looked around her despondently. She'd had so much hope about what she'd find today. After all the years of not asking questions and not knowing the things all kids knew about their families, she'd thought she'd figured out a way to get some answers without her mother knowing about the betrayal. But there were no answers in the pages of the anthology. She didn't mean to slam the book when she closed it, but she did.

From across the room, the nice young librarian caught her eye and gave her an encouraging smile. He seemed to be saying it was too soon to give up. She looked at the pile of books and the two folders in front of her and sighed again. The librarian was right; she had to be patient. Her mother was always telling her that. She picked up the folder with her grandmother's name on it and began sifting through the clippings.

An hour later, she gave up. The magazine and newspaper arti-

cles were even less help than the anthology had been. She decided
to go home early and make herself something to eat so she'd have
an excuse not to have dinner at the shelter. As she picked up the
two folders, a large manila envelope fell out of the one marked
"Bobby Manning." A stamp across the front of the envelope read,
"Photograph, do not bend." Carrie opened the envelope and took
out a large photo wrapped in a sleeve of protective paper. On the
bottom of the picture was a typed caption attached with Scotch
tape. A handwritten note clipped to the top of the picture said,
"Outtake for photo shoot for lead article in *Fashionable Woman
Today* magazine. February 12, 1969. Page One. "

Carrie pulled the picture out of its paper sleeve—and stared in
disbelief. The picture wasn't another shot of Bobby Manning;
this was a full-color photo of a glorious young girl with a mane of
gleaming red-gold hair, and thick false lashes fringing her spectacular green eyes—eyes that Carrie knew well.

"Rose Manning has a fabulous jewelry collection, but she says
she's proudest of the ring hubby Bobby gave her when they got
engaged," read the caption under the picture. And there was Carrie's mother posed in front of a white silk backdrop. She was wearing a sparkling white dress that was so short, her hair fell almost to
the hem of it. Over one shoulder she'd tossed a fluffy white fur
coat, and white high-heeled boots that came up to her knees completed the ensemble. She was looking at the camera with a pouty
expression, and she was holding out her left hand to show off a
massive diamond ring on her fourth finger. There was only one
word to describe her pose—sexy.

The Rose Manning that Carrie knew said diamonds were im-
moral; they were mined by people who were virtually slaves. She
said putting on makeup was a waste of valuable time—and it was a
sign of vanity. She would never, ever smile at a camera while wearing a dress that barely covered her underpants. Carrie shoved the

picture back in the envelope and began searching through the Bobby Manning folder for the rest of the article from *Fashionable Woman Today*. There was nothing. She took the picture to the librarian's desk and showed it to him.

"It says right here that this is the first page." Carrie pointed to the caption. "Doesn't that mean that there must be more?"

"Probably. But God knows where. People are always screwing up those folders. I spend my life straightening them out. Tell you what: I'm too busy to do it today, but I'll look around next week, and if I find the rest of the article, I'll give you a call." He shoved a piece of paper and a pencil at Carrie. "Write down your home number."

Visions of her mother answering the phone and hearing that Carrie was doing research at the Library for the Performing Arts at Lincoln Center ran through Carrie's head.

"That's okay," she said hastily. "I'll come back next Saturday." And before the librarian could ask any uncomfortable questions about her reluctance to leave her phone number, she smiled sweetly at him and hurried out. But going down to the main floor in the elevator, she was more confused than she had been when she walked into the darn library. Now she had this startling new image of her mother as Rose Manning the Sex Kitten to add to all her other unanswered questions.

WHEN SHE REACHED the plaza outside the library, she saw several concrete benches. Still slightly stunned, she sat on one of them. She was trying to puzzle out the significance of what she'd just seen when she noticed a stream of people headed for the building next to the library in the Lincoln Center complex. Curious, Carrie put the mystery of her mother's astonishing picture on hold, stood up, and trailed after the crowd.

There were two theaters in the building: the Vivian Beaumont

Theater and the Mitzi E. Newhouse Theater. The women—it was
mostly women hurrying across the plaza to the theater entrance—
were coming for a Saturday matinee at the Vivian Beaumont. Carrie had never seen a play in a theater, but Mrs. Forester loved to go
to shows, and she often took Zoe, which was how Carrie knew that
matinees were performed on Saturday afternoons.

Carrie walked around, mingling with the theatergoers until she
found two women chatting energetically as they waited to go into
the theater. One was old enough to be a grandmother; the other
was young enough to be the woman's daughter. Carrie did her best
to look as if she belonged to them and followed them through the
front entrance. When she was inside, she forgot everything except
the scene in front of her. This was what she'd been looking for in
the books and magazine articles in the library! This was a theater
audience! As they poured into the lobby of the Vivian Beaumont,
the place seemed to crackle with energy. Part of it was the noise of
a hundred different conversations going strong as everyone milled
around, waiting to go into the auditorium where the stage was—
Zoe's mother called it "the house." But it was more than just the
sound; it was the sense of anticipation, the feeling of a crowd of
people looking forward to something they knew was going to be
great. Carrie circled the room, breathing in the excitement.

A bell rang and a door opened at the back of the lobby—
presumably this was the entrance to the house. A woman appeared
at the door, and people began lining up to give her their theater
tickets. And Carrie wanted, no, she *needed* to get inside. Every instinct she had said it was the only way she was ever going to understand her father and her grandmother and what they had done.

She looked around for her mother-daughter duo; they had already joined the line and were still talking. Carrie turned to watch
the woman who was taking the tickets; she seemed bored with her
job, and she wasn't really paying attention. It was now or never.

Heart pounding, Carrie moved as close as she dared to her two decoy women, and moved with the line in the direction of the auditorium. In a matter of minutes they had reached the doorway where the ticket lady was standing. Carrie's heart was thumping so loudly, she couldn't believe the lady couldn't hear it. In another second, she'd drag Carrie out of the line and say she was a liar, or a stowaway or worse. She might even call Rose. Carrie clenched her fists and braced herself. But then she was passing by the ticket taker and the woman didn't even look up. Carrie walked a few more feet through the door. She was in! She made herself breathe. And she calmed down enough to take in her surroundings.

The auditorum of the Vivian Beaumont theater was big—that was the first thing that hit her. The stage at the back wall jutted out into the audience so that people could see it from three sides. The seats were arranged in five sections that surrounded the stage; taken together, they formed three quarters of a circle. The floor, covered with a thick carpet, slanted downward toward the stage so people in the back rows could see over the heads of those in front of them. There were more seats in a balcony that curved around the theater on three sides.

An usher approached Carrie's escorts to take them to their seats; Carrie quickly backed away. There was a group of people who seemed to be hanging around at the back of the theater. According to what Zoe had told her, these were the standees. Carrie melted into their ranks, and, feeling safe, for the moment, stared at the exposed stage on which several pieces of furniture had been set.

Meanwhile, the excitement in the auditorium was escalating. A couple of latecomers had just scrambled into their seats but everyone else was sitting, rattling playbills and talking. The conversations became a buzz that bounced around the walls. Then, suddenly, the lights began to dim. Instantly the house went silent. It was eerie how quickly it seemed to happen. Now all eyes were fixed on the stage.

The theater darkened to black, and the excitement was still growing until Carrie was sure the theater couldn't contain it. But then a second later the stage was flooded with light. There was a little intake of breath from the audience as the backdrop was illuminated and the furniture on the stage was revealed to be a part of a living room set. Then there was a burst of applause, and Carrie knew the magic had begun. Part of it was the way the lights played on the stage and made everything on it seem like it belonged to a fairy-tale world. Part of the magic was the way the audience was transformed. They had started out as strangers; when the lights came up on the stage they bonded together into one large mass. There was something childlike and eager about them. Carrie wanted to run down the aisle hugging as many of them as she could grab.

At that moment, the usher came over to Carrie, flicked on her flashlight, and demanded in a whisper to see Carrie's ticket. Seconds later Carrie was shooed out of the theater. Relieved that her punishment was nothing more than a momentary embarrassment, Carrie ran all the way back to her apartment. She'd gotten what she wanted. She'd felt the magic of live theater.

LATER THAT EVENING, after Carrie and Rose had helped out at the shelter and were back home, Carrie remembered the picture of her mother that she'd seen at the library. Rose had just come out of the bathroom wearing her old chenille robe—she always changed out of her clothes as soon as she walked in the door because that way they stayed new longer and didn't have to be replaced—and she still had on the low-heeled black pumps she wore every day. Carrie stared at her and tried to reconcile this present-day mother with the one from the past.

"Why are you looking at me like that?" Rose asked.

"No reason," Carrie said.

CHAPTER 3

New York City

2008

THE CAB LURCHED to a halt. Carrie pulled herself out of her daydream and looked out the window. They'd arrived at her mother's apartment building. She paid the driver, got out of the car, and looked up at the town house where she had lived for more than twenty years—she and her mother had moved in right after Bobby's death. The apartment was on the fifth floor—it was a walk-up—and it was laid out as a railroad flat, the outside door opening onto a small entryway, which gave way to a small living room. You walked through the living room to get to a tiny kitchen and an equally tiny bathroom, and beyond that was the only bedroom in the apartment. Rose had assigned the bedroom to Carrie, announcing that she herself would sleep in the living room on a foldout sofa. She did it for all the years that she and Carrie were in the apartment together, and never once complained about the arrangement. When Carrie was a little kid, the sight of her mother opening the bed every night and stashing her clothes in the coat closet had made her feel guilty. But by the time she reached her self-centered adolescence she'd been glad her mother had a martyr complex. After Carrie left home she was sure—although she hadn't asked—that her mother never had moved into the bedroom. When Rose was sick she'd insisted that her hospital bed be crammed into the living room next to the sofa.

Carrie began climbing up the six steps of the front stoop. It was clean, she noticed. The building had been sold to the tenants as a co-op in the eighties, and since that time maintenance of the place had vastly improved. When Carrie was a kid the stoop had been crusted with the dirt of the city—and other more disgusting deposits left by sick junkies. Rose had come out every morning with a mop and a pail of water to wash away the worst of the crud.

It wasn't just the transition from a rental building to a co-op that had changed the fortunes of Carrie's former home. In the pregentrification days when Rose had moved to West Eighty-third Street, this portion of the Upper West Side had been what the real estate woman referred to as a marginal neighborhood. Little Carrie had been warned not to ride a bike on the street—not that she owned one—because it could be ripped off. Her mother had been told to carry mugging money so she would always have something to hand over if she were attacked. The common wisdom of the street back then was to never frustrate a mugger.

Now there were chic little restaurants and shops all over the West Eighties. Nannies pushed babies in strollers that cost north of a thousand dollars on the sidewalks alongside affluent young singles walking trendy dogs.

Carrie had reached the top of the steps. She took a well-used key ring out of her pocketbook. It was time for her to let herself into the building, walk up the five flights of stairs, and sort through

Rose's possessions. Her mother had intended to do that herself. "After I come back from the hospital, I'm going to put labels on everything so you'll know which charity gets what," she'd whispered to Carrie on that last morning as they waited for the ambulance. But Rose hadn't come back from the hospital. Carrie tried to push away an image of her mother looking around the ugly little living room for the last time. "I've been so happy here," she'd said.

Carrie put the key ring back into her pocket and sat on the nearly clean stoop. *Wuss*, said a voice inside her head. But she couldn't go inside. Not yet. She leaned on the side wall of the stoop and continued her mental meanderings.

AS SHE HAD told the librarian she would, the week after she'd discovered her mother's picture Carrie had gone back to Lincoln Center. And true to his word, the man had found the rest of the missing article from *Fashionable Woman Today*.

"Some idiot filed it under 'Mary Martin,' " he said wearily. "I guess it's possible to confuse Martin and Manning—if you have the IQ of an artichoke." He handed Carrie the story.

The written part wasn't very long, but there were ten pages of photos—all featuring a glamorous young Rose Manning. Carrie had looked at the images in front of her and tried to remember the time when the pictures would have been taken. The time before Bobby Manning had died.

The first few shots were no help. There was one of Rose in huge sunglasses, with a scarf tied over her hair, sitting in a red convertible that Carrie didn't recognize, although according to the accompanying caption, Bobby had a black one just like it. The car photo was followed by two pages that featured Rose's jewelry col-

lection, every glittery piece a gift from Bobby. Each item com-
memorated one of his achievements: an opening night, an award.
Carrie didn't remember ever seeing any of the jewelry either.

On the next page a caption read, "Rose shows off the entrance
to her Park Avenue penthouse." The accompanying picture showed
Carrie's mother in the foyer of a palatial apartment. Behind her was
a sweeping mahogany staircase. Above her head was a huge chande-
lier dripping with crystals. The walls and ceiling of the foyer were
draped in purple paisley silk. Carrie had a sudden flash of touching exotic fabric that billowed like a balloon. She remembered—or
thought she did—sitting on the massive stairs and waving good-bye
to someone. She remembered—or thought she did—the scent of
lemony cologne. Carrie kept turning the pages. She saw a dining
room with walls covered in gold leaf, a living room with French
doors opening onto a wraparound terrace with a four-sided view
of the Manhattan skyline, a huge kitchen, and an immense master
bedroom. Some of this grandeur seemed familiar—but once
again, she couldn't be sure. Had the photos jogged her memory, or
her imagination?

Then, on the last page, she saw two rooms she knew she remembered: the rooms that had made up her nursery suite. Pink
ruffles trimmed with white lace had been everywhere—on the curtains, the crib, and the pretty little rocking chair. The bedroom was
where Carrie had slept; the second room was her playroom, where
her toys had been kept. There were stuffed animals, board games,
books, a child-size oven and refrigerator, little tea sets and tiny pots
and pans, a dollhouse, a playhouse, and a go-cart. There was a television and a stereo player with stacks of children's records. There
were mountains of dolls: baby dolls, Barbie dolls, Ken dolls, Skippy
dolls, Madame Alexander dolls, and rag dolls. Dolls with complete
wardrobes and their own houses and cars. German porcelain dolls
in period dress that would one day be collectors' items.

There were toys that Carrie had never played with, still in the original boxes, piled on shelves that reached from the floor of her playroom to the ceiling. As she sat in the Library for the Performing Arts, thirteen-year-old Carrie remembered them.

THE STOOP WAS hard and Carrie's butt was starting to hurt. But she didn't get up. She didn't take out the key ring, unlock the front door of the brownstone, and let herself inside. She still wasn't ready to climb those five flights of stairs to her mother's empty apartment.

"Didn't you ever ask your mother why she traded a Park Avenue penthouse for that little dump you lived in?" Zoe had demanded once when they were about sixteen or seventeen.

"She wouldn't have wanted me to ask," Carrie had said.

"You lived in a frigging palace, and she took it away. Didn't that ever make you mad?"

"She didn't think she was taking anything away from me. She thought she was giving me the perfect life."

"And you believed her? Talk about drinking the Kool-Aid."

But Carrie hadn't drunk the Kool-Aid. Not totally. She'd felt guilty about it, because she knew her mother's life of self-sacrifice was noble and admirable—everyone said it was—but Carrie *had* wanted to know about the days before Rose became noble and admirable. Over the years, she'd pieced together as much of her mother's history as she could using snippets she remembered and filling in the gaps with what she'd read. An awful lot had been written about Rose Manning.

The most recent article about Rose had appeared in *People* magazine the week after her death. It had been a clip job, put together fast to make a deadline, but it followed Rose's metamorphosis from glamorous showbiz wife to philanthropic wheeler-dealer in detail.

Carrie had crammed the issue of the magazine into her purse. Now she pulled it out, and even though she'd read it enough times to have memorized it, she turned to the story again.

"When Rose Manning was the chatelaine of her Park Avenue apartment," the article began, "she was a leader of that subsection of Manhattan where the arts, society, and money come together. She went to all the good parties, gave many dazzling bashes of her own, and she was a lunchtime regular at La Toque Blanche. For dinner it was usually Sardi's or one of the theatrical watering holes in town, always on her husband Bobby's arm—that would be Bobby Manning of Broadway musical fame. Rose was a fixture on the best-dressed list, and she and her husband showed up regularly on the society pages of all the major New York City newspapers. And, of course, they went to every opening night on Broadway.

"In those days, friends say, Rose wasn't a serious person, and her concerns seemed limited to the season's new hemlines. She was married to a theatrical powerhouse and was content with that role.

"Then in 1973 Bobby Manning had a heart attack and died. It happened during a hot weekend in July. He was staying at his mother-in-law's cottage in upstate New York, where he was putting the finishing touches on his new musical. The lights on Broadway were dimmed for five minutes the night they announced his demise, and his funeral at Campbell's was attended by 680 mourners. After the ceremony, Rose Manning seemed to disappear from sight. Friends assumed she was too grief-stricken to appear in public. Nobody dreamed that she was quietly selling her Park Avenue penthouse, her furs, her car, her jewels, and her entire designer wardrobe and giving the proceeds to the Archdiocese of New York. She moved herself and her daughter into a small apartment in a risky part of town so she could cut costs and have more money to give to the poor."

There was more to the article, but Carrie already knew the rest of the tale. It really hadn't been necessary for Rose to go to such lengths to do her good deeds. The royalties from Bobby Manning's musicals and songs were substantial. There was one cash cow, a Christmas song written for *The Lady*, that was a gift that kept on giving year after year. Bobby had spent whatever he earned during his lifetime—everyone knew that—but he was bringing in enough posthumously so that Rose could have kept her penthouse and contributed, within reason, to any number of pet charities. But Rose Manning had gone for broke. Literally. And it wasn't just the charity stuff. She'd cut herself off from all her friends and all her theater connections. It was as if she'd decided to be reborn. And no one knew why.

In the beginning Rose had intended to drop off the radar—Carrie had always believed that, no matter how much Zoe laughed at the idea. When Rose gave her huge check to the archdiocese she insisted that she wanted to remain anonymous. She had asked that the money be used to purchase an old house near her church that was to be used as a homeless shelter, but she wouldn't let Father Xavier, the priest in charge of the place, put her name on it. She wouldn't even let him add her name to the donors list in her parish newsletter.

At that time, Rose had planned to support herself and Carrie by getting a job. Bobby had set up his estate in a trust with all of the income going to Rose in monthly payments. Rose couldn't disband the trust, but she was determined that every dime it generated would go to the new shelter. She was going to work for a living, like the rest of the world. That was what she told Father Xavier. Later on, after she'd become an icon, he'd repeated this conversation to the adoring press. The story added greatly to her luster, even though she had never actually followed through on the getting-a-gig part.

The problem was, Rose had never earned a dime, and she hadn't gone to college. And since she refused to trade on Bobby's old connections—or her mother's—her options were somewhat limited. But, as Rose told Father Xavier, there were thousands of women in her predicament, and she wasn't any better than the rest of them.

While she was still trying to find her fantasy job she began volunteering at the shelter, and the staff quickly realized what an amazing resource she was. No task was too difficult for Rose. With her little daughter at her side, she served meals, read bedtime stories, and wiped away tears—childish and adult. When Carrie and Rose picked up head lice at the shelter, they stood in the shampoo line with the residents and Rose cracked jokes. She shamed high-end restaurants and grocery stores into donating their leftovers to the shelter kitchen, and she bullied a local cop precinct into coaching a baseball team for the shelter kids. She could also unclog the tricky toilet on the third floor. Throughout it all, she smiled radiantly, and when Father Xavier asked her once if she really wanted to expose little Carrie to so much sadness, Rose answered with total sincerity, "I couldn't give her a bigger gift, Father. She's learning about the joy of giving now, while she's young. I wish someone had done that for me. I had to wait so many years to discover it."

It was clear to everyone that Rose had found her calling, but she was still stubbornly insisting on earning her living. Father Xavier drew her aside and gave her a lecture on the sin of pride, reminding her that God has a plan for all of us and he was willing to bet that plan did not include Rose's working as a salesperson or a restaurant hostess when she was doing so much good with her volunteer service. The priest then quoted rather heavily from Mother Teresa and St. Francis.

When Rose left the shelter that day, she wasn't smiling. And in the middle of the night Carrie was awakened by the sound of someone crying. She ran into the living room. Her mother was looking out the window, so Carrie couldn't see her face, but she could hear the sounds Rose was making: high, breathy sobs.

"Mommy?" Carrie whispered from the doorway.

Rose whirled around and swiped at the tears on her face. "Go back to sleep, Carrie," she said. Then she turned back to the window. But Carrie's world had been rocked by the sight of her weeping mother. She ran to Rose and tried to throw her arms around her waist. Rose held her off. She wasn't rough—Carrie would always remember that—but the hands that grasped Carrie's arms were steely. "Leave me alone," Rose whispered. "Just leave me alone!" She turned away again and went back to staring out the window at Eighty-third Street. She seemed to have forgotten Carrie's existence. Carrie watched her for what seemed like a very long time, then Rose drew in a deep, shuddery breath. "All right," she said into the darkness. "I have to take his money." When Carrie tiptoed out of the living room and went back to her bed, Rose didn't turn around.

After that night, Rose's radiant smile vanished for a while. Carrie remembered being aware of her mother's darker mood—not in any specific way; she just had a general feeling that her mother was going through a bad time. But Rose's mood lifted as Christmas approached. She was full of plans for the shelter. She and Carrie would spend all of Christmas Day there, and in the morning they'd play Santa Claus. Rose bought warm coats, gloves, sneakers, underwear, and jeans for the residents—she was now calling them "our family." She bought necessities like soap and toothpaste, and little luxuries like Jean Naté toilet water, pretty scarves, and sparkly barrettes. She wanted Carrie to participate in the gift giving too. They had a serious talk, and Rose pointed out that there really wasn't room in their new apartment for all the toys Carrie had

brought from her nursery suite on Park Avenue; in fact, there were
cartons they hadn't unpacked that were full of toys in their original boxes because Carrie had never played with them. So didn't
Carrie think it would be in keeping with the spirit of the season to
donate those unused items to kids who had so little? Even though
they could have bought presents, that wasn't the point. Giving was
what the season was all about, and Rose just knew when Carrie saw
the joy on those children's faces she would so happy. Carrie was
four years old—she'd had her birthday that summer—and a lot of
things adults said slipped by her. But one thing was clear to her:
whatever they were talking about was making her mother happy.
So she agreed. With Rose's enthusiastic approval, she chose a few
well-loved toys to keep and sat down with her mother to wrap up
the rest of her hoard in red paper with reindeer on it.

From the get-go, Carrie could remember being a little uneasy
as her possessions disappeared into the mound of brightly colored
packages. But her mother was smiling, and Carrie didn't want to
make the unhappiness come back. Besides, she never thought she'd
be giving away her toys forever. In her mind, the whole exercise
was a kind of game in which her stuffed animals and dolls would
be wrapped, opened, and then returned to her, the rightful owner.

Carrie enjoyed wearing her Santa hat at the shelter when she
and her mother handed out their presents in the dayroom. She got
caught up in the happiness of the kids, who were tearing off the
wrapping paper and screaming with delight. Then, after all the
presents had been opened, she sat and waited for her property to
be handed back to her. When it didn't happen, she was a little per-
plexed but not really worried. As soon as the adults had retired to
the kitchen to put the final touches on the holiday dinner, she
began going around the dayroom collecting her belongings.

The kids at the shelter were used to disappointments, and most
of them gave the presents back without a fuss. But Angel Ro-

driguez, age five, was made of sterner stuff. He held on to his gift—a large and gorgeously plush dinosaur—for dear life.

The battle that ensued was surprisingly close considering that Angel was male, had a year on Carrie, and was used to protecting his few possessions from his siblings and friends, whereas Carrie had never been in a physical fight before. By the time the adults came racing into the dayroom, Carrie was on the ground, but she had discovered that her teeth could be used as a weapon, and Angel had dropped the dinosaur. It took several seconds for Rose and Angel's mom to separate them.

Rose was appalled. She picked up the toy and dragged Carrie to a corner. "How could you, Carrie?" she whispered. "How could you take anything away from that little boy?"

"It's mine," Carrie sobbed as she tried to grab for the dinosaur she'd won fair and square.

"We talked about this. You agreed to give away the things you never play with—"

"I want them back!" Carrie cried. "They're mine!"

A look composed of disappointment and sorrow filled her mother's beautiful green eyes. When she spoke, her voice was disappointed and sad too. "Carrie," she said, "Angel doesn't have a home. Before he came here he used to go to bed hungry. You've always had whatever you needed." Then her mother said the words that she would repeat for the next thirty-three years of Carrie's life. "I expect you to be better than this, Carrie." She handed Carrie the dinosaur. "I'm sure when you think about it you'll want to do the right thing." And she walked away.

Carrie did want to do the right thing. And she wanted to make her mother happy. But she didn't want to give up the dinosaur. Across the room, Angel was sitting in his mother's lap. He was sucking his thumb and his mother was whispering things in his ear, trying to soothe him. Carrie looked down at her shoes. They had buckles on them, and Carrie was pretty sure those buckles would hurt if she were to kick someone really hard. The fight for the dinosaur would be won in a matter of seconds.

Then Carrie looked up and saw that her mother had walked over to the enemy camp. Rose was smiling encouragement at her, waiting for her to give the toy back to Angel. Carrie stayed still as long as she dared. Rose continued to smile. Finally Carrie capitulated and walked slowly across the room. She held out the dinosaur. Angel's mother took one look at Carrie's face and stopped her son from grabbing the prize, but Rose said softly, "Carrie wants Angel to have it, don't you, darling?" Her eyes were shining. Carrie nodded her head. Angel grabbed the dinosaur and it was at that moment that the photographer who had been hired to record the shelter's first Christmas for the cardinal's holiday bulletin got a sweet shot of little Carrie Manning in her Santa hat handing over one of her very own toys to a kid named Angel Rodriguez. Angel clutched his booty and gave Carrie a sneer of triumph. Carrie wondered how hard she'd have to kick him to make him bleed.

But then the photographer got a second picture that was even sweeter than the first one when Carrie's beautiful mommy scooped up her little girl in her arms and said joyfully, "That's my girl! You're going to be so happy you did this, Carrie."

No one knew it yet, but those shots were the beginning of Rose's career as a humanitarian. They also started Carrie's career as a fraud.

CHAPTER 4

New York City

2008

CARRIE SHIFTED ON her stoop. After all the years, she still wondered what would have happened if the photographer hadn't been in the exact spot to take those first pictures. Because somehow those shots of Rose and Carrie were leaked to a little freebie newsletter that grocery stores and shops on the Upper West Side handed out to customers. Rose and Father Xavier never did find out how it happened—the photographer swore she hadn't done it—but the pictures caused a stir. Part of the reason was that the story of the mother-and-daughter philanthropists was so heartwarming. But most of the buzz was about Bobby Manning's widow, who had been out of the public eye for so long, suddenly resurfacing as an angel of mercy. Several other newspapers and a couple of talk radio shows picked up the story ("The society queen who became Lady Bountiful" was the way one of the radio shows led off). So many people wrote to the archdiocese to ask about Rose that she and Father Xavier created a boilerplate letter with her signature on it, which provided information about the shelter. People started donating money after reading about the suffering of the residents, and the higher-ups in the church took notice. Rose was asked to make a speech on behalf of the shelter at a luncheon given by the Starling Enterprise, one of the biggest charitable foundations in the city.

"I can't," she told Connie Haggerty, the social worker who donated a few nights a week to the shelter. "Father Xavier should do it." They were sitting in the director's office—which was empty because so far the shelter hadn't found a director who would work for free—and drinking instant coffee with powdered creamer. Connie Haggerty studied Rose for a moment. "What do you think of this place?" she asked. "You think it's doing a good job?"

Rose had been pondering that question for weeks, and she unloaded with passion. "We're putting Band-Aids on cancer. We give a woman and her children a roof for sixty days and we try to funnel them into city housing. Most of them will be back in a place like this within a year, because we didn't deal with the problems that landed them here in the first place. We should be offering job training, counseling, therapy, GED classes, language skills, treatment for drug addiction and alcoholism, day care for mothers who have gotten back on their feet . . ." She slowed down the litany. "And all of that costs. And most of the money for this place comes from me. And I'm a few million short of being able to provide all that. We need outside help."

"Say it just like that and you'll have the Starling people eating out of the palm of your hand," said Connie.

"But Father Xavier is much more knowledgeable—"

"Have you ever sat through one of his speeches? I never knew there were that many quotes from St. Francis. Besides, you'll photograph better than he will."

And so Rose gave her speech to the Starling Enterprise and walked out with one of the biggest checks the organization had ever given the Catholic Church. The archdiocese set up speaking engagements for Rose with three other foundations—by now she was speaking on behalf of the church's charities throughout the city. She brought home the bacon each time. The archdiocese asked her to become the director of the shelter because they wanted her to have a title when she spoke in public. They never expected her to actually take charge, but it turned out that she had a gift for administration. Connie Haggerty was hired full-time and the shelter began offering a variety of new services.

A couple of years into Rose's tenure as director, *New York* magazine asked to do an interview with her. She was torn, because it felt dangerously close to an ego trip. On the other hand, she knew publicity translated into bucks, and the level of publicity she'd get from *New York* magazine would be big. She put on her simplest blouse-and-skirt outfit, brought the reporter to her humble little home on the wrong side of town, fed him a salad she'd bought from the local deli, established that his name was Al and hers was Rose because she hated formality, and then, with her daughter, Carrie, sitting at her side, she told the man, who was by now thoroughly entranced, that he could ask her anything he liked.

He kicked off with the question she had been expecting because even though Bobby had been dead for two years, there was still a certain segment of New York that would always think of her as his widow. "Mrs. Manning," he said, "your late husband was one of the great men of Broadway, and your mother was a big star, yet you have chosen to walk away from all of that. I think most people would wonder why."

Rose had her answer ready. "Al, I want to show you something," she said, and she brought him into her little kitchen and stood in front of her refrigerator. The door was covered with children's artwork, all done in crayon. Some were brightly colored freehand pictures, while some had been ripped from coloring books and had been painstakingly filled in with pale pastels. "These are pictures the kids at the shelter have made for me," Rose said. "They give them to me to put on my refrigerator because none of them has one. I've promised them that their pictures will stay right here until each of them has a kitchen of their own. It's my mission, and the kids and I call it Project Fridge. Now, I want you to tell me what Broadway opening night, what designer dress or big party, could possibly be as important as the hope of these children for homes and a decent life? And I am privileged to share in their hope. What more could I ask for?"

Al the reporter couldn't write it all down fast enough, but Carrie could have given the man a slightly different perspective on Project Fridge if he had asked her.

PROJECT FRIDGE HAD evolved like so many things in Rose's life, by accident—or perhaps serendipity might be a better word. It had happened when Carrie was six. In addition to her duties as director of the shelter and unofficial spokesperson for the archdiocese charities, Rose still insisted on spending several hours a day with the homeless kids. "I need to remember why I'm doing this," she told Connie.

When Kenisha McKnight and her family came to the shelter, Rose took the sad-eyed little girl under her wing. The McKnights' story was different from those the staff usually heard. There was no history of drinking or addiction, no spousal abuse—just the slow death of a father who hadn't had health insurance, and a mother who couldn't earn enough to bail the family out after he was gone. Kenisha's two brothers had settled in to their new life at the shelter, but Kenisha sat alone, not speaking. Rose had seen it happen before: one child would take all the clan's defeat and heartbreak on his or her shoulders. Rose was determined to get through to Kenisha.

She finally had success when she gave Kenisha a coloring book and some crayons. The little girl picked the softest of the pastel colors, worked diligently to stay within the lines, and then handed her picture to Rose. Thrilled by her success, Rose said it was the best present she'd ever been given, and then in a moment of pure inspiration added that she was going to take it home and put it right in the middle of her refrigerator. Kenisha's sad eyes lit up. She turned out a second picture, which was lovingly taped on Rose's refrigerator, and Rose took a photo of it to give to Kenisha, who now was eating with the rest of the kids at mealtime. Soon other kids at the shelter wanted their pictures on the director's refrigerator, and thus Project Fridge was born. All of it made Rose very happy. For days she smiled the radiant smile her daughter loved. Carrie decided to put that smile on her mother's face herself. She too would make artwork for the refrigerator. But hers would not be some dumb little picture that was so pale you could barely see it. She was going to make a masterpiece.

Creativity was encouraged in Carrie's public school; there were three deep drawers full of art supplies in her first-grade classroom. Even so, Carrie's teacher, Ms. Margulies, was a little dubious about the size of the project Carrie was proposing and tried to persuade her to scale it down. Carrie refused.

"It's for my mommy," she explained.

Ms. Margulies agreed that in that case it had to be special, and wasn't Carrie's mother a lucky lady to be getting such a magnificent present? Carrie nodded proudly.

The final product *was* magnificent. It was large—big enough to cover the entire top section of the front of their refrigerator. There was no specific subject; Carrie had filled her painting with swooping free-form strokes of purple, yellow, orange, green, and blue. Then, still not satisfied, she cut gold and silver paper into stars and pasted them on. Finally, she'd mounted the whole thing onto the brightest red posterboard she could find. When it was finished, she stood back and looked at it, completely satisfied. This picture was worthy of her beautiful mother. This would make her mother happy.

"It's so good, I wish I could put it up on the bulletin board in the hallway," said Ms. Margulies. But of course Carrie was taking it home.

She wrapped it in newspaper to protect it when she walked from school to the apartment, and she waited impatiently for her mother to come in. When she did, as usual, Rose had a new offering for Project Fridge, and she headed straight for the kitchen to tape it to the refrigerator door. Barely able to contain her excitement, Carrie burst in after her.

"This is for you!" she announced breathlessly, and handed her mother the masterpiece. "Do you like it?"

"It's lovely," Rose said. She didn't smile her radiant smile that the shelter kids got, but she did give Carrie a hug. Then she looked more carefully at the picture. "They really do a wonderful job of fostering creativity at PS Sixteen, don't they?"

She handed the picture back to Carrie.

That's it? Carrie thought. After all the weeks of work, after all the hours spent anticipating her mother's delight, this couldn't be the only response.

"But do you like it?" she demanded. "Do you really like it?"

"Of course I do. And I'm so grateful we live in a neighborhood with one of the best elementary schools in the city. We just need to keep reminding ourselves how lucky we are."

And then, instead of taking the Project Fridge pictures off their refrigerator to make room for Carrie's gift, Rose brought it into the living room and propped it up on the chest of drawers where she kept her clothes. Carrie knew she could have asked her mother to put her painting on the refrigerator, but she wanted Rose to do it on her own—that was the whole point.

Carrie waited three days. For three days Rose brought home sketches and scribbles from the shelter, taped them on the refrigerator door—by now she had so many she had to rotate them—and took photos to bring back to the kids. Carrie's painting stayed propped up on the chest of drawers. On the fourth day, Carrie broke down and cried. When she was told the reason why, Rose was contrite. "But Carrie, why on earth would you want to be a part of Project Fridge?" she asked. "You and I have a kitchen—and a home." Then she added, "And you probably didn't think about this, but your painting is so big that we'd have to take down all the other children's drawings. I'm sure you wouldn't want that, would you?"

Carrie the fraud had taken a fast look at her mother's anxious frown, swallowed her tears, and said, "No. I wouldn't want that. Absolutely not." For her lie she was rewarded with the radiant smile the shelter children got.

A week later Carrie tore up her picture and threw it into the trash can on the corner of the street. As far as Carrie could tell, her mother never realized that it was gone. Certainly, she'd never mentioned it.

THE REPORTER FROM *New York* magazine had finished the interview, and he was putting his tape recorder away in his bag when suddenly he turned to Carrie. And as if he'd been reading her thoughts, he said, "Carrie, what do you think about Project Fridge?"

Naturally Carrie wasn't going to tell him she'd wanted her mother to take all the other pictures off the refrigerator and put hers up.

"I think it's a wonderful thing for me to have the Project Fridge refrigerator in my house," she said charmingly. "It reminds me of how lucky I am. Not just because of the material things I have; I'm so proud to have a mother who does so much to help people." She could see that the reporter was impressed; he was making notes again. But her mother wasn't looking very happy. "I'm just glad I get to be a part of my mother's work." She finished up quickly as she watched Rose.

Sure enough, after the reporter left, Rose sat on the sofa and motioned to Carrie to sit next to her. "Carrie, we need to have a talk about being in the public eye," she said in a troubled voice. "We get attention because of the things we do, but we can't let it go to our heads. I know sometimes that's a temptation, and I think you were giving in to it just now, which is why I'm trying to warn you. We talk to the press because it's publicity for the shelter and the families. It's not about us. If we forget that, we're just on a big ego trip."

OVER THE YEARS, Rose herself had to guard against the lurking dangers of the ego trip more and more. Her prowess as a fund-raiser was amazing. Celebrities and politicians liked to be seen on the same dais with her at philanthropic events. She was admired because she not only talked the humanitarian talk but walked the walk. At Christmas she and Carrie figured out what they would have spent on presents for themselves and donated the amount to charity. They did the same thing on their birthdays. When asked about this—usually by the adoring press—Rose said it made her happy to celebrate that way. Carrie the fraud agreed eagerly. Later on, when Carrie was a teenager, if she wanted a new pair of shoes or the latest CD, the look of disappointment would cross Rose's beautiful face and she would ask in her gently reproving voice, "Do you really need it, dear?" And Carrie would backtrack fast and say no, she really didn't—not when you thought about the needs of kids who didn't have enough to eat.

There was only one time when Carrie balked. She had gone to a public elementary school, but the public high schools in Manhattan were notoriously bad. Even Rose felt a little dubious about Carrie's continuing in the system, but she wanted Carrie to give it a try before they picked out a nice parochial school. Carrie refused. Her best friend, Zoe, would be attending a pricey academy known as the Dearborn School, and that was where Carrie wanted to go. No amount of guilt-tripping or arm twisting would change her mind. Rose lectured about kids they both knew—who were no less entitled than Carrie, after all—who had to bounce from school to school, never settling long enough in one place to get a decent education, because they were homeless. She threw in the plight of the youngsters who were forced to go to schools that were death traps in neighborhoods that were war zones. But Rose's look of disappointment and sorrow had no effect. Carrie said if her mother wouldn't pay for Dearborn, she was going to apply for a scholarship. Carrie was a straight-A student who aced any test that was put in front of her, so there was a good chance that she might actually follow through on her threat and deprive some child who really needed the help. Rose agreed to send Carrie to Dearborn.

It wasn't as wonderful as Carrie had thought it would be. The rich kids at her school had never been taught about the joy of self-sacrifice. They could understand why a scholarship kid didn't have the de rigueur jacket from Charivari and didn't go skiing in Aspen during Christmas break, but Carrie wasn't poor. The Dearborn kids tried to figure out where Carrie fit in their world, and came up empty. They labeled her weird and ignored her for six years. Her only real friend was Zoe.

CHAPTER 5

New York City

2008

LEANING AGAINST THE wall of the stoop had started to give Carrie a crick in her neck. She eased herself into an upright position and was feeling around in her pockets for her mother's key ring when she heard a familiar voice say, "I thought I'd find you here." Carrie looked up to see Zoe, sans hairnet and work pajamas, standing on the step below her.

"I went to that Starbucks on Amsterdam to look for you before I came here," Zoe said as she sat down on the stoop. "I figured when you realized you couldn't face your mother's apartment you'd stall by having a latte."

"Starbucks lattes are an evil force sent to destroy civilization as we know it," Carrie said. "Remember when you couldn't walk around the city without tripping over a Mrs. Fields cookie joint? Hundreds of little mom-and-pop bakeries died because those cookies—which were usually raw, by the way—crowded them out.

There was a Hungarian guy who had a bakery over on Columbus that had been there for forty years."

"Wasn't he closed down for selling drugs?"

"My point is, these plagues are sent to us from foreign lands like California and Spokane for the purpose of stripping the city of everything that makes it the city. Mrs. Fields is now an afterthought, and Starbucks will go the way of all fads, but first it will take out all the old Greek coffee shops, and—"

"And you still can't make yourself go into your mother's apartment," Zoe said. "Want to know how I know this? First, you're rambling; second, whenever you start pontificating about the Americanization of Manhattan, you're scared about something else; and third, you've been sitting on this filthy stoop for more than an hour."

"I'll have you know, they clean this stoop every morning."

"This is New York; they could clean it every five minutes and it still wouldn't be clean enough for you to take up permanent residence on it." Zoe stood up. "Carrie, either go into your mother's apartment with me now, or go home."

"Do you have the time?" Carrie asked.

"I made the time."

Carrie handed Zoe the key ring.

THE APARTMENT ALREADY had the feel of a place where no one lived. Rose hadn't had much furniture: the sofa where she slept, the dresser where she kept her clothes—where Carrie's masterpiece had languished—an old-fashioned trunk that had served as a coffee table, and two chairs. All of it had been jammed up against the walls to make way for the gurney when the paramedics had come to take Rose to the hospital that last time. Carrie had an impulse to drag the sofa back to its original spot. She could still see the depressions its legs had made in the ancient carpet. Then she looked at the floor more closely. There was something white and shiny hidden in the pile of the rug. She picked it up. And then she had to swallow very hard. She turned to Zoe and held out the object.

"It's Mother's rosary," she said. "It's the one her grandmother gave her when she made her First Communion. She always kept it in this little gold-plated case with a red velvet lining . . ." She had to do some more swallowing. "She started using it again when she got so sick."

Zoe, who had been raised by former hippies, had never gotten the religion thing. "Oh," she said politely.

"She must have dropped it when they took her to the hospital . . ." Carrie stopped herself because she was going to start crying again.

"Carrie," Zoe started to say, but Carrie shook her head. She jammed the rosary in her pocket.

"Mother kept most of her clothes in the closet, and the dresser," she said in her most matter-of-fact voice. "I'll take care of them. Would you check out the trunk?"

Zoe nodded and headed in silence for the trunk. Equally silent, Carrie opened the closet where Rose's blouses and skirts hung in a neat black-and-white row. Carrie realized with a start that it had been months since she'd seen her mother in her uniform—the vision of Rose at the end, in her hospital nightgown and her old chenille robe, flashed through Carrie's brain—and she had to fight an urge to run. She forced herself to reach into the closet and take a blouse from the hanger. It was easier, she found, once she was actually holding the thing in her hands. It was just a bunch of cloth; it didn't even smell like Rose. If it had, Carrie wasn't sure she could have taken that. She folded the blouse and started taking the rest of the clothes off the hangers.

In a matter of minutes the closet was empty—except for one item. It was hanging in the back, right where Carrie knew it would be. She reached in and carefully took out a beige chiffon evening gown. The bodice was cut like a shirtwaist, buttoned up to the neck, and it had long sleeves and a beige satin collar and cuffs. The skirt was full, with two layers of chiffon that swept the floor. The gown was the kind of classic garment that had never gone out of style because it had never really been in; Rose had purchased it in the early eighties and she had worn it for the next two and a half decades whenever she had to attend a black-tie outing. She had disliked the balls and glittery events at which the wealthy rewarded themselves for doing good works. "They could just donate the cash," she complained. "It would be cheaper for them and a lot less time-consuming for us." But the charity party circuit couldn't be avoided. So she'd bought her one gown and worn it season after season. And, as with everything she did, the gown became a part of her walking-the-walk image. The press took pictures of Rose in her vintage dress, and somehow her nobility seemed to rub off on everyone in the room. As Zoe once said, "That gown has gravitas." It hadn't hurt that Rose looked fabulous in beige.

Carrie held up the gown so the hem wouldn't pick up any dust from the carpet. "It looks as if it's never been worn, doesn't it?" she said to Zoe. "After twenty-five years, how the hell did she do that?"

When Zoe answered, her voice sounded a little strange. "Uh . . . Carrie," she said, "you might want to come here and look at something." Carrie put the gown back in the closet and hurried over. Zoe had taken something out of the trunk, something that was carefully wrapped in tissue paper so it wouldn't wrinkle. Carrie pushed the tissue aside and saw a beige chiffon gown cut like a shirtwaist with long sleeves, a floor-length skirt, and satin collar and cuffs. She took it out of the paper and shook it out.

"It's a clone," she said.

Zoe nodded.

"She had the gown reproduced."

"Several times," said Zoe. "There are two others in the trunk."

"That's how she kept it looking so good. It was her signature getup, so she had it copied. Everyone thought she had just one . . ."

"There's something else," Zoe said.

"If you're going to tell me she wore mascara and lip gloss, I already knew that," Carrie snapped. She couldn't seem to take her eyes off the clone gown.

"Here," Zoe said, and shoved something at her. It was a book with a fake white leather cover that looked like an album—or a scrapbook. Carrie dropped the gown on the floor and took it. It was full of press clippings. Rose Manning's press clippings.

Carrie sat on the floor near the gown. "She kept the stories they wrote about her," she heard herself say.

Zoe slid down to the floor next to her. "It looks as if she didn't start until the eighties," she said in a soothing voice. "So you were right. In the beginning she meant to keep a low profile."

"She said when people told us how terrific we were, we couldn't let it turn into an ego trip . . ."

"So she kept a few newspaper articles. Carrie, she helped a lot of people . . ."

"She said we had to remember that we weren't doing it for ourselves. It was for the shelter and the families. Our motives had to be pure. I thought she meant it."

"She did. She just wasn't quite as pure as you thought."

"But she told me she was," Carrie said childishly.

"It's just a scrapbook . . ."

"I believed her. Everyone believed her."

"Why don't we get out of here for a while?" Clearly Zoe had decided Carrie was fragile.

Carrie pulled the rosary out of her pocket. "Mother never went to Communion," she said.

"We don't have to clear out the whole apartment today."

"I never told you about Mother not going to Communion—did I?"

"We can come back when you're up to it—"

"She went to Mass every Sunday—sometimes she went during the week too. I went with her—"

"We'll go get some lunch—"

"I went up for Communion, but she never did. Not once."

"There's a great little greasy spoon on Eighty-sixth and Broadway . . ."

"When everyone else went up to the altar she'd get this look on her face, like she was really hurting . . . and then she'd stay in her seat, praying."

"Okay, praying is a good thing—right?"

"It's not a substitute for going to Communion! In the old days not going to Communion was a heavy-duty sin for Catholics."

"Carrie . . ."

"I never asked her about it. I never asked her about my father, or my grandmother . . . I never asked her about anything."

"I know, Carrie."

"Who was she? She was the most important person in my life, and I never knew anything about her."

"So find out. It's time."

In the end, Carrie had given up on the apartment and gone with Zoe to the greasy spoon, where she'd broken her potato-chip fast with a bagel and a schmear. But she'd insisted on bringing the scrapbook, the rosary, and the three gowns with her. She'd crammed them into shopping bags so when she and Zoe sat in the booth at the Star Coffee Shop they were surrounded by a sea of beige chiffon, and then she had schlepped the bags back to her apartment. Now, having taken them into her bedroom, Carrie was wondering what to do next. The contents of the scrapbook would be toast as soon as she could buy a shredder, the rosary went into a drawer, but how was she going to get rid of three identical beige gowns? Giving them to a thrift shop was out of the question, because someone might recognize them.

Protecting Mommy's dirty little secrets? sneered a nasty voice inside her head. She told it to go to hell, stashed the shopping bags under her bed, and lay down on top of it. In the coffee shop, Zoe had said again that Carrie owed it to herself to find out more about her mother's past. It was one of those pieces of advice that seemed to be healthy and obvious—until you asked yourself how you were going to do it. There were probably hundreds of people in New York who had claimed Rose Manning as an acquaintance, but had any of them really known her? Carrie thought back to Rose's memorial service, which had been one long tribute to her work, without a personal note. Except for . . .

Carrie sat up, climbed off the bed, and ran into the living room. The basket of white roses was in the corner where she'd left it. There was a card attached to a tulle bow on the handle. Carrie ripped it open and read it quickly. The flowers had been sent by someone named Uncle Paulie. But Rose had been an only child—she hadn't had any brothers who could now be calling themselves Carrie's uncle. Same thing for Bobby Manning. Carrie looked at the card again, this time taking her time to decipher the florist's handwriting. It said, *For Little Rose, with love from her Uncle Paulie.* The sender was *Rose's* uncle. Carrie tried to think back to the research she had done when she was thirteen. As far as she could remember, Lu Lawson had had six brothers, and the family had originally come from New Haven, Connecticut. Lu's real name had been Lucia Leporello. It wasn't a lot to go on, but it was worth a try. Carrie picked up the phone and dialed Connecticut information.

CHAPTER 6

Connecticut

2008

DRIVING WAS NOT one of Carrie's skills. As a Manhattan kid used to public transportation, the first car as a rite-of-passage tradition hadn't registered with her—which was a good thing, since there was no way in hell Rose would ever have bought her a vehicle. Carrie had finally taken driving lessons when she was attending cooking school because the Culinary Institute was located in upstate New York, where there were no subways, but she never really relaxed when she was behind the wheel. She couldn't forget that she was operating a machine that could maim and kill. After quitting the institute, her first act had been to sell her car and stop driving as a public service.

But now, once again, she was behind the wheel—this time of a rented Volvo because someone had told her they were safe cars—on her way to a satellite suburb of New Haven, where she was going to meet her great-uncle Paulie. Finding him had proved to be easy. He'd stayed in the city of his birth and there was only one Paul Leporello listed with New Haven information. Carrie had dialed his number and he had picked up on the second ring. He lived in a place called Seaview Manor—he called it "the joint"— and he would be happy to talk to Carrie about her family.

"It's going to be a total waste of time," Carrie had moaned to Zoe. "Seaview Manor is a nursing home, and Uncle Paulie's eighty-three. I'm going all the way out to the wilds of Connecticut to ask an old man who probably can't remember his name why my mother cloned her gown and kept a secret stash of press clippings. He's not going to be a help. He's not going to know why my mother and my grandmother didn't speak to each other for thirty-four years."

"You are not allowed to back out on this," Zoe had said sternly.

"Did I mention I'll be driving on major highways? The speed limit will probably be astronomical."

"We're talking about Connecticut, not the autobahn. Stay in the slow lane."

"Clearly, the man didn't know anything about my mother. Sending those roses, for God's sake."

"Okay, forget Uncle Paulie. Call Lu Lawson and get the story from her."

"Are you and Howie channeling each other these days? Because he keeps telling me the same thing."

"Howie's a smart guy."

"But Lu's old too. She probably can't remember any more than Uncle Paulie."

"She's three years younger than he is. And she's together enough to live in her own home."

But calling her grandmother was impossible. It was bad enough that Carrie was poking around her mother's past trying to uncover secrets Rose had wanted to keep hidden. Calling the woman against whom her mother had issued a lifetime fatwa would be a postmortem betrayal Carrie couldn't handle.

"I know in the World According to Rose, Lu Lawson was the enemy," Zoe went on, "but you're going to have to talk to your grandmother someday. She is your family, after all."

Carrie looked at her best friend. Zoe's mother and grandmother had gone on peace marches together in the sixties. When Zoe was a kid, she and Mrs. Forester had bonded at Saturday matinees. Zoe was Carrie's oldest and dearest friend, but there were some things she'd never understand.

"I can't go see Lu because . . . I can't change my plans," Carrie had said. "I told Uncle Paulie I was coming, and I bought a map of Connecticut."

"You are aware that that excuse is not only lame, but it doesn't make sense—right?"

"Yeah, but it's the best I've got."

So now Carrie was trying to stay in the slow lane of the Merritt Parkway—which was also the lane where cars merged, and she could never remember if she was supposed to slow down or outspeed them—as she drove past the towns of Connecticut looking for an exit she knew she was going to miss. She cursed herself for going on a fool's errand.

SEAVIEW MANOR WAS not the Dickensian nursing home Carrie had been picturing. It featured a large white clapboard building that looked more like a Victorian mansion than a warehouse for the elderly. It had been built on a cliff overlooking the ocean, and even from the car, the view was spectacular. Carrie opened her window and breathed in salt air.

The interior decor continued the Victorian mansion motif—there was a lot of lacy wicker furniture with comfortable cushions, and large pots of colorful flowers were scattered everywhere. Two card games were going strong at tables near the front windows, and there was a television at the far end of the room where several people had congregated to watch a cooking show. It was only after a second look that Carrie realized how many walkers and canes were leaning up against chairs and how many of the chairs had wheels. She made her way to the main desk, but before she could speak, a voice called out, "Carrie?"

Uncle Paulie was spry on his feet; no cane or walker for him. And he was a natty dresser—which Carrie liked in a man. His cotton sweater vest was coral, the shirt underneath it was the same color with white stripes. He wore a coral silk ascot—one tone darker than the sweater—and impeccable white slacks and loafers completed his ensemble. His hair had been dyed brown, but the thick curls were all his own. His only accommodation to age seemed to be a pair of glasses and a hearing aid stuck in each ear.

Uncle Paulie pulled Carrie into a hug so strong, it almost knocked her off her feet and said, "I'da known you anywhere. You're the spitting image of Lu!"

"So are you," she said after she'd regained her balance. They both laughed awkwardly.

"It's the nose," he said. "And the mouth and the chin. And I'm a runt—only five-seven. Well, I used to be. Now I don't like to ask when the doc measures me anymore, because I've been shrinking." He patted a small paunch ruefully. "Not everywhere, unfortunately." He looked at Carrie and his eyes filled up. "It's good to make your acquaintance, Carrie," he said softly.

Carrie felt her own eyes fill. "You too," she said.

He took her out to a terrace that overlooked the sea, and after some deliberation seated her at a table that commanded an almost perfect 180-degree view of the water. There was an umbrella in the middle of the table, and he spent several minutes angling it so the sun wouldn't get in her eyes. He didn't need the shade himself; the fashionable glasses he was wearing were the kind that went dark in bright light.

Carrie watched him bustle around with the agility of a man half his age, and finally she couldn't restrain herself. "Why are you living in a place like this?" she demanded. "You don't need help. You're just fine." Then she added quickly, "I'm sorry. That's none of my business—"

But Uncle Paulie was delighted. "Yeah," he said happily, "I'm still sharp as a tack. I get around pretty good too—not like I used to, but what the hey, who does?" He turned himself so his back was to the sun, and his dark glasses lightened enough that she could see his eyes. "Truth is, I don't need to be here. But I got this friend, Dom. A couple of years ago I start noticing he can't remember if it's Tuesday or Sunday. He's screwing up his medicine, he drives his car into a tree. Well, his wife has passed on, rest her soul, and all of his kids have left New Haven, and they're going crazy worrying about him. Dom won't move in with any of them, but he's going to kill himself the way he's going.

"So I start wondering about myself. I think, sure, I can live on my own for now, but how long is that going to last? The lady I was with for ten years died too, and do I want to wait until I'm like Dom? So I call him up and I say, 'Hey buddy, we're getting too old for this crapola. You know that assisted living place on the water we heard about? I'll go there if you will.' And that's what we did. It's not bad here. Couple of nights a week we go to the casinos over in Trumbull, and there's a bus that takes us down to the old neighborhood when we want to play bocce. The docs here let Dom have a lot of freedom because they know I'll look out for him." He grinned. "And you can't beat the ratio of men to women in this joint."

His fake brown hair had a reddish tinge, but the eyes that shone behind his dark glasses were kind, and his smile was one of the sweetest Carrie had ever seen. *Let's hear it for the Leporellos,* she thought.

"You're a great friend," she said.

Uncle Paulie waved it away with a dismissive gesture. But she could tell he was pleased. "I do what I can. But you didn't come here to hear about me."

"Well, there were some things I wanted to know . . ." But then, she didn't know how to start the conversation they needed to have.

Uncle Paulie was studying her as if he had something to say, but apparently he didn't know how to begin either. Finally, he decided to risk it. "Before, when you said I looked like Lu . . . have you . . . ? I mean, did Rose ever . . . ?" He left the question dangling.

Carrie shook her head. "No, I've never met Lu. Not that I can remember, anyway. I've seen pictures of her, that's all."

He sighed. "Well, there were always plenty of pictures of Lu around."

"Not in my house," Carrie said. "I had to go to the library to see them."

"And that's why you're here. You want to know what happened between your mother and your grandmother."

"Yes."

"I can't tell you that. I don't know what the fight was about . . . I guess there was a fight, but I'm not even sure about that." He looked out at the ocean for a while. "What do you know about your great-grandmother? My mother?" he asked.

It was an unexpected turn. "Nothing, really," Carrie said.

"She was born in Italy—in a small town outside Naples. She was raised in a convent and she came to this country when she was sixteen. She came over to marry my father—it was an arranged marriage. He paid her way to this country. He was nineteen years older than she was—a grown man—and she was just a girl." Uncle Paulie shook his head and looked out at the ocean again. "I used to wonder sometimes what went through her mind when she got off that boat and saw him for the first time."

"Why did she agree to do it?" Carrie asked.

Uncle Paulie turned to her and took off his glasses to rub his eyes. "In the old country she wasn't a catch. She was pretty, and she was smart. She could read and write—the nuns saw to that. But the story was, her mother was an opera singer from the big city—Naples. And she wasn't married to Mama's father. That's why she gave Mama to the nuns to raise."

"My great-grandmother was illegitimate?" Carrie said, fascinated by this colorful tidbit of her history.

"I know it's not a big thing today. Half the weddings in Hollywood, the best man is the couple's three-year-old kid . . . but back then, oh, it was such a disgrace! And no matter how terrific Mama was, she could never forget it." He put on his glasses, stood up, and held out his hand to her. "You've got wheels, right?" he asked. She nodded and let him help her to her feet. "Let's take a little drive. I want to show you something."

THE ROUTE UNCLE PAULIE chose took them through New Haven. Carrie white-knuckled her way through a maze of one-way streets and did a lot of praying, but her passenger didn't seem to notice how many near misses they had. He'd designated himself tour guide, pointing out little pockets of the city that hadn't been touched by the disastrous urban renewal of the sixties, giving a quickie history of each. They saw part of the Yale campus—a potpourri of architectural styles in which Gothic and Georgian seemed to predominate—and they drove past a green with three churches in its center, which, Uncle Paulie informed Carrie, was on the National Registry of Historic Places. Finally, when it seemed to Carrie that her hands had permanently welded themselves to her steering, wheel, he announced that they could stop. They were on a broad street lined with houses that looked like they'd been built in the early part of the last century. Ample, welcoming porches curved around the homes, which were so close to the sidewalk that there was only room for a few shrubs in the front. The neighborhood seemed to be a mixed bag in terms of upkeep, some of the places sparkling with new paint and roofs, others badly in need of TLC.

"This street went through a bad time for about twenty years—in the sixties and the seventies," Uncle Paulie said. "But now all these youngsters—I guess you could call them yuppies—they're seeing how beautiful it could be and they're buying the old houses and fixing them up. Look at that one." He pointed across the street to a large lucky house that had gotten a makeover. It had been painted a soft gray with dark green trim, and it had a beautifully refinished front door with gleaming brass fixtures. A stained-glass window arched over the top of the door, and a brass number was prominently displayed on the side.

"It's big," said Carrie, the apartment dweller.

Uncle Paulie nodded. "Yeah. This was a ritzy house for an Italian family when I was a kid—a ritzy neighborhood too. Most of our people lived over on Wooster Street, and Franklin Avenue—our Little Italy. But I guess you could say my folks were upwardly mobile."

"This was your house?"

"It was Lu's house too. And your mother's, when she was little."

"I never imagined anything like this." Carrie moved closer to the gray-and-green beauty.

"Pop could afford it because he was successful," Uncle Paulie went on. "He had three grocery stores by the time he died. His family came to this country early, right after the Civil War. So even though they were poor, he still had a leg up, you see? And he was a smart businessman."

Carrie tore her eyes away from the house and looked up and

down the block. "This was your street," she said, trying to impress it on her brain. "This was where all of you grew up."

Uncle Paulie nodded. "Pop and Mama moved here in the twenties. It was mostly an Irish neighborhood, and farther up the street there were some old Yankee families, Griswolds, Russells, and like that. There's a Polish church two blocks over. In the fifties, when the Communists took over Poland, the priest in St. Stanislaus used to play the Polish national anthem at the end of Mass and all these little old ladies would stand there wearing their babushkas, singing, with the tears streaming down their faces."

Carrie turned back to her ancestral home. "Your house is beautiful. I like the colors."

"The couple who bought it—two boys, can you believe how things have changed? Dom and me, we got to know them, and we taught them to play bocce. Anyway, they wanted to know what the place used to look like in the old days. They found my name and called me. I told them Mama always had it painted gray and green every two years." He gazed at the house, seeing another time. "It looks just like it used to," he said. "She'd be happy about that. This place was . . ." He turned to Carrie and smiled. "I guess you couldn't call it her kingdom . . . her queendom, maybe?"

"Sounds right to me," Carrie said.

Uncle Paulie looked back at the house and stared at it silently for a while. "You said you wanted to know what happened between your mother and your grandmother," he said at last. "You've got to go back further than them. It started with my mother. Whenever I think of them; Mama—her name was Mifalda—Lu, and Rose, it's like they're standing in a line. Three young girls, handing down all the good and the bad from one generation to the next. They couldn't get away from each other—and I know there were times when they all wanted to. But if you want to go back to the beginning of the story, you gotta start with Mama."

CHAPTER 7

New Haven, Connecticut

1936

THE AIR IN the kitchen was hot and thick. It was Monday—washing day. The day of the week that Mifalda hated the most. She straightened up and stretched her aching back—she had a new washing machine, but she still had to bend over the deep sink full of scalding water and bleach and scrub out the stains and spots with her washboard before she could put the laundry into the machine. That was a little detail the advertisements in the newspaper didn't mention. With six kids—five of them boys—there were a lot of stains and spots.

The small space that served as her laundry room was right off the kitchen. There was no ventilation, and the steam from the washing machine mixed with the smell of bleach and made it hard to breathe. Mifalda turned to the woman working at her side. After she'd had her fourth son, her husband, Carmine, had said she had to have a girl to help her in the house. He had hired Ana, a greenhorn, whose family came from Poland and had been in America for only a short time. At first, Mifalda had begged Carmine to get someone who spoke Italian so she could speak the language she still missed. But Ana came cheap, and although Carmine spoiled his young wife—his mother said so until the day she died—he was no fool when it came to money.

In the end, Mifalda had come to like the Polish greenhorn. Ana was Mifalda's age, which meant they had things in common, and since Mifalda had been in the country so much longer than Ana— she'd been a citizen for fourteen years by then—she was able to give Ana little tips on being an American when they took a break from their work every afternoon to have coffee. It was nice, she discovered, to be an old-timer. Plus, Ana did all the hardest chores without complaining.

The air in the little laundry room had become unbearable. "I'm going to check the sauce," Mifalda told Ana, and escaped into the kitchen. The laundry smells were here too, but at least she didn't feel like the walls were closing in. She sat at the kitchen table and fanned herself. It was freezing outside, and much as she would have liked to, she couldn't open a window and let out all the heat, not with coal costing what it did. Her kitchen was huge—when they'd bought the house, Carmine had had the wall separating it from the dining room knocked down to make it bigger—and all of Mifalda's appliances were up to the minute. She had a gas range, a sewing machine, a coil-top refrigerator, an electric toaster, and in the little laundry room there was an electric iron—the latest model—sitting on the shelf. Any time Carmine heard of something new for the house, he bought it. Part of the reason for this, she knew, was that he loved her and he wanted her to be happy. But the splendor of her possessions was also a mark of his success. He enjoyed talking to his cronies about the things he bought for

Mifalda and mentioning—very casually—that she had a Polish girl working for her. He liked it when a friend dropped by and his pretty young wife in her starched housedress served pie she'd made according to the recipe his mother had taught her. He liked knowing that when he and his friend went outside to sit on the front porch and talk about politics and business, his wife was inside crocheting the lace that would be stitched onto the pillowcases in his daughter's hope chest.

Carmine deserved all his domestic happiness. His father had died when he was a child, and Carmine had worked to support his mother from the time he was twelve. He had lived at home and put off marriage until he had established his first grocery store. He held off some more on wedded bliss until he owned the building where his store was and he could move himself and his mother into the spacious apartment above it. Then he continued to hold off until he was the proud owner of two more stores. When Carmine finally decided to marry, he was in the position to buy a beautiful house for his new wife.

Of course, all the success came at a price; Carmine worked long hours. Every morning before dawn he was at the market down by the wharf, buying his fresh produce, and sometimes he didn't get home until after midnight. He took regular trips to New York to check with the importers of the olive oil and other specialties he sold. That was how he managed to stay in business in spite of the big new supermarkets; he offered quality products his customers couldn't buy at the A&P. He kept costs down by doing most of the work himself. And it had paid off—even during the worst of the Depression, Mifalda's household allowance had come down only a few dollars a week. The one sacrifice she'd made was buying a cheap wool fabric for her daughter's winter coat.

Mifalda stood up, looked around her handsome kitchen, and

told herself—as she did every day—how lucky she was. A good provider like Carmine could have had his pick of New Haven women. But even though he was American born, he had wanted to marry from the old country. And it had been a plus, as far as he was concerned, that his future bride had been raised by the nuns.

"You're an old-fashioned girl. I like that," he said to Mifalda when they were alone for the first time. He spoke Italian like she did, with the Neapolitan dialect. What he meant was *I want an old-fashioned wife who has been taught to know her place. I want a wife who is quiet and won't push herself forward.* He didn't say it, but she knew that was why he had agreed to an arranged marriage with a girl he'd never met. A girl who was not even half his age.

And she had been grateful to get away from the dusty little town in Italy where she'd been born and the convent where she'd been raised. The area had been too poor to support an orphanage, and she had been the only child living with the nuns. She'd prayed when they did, eaten the same limited rations—she was always hungry in those days—and worn shapeless smocks made of the same scratchy black fabric they used for their habits. Two of these garments would be sewn for her at a time, and she was expected to wear them until they were so frayed they couldn't be darned, or she outgrew them. The ugly outfits marked her in a community where she already stood out as a charity child and the daughter of a shameless woman. Walking to school each day was a special agony; the pathway from the convent to the street was a favorite congregating spot for the local toughs, and if they spotted her the taunting hurt worse than knives.

"Look at her, all bones in a sack." "She smells bad too." And then someone would start saying the really terrible things. "Daughter of a whore." *"Putana!"*

Once when she was young Mifalda had picked up a clod of dirt and thrown it at her tormentors. The nuns had beaten her for that. "You have your mother's bad blood," they told her between blows. "You must always be on the watch for it. You must recognize your sufferings as a gift from Our Lord to teach you humility and bear them meekly."

Madonna, those nuns could be hard!

Mifalda stood up and went to the window. Out in her garden she had an arbor where her boys grew the grapes Carmine used for making the family wine, and a tomato patch. Both were now buried under snow and ice. In this weather the wash would freeze if she tried to dry it outside, so she and Ana would have to hang it in the basement, where her sons had strung up a line for her.

She moved to the stove to stir the sauce—her mother-in-law's recipe. The eggplant parmigiana she'd made at five o'clock that morning was cooling in the pan. She'd cut it into squares and make it into sandwiches for the children's lunch when they came home from school at the noon break. In the laundry room, Ana was feeding a shirt into the wringer, folding it so the buttons wouldn't get caught and break. Everything in her world was in order. Everything was perfect.

I'm so lucky, she told herself. *I don't deserve everything I have.*

But if she didn't get away from the smell of wet wash and her mother-in-law's tomato sauce, she was going to start throwing things. She looked up at the clock on the kitchen wall. It was only a little after ten, and the children wouldn't be home for two hours. If she hurried . . . She grabbed a coat and ran for the door. Over her shoulder she called out to Ana, "I just remembered, I need something from the store." Ana knew all she had to do was call Carmine and ask him to bring home whatever she wanted, but the woman gave her a grim little smile. Maybe she understood how it could get when you were trapped in your perfect house all day—day after day.

* * *

IT WAS TOO cold outdoors for the thin coat Mifalda had taken. But the stinging dry air felt good after the humidity of the kitchen. For one reckless moment she wanted to run, to see if she could still go as fast as she had when she was a child. But she was not a child anymore, and she was wearing shoes meant for a grown woman who had six children. Besides, even when she was a child, the nuns hadn't let her run free—that was not allowed for a girl who had to be extra careful not to draw attention to herself. A girl who must not ever do anything that would remind anyone of her shame.

The park was only three blocks away from her house. Mifalda reached it quickly and then gave a little cry of dismay. The path that ran through it was still covered with snow. She could walk on it—the snow had been packed down—but if the city hadn't sent people to clean the pathways, there was a chance that the big pond in the center of the park hadn't been shoveled off. That pond was her destination. After she'd finally made her escape it would be too mean of God to let it be covered with snow. She ran down the slippery path.

The pond had been cleared off! She scanned its frozen surface eagerly. For a moment she thought God had decided to be mean after all and that there was no one there, but then a girl skated out onto the ice. She was wearing a red dress that came to her knees; the collar and the edge of the skirt were trimmed with white fur. A little red hat with more white fur protected her ears from the cold. Mifalda was too far away to see her face, but she knew from other times that the girl's eyes were blue, her nose turned up, and her hair was carrot red. It was a typical Irish face, and in her mind, Mifalda called her the Irish Girl.

The Irish, she had learned when she first came to America, had been in the country longer than the Italians. They ran the Catholic churches and the parochial schools, and they lorded it over the newcomers from the Mediterranean. The newcomers responded by hating them heartily. But no matter what bad things her husband said about them, Mifalda knew in her heart that the Irish, who put butter on their bread instead of olive oil, were more American than she and Carmine were. It was no surprise to her that the Irish Girl knew how to ice-skate.

The girl worked hard at it; she was out every morning practicing. Mifalda knew this because whenever she could sneak away she came to the pond to watch the Irish Girl. Sometimes the girl went around in circles on one foot, stopping every once in a while to check the markings she'd made on the ice. She was graceful when she made the circles, with her hands held out just so and her toes pointed, but that wasn't what Mifalda waited to see. Eventually the Irish Girl would start skating in curved strokes that went so fast, she barely seemed to touch the surface of the pond. Her arms extended, her skirt would ruffle around her legs in the wind she made. That was what brought Mifalda to the park.

Today the girl dispensed with the circles and started going fast right away. What was it like to be free like that? To show off your pretty legs in a short skirt and fly? *She's younger than I am, but I already had a husband to care for and a house to tend when I was her age,* Mifalda thought. *I never had a chance to be free. And my legs are as pretty as hers.*

Suddenly, the Irish Girl turned backwards and stuck her toe in the ice so she could jump. Then, Mifalda knew, she would turn around in the air and land on one skate going forward. Mifalda held her breath; the girl had tried to do this many times before, and often when she did, she fell. But it seemed that this was going to be one of the good times. The girl jumped, turned, came down as gently as a bird landing on a tree branch, and swooped off again. Mifalda watched her triumph and she felt as if she and the Irish Girl were skating together—two wild, free creatures who didn't have laundry to wash or floors to scrub, they were just flying and showing off their pretty legs. Mifalda laughed out loud at the joy of it.

The Irish Girl heard her and was startled, not aware that she was being watched. She stopped skating and stood in the middle of the pond, looking around. Mifalda wanted to run, but she couldn't move.

The Irish Girl spotted her. "Hey," she called out.

Whatever had been holding Mifalda back released her and she started to run up the snowy path. She ran away from the pond and the Irish Girl, who was still calling to her. She ran out of the park and through the streets until she was standing in front of her house. The big, warm house her good husband provided for her and her children to be safe. The house she did not deserve. She shivered—and not just from the cold.

The truth was, there had always been something wrong inside her—the nuns had been right about that. Mifalda loved her husband in her way, and she loved her children so much that it hurt. The five boys had been easier for her than the girl; maybe because her daughter was too much like her, or maybe it was always that way with two females, but all of them—the boys and the girl—were what made her life worthwhile.

She could remember them as newborn babies, each one a small miracle, with satiny skin and a soft round face and little fat hands and feet. She had cherished them when they were wobbling around on those tiny feet; she'd felt a deep satisfaction as they grew to be sturdy and strong on the good American food she was able to give them, and she'd swelled with pride when her handsome family was dressed and assembled for church on Sundays. If she ever doubted the goodness of God—and there were times when the washing and the cleaning got to be too much and she did wonder if He had any love for women at all—her healthy, glowing youngsters made all the rest worthwhile.

What she hated was housework. She didn't mind cooking for her family, but she didn't want to be the one who had to wash the pots, dishes, silverware, glasses, and linens afterward. She didn't want to make the beds, or wash the windows, or iron the sheets like a good wife and mother should. The never-ending monotony of those same chores done over and over, day after day, week after week, could make her want to scream until the rooms of her nice safe house echoed. And that was wrong.

Sometimes she thought if she'd had more daughters to help her—you couldn't ask boys to do housework—she might have been a better person. Or if she'd had family nearby, sisters who could visit and gossip and laugh, maybe that would have made her more able to accept her lot. But she didn't have any of that. And besides, whatever was wrong inside her went deeper than washing and cleaning.

She didn't want to smile and agree with Carmine when he said President Roosevelt was ruining the country, and she didn't want to sit quietly crocheting lace while her sons and their friends talked about baseball. In the years that she had been in America she had taught herself not only to speak English but to read and write it. She went through the newspaper every day, and she had opinions about things. She didn't want to be a part of the background; she wanted attention. She wanted people to listen when she talked, to laugh at her jokes, and—it was shameful to admit—she wanted to be admired. But those were not the feelings of a good woman. Those were the feelings of a *putana*—an opera singer who had had a child she couldn't keep because there was no father.

There was something warm trickling down her shin. Mifalda looked down and saw blood. She'd fallen on the packed snow when she was racing through the park and she must have hurt her knee, although she didn't remember it. Her stocking was ripped too. It served her right for running off in the middle of the day. It served her right for wishing—even for a moment—that she was young and free.

She hurried inside the house. After she'd bandaged her knee, there would still be time to make a fresh applesauce cake before the children came home from school. If she could get it cool enough, she'd put a lemon icing on it—the boys liked that.

IT WASN'T UNTIL late in the day that Mifalda and Ana finished washing the last of the sheets. As they piled the wet mass into the laundry basket, Mifalda heard the back door to the kitchen slam shut. A high, sweet voice was singing, *"Panis angelicus fit panis hominum; Dat panis coelicus figuris terminum."* Mifalda's daughter was home. The little girl had been named Lucia after Carmine's mother. But she had informed all of them that they were not to call her that foreign-sounding name anymore. Nine-year-old Lucia was now, if you please, Lu.

"Like that character in the funny papers?" Mifalda had asked sarcastically. But her daughter had informed her with a giggle that she was thinking of Little Lulu.

Her daughter's rejection of her grandmother's name had annoyed Mifalda. True, she hadn't liked her mother-in-law, but there was respectability and tradition in the handing down of a family name. Her spoiled daughter didn't know what life could be like without that sense of belonging.

Carmine had pointed out that the boys had Americanized their names—Francesco had become Frank, Ezio called himself Ed, Nico was Nick, Paolo was Paulie; only Carmine Jr. had stuck by the name given to him at birth. It was her husband's opinion that Mifalda was making a mountain out of a molehill—a particularly American expression that Mifalda hated. Carmine was too soft with their daughter, partly because she was a girl and the baby of the family, and partly because he was getting old. Carmine was in his fifties now and he didn't have the energy to discipline the girl. That fell more and more to Mifalda. And Lucia—all right, call her Lu if that was what she wanted—needed discipline. She was, after all, her mother's daughter.

"O *res mirabilis! Manducat Dominum,*" Lu sang as she put down her books and checked the refrigerator for a snack. "*Pauper, pauper, servus et humilis.*" Her pure, sweet voice rose to the high notes with the ease of someone flying. Like a skater skimming across the ice, graceful and free . . .

"Lu, we're going down to the cellar to hang the sheets; come help," Mifalda called out. The singing stopped. Lu stuck her head into the laundry room. She was bursting with excitement, Mifalda could see. But Lu always waited to tell you something until the right moment—when she had your undivided attention.

"I can't, Mama," she said. "I just came home for half an hour." She paused, then walked away, saying much too casually, "Then I have to go back to school and start rehearsing."

That brought Mifalda out of the laundry room. "Rehearse for what?" she demanded.

Lu turned, and, Madonna, how the child's face could light up when she was happy! "I'm going to sing a solo for the crowning of the Blessed Mother!" she announced dramatically.

The crowning of Mary was an important event at the parochial school Mifalda's children attended. The school was attached to St. Mary's Church, and every year in May—Mary's month—the parish held a celebration in which a statue of the Virgin was crowned with a wreath of flowers. There were readings from the saints, usually done by someone very important in the parish, a blessing was given by a delegate of the bishop, the children of St. Mary's School marched in a procession to the statue, and then there was music. In the past professionals had been hired to sing, but if Lu was to be believed, this year was different.

"Miss Gaspari says our school choir at St. Mary's is as good as any of the children's choirs in Italy," Lu was gushing happily. "She should know—she's been there, and she's heard them!"

Gaspari was a familiar name. Mifalda knew she'd heard it before, but she couldn't place it.

"Miss Gaspari says this year we children are going to sing all the music for the coronation," Lu continued.

Suddenly Mifalda remembered how she knew the name. The Gasparis were one of the most influential Italian families in New Haven. The grandfather of the clan, Gaetano Gaspari, had had a circuit of vaudeville houses throughout Connecticut and Massachusetts in the early nineteen hundreds. He'd sold them before the Depression—he got out in the nick of time was what Carmine said—so he was very rich, and he'd built a family compound of twelve mansions out on the shore, where he now lived with his grandchildren and his children. His sons owned restaurants, hotels, and several blocks of downtown New Haven, and his daughters all married bigwigs in lavish weddings that were mentioned in the New York society pages. But what did a Gaspari have to do with Mifalda's daughter?

"Miss Gaspari is the music teacher for all of St. Mary's—the grammar school and the high school," Lu answered the unspoken question.

"I thought the nuns teach you."

"Miss Gaspari is special. She's teaching us for free because she wants to bring cultural enrichment to the children of the Italian community who haven't had her advantages, " Lu said in a highfalutin voice that had to be mimicking her teacher's. Lu didn't mimic people to make fun of them; it was just the way she heard things. "I'm the only one who has a solo," she babbled on joyously.

"I'm singing the Panis Angelicus. Miss Gaspari only had to play it for me twice and I learned all of it. She says she's never seen anyone who can learn music as fast as I can. She says I have a remarkable ear, and—"

"Why are you the only one who has a solo?" Mifalda broke in. Sometimes Lu talked too fast for her.

"Miss Gaspari says my voice is the best in the school—she says I have an exquisite instrument. And I really do, Mama! Sister Mary Joseph says my voice is a joy to listen to, and everybody knows she hates us kids."

Lu didn't intend to brag, Mifalda was sure of that. But it was clear that all the attention was turning her head, and that was dangerous. Of course, the two women who were encouraging Lu wouldn't think of that. One was a rich schoolteacher with fancy ideas, and one was a nun! They had no idea how careful you had to be to fight your own weakness—the wildness in your blood that you controlled every day of your life—when you saw it in your child. They didn't know what a responsibility it was to keep your daughter safe.

"I don't know if it's right, to sing alone and show off . . ." Mifalda began slowly.

"Mama, didn't you hear me? No one else is as good as I am. Miss Gaspari says I have a great gift. She says in a few years I should start studying with Maestro DiTullio."

"Who?"

"Rosa Ponselle took some lessons from him—you know, the opera singer . . ."

Mifalda did know about Rosa Ponsell. Everyone in the Italian community of New Haven knew about the Connecticut-born girl who had gotten her start entertaining in their city and was one of the very few American opera singers good enough to perform at the Metropolitan Opera House with European stars like Enrico

Caruso. Madame Ponsell might be a fine artist and the pride of her state, but Mifalda Leporello was not about to let her daughter have singing lessons—or any other kind of lessons—alone with a man. A girl's biggest asset was her purity; it was the gift she would give her husband one day, and without it no man would want her. Mifalda knew it was the fashion for young women to be careless about things like a good reputation, but she also knew the hard way what life was like when you didn't have one. And then too, Lu had that legacy of wild blood.

More important, no daughter of Mifalda's was going to learn to sing so she could go on the stage—or even think about such a thing. What right did an old maid and a nun have to fill her child's head with nonsense? Didn't they understand, educated ladies that they were, that that was the way to ruin a girl's life?

For the second time that day, Mifalda grabbed her coat and headed for the back door. A determined little figure blocked her way.

"Where are you going?" Lu demanded.

"Move away from the door, Lucia."

"Mama, if you spoil this for me, I don't know if I'll be able to forgive you," said her youngest child. It was not a baby's threat. Lu said it seriously, almost thoughtfully. For a second Mifalda was stunned. None of her boys had ever talked to her like that. But then, her boys didn't fight with her the way Lu always had. "I mean it, Mama," her daughter warned.

Mifalda did not believe in hitting children—she'd been hit too much herself when she was young—but she couldn't let this kind of defiance go unpunished. She drew back her hand. Then she looked at her daughter's little body, held ramrod straight, and she looked at Lu's unwavering gaze. *It's not her fault*, she thought. *She's just like me.* When she leaned down and moved the child away from the door, her hands were gentle. "Set the table, Lu," she said. "Your brothers and your father will be coming home soon."

As she ran out of the house, she could feel Lu staring after her.

MIFALDA HAD NEVER gone to her children's school, because there had never been any need. Her sons were good boys— perhaps not the brightest students, but they worked hard and were reasonably well behaved. It was somehow logical that the first time Mifalda was having trouble at St. Mary's it was because of Lu.

She found the auditorium—that was what the girl behind the desk in the front called it—where the children's choir was practic- ing. Mifalda walked in quietly and sat in the back. The youngsters were singing the Panis Angelicus. The woman conducting them was maybe ten years younger than Mifalda. She was tall, with fair skin and reddish-blond hair—strawberry blond, people called that color. It was the coloring of the northern Italians; the Piedmontsi, or maybe the Veneziani. Back in Italy, the north was the wealthy, cultured part of the country, and people from that region looked down their noses at southerners like Mifalda, considering them uneducated peasants.

Miss Gaspari seemed to be checking over her shoulder for someone as the children sang. She had them repeat the piece twice, making suggestions, which as far as Mifalda could see didn't change anything very much, and then she looked at her watch. "It seems our soloist won't be with us today," she said in a fake- cheerful voice. "So I'll sing the part with you."

The choir started again and after a few seconds the teacher joined in. When she started, it sounded almost like a children's round, like they were singing "Row, row, row your boat." Except, of course, this was God's music, and it was beautiful. Miss Gaspari had a nice voice—not spectacular like Lu's, but even with her taking the lead the song was a joy to listen to. Mifalda could imagine how lovely it would be with Lu's soaring soprano weaving in and out of the choir's singing. It was too bad that she wouldn't have the opportunity.

The piece ended and Miss Gaspari looked over her shoulder one last time, then gave a big sigh and dismissed the children, who ran off like they'd just been let out of jail. As Miss Gaspari gathered up her music, Mifalda started down the aisle toward her.

"Miss Gaspari?" she asked. The schoolteacher looked up. Madonna, she was tall—Mifalda pulled herself up to her full five feet, one inch—and oh, the suit Miss Gaspari was wearing! It was navy blue, perfectly cut, the fabric soft as butter. Under the jacket was a silk blouse—pink and navy blue striped—with a bow at the collar. Her stockings were silk too. Mifalda was aware of her housedress, freshly starched and ironed that morning, but still a housedress, the apron she'd forgotten to take off, and her bandaged knee under her cotton stockings.

Miss Gaspari smiled benevolently at Mifalda. "May I help you?" she asked in the highfalutin voice Lu had mimicked. Hundreds of years of animosity between the north and south of Italy—animosity that should have stayed back in the old country—welled up inside Mifalda.

"I am Mrs. Carmine Leporello," she said in her own highfalutin voice.

"You're Lu's mother!" the young woman said. "Is she all right? She didn't come to rehearsal and I was worried."

The worry seemed to be real. *Still, she thinks I'm a peasant,* Mifalda thought. "My daughter, Lucia, is fine," she said formally, but somehow her accent had gotten thicker. "She's at home getting the dinner ready for her brothers and her father." *And now I sound like an ignorant peasant—one of those that pull their children out of school to go work in the fields.* "All of her brothers are going to college," she added, knowing it was a stupid thing to say but unable to stop herself. "My husband and I agreed. And we want Lucia to get a good education too. But she has her chores and . . ."

"Mrs. Leporello, please sit down, won't you?" The schoolteacher was smiling at her again—in a kindly way that made Mifalda want to slap her. But it would be rude to refuse, so she sat in a chair in the front row of the theater. Miss Gaspari sat two seats away and clasped her hands together as if she was going to pray. She was trying to find a way to talk to the ignorant peasant in front of her.

"Mrs. Leporello, I think I know what the problem is," the young woman finally began. "My grandmother came from Italy, and when I said I wanted to train to be a teacher so I could get a job, she was horrified. I don't need the money, and as far as she was concerned that was the only reason a woman should work. In her mind, a woman stays in her father's home and he supports her until her husband takes over. But that wasn't enough for me."

For a second Mifalda wanted to say, *Me too! It isn't enough for me either!* She wondered what it would feel like to tell this self-possessed young woman about all the shadowy yearnings she couldn't find words for—yearnings for adventure and attention that had nothing to do with cooking and cleaning. But then she looked into Miss Gaspari's beautiful face—and the schoolteacher was extraordinarily beautiful, with huge green eyes—and she saw the condescending smile. And she knew a rich girl who was working for the fun of it would never understand.

"Times are changing, Mrs. Leporello," Miss Gaspari went on in a voice that was patient and kind—and infuriating. "Women have choices these days, and—"

"Lu can't sing at the Holy Mother's Coronation because she's going to New York City with her papa that day." Mifalda broke in.

"My husband goes all the time—he has business there—and Lu is going with him. New York is such a big city and there are so many things to do. Educational things. You know?" Mifalda stood up and straightened her apron around her waist. "I'm sorry she can't sing for you. But I'm sure you can find someone else. It's not an important feast day, after all. " And she swept out of the auditorium.

CHAPTER 8

New Haven

2008

UNCLE PAULIE WAS leaning against the rental car, arms crossed over his chest, lost in the past and the story he'd been telling as he stared up at the gray-and-green house.

"Did Lu go to New York with your father?" Carrie asked.

The spell broke and he turned to look at her. "Oh, yeah," he said. "See, if Lu didn't go, then that made Mama a liar. And lying was wrong. Mama was real strict about right and wrong." He looked back at the house, shook his head, and started to laugh. "But the thing was, that first trip for Lu? That was the beginning of the end for Mama."

"What do you mean?"

"Pop got a big kick out of taking Lu to New York. She loved the city—from the first minute she saw it, it was her town. So from then on, whenever he goes there, Pop brings her with him. And then one time Pop takes her to see a show—a musical written by Mr. Cole Porter. Well, Lu goes crazy for it. All the way home on the train, she's humming the songs from the show—and then she's making up words to go with the melody. She always had this thing she could do, it was like a trick memory—she'd hear a song once and she knew the music. The words didn't come quite so fast; she usually had to see them written out. But you could sing any tune to her and she'd sing it back to you.

"So Lu and Pop are going home on the train and Lu is singing her own words to the songs and doing gestures like she remembers from the show and trying to dance in the aisles and Pop thinks she's real cute. And after that, they go to a show every time they're in New York—not telling Mama, of course.

"A couple of years go by with them going to the theater behind Mama's back, and then Miss Gaspari—she's still teaching Lu at the school—wants to set up an appointment to see if Maestro DiTullio will take Lu as a pupil. Lu doesn't even ask Mama; she goes straight to Pop and he says, yeah, sure, why not? Mama gets real mad when she hears about it, but what can she do? Pop is the man of the house.

"DiTullio hears her sing, and says he'll take her. But to make Mama not be so mad, the deal is, I've got to go with Lu to her lesson every week. I've got to sit there for the whole hour until she's finished, then walk her home. Every Saturday morning when all my friends are outside playing ball!" He paused for a moment, then added, "But even I know DiTullio's real picky about who he takes—so being his pupil, that's a real feather in Lu's cap.

"See, to people in New Haven who care about art and music and that kind of thing, DiTullio is a big cheese. Every year he has a recital for his students and people buy tickets like it's a regular show. Mama doesn't want Lu to do it, because it's too much like being an actress Mama thinks and that's a profession for girls who

aren't, well . . . nice, if you know what I mean. But Pop says
Mama's making a mountain out of a molehill, so Lu sings at the
recital, and she's the best in the whole thing. By far." Uncle Paulie
stopped to uncross and recross his arms. Carrie held her breath so
she wouldn't distract him from his narrative.

"Now, back in those days DiTullio's pupils were in demand to
sing at functions like weddings and birthdays," he went on. "And
after that first recital, everyone in New Haven wants Lu to sing for
them. And Pop says sure, why not? As long as it's in the daytime
when it's light outside, and she never, ever does it for money. Even
Pop's not gonna go that far. On top of which, I have to go with her
and stay nearby while she's doing her act so people will know she's
the kind of girl who has a family that watches out for her.

"Only by now I've had it with babysitting for her when she's
singing. I start cutting out early to go with my friends. I tell her
where I'll be so she can meet me after she's done and we go home
together like everything's on the up and up. But I'm not watching
her anymore." He paused and looked off into the distance. "And
come to find out, Mama was right. I should have."

"Why? What happened?"

Uncle Paulie pulled away from the car and looked at his watch.
"You hungry?" he asked.

"Now that you mention it, I'm starving."

Uncle Paulie got into the car on the passenger side and carefully buckled his seat belt. "Come on," he said. "I'll take you to the
best food in town."

They made their way through more scary one-way streets until
they reached what looked like a very old section of the city. Uncle
Paulie directed Carrie into a small parking lot behind a group of
shops and restaurants and extricated himself from his seat belt with
a low whistle. "Driving really isn't your thing, honey, is it?" he
asked as he got out of the car.

He led her to a little hole-in-the-wall eatery. MAURIZIO'S was stenciled in red on the front window. Underneath the name was a simple declarative statement: "The Best Pizza in the World."

"And it is," Uncle Paulie said as he led the way inside. He and Carrie sat in a booth next to a wall on which a mural of the Bay of Naples had been painted. The mural on the opposite side was of the Amalfi coast. Uncle Paulie ordered a large plain pizza without consulting Carrie. "You'll love it," he promised. "Maurizio's family had one of the first pizza places in New Haven. Back then we used to call it 'apizza pie,' which wasn't correct Italian, because that's what *pizza* means—pie. Maurizio makes the crust just like his grandparents used to . . . but he's changed with the times. Back then, they used to put just sauce, grated cheese, olive oil, and a little dried oregano on the dough. No mozzarella, no meat, nothing like that. When I was growing up you'd hear the old people complaining." Uncle Paulie slouched in his seat and hunched up his shoulders. " 'Eh, why do they put mozarell' onna tomato pie?' " he said in a heavy accent. " 'We didn't make it like that back on Franklin Street!' " He laughed at his own joke. Then he shrugged. "Personally, I like pizza with mozzarella on it. Lu and me, we always were for anything new."

"Speaking of Lu, you were going to tell me—"

"How I let her down—I know." He took a moment to sigh deeply. Then he plunged in. "It was when she was sixteen—in 1943. A lot had changed by then. For one thing, Pop had died in 1940. He had a heart attack. He'd never been sick a day in his life, but all of a sudden he was gone and Mama was the head of the house. You can't imagine what a big thing that was for our family, because Pop had handled everything. And then there was the war—World War Two. That changed the whole darned universe. "

CHAPTER 9

New Haven

1943

MIFALDA PUT ON her straw hat and began looking for
the little hoe she'd left in the back hall. She'd taken to
keeping it there since it was now her job to plant and
weed the tomatoes. Before the war Carmine would have hired a
boy from the neighborhood to do the heavy work for her, but
now all the boys were in the army—including Mifalda's sons. Her
oldest, Carmine Jr., was in the coast guard, and Nick was stationed
in Washington, so she wasn't too worried about them—although
Nick could be sent overseas anytime. But Frank was working in a
motor pool somewhere in England, which was frightening because
of all the bombing over there. And Eddie—her brilliant Eddie,
who had gone all the way through medical school on scholarships
and become a doctor—was in the air force out in California and
was going to be shipped out to some island in the Pacific to be a
flight surgeon, but no one knew when or where. That had been

keeping Mifalda awake nights already, and then, just when she'd thought things couldn't get any worse, she'd gotten a letter from Eddie.

Mifalda gave up the search for the hoe and took off her hat. Let the tomatoes wait. She went inside to pour herself a glass of lemonade from the refrigerator and sat at the table.

The letter from Eddie had been typical of the madness that was going on all over. He said he'd met a girl—not Italian, but she was Catholic, thank God—and he was going to marry her. No time for a wedding, no time to meet the family; he was going to war and he wanted to get married. And he'd done it. Just like that, Mifalda had a daughter-in-law she'd never met. She sipped the sweet, tart liquid and shook her head. These were crazy times—crazy and bad.

On top of all her other woes, she still hadn't gotten over the shock of losing her husband to a heart attack, even though she'd always known that he would probably go first because he was so much older than she was, rest his soul. And now she had to find someone to run the business. She couldn't do it herself because she was a woman, and Paulie, who was the only boy she had left at home, was only seventeen and planning to join up as soon as he could. She'd finally asked their accountant to take over with the stores, but she knew he was an idiot. So maybe that was why she hadn't been paying as much attention as she should to Lu.

As far as Mifalda was concerned, Lu was out of control. She'd been branching out with her singing and performing. It had started when people began asking her to say a little speech or sometimes do a little skit when she was entertaining at their party or at their christening. Lu was glad to oblige, and everyone said she was a natural at acting. A little local theater in town that did shows for children on Saturday mornings was told about her, and all of a sudden Mifalda heard that her daughter was taking the lead in a children's play called *Puss in Boots*. Then the next thing Mifalda heard, Lu was spicing up her performance by doing cartwheels, exiting from the stage after her final song by flipping head over heels. Everyone talked about that too—and of course they loved it. There was an offer for Lu from another amateur theater group in town—this one performed plays for the adults—but Mifalda had gotten wind of that in time to put her foot down.

Then the people at the USO had asked Lu to sing. The army had turned Yale University into a training school for officers—Mifalda wasn't quite sure how it had all worked—but suddenly the town was full of young cadets who were going off to fight, and everyone wanted to keep their spirits up. Entertaining these young men was a patriotic thing to do. At least, that was what Lu kept saying. To Mifalda, the young men were the problem. She didn't want her daughter parading around in front of them—or flipping head over heels—no matter how unpatriotic that sounded. She and Lu had screaming matches about this that usually ended in their not speaking to each other and Mifalda having to say things to Paulie like "Ask your sister to pass the grated cheese."

In desperation, she'd finally sent Lu off to California to visit Eddie and his new wife, hoping that maybe while she was gone people would find someone else to entertain them by singing and making jokes and doing cartwheels. Or maybe Lu herself would forget about it. But people hadn't found anyone else, and Lu hadn't forgotten. As soon as she returned home there was an invitation to perform that even Mifalda couldn't say no to. There was no money involved, and she'd be singing at a family wedding; it was the kind of thing she'd done a hundred times before. And of course Paulie would be there to watch out for her.

Mifalda drained her glass and went to the sink to rinse it. Later, after everything had happened—after she'd learned that Paulie wasn't watching out for Lu, and Lu wasn't watching out for herself—she would wonder if Lu would have done what she did if

Carmine had still been alive. Lu loved Mifalda—for all of their fighting, Mifalda knew that—but the girl had worshipped her father. She wouldn't have wanted to hurt him.

But those were questions that would come later. At that moment Mifalda checked her kitchen clock and saw that it was time for Lu to start her performance at the wedding. And even though Mifalda had never seen her daughter sing in public, she pictured Lu pulling herself up straight and tall so she'd have that extra little bit of height that mattered so much to her, and then, with her eyes shining, walking out in front of a crowd of people.

CHAPTER 10

New Haven

1943

LU WALKED OUT onto the little raised platform that served as a stage in the Villa Veneto restaurant and looked out over the crowd. Before the war she would have thought it was small for a wedding reception. But these days, with the rationing and with so many families having boys overseas, people weren't giving big parties like they used to. Any size gathering was impressive in 1943. And even though there wasn't any butter for the table and most of the guests had traveled to the restaurant via the trolley instead of wasting precious gasoline, there was a band complete with a pianist. And there was Lu. She'd been asked to perform by the bride, who was none other than her beloved Miss Gaspari. Lu had been thrilled by the honor—until she'd seen the list of selections Miss Gaspari wanted her to sing.

Lu sighed and looked out at the room full of her teacher's

friends and relatives. She was about to try to entertain them, and they were not going to like it. Even Maestro DiTullio, who loved Miss Gaspari—her name was Mrs. Benedetto now, although he called her by her given name of Adele—had been dismayed when he saw the first piece on the bride's proposed list.

"She wants you to sing church music at a wedding reception?" he'd said.

Lu had nodded miserably. "She taught me the Panis Angelicus when I was just a kid. She says it has special meaning for us."

"But it's going to put everyone else to sleep. Especially at two o'clock in the afternoon when they've been drinking since eleven." He shook his head in disbelief. "Adele is a good person—one of the best I know. But she overestimates people." He'd slammed over the remaining selections. "If you can soften up the audience, you can get away with the rest of these songs," he'd said. Then he'd rolled his eyes. "Although how you're going to get them in a good mood by singing the Panis Angelicus . . ." he'd trailed off. "Eh, never mind. Every once in a while the crowd just doesn't want you. It happens to everyone."

But not to me! Lu thought as she stood in front of the microphone in the middle of the little platform in the Villa Veneto restaurant. Audiences always loved her, because she loved them and they could sense that she wanted to make them happy. She had tried to explain it once to Paulie: "If I make them forget for a little while about the boy they've got in the war or the scary things they read in the newspaper, that's like being God." Then she'd giggled, because that was such a vain thing to say. "It's better than being God because God does things that make them suffer," she added jokingly. But there was a part of her that meant it.

And now she was going to sing, and while the audience wasn't going to suffer, she wasn't going to make them forget the son who was gone, or all the scary things in the newspaper. And that was going to make her feel bad. Feeling bad was something Lu always tried to avoid. Mama felt bad about a lot of things in her life, Lu could tell, but Mama just accepted it, and Lu couldn't see where that had gotten her.

Lu looked at the crowd again. They were in a mood for fun, and the obvious choice for them would be something jazzy like "Don't Sit Under the Apple Tree." But maybe there was a way to turn them. After all, this was a wedding, and people got sentimental at weddings. And, as the maestro had predicted, they had been drinking since before noon. So if she could just find a way to make them all a little teary . . . She turned to look at Miss Gaspari—now Mrs. Benedetto—who was sitting at the head table. She was staring at Lu with a big smile, waiting for the Panis Angelicus. Lu knew what she had to do. She leaned into the microphone and said to the room, "Ladies and gentlemen, on this happy day, my teacher—the new Mrs. Benedetto—has asked me to perform a special song that she taught me. I'm going to ask her to come up here now and we'll do it together for you." If listening to the bride sing on her own wedding day didn't soften up this house, Lu didn't know what would.

It took very little to persuade Mrs. Benedetto to come to the platform to sing. Almost before Lu knew it, the woman who had been so much more than a teacher to her, who had believed in her more than anyone, even Pop, was at her side. And as they waited for the music to start, Lu realized she wasn't thinking about softening up the house anymore. It hit her that she was going to lose Mrs. Benedetto because she was married now and married women didn't teach. After they left the restaurant today, Lu would never be Mrs. Benedetto's star pupil again.

The pianist started the opening chords of the Panis Angelicus. Lu and her teacher turned to each other, and Lu could see in Mrs. Benedetto's big green eyes that she knew what she was losing too. They smiled at each other because if they didn't they would cry. And then they started to sing. They sang the music one of them had chosen for the other to learn, music that came from their church and their childhood. They were two Italian women—never mind the difference in age, now—singing side by side, because that was what their people did. When you were Italian that was how you laughed and cried and prayed. They sang to forget that something precious was ending for them, and they sang to celebrate what it had been. Then, because she could never ignore an audience, Lu turned to the crowd. The melody of the Panis Angelicus was swirling upward now, melding with the old Latin text of the piece, and Lu's voice floated higher and higher as she sang the ancient words, while in her mind she was urging the people in front of her to surrender to the beauty of this music and this moment. *Come with me*, she commanded them with all the strength she could muster. *Come way up high with me and forget all the things that make you sad. Come and remember how roses smell, and stars shine in the black night sky, and the way the world feels when it's springtime. Come, and remember everything that makes you happy.* Her voice rose like a balloon, and underneath her, her teacher's voice was keeping her tied to the earth for when she was ready to come back down.

When the duet ended there wasn't a dry eye in the house. And after Mrs. Benedetto had gone back to her seat to cheering and applause, the audience was in the right mood to hear the rest of the songs on Lu's program.

FORTY-FIVE MINUTES later, when her performance was over and Lu had received her applause, she stepped down from the platform and looked for the exit to the kitchen. There was a small pantry behind it where the musicians rested between sets, and that was where she planned to spend the rest of the afternoon. Mrs. Benedetto had wanted her to sit at the bride's table and meet everyone and not run off like the hired help, but Lu had refused.

The truth was, when she wasn't onstage Lu was a little shy. But it wasn't just shyness that made her want to duck out of the restaurant dining room. She wasn't sure why she insisted on staying by herself before and after a performance, but she knew if she had to meet people face-to-face after she'd entertained them, some of the magic would be gone—for her and for them. And the magic was everything. So she hurried to the back of the dining room before Mrs. Benedetto could catch her eye.

"Come with me," said a voice at her side. She whirled around and saw a young man walking fast to keep up with her. "I'll take you to the kitchen," he said. "I bet you haven't eaten anything." She looked at him more closely. He was slim, but not skinny—she could see the muscles in his arms through his jacket—and he had an olive complexion and thick dark hair that curled around his thin face. His nose was on the large side, although it wasn't so big that it was ugly, his mouth was full, and there was something a little cynical in his dark eyes. And he was smiling at her.

"I can't eat before I sing," she admitted. Something about him made her feel comfortable although she had never seen him before.

"The greats never can," he said knowledgeably. "You've got to be hungry."

And then she felt really shy. "They've . . . stopped serving food . . ." she said, and trailed off as his smile got even bigger. He wasn't as old as she'd first thought he was.

"Yeah, but I've got pull," he said. "My dad owns this place." He held out his hand. "Your teacher is my aunt Adele. I'm Ricky Gaspari."

*   *   *

RICKY'S BRANCH OF the Gaspari clan was well known in New
Haven; his father was Vincent Gaspari, the owner of three popular restaurants. The jewel of the trio was the Villa Veneto. It
perched on a bluff above the West Haven shoreline, and if you had
dinner on the back terrace, the water seemed so close, it was like
you were eating on the beach. In addition to the spectacular view
and great food, Ricky's father had guaranteed the success of his
biggest restaurant by building it on the trolley line from downtown New Haven. It was as easy to get to the Villa Veneto as it was
to get to Savin Rock, the amusement park nearby.

Vincent himself was also a draw at the restaurant, greeting his
patrons at the door, remembering their names, flirting with the
women, and treating them all like dear personal friends. Of course
it was all an act; everyone in the Italian community knew that Vincent Gaspari was actually a calculating man driven by a boundless
ambition for his family, but the show he put on was so good that
no one cared if it was real.

As for Ricky's mother, she wasn't well liked, although it was
generally agreed that she was an upright, devout woman. She
gave to the church and was always there if the nuns needed a new
water heater for the convent, or a new roof. But people said there
was something cold about Guisipinna Gaspari. In the old country
her family had been a very big deal—they were northerners, of
course—and she never let you forget it.

Ricky's two older brothers were a different story. Joe and
Tommy Gaspari were twins. And to the first-generation Italian
American kids of New Haven the Gaspari twins were heroes. The
boys had earned their fame in high school on the football field.
After graduation they'd both gone on to Yale, where they had ce-
mented their reputations on the Yale team. It was that Ivy League
connection that had made them glamorous to the youngsters of
Lu's generation.

It was common knowledge that Yale had a quota for young men with too many vowels in their last names. The school did take in young men of "foreign," that is, non-Yankee backgrounds, and there were a handful of Italian American families in New Haven that boasted a Yale graduate in their midst. But most of those boys were hardworking day students who lived at home and didn't participate in campus social life. The sons of Eli didn't fraternize with the sons of immigrants, and the sons of immigrants were expected to understand that. But not the Gaspari twins. Not only had they shared a suite in Saybrook College on the Yale campus, but they had pledged one of Yale's best fraternities. Tommy was known to have dated a girl whose New England pedigree went back to the signing of the Declaration of Independence. It helped that the Gaspari family was rich, and that the clan had been in the country for generations. Still, the people of Italian New Haven—even those who said the Gasparis were snobs—were proud. Then after Pearl Harbor, the twins had signed up the very next day—Joe for the navy, Tommy to become a paratrooper—and the pride knew no bounds.

Ricky led Lu to the restaurant kitchen, where he seated her at a large wooden table and served her a dish of lasagna that smelled as good as her mom's. "You must have heard of my brothers," he said, with the younger brother's worshipful tone she recognized from her own tribe. Then, to cover, he added quickly, "They're both a couple of jerks."

She nodded.

"If Tommy and Joe looked like me, they wouldn't have made it nearly so big," Ricky went on. "They've got the Gaspari looks, all white skin, red hair, and green eyes. Me? No one knows where I came from." It was true; he didn't look anything like the pictures Lu had seen in the *New Haven Register* of his strapping, godlike brothers. "I'm the dark horse," he went on. She was about to tell him that he was a very attractive person when it occurred to her that there wasn't anyone else in this part of the kitchen and she couldn't remember ever being alone with a boy who wasn't a relative. The newness of the situation made her feel nervous, and for a second she wondered if she and Paulie had been right to ignore Mama's rules. Then Ricky reached into his pocket for a pack of cigarettes and she saw how long and strong his fingers were and the dusting of dark hair on his arm where it came out of the sleeve of his jacket, and she stopped thinking about Mama.

She watched Ricky light his cigarette with a practiced flip of match to matchbook and then blow the smoke away so it wouldn't bother her. When Lu's brothers and their friends snuck a quick cigarette on the street corner, it had always seemed like a crude and unappealing thing to do, but somehow Ricky made it look smooth . . . and classy . . . and . . . suddenly she wasn't hungry anymore. She pushed her plate of lasagna away. Ricky seemed to read her mind.

"How old are you?" he asked in a voice that had suddenly gotten husky—from the cigarette smoke, she told herself.

"Sixteen. How old are you?" she managed.

"Seventeen."

"You seem older."

He looked at her for what seemed like a very long time, then crushed out his cigarette, stood up, and held out his hand to her. "Let's get out of here," he said. She took his hand with the long fingers. It was warm and strong. She didn't ask him where they were going as he opened the back door of the kitchen so she could follow him outside. The nervous feeling was back. But it was a pleasant nervous feeling—like the kind that made you shiver with excitement backstage because you were so eager to go out and sing.

*   *   *

THERE WAS A lawn leading up to the front entrance of the Villa Veneto, and chairs, benches, and a couple of swings on frames were scattered on it. But to Lu's surprise, Ricky headed in the opposite direction. The warm, strong hand that was still holding hers led her to the parking lot at the side of the restaurant. They walked over to a motorcycle. "It's mine," he said proudly. "You want to go for a spin?"

Lu had never been on a motorcycle, but she knew what she would have to do if she took him up on his offer. She'd seen a girl in the neighborhood riding behind her boyfriend, her arms around his waist, her legs on either side of him, the front of her body pressed against his back. Whenever they sped past Lu on the street, they were laughing and they seemed to be having so much fun that Lu had envied them. Now all she could think of was Mama saying that the girl was a disgrace.

Ricky threw his leg over the machine like he was John Wayne climbing up on his horse, and settled in to the seat. "Hop on," he said. "It's real easy to balance. All you have to do is hold on to me, and . . ." But he stopped in the middle of his sentence, and she knew they were both thinking about where her arms would go . . . and her legs. Ricky's face reddened. "Hey, if you'd rather not . . ."

"No," she said quickly. "I want to." And she wasn't lying. She pulled her dress up above her knees so she could sit behind him.

It took only a couple of turns around the parking lot for her to learn how to balance. She held herself erect and made sure there was a distance between herself and Ricky; not at all like the girl in the neighborhood. But she did have to hold on to him. And she did have to move her body with his in a way she'd never done before—not even when she was dancing. Mama would have said she was a disgrace. But Mama wasn't there. They roared out of the parking lot and headed south on a road that hugged the shoreline.

"Where are we going?" Lu shouted into the wind.

"Savin Rock," he shouted back.

Savin Rock was known as a place where boys took their sweethearts.

The amusement park wasn't far from the Villa Veneto; Lu and Ricky could have walked it. But sitting behind him on the motorcycle, she could feel the warmth of his back as they roared along the road, and watch the wind ruffle the curls at the back of his neck. Curls she could have touched. They went around a curve and she held him a little more tightly.

When they finally stopped in the heart of Savin Rock, Ricky seemed a little quiet, as if something had happened on the ride that he hadn't been expecting. He parked the motorcycle, lit another cigarette, and smoked it in silence, while she breathed in the fresh salt air and waited for him to make up his mind about what he wanted to do next. Finally, just as she was about to ask if he'd changed his mind and wanted to go back to Villa Veneto, he grabbed her hand and they started wandering down the street.

By 1943, Savin Rock Amusement Park had seen better days. Forty years earlier it had been a glorious fantasyland of roller coasters, water chutes, bumper cars, fancy restaurants, quickie food stalls, vaudeville shows, firework displays, boardwalks, colonnades, and several carousels, including the magnificent one known as the Flying Horses of Beach Street. Sadly, fires had destroyed many of the attractions over the years, and several of the fine restaurants had been built on piers, which had been blown away during hurricanes. And like so many places of entertainment, the old park had never totally recovered from the Depression. But thanks to the nearby trolley, it was still popular with young people—especially now that gas rationing made public transportation a must. There were groups of kids—many of the boys wearing uniforms—laughing, joking, and eating as they strolled past the cotton candy stands, shooting galleries, arcade games, and postcard stalls. There were couples too, some with their arms around each other, some holding hands. Sometimes the boy looked solemn and the girl looked like she might cry. When the boy was wearing a uniform it was easy to imagine why.

Ricky wove his way through the crowd, leading Lu. Usually she wasn't the type who followed anyone without knowing where she was going, but this time, with this boy, it was different.

They rode the merry-go-round. Her horse was a beautiful caramel color with pink roses on the side, and Ricky's horse was white with flaring nostrils and gold leaf on its bridle. Ricky won them a free ride by grabbing the brass ring. He was very serious about getting it, positioning himself carefully so he could snatch a ring—most of which were steel—each time he went around. Lu couldn't help feeling proud to be with him. His seriousness said something about him that she liked.

She'd never been to Savin Rock. Mama wasn't one for amusement parks and Pop had always been too busy to take the family. Lu knew she should have felt guilty about sneaking off like this with a boy she didn't know. But she wasn't. Not even a little bit.

Ricky took her to a food stand called Jimmie's for hot dogs because he said you couldn't go to Savin Rock without a stop at Jimmie's. He bought her cotton candy and a frozen custard, which they shared, laughing when it melted, and she didn't even mind when she got some on her skirt. But then, even though there were more rides and other kinds of food to try, he took her hand again and they walked down to the beach. Ricky spread his jacket on the sand for them to sit on, and they looked out at the sea. When he kissed her it wasn't a surprise. Not really. Even though it had never happened to her before. At first she wasn't sure what to do, but his mouth was soft and he opened it a little and it seemed like the most natural thing in the world to open hers too. He tasted like tobacco and frozen custard. The taste made her dizzy. She pressed herself against him; she wanted him to go on doing this forever. But in a minute, Ricky pushed her away.

"No," he said in a scratchy voice. "You're not the kind of girl I kiss that way."

"Why not?" she demanded. But he looked at her with a glare that made her turn away.

"You know why," he said, as if he was angry at her. She wanted to cry, but then he reached out to stroke her cheek very gently, and that made it all right. They turned back to the sea, and there was sand on her face from his fingers.

After a couple of minutes he said, "You're going to be a star, you know," as if they'd been talking about it for a long time and it was a conclusion he'd come to. He turned to look at her, squinting a little in the sunshine. "It's not just that you have a beautiful voice. What you did today with Aunt Adele—that was what a star would do. The way a star would think. No one can teach you that."

She thought about saying what she'd done was no big thing. Her brothers went on all the time about how there was nothing worse than a girl who was too full of herself, and when a boy gave you a compliment you were supposed to brush it off and find a way to turn it back on him. But her instincts told her Ricky would be disappointed if she played games with him. And talking about her future as an actress was too important to lie about.

"I do want to be a star," she said seriously. "On Broadway. And I think I'm the kind of person who gets what she wants."

"So am I," he said.

"I know." He didn't ask her how she knew, because he didn't have to. They understood each other.

"I'm not going to Yale like Tommy and Joe," Ricky went on. "In a month I'm going to be eighteen and I'm going to join up so I can do my part for the war and put it behind me. After I get out of the army, I'm going to California to work in the movies."

"You want to be an actor?" It was the first time she thought he was making a mistake about something. The performer in her knew that he wasn't one.

He smiled. "You don't have to be polite; I know I'd stink at acting. I'm going out there to be a cameraman. The family still has a few connections in show business, and one of my grandpop's friends said he'll get me a job."

She looked at him, his strong profile silhouetted against the background of the sky and sea. "I don't think a job working for someone else will be enough for you," she said thoughtfully. "You need to be top dog."

He laughed. Then he hugged her. "I'm going to work my way up, learn the ropes as I go. Being a cameraman is just the beginning. Someday I'm going to be a producer, and have my own studio." He tightened his arm around her. "And you'll come out to California and star in one of my movies."

"If I can get away from Broadway," she said. Even in a daydream she didn't like the idea of anyone taking her for granted.

"Oh, I'll make it worth your while, " he said confidently. He turned back to the ocean again. "Mom's going to hate it—me going into show business. Tommy and Joe are both going to be doctors. According to Mom, that's a noble calling. A career like that is worthy of a Gaspari."

"I thought boys got to do whatever they wanted to do. It's girls who have rules."

"We Gaspari boys have been privileged, you see. We have to give back. When I was seven—after I made my First Communion— I thought I wanted to be a priest. Mom loved that."

"What changed your mind?"

He turned to her and grinned, but his face was red. "I discovered girls . . ."

She felt a little dizzy again, the way she had when he kissed her.

"Oh," she said, and wished she could have come up with a more sophisticated response. "What about your father? What does he want for you?"

"Dad has different ambitions. He wants us to get married—preferably to nice Yankee girls from old American families who don't know how to cook macaroni—and start a dynasty of Gasparis who go to Yale." He shook his head. "I don't want that either. I don't want anything to tie me down."

"Me neither, " Lu said. And as she heard herself, she realized how much she meant it. "Mama gives up everything for us, and I hate watching her. I don't want to give up my life for anyone."

That was when he kissed her again. Then they walked back to his motorcycle without saying a word. And this time when they rode home she held him tight.

When they entered the lobby of the Villa Veneto, Mrs. Benedetto was dressed in her going-away suit and everyone was hugging her and crying. The wedding was almost over. Lu started toward the crowd of weeping well-wishers, but Ricky pulled her back. "I want to see you again," he muttered. "Can I call you?"

But Lu couldn't even imagine what would happen if Mama knew a boy was calling her. "I'll come out to Savin Rock on the trolley," she said. "Next Saturday."

AND SO IT began. Because it was summer, Lu had a lot more free time than she would have had during the school year, and sneaking off to be with Ricky turned out to be easier than she'd expected. Paulie was having a fling of his own—with the neighborhood girl Mama said was a disgrace—and he and Lu covered for each other. And Mama was distracted. Eddie had finally gotten his orders and was somewhere in the Pacific, but they hadn't gotten any mail from him yet. And the accountant Mama had hired to run the grocery stores was making a mess of the business, so Mama worried about that too. With Mama's attention so scattered, Lu was able to sneak entire afternoons with Ricky.

They always spent their time together in public places—Ricky insisted on that. His brothers owned a cottage on the beach near Savin Rock, and before they'd left for the army they'd given Ricky the keys. He could have taken Lu there anytime, but he never suggested it. Instead they met in the amusement park, where they walked around aimlessly before they headed to the beach. There they would kiss and drive each other crazy until one of them—usually Ricky—would stop it. Sometimes he took her to the movies, but neither of them could have told anyone what picture they'd seen. They wandered around neighborhoods where neither of them knew anyone until they found a deserted park where they could be alone. Sometimes the kissing and touching went further than they meant it to, and when they had to pull away from each other, Ricky would curse and Lu would want to cry. Ricky would say that they had to stop this. He'd swear that the next time they would actually watch the movie. They would look at the flowers and the trees in the park. They would talk—nothing more. But when they were together the kissing would start again. It seemed to Lu that they were marking time, waiting for something inevitable. It turned out that she was right.

One afternoon, they had arranged to meet for a matinee at the Loews Poli movie theater in downtown New Haven, and Lu arrived there first. That had happened before. Ricky often stayed at the beach in his brothers' cottage, and he had to take the trolley or ride his motorcycle into town. Since there was no telephone at the cottage, he had no way of calling if he was late. So Lu wasn't worried—at first. Then the minutes stretched into an hour. Then two hours. Then four. Lu waited through three showings of the movie. Finally, unable to bear the pitying looks from the ticket taker, she left.

It occurred to Lu that maybe she had been stood up—or even dropped. Maybe the long, frustrating afternoons had gotten to be too much for Ricky. But then she rejected the idea. If Ricky had wanted to stop seeing her, he would have told her. He wouldn't have made a plan to meet her and then let her cool her heels at a movie theater until she got the hint. Besides, Ricky didn't want to stop seeing her, she was sure of that. But still . . . he hadn't shown up. By the time she reached her house, she was getting scared. There were so many things that could have happened to him. He could be sick. He could have had an accident on the motorcycle . . . he drove it way too fast . . . She was desperate to know what had happened to him, but she couldn't call his house. No one in his family knew about her.

She helped her mother set the table and took her place for dinner, wondering if she should call Mrs. Benedetto. But what would she say? She couldn't very well tell her former teacher who had loved and believed in her that she'd been sneaking around seeing Ricky for months.

Paulie's voice broke into her thoughts. "Tommy Gaspari is missing in action," he announced.

"Madonna!" Mama dropped her knife and fork on her plate with a clatter. War talk upset her.

"Are you sure? How do you know?" Lu demanded.

"I heard it today at the ballpark."

"How long has he been missing?" Lu fired the question, even though Mama's face was dead white. Normally she would have changed the subject, but this was about Ricky's brother. No wonder he hadn't shown up at the movie theater!

"The guys at the park didn't know for sure," Paulie said.

"Tommy's Seventh Army. That's Patton. And Tommy's a para-trooper—so everyone's saying he could have been in the invasion of Sicily." Paulie threw a quick look at Mama. "They say the Gasparis just heard about it today and the old man is trying to pull strings in Washington to find out what's going on—"

"Eat," Mama cut in, her voice shrill. "Your ziti will get cold."

After the dinner dishes had been washed and put away, Paulie signaled to Lu to come upstairs to his room. She found him sitting on his bed with a map spread in front of him. Whispering so Mama wouldn't hear, he showed Lu the Pachino Peninsula, the Gulf of Gela, and the Gulf of Noto. He threw around words like "Sherman tanks," "DUKWs," "battalions," and "platoons." Lu barely heard him. While her brother told her about beachheads and landing craft, she remembered the look in Ricky's eyes whenever he talked about the twins—especially Tommy.

EARLY THE NEXT morning, Lu left the house and boarded the trolley for the beach. She found the twins' cottage easily—Ricky had shown it to her once—and knocked on the door. If Ricky wasn't there she would have to go to his family's home in the Gaspari compound to try to find him. But Ricky answered the door. He'd been crying.

"I'm sorry," she said. He stood in front of her like a hurt little kid. She put her arms around him and closed the door behind them.

The cottage wasn't fancy; just a little living room with a fireplace, a kitchen, and two small bedrooms. The furniture was beat up and old, mostly made of wicker and wood. The floor was linoleum, to make it easier to sweep up the sand that was tracked in from the beach, and the sofa in the living room was faded and a little saggy. Lu was aware of all of this, but she couldn't take it in.

All she knew then was that she was holding Ricky so tight, it was as if she was trying to take the pain out of him and into her own body. When the kissing started afterward, it was different than it had ever been before. And when they made their way to one of the small bedrooms, it felt right.

"We can stop . . ." he whispered at the doorway.

"I don't want to," she said.

TOMMY GASPARI WAS found safe and sound three weeks later. But by that time everything had changed for Lu and Ricky, and they couldn't go back to what they had been before.

Lu was never really sure of the point in time when she realized that she and Ricky weren't in love—not in the way that made you want to spend the rest of your life together. They liked going to bed with each other, and she got to know the little cottage at the beach very well because Ricky had finally agreed that they didn't have to wander around New Haven and Savin Rock anymore. But when he talked about his future in California he never used the word *we*. And when she dreamed about her star-studded life in New York she never pictured him with her. They were too young to settle down— she knew that was part of it. But there was something else too. They were both selfish. They wanted so much for themselves, and it was going to be years before either of them had time to be in love. For some reason that they never had to discuss, they understood that about each other. It was probably why they were so fond of each other, and why it was so easy for them to be together.

So the summer rolled on, and when Lu wasn't singing or taking lessons she spent her time in the little sun-drenched bedroom in the cottage at the beach. It was during one of these afternoons that Ricky asked her if she'd like to audition for a New York show.

"One of Grandpop's old friends from the vaudeville days is reviving an operetta that was done in the twenties called *The Maiden Ship*, and they need singers for a couple of bit parts," he said. "The show is going to play in a little theater down in Greenwich Village. It's not Broadway, exactly, but . . ."

"Yes!" she broke in. "Yes! Yes! Yes!"

"Don't you even want to know what kind of singers they're looking for?"

"Whatever they want, I'll be it!"

"They're looking for sopranos."

"And here I am! Ricky, you're an angel! You're better than an angel! You're Santa Claus and Ziegfeld and Billy Rose all rolled into one! You're . . ."

"I'm Louis B. Mayer. And don't you forget it."

They decided that Ricky would meet her on the street corner near her house on the morning of the audition and take her to the train station.

"I wish I could go with you to the city, but I can't," he said. "If I did, I'd have to tell my parents I set up your audition and they'd know I'm still in touch with some of Grandpop's old showbiz pals."

Lu nodded; she knew she wasn't the only one who kept pieces of her life secret from her family. But she also knew that wasn't the only reason Ricky wasn't going with her. Their golden summer was almost over; in a few weeks he'd be eighteen and he'd be joining the army. And she was looking to the future too. If all went well at her audition, she'd be going to New York to start her new life. She'd miss Ricky, but since their romance had to end sometime, it seemed to her that this was the best possible way for it to happen. Especially if her audition panned out.

It wasn't until Lu was on her way back to New Haven with the time and place of the audition written out on a piece of paper in her hand that she thought about Mama. The round trip to New

York, plus the audition, would take most of the day; it wasn't the same thing as vanishing for a couple of hours to be with Ricky in West Haven. No matter how distracted Mama was, she'd notice an absence that lasted all day. There was no way to keep this from Mama; Lu just had to pray she wouldn't find out about the audition until after it was over.

THE NIGHT BEFORE her audition, Lu gathered up everything she would need to get herself dolled up for her big day: her brand-new suit, best shoes, a card of bobby pins, a hand mirror, a tube of lipstick, an eyeliner pencil, and a bottle of leg makeup, which girls used to make their legs look less bare because nylon was rationed and no one could buy stockings. She put it all in a pillowcase and hid the bundle in the laundry off the kitchen. The bedrooms were on the second floor of the house, and Mama was a light sleeper who still heard every sound her kids made. Getting dressed downstairs on the first floor was safer.

The next morning, Lu woke up while it was still dark out and tiptoed down the back stairs to the laundry room, where she pinned up her hair and dressed in her brand new suit. It was going to get wrinkled sitting on the train, but she couldn't help that; there was no place in New York where she could change her clothes. She put on her lipstick—Mama didn't know she owned the contraband tube, but she always wore it when she performed—and then propped first one foot and then the other on the washing machine to smear on the leg makeup, praying it wasn't streaking.

She was slipping into her shoes when she heard a noise in the kitchen. Her heart started to race. Hoping against hope that it was Paulie who had awakened early, she walked out of the laundry room.

Mama wasn't dressed. Lu couldn't remember the last time she'd seen her mother in a robe and slippers with her long hair falling in a single braid down her back. No matter how early breakfast was, Mifalda appeared wearing a housedress, with her hair pulled back in a bun at the nape of her neck and secured with large tortoise-shell hairpins. But not this morning.

How did she know? Lu thought. *I was so quiet, so careful. How does she always, always know?*

Her mother didn't look up. In her hands was the book of music Lu had accidentally left on the kitchen table. Only the day before, Maestro DiTullio had noted all of her key and tempo changes on the page of the song she was planning to sing so the accompanist at the audition in New York would know how to play it for her. Mama was holding the music book so hard, she was wrinkling the cover.

Lu braced herself for the battle about to happen. She tried to tell herself that it was better to get it over with, but she knew it wasn't. She liked to be peaceful on the inside when she sang, and a fight would make her feel all jangled up. But there was no way out.

"Good morning, Mama, " she said.

Her mother dropped the music on the table and drew in a deep breath. Before she could start yelling, Lu beat her to the punch and confessed about the audition. "I'm going to New York today to sing, Mama," she ended breathlessly. "I'm going to be an actress. And this is my big chance." She pulled herself up to her full height and waited for the bomb to go off.

But Mama surprised her. There was no explosion, no yelling. Her mother was staring at her calmly, as if in some way she'd been expecting this. Had she? Did Mama understand? It was a startling thought. Mama always seemed to be made out of rock, an obstacle that Lu had to get around to live her own life. Did her mother know what it felt like to be young and have dreams? Could she be proud of the daughter everyone else said was so talented? Tears stung in Lu's eyes. *Oh, Mama, if you can just be on my side,* she thought, *I'll make it all up to you. You'll be the mother of a Broadway star, and all the sacrifices you've made will be worth it.*

"So," her mother said. Her voice was as calm as her face, but all of a sudden the calmness wasn't comforting. It was scary. "This 'big chance' of yours, how did it happen?"

"I don't . . . understand . . ." Lu stumbled.

"Who is he?" Mama demanded. "Who is the man who gave you this 'big chance'?"

And that was when Lu knew how dumb she'd been for ever thinking that Mama could be on her side. Because of course her mother immediately jumped to the conclusion that some man was trying to take advantage of Lu. That was how Mama's mind worked. And for the first time since she and Ricky started sleeping together in the cottage on the beach, Lu saw them the way Mama would. Mama wouldn't see a girl who had tried to comfort a boy, or a boy and a girl who were fond of each other but were too smart to kid themselves that they were ready for marriage. Mama wouldn't understand that Ricky cared about her and he'd set up the audition because he believed in her. Mama would see a girl who got her "big chance" by giving herself to a rich boy who tossed her a bone on his way out the door. To Mama, Lu was being wild and cheap. And stupid.

Lu stood even taller and looked her mother in the eye. "A friend of mine called some people and asked them to hear me sing," she said.

"What is the friend's name?"

"Mama, I have to go or I'll miss my train." Lu started for the kitchen table to pick up her music, but a hand that was far stronger than Lu could ever have imagined grabbed her arm and whirled her around. The force stunned her.

"You are not leaving this house!" Her mother's voice wasn't scary calm anymore. Mifalda was shouting now. "You're going to your room and you're going to stay there until I tell you."

"No, Mama." Lu heard the steel in her own voice and was surprised by it.

"I am your mother and I'm telling you . . ."

Lu yanked her arm out of her mother's grasp. "I won't do what you tell me to, Mama. Not anymore. Because you want me to be just like you, and I won't. Pop and the boys always thought you were so happy taking care of us, but I knew—"

Without any warning, Mifalda slapped her across the face. Hard. The movement was so swift, for a second Lu wasn't sure it had happened. Then the wave of pain came. For the second time that day, tears filled Lu's eyes. But the cause was shock as much as the slap itself. No one had ever done anything like it to her before. Mama always said she didn't believe in hitting her children—she was proud that she didn't—and Pop wouldn't have laid a finger on his little girl. But Mama had slapped her. Lu's face was stinging and she could feel the blood pumping through her veins. Her teeth had cut into her upper lip—not enough to cause bleeding, but there could be some swelling. And her head was going to ache. But she wasn't going to cry.

"You'll have to hit me a lot harder than that to keep me from going, Mama," she said, forming each syllable carefully in spite of lips that felt too thick. She walked to the table and scooped up her music.

"You are not going to New York," her mother said, but the tears were streaming down her face, and Lu's face was dry.

"How are you going to stop me?" she asked gently. Then she turned and walked out of the house.

CHAPTER 11

New Haven

1943

LU DIDN'T TELL Ricky about the fight with Mama. She met him at the corner as they'd planned, and climbed on the back of his motorcycle fast so he wouldn't see the marks on her face. By the time they reached the train station, she was sure the redness had died down, because Ricky didn't say anything about it. He did say she looked beautiful and she should wear lipstick all the time. But when they were inside the terminal buying her ticket, Lu's hands started to shake. She still couldn't tell him why. "I think I'm a little nervous," she said.

Ricky bought her a *McCall's* magazine to read on the trip, to take her mind off the audition, he said. She took the magazine from him, and her teeth started to chatter. He put his jacket around her to warm her up as they walked out to the platform to wait for the train. He rubbed her shaking hands, but nothing helped. Finally, as the train was rolling into the station, he said sharply, "Lu, you've got to get a hold of yourself. No matter how scared you are, you've got to be great at this audition. These producers do a lot of shows in the city—not just this one. You don't want to make a bad impression on them."

It was the wrong thing for him to say. She'd just had her face slapped and now Ricky, who always told her he knew she was going to knock 'em dead, was warning her about making a bad impression? It had never occurred to Lu that she might fail. She'd been so focused on getting out of the house without Mama knowing that she'd never thought about something going wrong with the audition. But when she saw how worried Ricky was, fear crashed in on her.

Suddenly she realized that this was going to be very different from singing for the director of the New Haven Children's Theater Workshop. Today the men who were going to hear her were professionals. They could make or break her, and they didn't know she was Maestro DiTullio's best pupil. They'd never heard of the maestro. An icy sweat started under Lu's arms and trickled down her sides.

"Hey, I'm going to knock 'em dead," she said, and she managed to produce a jittery smile. Ricky didn't look convinced.

The train stopped and the conductor yelled for people to get on board. Lu gave Ricky a quick kiss, climbed the metal steps, and found a seat, the way she had so many times when she and Pop used to go to Manhattan. She wished Pop was with her now. She wished Paulie was with her. For a moment she even wished Mama was there. She looked out the window and saw Ricky standing on the platform. As the train pulled out of the station, she waved frantically at him until he was out of sight. Then she opened the *McCall's* magazine and began reading as if her life depended on it.

The train trip to Manhattan was the longest one she'd ever taken. She knew she was having a massive attack of stage fright, and the problem was, this was her first experience with it. When she'd appeared in Maestro DiTullio's recitals, she'd seen other students become mindless with terror before they went on; some of them even threw up. She could never figure out why—she couldn't wait to get in front of an audience. But that was before Mama slapped her and Ricky warned her about making a bad impression. When the train finally roared into Grand Central Terminal, Lu's brain was frozen. There had even been a couple of times when she'd been afraid she might throw up. The conductor had to tell her twice that it was the last stop before she could make herself get off the train.

LU HAD NEVER played a real theater. The Children's Workshop performed in the auditorium at St. Mary's High School, and Maestro DiTullio held his recitals in the hall at St. Anthony's Social Club. Ricky had tried to prepare her for what she would find backstage at a professional house.

"The stage will be deeper than what you're used to," he'd said. "The wings will be wider, and it'll feel like there isn't any ceiling when you look up. That's because they hang the backdrops and the curtains above the stage on riggings—the space up there is called the flies. Even though the theater where you're going to audition isn't a big Broadway house, it's going to seem huge to you, so don't let it throw you."

Unfortunately there were some things about auditioning that Ricky hadn't warned her about. He hadn't mentioned that there would be at least thirty young women—presumably all sopranos—standing in the wings, clutching their sheet music, in various stages of panic. He hadn't said that the accompanist would be on the stage with the auditioning singers so the tinny old upright piano could drown them out if they stood too close to it. Ricky hadn't warned

Lu that there would be enough light on the stage so the singers could see the faces—dimly—of the three men in the audience who were going to judge them, and he hadn't told her that those three men would be too busy talking about their lunch that had just been delivered to pay any attention to the frightened performers. Lu watched as a girl who had been brought out on stage waited to sing. She stood there smiling desperately.

"Go on, dearie," one of the threesome in the house commanded.

Rattled, the girl nodded, smiled even more desperately, and said loudly, "Good afternoon, gentlemen . . ."

"I told you I didn't order the tongue," said the man to one of his colleagues. "Why would I order tongue? I hate it."

Those guys are nothing but a bunch of cafones, Lu thought. *I don't care how important they are.* And her brain started to defrost. It seemed that getting angry was a good weapon against stage fright.

"I'm going to sing the song 'Spanish Nights' from *The Maiden Ship*," the singer barreled on bravely. As the bored accompanist began playing the intro to a song with a vaguely Latin beat, Lu's brain continued defrosting. She looked around her and registered something that had been bothering her since she'd walked through the stage door. Most of her fellow auditioners were wearing ensembles that suggested if not Spain, someplace south of the border. Skirts were draped with brightly colored scarves, and shawls and blouses with puffy sleeves prevailed. There were a lot of flowers tucked behind ears. Clearly, the trio in the audience was looking for a Spanish type. Lu looked down at her dark blue suit and her ruffled white blouse with the high neck. She looked at her alligator pumps. It had never occurred to her to try to dress for the part she was trying to get—or to find out what the part was. She hadn't thought to learn a song from *The Maiden Ship* as the singer on stage had done. Lu was going to look like a total amateur when it was her turn.

Why didn't Ricky tell me about all of this? she thought furiously. But then she realized he probably didn't know. After all, he was an amateur too.

Lu listened to the tune the girl on the stage was singing. In other circumstances she would have said the music was silly; it was a soprano aria written in a rumba rhythm. And at the end of the piece, the girl launched into a coloratura cadenza that ended in a trill—and shouted *"Olé!"* Maestro DiTullio would never have allowed Lu to work on such garbage.

She was to hear the song three more times before she was called on the stage to sing herself. By that point she wasn't nervous anymore, but a feeling of doom had come over her. Her clothes were wrong, her hair was wrong, and her material was wrong. Her big chance was going to be a big flop. She'd gotten herself slapped in the face for nothing.

Still, she strode out onto the stage the way she'd seen all the other girls do, and, as she placed her book on the rack of the upright piano, she said to the semi-comatose accompanist, "The song is on page sixty-three. You'll find all my key changes are noted." Then she walked as far away from the piano as she could and turned to the house. "Good afternoon, gentlemen," she said to the men, who had finished their lunch and were now engrossed in a conversation about the check. She knew better than to wait for them to look up. "I am going to sing . . ." she began, but a snicker from the piano stopped her. "I am going to sing . . ." she began again, but the accompanist stepped in.

"Honey, could you come over here for a sec?" he called out.

Lu's brain threatened to freeze again. She sidled over to the piano.

The accompanist was actually showing signs of life. "I'm good," he said with a chuckle, "but even I can't play *McCall's* magazine." He held out the booklet she had placed on the rack of the piano with such authority and bravado. Horrified, Lu read the title on the cover.

"You got your music?" the accompanist asked.

She didn't. When she'd walked out of Grand Central Terminal, she'd carried only one item in her sweaty, cold hands. She'd thought it was her sheet music, but in those last panicky moments on the train she must have picked up the magazine instead. And during the cab ride to the theater she hadn't bothered to check because she was too busy trying not to be sick.

"Your music, honey?" the accompanist prodded.

She shook her head.

"Too bad," he said, and started to signal the stage manager to send out the next girl. Something inside Lu snapped. She hadn't endured two hours of terror and nausea on a train and in a cab—plus a slap in the face—to go back home without auditioning.

"Wait," she heard herself say to the accompanist. She grabbed the magazine he was still holding out to her. "Play that song everyone's been singing," she told him.

The look he gave her was sympathetic. "Kiddo, you can't sing that thing if you don't know it. God knows you could try to wing it, but it's tricky, and . . ."

"I know it, " Lu broke in. That was only partly true: she didn't know the lyrics because she hadn't been paying enough attention, but the melody had embedded itself in her mind. "Can you play it without sheet music?"

He shrugged. "In my sleep. What key?"

"Pick one for me." She moved to the center of the stage and flipped quickly through the magazine until she found what she wanted. What she was about to do was really nuts, but she was going to sing no matter what. Besides, Ricky said she thought on her feet like a star, and she was gambling that he was right. "I'm gonna sing a song about food," she announced in an accent she meant to be Spanish but which really sounded a lot like Mama. The men in the house stopped talking to each other and directed their attention to the stage for the first time. So far, so good.

The accompanist began playing, and Lu began singing her selection from *McCall's*—the ingredients and instructions for a recipe for Spanish meatloaf. She fit the words to the dumb operetta aria as she went. Whenever there weren't enough syllables to fill out a musical phrase, she filled in the dead space by stomping flamenco-style on the stage floor and shouting *"Olé."* For three quarters of the song she managed to make each line work. Then her recipe ran out. Lu went into the cadenza with the silly trill, singing it a capella because the accompanist, who was watching her with openmouthed awe, had given up trying to follow her. When she finished the trill, she had nowhere else to go and no way to get herself gracefully off the stage. In a moment of pure inspiration, she kicked off her shoes and did three of her *Puss in Boots* cartwheels into the wings. Then she had to run back onstage to collect her shoes, killing her exit, so she shouted three triumphant *"Olés"* at the men in the audience and exited again.

She wasn't sure exactly what she'd been hoping for—maybe some laughter, because she knew what she'd done was funny, or maybe a little applause for her courage. Maybe the producers would decide she thought like a star and ask for her name and her contact information.

There was a stony silence from the house. Backstage, the fake señoritas were staring at her in horror. A couple of them backed away from her as if whatever madness had just possessed her might be catching.

Come on, she wanted to shout at them. *It's a stupid song. And those men are rude. They deserved what they got.* But the silence in the theater had become a roar. And she remembered Ricky saying that the men in front produced a lot of Broadway shows and she mustn't make a bad impression. Lu's hands started shaking again—there was no way she could get her shoes on. Every eye was on her. With her head held high, clutching her magazine and her alligator pumps, she marched out of the theater barefoot.

The stage door opened onto an alley, and Lu slumped against the side of the theater. She'd failed. Her career was over before it had started. Now she had to hail a cab, get back on the train, and go home to face Mama. And Ricky. It was hard to decide which was going to be worse.

Behind her, the stage door opened and closed. She heard the sound of laughter—shrieking, out-of-control laughter. She turned to see the accompanist doubled up and grasping a trash barrel for support. His eyes were streaming.

"Oh God," he gasped. "Oh God, I've been playing that idiot song for three days straight and I thought it was going to be in my nightmares for the rest of my life. Then you come along and . . . Oh God!"

Being laughed at was more than Lu could bear. She crammed her feet into the pumps and started down the alley.

"Hold on. Where are you going?" the accompanist called out.

"I'm glad you thought it was funny to watch me die in front of the most important men in show business," she said. "At least one of us got something out of it."

"What 'most important men in show business'?" he demanded. "You mean Larry, Moe, and Curly in there? Those guys haven't had a hit since the twenties. God knows where they got the backers for that old warhorse they're putting on."

For the first time, she really looked at him. He was probably a couple of years older than she was, tall—well over six feet—and a little chubby. His hair was blond and so curly, no amount of brushing was going to keep it off his face. His eyes were blue and he wore thick glasses with black frames. But what was most remarkable about him was the way he was dressed. Because of the war, everyone—men and women—wore fitted clothes to conserve precious cloth, but the accompanist was wearing a zoot suit with an oversize jacket, wide lapels, and baggy pants that narrowed at the ankles. It was an old-fashioned look, but given his size Lu felt it was a good choice.

"You didn't want that job." He'd stopped laughing and now he clapped one hand dramatically over his chest and held the other up to the sky. "Believe me."

And in spite of his theatrics, she did. If the song "Spanish Nights" was an example of the score for *The Maiden Ship*, he was right—that operetta was an old warhorse. And she was happy to believe that the men in the house were over the hill and hadn't had a hit in twenty years. For a moment she felt sorry for Ricky, who had put so much faith in his grandpop's old pals, but Ricky would figure out that they were the Three Stooges for himself. Ricky was tough. She grinned at the accompanist. "So I haven't ruined my chances in show business?"

"You might have, if you'd gotten a part in *The Maiden Ship*," he said. "But this is your lucky day." He pulled a piece of paper out of his pocket. "I've written down the name of an agent for you—Max Lieberman. I've sent him other people who were good, and he trusts me. He'll see you if you use my name." He held out the piece of paper to Lu. "He's legit; you can check with Actors' Equity."

Lu looked at the paper, but she didn't take it. "Why are you doing this?" she asked.

He grinned. "Because you're the funniest thing I've seen on two feet. And I want to be able to say I knew you when."

Things were moving too fast—the sick feeling came back—and for a moment Lu had to close her eyes. Five minutes before she'd been trying to figure out how she was going to tell Ricky that she'd failed. Now this total stranger was offering her a second chance.

She opened her eyes. The accompanist was standing in front of her, still holding out the piece of paper. "Max is going to be out of town for three weeks," he said. "Call him when he gets back and ask if you can sing for him. I gave you my number too. There'll be someone in Max's office who will play for you, but I can rehearse you first." He wasn't kidding around; he really wanted to help her. She took the piece of paper with the phone numbers from him and held out her hand. "Hi," she said. "I'm Lu Leporello."

He shook her hand and said, "George. George Standish." He frowned. "You're going to have to change the Leporello to something more American. Something that'll look good on a marquee." He thought for a second, and then he said, "How about Lawson? It's always good to keep it close to your own name. I used to be Gregory Stantonkovsky."

THE TRAIN TRIP home was the opposite of the frozen journey Lu had endured that morning. True, she hadn't gotten a job. But she had made friends with a person who accompanied at Broadway auditions. And she had the phone number of a real New York agent. She wasn't sure how she'd get around Mama and come back to New York, but that didn't matter now. She was on her way. Or so she thought.

THE NEXT MORNING when Lu woke up, she almost didn't make it to the bathroom before she got sick. She told herself it was because she'd been so scared the day before. When the same thing happened the next morning, she tried to tell herself she was upset because she and Mama were not speaking to each other—although their fights had never bothered her like that before. When she continued to get sick every morning for the next two weeks, she told Ricky. He bought two rings that looked like wedding bands and took her to a doctor in Danbury, which was a few towns away from New Haven. The doctor told them that contrary to what Ricky had been led to believe, there was no such thing as an absolutely safe time of the month. But, the doctor added brightly, Lu's morning sickness should start tapering off in the next few weeks.

CHAPTER 12

New Haven

2008

"LU GOT PREGNANT with my mother by Ricky Gaspari?" Carrie demanded. Maurizio's pizza—truly one of the best Carrie had ever eaten—had been reduced to a small pile of crusts, and Uncle Paulie had already signaled for the check. "The way I always heard it, Mother was born in California."

"Yeah, she was." Uncle Paulie nodded. "Born there. But not . . . you know . . ." He blushed.

"But she wasn't conceived there." Carrie finished the thought for him. "So what happened to Ricky—did he duck out on Lu?"

"No."

"But he wasn't the daddy of record."

"No."

"The way I always heard it, Mother's father was a soldier from California who was killed in World War Two. He died before Mother was born and his last name was Lawson."

"That was the story," Uncle Paulie said. But he looked uncomfortable, as if his collar had suddenly gotten too tight.

"But now you're telling me there was no soldier out in California who was killed tragically in the war?"

"No." Paulie pulled at his collar.

"So what happened to Ricky?"

"Look, you should call Lu and ask her about all of this. I can give you her number . . ." He trailed off expectantly, waiting for her to agree. Carrie thought about trying to explain her mother's code of loyalty, but even that felt like putting the frosting on the betrayal cupcake. She looked down at the pizza crusts. Paulie reached out and took her hand. "You can't call Lu because of your mama—right?" Carrie nodded. "Women," he sighed. "Come to think of it, if my mother knew I was talking about this, even after all these years, she'd kill me."

"Could you tell me what you *do* know about Ricky Gaspari?" Carrie asked.

Now it was his turn to look down at the pizza crusts. Paulie picked one up as if he was going to chew it, dropped it back in the pan, and then he leaned back in the booth. "All I know is, the boy was going to do the right thing. He and Lu told Mama before they told his family—Lu wanted to get that over with first. The only thing that calmed Mama down a little was that Ricky kept saying he was going to make an honest woman of Lu." The waiter appeared at the table with the bill, and Uncle Paulie waved away Carrie's credit card, handing the boy a wad of cash. "Then on the day that Mama and Lu and Ricky were supposed to go to his house to tell his family about the baby and Lu and Ricky getting married," Paulie went on, "on that very morning, everything changed. And to this day, I don't know what the hell happened."

CHAPTER 13

New Haven

1943

MIFALDA WOKE UP with a jolt. Something black and nameless threatened to swamp her, and for a moment she couldn't remember the cause. Then it came to her. This was the day she and Lu would meet Ricky Gaspari's family. The boy was coming to the house at eleven to take them to one of the big mansions in the Gaspari compound—Mifalda didn't know which one belonged to his parents—so all of them could be there when Ricky told his mother and father about Lu being pregnant and the plans for a marriage. Mifalda looked at the clock on her bedside table. It was five-thirty—she'd slept longer than she thought she would. Still, it was early, so she turned on her side and pulled up the covers. She wasn't ready for the day to start yet.

A picture flashed through her mind of Lu standing next to Ricky, announcing in a clear voice that she was going to have his baby. A bastard. Mifalda's daughter was no better than the opera singer who had given birth to a child without being married and left that child in a convent, where the other children called it names and threw rocks at it.

It's my wild blood that caused this. The blood Lu got from me, Mifalda thought. But she knew this wasn't just about blood. *I was too strict with Lu. I didn't give her enough attention so she looked for it in other places.* And most damning of all: *I let her see that I wasn't happy with a woman's place in life.*

Mifalda dragged herself out of bed. Her body felt heavy, and difficult to move—it was hard to remember that only a couple of days ago she'd been bustling around her kitchen, canning her tomatoes. She started to dress. She loosened her long hair out of its nighttime braid, brushed it, and pinned it in a bun at the nape of her neck. Next came the corset to give a semblance of a waist- line to a figure that had spread over the years, since there was no man to keep it for. And finally her housedress, which she would change later in the morning before the boy came to take them to his family. She reached into her closet and pulled out the dress she'd bought to wear for her twentieth wedding anniversary. Her husband had wanted to have a big party at a social hall, which she had thought silly when their twenty-fifth was only five years away. But he had died before they reached their twenty-third, so she was glad she hadn't said anything.

The dress was pale lavender, made of a jacquard silk—you couldn't find such a fabric in the shops today, with the war on— and it still fit. She knew because she had already tried it on. She wasn't going to meet the mother of the boy who was going to marry her daughter wearing a dress that was too tight. And she would wear the hat with little violets on it that had been made to go with the dress. She would show the Gasparis that they were dealing with a woman of dignity . . . a woman with pride . . .

A woman whose daughter gave herself to their son like a common whore!

Suddenly Mifalda was dizzy. She dropped the dress on the floor, sat on the side of the bed, and bent over as far as the corset would let her. She stayed that way until the light-headedness passed, and then she picked the dress up from the floor, brushed it off, and spread it on the bed.

Lu was going to have a hard time with the Gaspari family; there was no use in pretending otherwise. All of New Haven knew that the mother was a virtuous woman, but cold as ice. She would agree that her son had to marry Lu, even if it ruined all her hopes for him, and she'd bear the blow God had sent her like a good martyr. She'd be polite to her unwanted daughter-in-law. She'd never raise her voice or spit out the accusations in her heart. But her coldness would hurt more than a beating. As for Ricky's father, people gossiped all the time about how ambitious he was. A girl whose father had been a grocer and whose mother still spoke English with an Italian accent—a girl whose people came from the wrong part of the old country—would not be the bride he wanted for one of his sons. He was going to hate the idea of this marriage. And if the rumors about him were true, he wouldn't be quiet about it.

But worst of all was the boy, Ricky. Right now, he was embarrassed and guilty, so he was trying to tell himself he wanted to marry Lu. But anyone could see he didn't. How long would it be before he started to resent the girl who had trapped him—even if she didn't mean to do it? Mifalda had a vision of Lu standing as straight and as tall as she could make herself, full of spirit, her eyes shining with happiness. How many years of living with Ricky's mother and her silent blame was it going to take to break that spirit? How many years of the angry father and the resentful husband would it take to dim the light in those eyes for good?

Mifalda gave herself a little shake. None of that mattered now. There was a baby on the way and it must have two parents and a home. A respectable home. There would be no more bastards in Mifalda's family. No more orphans. And if Lu had to pay the price—so be it. She had brought this on herself. Mifalda put the lavender silk back in the closet so it wouldn't get wrinkled, and went downstairs to the kitchen.

She stopped at the doorway. Lu was sitting at the kitchen table. She was hunched over as if her stomach hurt—which it probably did after all the morning sickness she'd been having. Something rose up inside Mifalda as she stood in the doorway looking at the girl—something deeper than anger.

I told Carmine something like this would happen. Letting her sing in public, taking her to New York to go to shows and fill her head with garbage—I told him nothing good was going to come from that. And he said, "You're making a mountain out of a molehill." Well, who was right, Carmine? And now who's got to clean up the mess you made? I'm the one who has to send my daughter to a bad marriage. My daughter, who faces the world with a smile. I'm the one who has to send her to a bad life.

Lu turned around. Her face was pale, and there were salty little lines down her cheeks where the tears had dried. "I'm sorry if I woke you up, Mama," she said.

An explosion was on the tip of Mifalda's tongue. *You think I can sleep after what you did?* she wanted to shout. *I'll never have another peaceful night again. And I don't deserve this.* But Lu was still hunched over. She looked . . . beaten. Mifalda moved to her. She was close enough to stroke the curly hair on Lu's head, but she kept her hand to herself. "It'll be all right," she said. "It looks bad now, but it will be all right."

Lu looked up at her with haunted eyes. "I'm scared, Mama," she said.

Lu's head was so close—it would have taken nothing to reach out and touch it. Mifalda turned away and went to the stove to start the coffee. "Don't worry," she said briskly. "The boy—Ricky—he'll do what he has to. The baby will have a name."

She heard Lu stand, felt her come over to the stove, but she didn't turn to meet Lu's eyes. She didn't want to see her daughter's haunted look.

"That's not what I'm afraid of," Lu said. "I know Ricky will marry me. It's the baby."

Concentrate on the coffee, a voice in Mifalda's brain commanded. *Measure the grounds and put them into the metal basket in the pot. If you concentrate on the coffee, you don't have to look at those eyes.*

But then Lu was whispering, "I don't think I'm going to be able to love this baby, Mama. I know I can't." And there was no avoiding looking at her daughter.

"You'll love the baby because you have to," Mifalda said.

Lu shook her head. The haunted look in her eyes was deep. "I'm not like you, Mama," she said. "I can't give up my life for something I don't want and tell myself it's okay. This baby is taking away everything I've ever dreamed of. I don't want to dislike a poor helpless little child, but I'm afraid I will."

"When it's born . . . you'll change." Mifalda heard herself stumble, the words sounding uncertain even to her. She had welcomed her babies, no matter what else she'd felt about her life, but Lu was very different from her. "You'll learn to love it . . ."

"Really, Mama?" Lu demanded, and now her voice was strong. "Really? Can you promise me I'm not going to be angry? Can you promise me I'm not going to take it out on this child?"

And as she looked at her daughter, for no reason in the world a picture flashed through Mifalda's mind of a girl with carrot-colored hair skating on a pond, in a red dress that showed off her knees.

The girl twirled and swooped, flying across the ice, free to go as fast and as far as her pretty legs would carry her. The image lasted only for a second, but it was long enough. In a flash Mifalda knew what she had to do.

"Sit," she told her daughter. For once, Lu did as she was told. She went back to the table and sat down. Mifalda finished making the coffee, her mind racing as she went over the outrageous plan that had just come to her, checking it for flaws, for anything that could possibly go wrong. When she was sure there was nothing she'd overlooked, she poured two cups of the coffee, brought them to the table, and sat opposite her daughter. "Here's how it's going to be," she said. She stopped to add some cream to her cup. Her voice was so calm, it shocked her. "Ricky is not going to tell his parents about the baby today. You are not going to marry him."

"Mama, what—"

"Quiet!" said the calm voice Mifalda didn't recognize as her own. "You're going to California. We'll say that when you were there visiting Eddie's wife last spring you met a boy and you fell in love with him. You're going out there to get married. You're going to do it fast, because the boy is going to go into the army. Like your brother Eddie." Her voice was still calm. She took a sip of her coffee and her hands were steady. "After you're married, you're going to find out that you and your husband are going to have a baby. But your husband will die in the war before the baby is born, and you'll come home. And because you're so young, I'm going to raise your baby. You're going to New York to do what you want to do."

Lu's mouth was a shocked little circle in her face. Her eyes were huge—but the haunted look was starting to leave them. *So, your mama can surprise you,* Mifalda thought. *Your mama has a few tricks up her sleeve.*

"Mama, we can't—" Lu started to say.

"Who's going to stop us? Ricky? That one will be so happy to be out of this, he'll be dancing in the street for joy. If he does give us any trouble, we'll tell that snooty father of his. The man will pay us to save his son from having to marry you. Now, besides Ricky and your brother Paulie—who will keep his mouth shut because I'll tell him to—does anyone else know?"

"No one," Lu breathed. "I never told anyone about Ricky and me. And he never said anything either."

"So, it's settled."

"Mama . . . do you want to do this?"

"Do you want to take care of a baby?"

There was no hesitation. "No," Lu said.

"Then I'll be fine."

Lu wanted to hug her—Mifalda could feel how much she wanted to—but she sat where she was. "I love you, Mama," she said.

"Every Sunday, from New York, you'll come home to visit me and the baby," Mifalda said. "You'll get here in time to go to Mass with us."

Lu nodded. She was sitting up straight and her eyes were glowing with happiness.

AFTER A YEAR and a half in California, Lu came home to New Haven as a widow. In her arms she carried a baby—a little girl with reddish gold hair and big, beautiful green eyes. *We'll have to say the father was Irish*, Mifalda thought. *That will serve you right, Carmine.* Then she held out her arms to take the child. But Lu was still holding on to her.

"This is Rose, Mama," she said, and there was a quiver in that voice that was usually so firm and sure. Mifalda let her arms fall to her sides.

"You remember I wrote you? I named her after Pop's aunt in

Italy—the one who was named Rosella." Lu's voice was shaking now, and her eyes were filling up. "He told me about her once. She stayed in the old country when everyone else came here— I thought he'd like it if the baby was named after her . . ." The tears were spilling over now. Lu nuzzled the baby's cheek. "She's pretty, isn't she, Mama? Isn't my baby pretty?" And Mifalda could only nod because her throat had suddenly tightened too much to talk. "I dress her in blue and green most of the time—I think those are the best colors with her eyes. All her clothes are in the suitcase . . ."

"Lu." Mifalda forced the name out. "Have you changed your mind?" At the same moment the baby turned to her and smiled. And she knew her heart would break if Lu said yes. She wanted her house that was so empty and quiet now to be full of baby sounds again. She wanted baby toys on the floor and the smell of baby powder in the air.

But Lu was her child, so Mifalda had to ask. "Do you want to keep Rose?"

Please, Blessed Mother, let her say no. Let me have this beautiful child to fill my days and my life.

The silence lasted an eternity. But then Lu looked at the child for a moment and at last shook her head. "No," she said softly. "It wouldn't be fair to her." She handed the child to Mifalda, who now had tears streaming down her cheeks as well.

Later that night, after Lu had gone to bed, Mifalda lifted the sleeping Rose out of her crib.

"I'm your nonna, sweetheart," Mifalda whispered to the child. "And you're my little Rose."

And as she looked down at the little round face, she thought, *I'm older now. My wild blood has finally cooled down. This time I'll do it right. I'll give this little one so much attention, she won't have to go look-*

*ing for it from strangers. I'll show her that a woman can be content in
her own home. She will see that I am finally happy with my life. And she
will have my whole heart.*

When Rose was five years old her nonna took her to the New
Haven Rink and signed her up for figure skating lessons.

CHAPTER 14

New Haven

2008

CARRIE AND HER uncle had come full circle back to Seaview Manor. They stood on the terrace again. Behind them the sun had started to set; bands of pink and orange in the sky reflected like gleaming ribbons on the blue-gray surface of the ocean.

"This has to be one of the most beautiful places I've ever seen," Carrie said.

"Yeah, the Gasparis always went for the best."

"The Gasparis?"

Uncle Paulie chuckled. "I thought maybe you'd figure it out—this place used to be the Villa Veneto. The assisted living people added another floor to it and a wing on the side. But the lobby where you came in? That used to be the main dining room. That's where your grandmother and your grandfather met."

It was the first time in the long afternoon of storytelling and listening that Carrie had thought of Lu's boyfriend as her grandfather. "What happened to Ricky Gaspari?" she asked. "Did he ever try to see Mother? She was his child . . ."

Uncle Paulie shook his head. "Ricky got through the war. But he didn't stay in New Haven; he went to California right away like he said he was going to. I always thought he left so fast because he didn't want to see the baby he gave up, but who knows?

"He was starting to make it out in Hollywood—that's what we heard—and then he had an accident. He was on his motorcycle on the highway that goes up the coast and some car slammed into him and killed him. That was maybe 'fifty or 'fifty-one. There was a memorial service for him in New Haven and Lu came up from New York for it. She was sad about what had happened, I knew that, but by then it was—what, seven or eight years since she'd seen Ricky? I think she felt the way you would if you heard someone you dated in high school had died—not the father of your baby."

"How warm and fuzzy of her."

Uncle Paulie sighed—a sigh that was full of gentle reproach. "Lu was never warm and fuzzy," he said. "She didn't pretend to be. But there was a lot about her that Rose never told you. Like, from the time Rose was six years old, Lu was supporting Mama and Rose and the house in New Haven—the whole shebang. I guess you could say Lu was a star by that point, but getting the next job in the theater is always a crapshoot. It must have been hard for her, carrying all that on her back, but she never complained."

"I thought the family was well off—what about the grocery stores?"

"Pop's accountant was as lousy at the business as Mama had been afraid he would be. And when my brother Carmine junior came back from the war to take over . . . well, he was a nice guy—rest his soul, he died ten years ago—but he was even worse. The economy was flying after the war, with the boys coming home and getting married and having kids. It took talent to go belly-up in those days, but Carmine did it. He lost all three of Pop's stores. And Mama just didn't understand that she couldn't spend the way she could when Pop was bringing in the bucks. She wanted the best of everything for Rose, because that little girl was the light of her life. Lu had to come up with a pretty penny each month to keep them going." He shook his head. "To tell you the truth, she carried a couple of us. When I got out of the service, I went down south to start a business with a buddy of mine—a hamburger joint that didn't pan out—and Lu staked us. Then Eddie quit the doctor racket because he wanted to find himself—only we didn't say it that way back then. We called it being lazy. His wife left him for a year until he came back to his senses, and Lu picked up the tab for her and Eddie's three kids the whole time.

"Lu came to New Haven when she could, but she didn't make it every Sunday like Mama wanted—not even close. And I'm not going to tell you she spent a lot of time with Rose during those years, because she didn't. But Mama was to blame for part of that. She never would take Rose to New York to see Lu. She didn't like show business, and that was Lu's life. Mama said she didn't want the baby exposed to it. She wouldn't even go to the Shubert Theater in New Haven when one of Lu's shows was trying out before it went to New York. Lu had to come to Mama's house—that was how Mama saw it. Lu never said a word about any of it; she just kept on paying the freight." Paulie pulled off his dark glasses. The sun had set and the sky was an eerie yellow-gray blending into the gray ocean. Soon it would be dark and the stars would come out. "Things went along like that until Rose was thirteen," Uncle Paulie said. "Then Mama died. And Rose had to go live with Lu."

Carrie pictured a bereaved thirteen-year-old girl showing up on the doorstep of the woman who hadn't wanted her. "That must have been rough," she said. "Poor Mother."

"I don't think it was easy for either of them," said Uncle Paulie. "But I wasn't there."

"What have you heard?"

"You know, there is one person who could tell you . . ."

"Uncle Paulie, I can't call my grandmother."

"I know. You gotta be a good daughter." He did another of his mournful, reproachful sighs. The man could lay on a hell of a guilt trip. "If I think of anyone else who could help you, I'll let you know," he said.

Uncle Paulie walked Carrie to the parking lot. He helped her into her car as if she were made of fine porcelain, and kissed her hand. *Chivalry is alive and well and living in my family*, Carrie thought as she started the car. Then she realized how good the words *my family* felt. And there was one person in the whole world she wanted to—*had* to—tell about it. Well, two people. Zoe, of course, because Zoe would be waiting by the phone. But even more than Zoe, she wanted to tell Howie. Because he would get it, totally and completely. The way he always had gotten everything. Before she'd let him go. For his own good.

She turned out of the driveway of Seaview Manor, formerly known as the Villa Veneto, and began the drive back to Manhattan from New Haven, making the journey her grandmother had made so many years ago. Howie would get the symbolism of that too.

CARRIE HAD KNOWN Howie for three years, four months, two weeks, and six days. They'd met because Carrie's dentist, who had seen her through adolescence and early adulthood, had retired. Thoughtful Dr. Lightman had given all of his patients a list of possible replacements—although, in his opinion, none of these new young guys could hold a candle to an old-school pro like himself—so when it came time for Carrie's semi-annual teeth cleaning, she found herself ringing the buzzer for the office of Dr. Howard C. Bendel.

"The names on Dr. Lightman's list were alphabetized, and you were the second one because you begin with *B*," she explained somewhat disjointedly once she'd settled into Howie's dentist's chair. "The dentist ahead of you was Ahearn, and her office is in Queens, which is too far because I live in Manhattan. And your receptionist said on the phone that you have a hygienist who does the cleaning for you and I thought maybe I'd like that, because Dr. Lightman always did it himself—the cleaning, that is—which wasn't always such a good thing, because in the last few years his hands could get a little shaky, and a couple of times he got my gums with that sharp little thing you use to scrape off the tartar. The last time it happened he said it was my fault, but it was really a cramp in his fingers and there was blood all over . . ." She looked over at her new dentist. Dr. Bendel was wearing his white coat but he hadn't put on his goggles or his mask yet. He was leaning against the wall, watching her. He wasn't tall, maybe around five foot ten, but he was slim with curly brown hair and very blue eyes and a mouth that looked like it was made for laughing. One of his legs was crossed over the other, and his arms were crossed too, but he looked casual, not closed off. He was smiling.

"I'm very afraid of the dentist," Carrie told him.

"I never would have guessed," Dr. Bendel said.

"Well, I'm the stoic type. I believe in hiding these things."

"And you do it brilliantly."

After her teeth had been cleaned and he'd finished poking at them and assured her that she had no cavities even though she'd been eating a ton of chocolate because she was going into the truffle-making business and there was no way to test a new recipe except to taste it, he looked at his watch and said, "I should be taking off for lunch in about fifteen minutes—would you like to go with me?" And when Carrie hesitated he said, "I know this is sudden, but I've found that the white coat and the Creature from the Deep getup the law says I have to wear is a little off-putting, and the sooner I can counteract that first impression the better off I am. I'm a snazzy dresser. And I want you to think of me as a guy with really good taste who's taking you to a fancy lunch."

And because she had no dignity, she asked, "How fancy?"

"I was thinking Luc Latesse."

"You have to wait months for a table there."

"Actually, I don't. I'm . . . sort of like a regular." He sounded apologetic, which was really sweet.

"The dentist business must be awfully good."

"It's not bad, but that's not the secret to my success at Luc Latesse. The maître d' has a daughter—a cute kid, but man, when I first met her that underbite was something else. It took us four years with two different sets of braces, but now I understand she's just won her first pageant out in New Jersey. Miss Fort Lee, I think. So will you have lunch with me?"

She did. She waited for him at the bar at Luc Latesse, and when he showed up he was wearing a caramel-colored cashmere jacket that fit his slim frame like a dream, and a blue shirt that mirrored his eyes.

"You're right," she said.

"About my clout at Luc Latesse?"

"About being a snazzy dresser."

Three weeks later, Carrie had yet another new dentist because Howie was a stickler for the rules and he would not date a patient.

He said he fell for Carrie when she did her riff on his name and dental hygiene. She told him he was deranged, but she loved that he liked her ditzy side. Up to that point, she had dated serious young men who were out to save the world. They practiced storefront law in inner-city neighborhoods with high crime rates, or they spent part of each year practicing medicine in countries that had no running water. Howie admitted that he'd gone to dental school because he thought it would be easier than medical school—although now that he was a dentist he liked the job. He took Carrie to Radio City Musical Hall to see the Rockettes and to the Bronx Zoo, and to every home game the Yankees played. He liked good restaurants, nice clothes, action movies—particularly if they were funny—and *Law and Order* reruns. "I like knowing I can find an episode any time of the day or night," he explained. "And the good guys win eighty-five percent of the time. If it were a hundred percent I couldn't go with it, but eighty-five percent makes for great mind candy."

She couldn't believe he'd admit out loud that he liked mind candy. "You really want to enjoy yourself, don't you?" she asked.

"Doesn't everyone?"

Carrie thought about telling him that she had a mother who slept on the sofa so there would be more money to give to the homeless shelter. She discarded the idea.

Howie enjoyed himself when he made love. There was no angst involved, no bravado, and no after-the-fact *Was it good for you?* questioning that Carrie understood was supposed to be sensitive but always sounded to her like a bid for applause. Waking up at Howie's place—nicely furnished with lots of light woods, and blue and brown upholstery—she thought that being with him was like sinking into a cushy oversize sofa.

Howie invited Carrie to have Thanksgiving with his family. "Mom cooks everything just like she used to do when we were kids. But she still lives in the city and there's not enough room for the whole family in her apartment, and my brother, Mike, and his wife have a house in Katonah, so he sends a car for Mom and the food. We can probably hitch a ride with her, if you don't mind balancing a turkey on your knees."

It was a dream Carrie had had since she was a kid, to have a real Thanksgiving dinner in someone's home—she'd given up on the hope of it being her own home at the age of seven. But now that she was faced with the possibility of actually eating her holiday meal at a dining room table with a family, she couldn't do it.

"My mother and I always spend Thanksgiving together . . ."

"She can come with us."

Carrie tried to imagine telling her mother they were going to Katonah in a chauffeur-driven car, and shuddered. "We always serve dinner, in the shelter, and I don't think—"

"What time?"

"We usually get there at around ten in the morning to help set up, and then we serve at noon and we're done around one-thirty—"

"Perfect," he said. "By the time my sisters get the kids rounded up, we never start eating before two. I'll tell Mom to make it a little later this year and I'll go help you and your mother serve dinner at the shelter. Then you and I will hop a train for the 'burbs."

He made it sound so easy, but it wasn't. There was no way Carrie could simply "hop a train for the 'burbs," because Rose thought it was demeaning and insulting when people showed up at the shelter to serve food for a couple of hours on Thanksgiving and Christmas and then split before the pie was served. "The residents don't need that kind of tokenism," she always said. "They don't need to be reminded that other people have homes and lives they're running back to. Share the entire holiday with them or stay home. Don't get rid of your guilt at their expense."

But Howie was saying, "I really want my sister Claire to meet you. She doesn't believe her dorky baby brother actually managed to find someone as incredible as you."

So Carrie said yes. She tried to tell herself if she got to the shelter even earlier than normal, that would make up for leaving early. She tried to tell herself that just this once her mother would understand.

Howie was a big hit with the shelter staff and the residents. He rolled up the sleeves of his monogrammed shirt—his family always liked to get a little dressed up for the holidays—and lifted the big pots of candied sweet potatoes and gravy off the stove. He set tables, carved turkey, and dished out mashed potatoes. Every once in a while, to the delight of the kids, he raced into the common room to catch the Thanksgiving Day parade on television.

But before the pumpkin pie and the coffee had been served, he rolled down his shirtsleeves and helped Carrie into her coat, saying, "We've got to run if we're going to make our train." And when everyone else exchanged hugs and kisses with them and told them to hurry, Rose retreated to the kitchen to scrub the dirty roasting pan.

"She didn't say good-bye to me," Carrie said when she and Howie were out on the street. "She barely said a word to you all day long. . . ."

"Give her time," Howie said. "She's never had to share you before. She doesn't like it." He put his arms around Carrie and held her. "She'll come around. Or she won't. That's up to her."

ROSE DIDN'T COME around. And it wasn't just that she didn't want to share Carrie.

All-or-nothing Rose could never understand what her daughter saw in laid-back Howie. "Is there anything, anywhere, he's passionate about?" Rose demanded soon after Thanksgiving. "Anything he'd make a sacrifice for?"

But Howie wasn't into sacrifice—not if he could find a way around it. And he definitely wasn't into guilt. Unfortunately, Carrie couldn't shake hers. They'd be in bed eating Ben and Jerry's Chunky Monkey ice cream, watching Jerry Orbach and Sam Waterston, on *Law and Order*, and Carrie would hear a sweet, familiar voice in her head. "Aren't you being just a little selfish, love?" a phantom Rose would ask. "Just a little self-indulgent?" At other times the phantom would be more militant. "At the very least, you could be reading a good book!" it would say. Later that day, in her office at the shelter, the real Rose would say, oh so casually, "Don't you think Howie's a little . . . well . . . shallow?"

Oddly, Howie understood Rose. "Your mother is a high-wire act," he said. "She thinks I'm boring. In her way, she's right—"

"No, she's not," Carrie broke in, eager to reassure, but he didn't need it.

"Sure I am—up against someone like Rose Manning." Then he grinned. "But the world needs boring people. Can you imagine what it would be like if everyone was as intense as you and your mother?"

"I am not like my mother! How can you say that?"

He rubbed the top of her head with his chin. "You don't know what you are, sweetheart. Not yet."

"My track record says I'm not much."

"Never discount genetics. You come from women who are major overachievers."

Not that Howie cared if she overachieved or underachieved. He just wanted to be happy with her. And that was the problem.

"I don't know if I can be happy," Carrie told Zoe in a desperate late-night phone call. "I wasn't trained for it. And besides, who says being happy is the way to go? Shouldn't we care more about what we do while we're here on earth and the footprints we leave behind?"

"Nah," said her best friend.

But the doubts and fears grew worse.

"Relax, Carrie, honey," Howie said.

But she didn't know how to do that either. When they'd been dating for a year, Howie had asked her to marry him, and she'd said yes, because she couldn't say no. For several months she'd floated around Manhattan in a little bubble of what she recognized was happiness—it seemed you didn't need any training for it, after all, just the right guy. But then she'd started to feel the old familiar locked-in feeling. The feeling that she was going to fail at something else. And this time Howie, who was way too good for her, would fail along with her.

The wedding plans finally did it. Howie wanted a big party. "I've got a ton of family and friends," he said. "You and your mother must have a lot of people you'd like to invite too. This shindig will be amazing." Carrie tried to imagine the press coverage when it was announced that Rose Manning's daughter was throwing a wedding for two hundred people. Rose Manning, who—as the archdiocese publicity department constantly reminded everyone—slept on a sofa so she could give extra money to the children in the shelter. Rose Manning, the Angel of Manhattan, who walked the philanthropy walk while she talked the philanthropy talk. "There's so much need out there," Rose said in an interview shortly after Carrie and Howie became engaged. "How could I even think about spending money on something frivolous when I know there are children who go to bed hungry?"

Meanwhile, Howie was talking about maybe inviting two hundred and fifty wedding guests.

Carrie decided Howie had a right to marry someone who wasn't screwed up. "I come from people who hurt each other," she said after she'd told him the wedding was off. "I won't want to do it to you, but I will."

Nothing he could say changed her mind. Carrie didn't even cry during their good-bye. She waited until he'd gone. Then she cried so hard, she thought she'd never stop.

Carrie was in the home stretch; she'd survived I-95, and the Cross Bronx Expressway, and she'd managed to avoid going to New Jersey by mistake when getting on the Henry Hudson. So naturally, just as she was congratulating herself on her success, her cell phone rang. There was no way she was going to answer it while she was driving—forget that it was illegal, she didn't have the motor skills for that kind of multitasking—so she pulled off on 168th Street and managed to fish the damn thing out of her purse just as it stopped ringing.

Uncle Paulie had called and left a message. "I've thought of someone who can give you a lot of info." His voice was triumphant. "His name is George Standish. Whenever Lu was in a show, George conducted the orchestra. But he was more than that; he was her best friend. He'd know what went on with Lu and Rose during those early years. I'll find his phone number and call you back. He's even older than I am, but he's still as sharp as a tack, so it'll be as good as talking to me."

Carrie started the car again. It was nice to have family helping her out, she decided.

"HOWIE, I'm doing it. "

"Carrie? Is that you?"

"I just wanted you to know, I'm getting closure. Or roots. Or mental health—whatever. I drove to New Haven yesterday. I drove a car, Howie. I called this uncle of mine—actually, he's my great-uncle—and I did what you've always told me to do, I asked a billion questions about Mother and her mother and my family and I got a lot of answers. They lived in this great old house, Uncle Paulie took me to see it, and we had the best pizza—in the old days they never put mozzarella on pizza, I never knew that— and he told me about Lu and this boy—well, actually he was my grandfather . . ."

"Carrie—"

"You and Zoe were right. I need to know this stuff. I'm going to call a man who used to be Lu's conductor. Can you believe that, Howie? My grandmother had enough power to demand her own conductor when she did a show. Uncle Paulie says this George person can tell me—"

"Carrie, what time is it?"

"It's after seven. In the AM, slacker. If you weren't awake, you should have been. Want to make yourself some coffee? I'll wait."

"Uh . . . the thing is . . . this isn't a good time."

That was when she heard the murmuring. Female murmuring. "Oh," Carrie said, wishing she were the kind of woman who could come up with a snappy comeback at moments like this. Not that she ever wanted to have another moment like this. That was what was so surprising—how bad this felt. "Oh," she repeated. And just to prove that she couldn't come up with even a half-assed comment, she added, "Well, all righty, I'll let you go then." And hung up.

THE SECOND PHONE call of the morning was not one she instigated. After the Howie debacle, Carrie did not dial Zoe's number to vent. Howie hadn't done anything wrong, so Carrie had no reason to vent. She told herself she got points for realizing that. She did raid her stash of sour-cream-and-cheddar potato chips, but she didn't cry—for which she was pretty sure she got more points—and when the phone rang a few minutes after eight, it was Zoe who was calling her.

"How are you?" Zoe asked.

"No, how are you?" Carrie shot back. Maybe she could get the hang of the snappy-repartee comeback thing after all. "Let's talk about you. What's your day been like?"

"I just dipped six dozen rosewater truffles. What happened yesterday in New Haven?"

"Six dozen truffles? Wow! You must be going through cocoa powder by the ton!"

"Yeah, and the weather is swell. Why are we doing bullshit party talk? What's wrong?"

"You are not going to play Rhoda to my Mary. Or Ethel to my Lucy. Or Vicki Lawrence to my Carol Burnett . . ."

"You really need to stop watching Nick at Night."

"I am not going to be the neurotic self-absorbed heroine who makes her best friend into a sidekick. Barbra Streisand played her in all those movies in the seventies . . ."

"You might want to drop the classic movie channel, too."

"You know what I'm talking about."

"Carrie, I'm here for you. You are the friend who listened to me for three years while I waited for the Jerk to divorce his wife. It took you thirty-six months to convince me to stop giving him the benefit of the doubt. Two phone calls a day. My personal best was the night I called you five times."

"That was different."

"I phoned you in the hospital after you'd just had your appendix out. You were still on Demerol. I repeat: what's wrong?"

"I called Howie this morning to tell him about New Haven."

"Okay, it's probably a little early for a chat, but I don't see—"

"He was with someone."

There was a pause while Zoe digested the news. "When you say someone . . . ?"

"There was murmuring in the background. A woman's voice."

"Oh." Zoe digested again. Then she spoke very carefully. "Uh, Carrie, isn't this what you wanted? I mean, you were the one who walked out three days before the wedding because you didn't know who you were and you were afraid you'd wind up failing him."

"I know that."

"When he bought that house in Katonah you said you were glad because you wanted him to get on with his life."

"Yes. And I do, " Carrie said. "I'm just a little . . . thrown."

"Right."

"Maybe a little sad."

"Right."

"It's a perfectly normal reaction."

The silence on the other end of the phone was long. When Zoe spoke again, it was with the authoritative voice she used with the deadbeats at gourmet stores who hadn't paid their bill. "Call your grandmother, " she said.

"Did I miss something? When did we start talking about her?"

"We're talking about you. You need to get your act together, fast."

"I don't see why—"

"I know you don't. Trust me on this. Find Lu. Go talk to her."

"Actually, I'm going to call the guy who was Lu's conductor. I think he could be very helpful and—"

Zoe broke in by making a sound like a chicken squawking.

"That was mature," Carrie said.

"Hear your grandmother's side of the story," Zoe commanded. "Hell, hear the story. Maybe Lu will actually tell you what happened between your mother and her. Wouldn't that be refreshing?"

"I can't. I don't know what Lu did, but she really hurt my mother."

"Mothers have been doing that since the first cavewoman told her daughter that bearskin made her hips look big. Most daughters forgive them."

"Mother couldn't. Whatever happened was too important."

There was more silence from Zoe, then a resigned "When are you going to see this conductor person?"

"His name is George Standish. I'm calling him this morning."

"Good luck, Mary."

"Thanks, Rhoda."

CHAPTER 15

New York

2008

GEORGE STANDISH WAS big—Carrie figured he was at least six-five—and he probably weighed in at around three hundred pounds. He was bald, except for a fringe of gray curls that circled his head, and he wore thick glasses with dark frames. He was dressed all in black; black slacks, a black leather belt with a discreet black buckle, and a black collarless shirt. The look just missed being clerical because of the accessories he sported: a four-inch gold cuff on his right wrist, several gold earrings in both lobes, and rings on most of his fingers. George was into bling. And although he had to be in his eighties, he was, as Uncle Paulie had said, as sharp as a tack.

He lived in a majestic pre-war apartment house on West Fifty-seventh Street, across from the Russian Tea Room.

"Of course, I knew it back when it really *was* the Russian Tea Room," he sniffed to Carrie as an elevator, which was heavy on wood paneling, with a plush carpet and a huge gilt-edged mirror on the back wall, whisked them up to the seventeenth floor and the co-op he had referred to as his hideaway. "When I moved into this neighborhood, the Russian Tea Room was the place to be, baby. Stanley Marks took his lunch calls there every day—from his booth across from the coat check." He glanced at Carrie. "You don't know who I'm talking about, do you?" Carrie shook her head. "Stanley was the biggest talent agent in Manhattan. He repped Lu for years. I thought you'd know . . . But I keep forgetting about that mother of yours." George looked heavenward. "Anyway, the Russian Tea Room was Stanley's office away from the office. Everyone ate there: Woody and Kissinger, Nureyev and Jackie O. And it wasn't for the food, let me tell you, because on a good day it was mediocre. But the city had soul back then. People went to the Russian Tea Room because Lenny Bernstein wrote the first bars of *Fancy Free* by the reflected light of the samovars in that dining room. We went for the sentiment, baby—we appreciated the glam. Today people think glamour means a drunken little TV star going into rehab." The elevator stopped and the doors opened. George glided out—he was light on his feet given his bulk and age—and headed down a carpeted hallway without missing a beat in his lecture. "Fifty-seventh Street used to be Showbiz Alley. There were dance classes, singing teachers, and agents' offices all up and down the street. You'd see the actors with their headshots and résumés going into Chock Full o' Nuts for an olive-and-cream-cheese sandwich. There was a health food place where the ballet girls would grab their celery juice between classes at the Carnegie Rehearsal Hall, and the kids who were trying to be Beverly Sills would walk along humming 'Vissi d'Arte.'

"That's all gone now. It's nothing but tourist traps and those ghastly outposts of bad Hollywood restaurants. 'Family-friendly,' they call them. When did New York City become the vacation spot for families from the boonies? Most of us came here to get *away* from our families in the boonies." As a connoisseur of rants against the new New York, Carrie felt like giving him a round of applause, but at that moment they had reached the door of his apartment.

George took out his key. "I should move," he said. "I've thought about it so many times, but I just can't." He unlocked the door and ushered Carrie in. The foyer was the size of Carrie's entire apartment, and she figured that the ceiling was at least sixteen feet high. The floor was an intricate parquet, and two ornate columns that didn't seem to be holding up anything flanked the entrance leading to the rest of George's "hideaway."

"The reason I can't leave is this," George said, and he waved his hand toward one wall. There, dominating everything else, was a life-size portrait of a man who appeared to be in his middle thirties. He was smiling so broadly, he gave new meaning to the phrase *grinning from ear to ear*, and he was wearing what appeared to be a crazy quilt that someone had made into a kimono. Garish patches of mismatched fabric with what looked like logos embroidered on them made up the body of the garment. The mad quilter had also sewn a small stuffed dog to one sleeve of the thing, and an American flag and a bunch of roses had been stitched onto the other sleeve, so these weird artifacts were actually a part of the robe.

"That's Davy," George announced with another hand wave. "My lover. I know the kids today like to say they're 'partners,' but we were lovers. For thirty years he was the love of my life." He snorted angrily. "And now the son of a bitch is keeping me incarcerated in this mausoleum. Because his damn picture is on that wall, and I can't leave it."

"There's no way you can move it?" Carrie asked, fascinated.

"It's a mural! The frame around it is fake. We had it painted directly onto the plaster because we wanted it to be there as long as the building was standing. We didn't know Fifty-seventh Street was going to turn into bloody Disneyland on the Hudson. And," George added more gently, "we didn't know Davy was going to die first and I'd be stuck with this frigging wall art."

"It's . . . amazing," Carrie said.

"It's tacky, baby. But what can I tell you? Davy had just gotten the Gypsy Robe after almost twenty years in the business and we wanted to do something grand. And, let's face it, we *were* tacky."

"What is the Gypsy Robe?"

"You don't know?" he was incredulous. "And you're Lu Lawson's granddaughter." He led her closer to the painted wall. "The Gypsy Robe, my infant, is a glorious Broadway tradition designed to acknowledge the kids of the chorus. You do know that the chorus kids in a musical are known as the gypsies—right?"

Carrie didn't, but she nodded.

"Thank God. At least you have a grasp of the basics," he said fervently. "The robe ritual has been around since the fifties. Each time a new musical opens on Broadway, one member of the chorus—usually the one who has worked the most shows and has the most credits—is given the Gypsy Robe. On opening night that chorus member dons the robe and officially becomes the king or queen of Broadway. He or she parades around the stage in a circle and each member of the cast touches the robe for luck. When another musical opens, the robe is passed on. The chorus ponies in each show stitch a memento onto the robe while it's in their possession. The chorus of *The Sound of Music* sewed a nun's headdress to it—that was one of the more famous ones."

"So it was an honor for your . . ." Carrie stopped herself from saying "partner." "For your lover."

"It meant everything to him." George looked down at the cuff on his wrist. There was an inscription on it, and he traced it with his finger. "Davy was a dancer," he said. "He never wanted anything more. Just being in show business was enough for him. It was for me too. I never had any big ambitions."

"But you were a conductor—isn't that big?"

"That was Lu's doing. Don't get me wrong, I was a good musician. I got my degree in piano from the Curtis Institute and that wasn't shabby; a lot of concert careers came out of Curtis. But I knew I didn't have what it took. My mother wanted me to come home and teach school, but I was out of the closet, which could get you killed in redneck Pennsylvania back then. And I loved musicals. I came to New York in 'forty-one and I figured I'd get work as an accompanist." He laughed. "Me and about a million other kids who could play the piano and didn't want to live at home. It was a crowded field, baby. I would have starved if the war hadn't broken out. I couldn't go into the army because my eyes were bad, so I was one of the few men my age left in the city. I started working, and then I met Lu, and the rest is history." He traced the inscription on his cuff some more. "But if Lu hadn't come along, I'd have stayed in New York in a crummy apartment somewhere, coaching wannabe singers as long as my fingers held out. Davy and I were just a couple of stagestruck boys from the sticks who wanted to be near the bright lights."

Carrie looked up at the picture of the young man wearing his triumphant smile and the crazy robe. Her mind flashed back to the two Saturdays long ago that she'd spent secretly looking up her father and her grandmother in the library at Lincoln Center. She remembered the hunger she'd felt to know their world, and how frustrated she'd been because she couldn't get a feel for it from the books and press clippings. She remembered sneaking into the Vivian Beaumont Theater and the magic she'd found there. "Thank you," she said. "I don't know anything about the theater—the insider part of it. I always wanted to, but . . . it just didn't happen."

George understood what she wasn't saying. "In your mother's

defense," he said, "it had to be a rough gig being Bobby Manning's wife—and Lu Lawson's daughter. They were two of the great ones. But they weren't good family people and they probably weren't easy to live with. There's a price tag on greatness. I don't know how high it should be—I've never figured that out—but I do know when people do what Bobby and Lu did, that doesn't come for free." For a moment Carrie thought George was about to burst into song—or tears. But then he held up his hands in mock preacher style and intoned, "And, my brethren, thus endeth the gospel in bullshit for the day. Let me take you on the grand tour of the Hideaway."

The apartment consisted of seven rooms full of regal architectural details such as original crown moldings that looked like they'd been squeezed out of a mammoth pastry tube. But the décor suggested that George and Davy had never really left their crummy-apartment roots; the grand rooms were filled with a hodgepodge of furniture that seemed to have no particular color scheme or style. "Davy lifted most of it," George said, beaming proudly. "When he was in a show that flopped and they were hauling away the furniture from the set, he'd take what we needed before it all went to the dump."

In addition to the flop show furniture, George's home was stuffed with theater memorabilia. Covering the walls were theater posters, framed copies of playbills, albums of Broadway musicals, and hundreds of pictures of people George and Davy had worked with. A glass case in the library featured pictures of Davy playing first base for the Broadway Softball League. There were shelves packed tight with scripts, musical scores, and scrapbooks. Every available surface was covered with souvenirs from cities they had toured, as well as what seemed to be an endless collection of snow globes, toys, stuffed animals, and other knickknacks, which, George informed Carrie, had been opening night presents. Framed opening night telegrams had been pasted on the walls of a guest bathroom. As far as Carrie could see, there wasn't one book in the entire apartment.

"On to lunch," George sang out, "before we wilt from starvation."

Three tiny Yorkies joined them in the kitchen.

"They're so quiet, I didn't know they were here," Carrie said.

"They stay in the bedroom when Daddy has company," George said. "Davy and I always took our puppies to rehearsals with us, so they had to learn to speak only when they were spoken to. I don't rehearse anything anymore, but I still train my dogs."

George had made chili—a killer recipe—that he served with mounds of sour cream to kill the sting, and ice cold beer. Then, as the dogs curled up to sleep at his feet, he said, "You said on the phone you had questions for me. Fire away."

Carrie *did* have questions—dozens that she'd practically memorized because she'd thought about them so much. But now only one popped into her head. "On opening nights, when people touched the Gypsy Robe for luck, did Lu do it too?"

George frowned. "Everyone touched the Gypsy Robe. What makes you think Lu wouldn't?".

"Because she was the star. Maybe she was above mixing with the kids in the chorus." *My mother said Lu was an egomaniac. Uncle Paulie says she isn't, but he's her brother.* "I've gotten some conflicting stories about Lu," she added.

George knew who the negative stories had come from. "Give me strength," he muttered. Then he looked directly into Carrie's eyes. "I want you to get this if you don't get anything else: Lu Lawson was a star, but she never did a star trip. Hell, baby, no one had to fight harder to make it than she did, and she never forgot that. When she came to town—it was late in 'forty-four—I was the only person she knew. She was broke—she slept on my sofa for six months because she couldn't pay her rent—and, as we say in the biz, she couldn't get arrested. People started calling her Audition Lu because she went up for everything: cattle calls, chorus gigs, any audition my friends and I could sneak her into. There were a couple of agents who sent her out too. Everyone could see there was something special about her, but she just didn't fit the mold." He paused to load up his spoon with chili and a dollop of sour cream.

"Back in the late forties and early fifties, the roles for women in Broadway musicals pretty much fell into two categories. There were the romantic heroines who always got their man because they were beautiful and really stupid. Those parts were played by legit singers who had classically trained voices—usually sopranos. Then there were the funny girls. They played the wisecracking underdogs who weren't beautiful but got the guy in the end because they were fun. Those parts called for a lower singing voice— big and brassy—what we call in the trade a 'belt sound.' Belting was a much rougher way of singing, and most sopranos wouldn't do it because it was hard on the vocal cords.

"When Lu came to New York, she could sing the hell out of the soprano repertoire, but she couldn't play a romantic heroine. She was cute, but she wasn't a beauty in that kind of peaches-and-cream way that people wanted. More important, she couldn't dumb down enough. She was smart and funny and no one wanted a wiseass singing 'If I Loved You.'

"I kept nagging her to change her singing style, but Lu loved whipping off all those pretty high notes. When she finally gave in and let me teach her how to lower her voice, she cried. And the truth was, she never really did have a natural belt like Ethel Merman. But she developed a nice edge on her tone and it suited her acting. She began to work regularly. She got a few good reviews and a couple of small breaks, and then she finally made it big in a show called *Time Out for Love*. Lu was the second banana but she had this fabulous number in the second act and she stole the show. It was grand larceny, baby! After that, Lu was a star and she wasn't going to be doing any more legit singing because she was known as a funny girl who belted.

"But she was always afraid of hurting her voice. That's why as soon as she had enough juice she always insisted on my being her conductor. She knew I'd keep the orchestra under control and protect her vocal cords. And every day she did the singing exercises her old teacher in New Haven had taught her. When she warmed up before a performance—and this I never got—she sang church music." George took a long swig of his beer. "Does that sound like a diva to you?" he demanded.

"No," Carrie said.

But somehow she was a part of what happened to my mother—my mother, who couldn't go to Communion. Whatever happened to her, I know it started with Lu.

"I never saw Lu phone in a performance," George continued. "Not even on Wednesday matinees in August when the theater didn't have air-conditioning. It would be a hundred and ten degrees under the lights and Lu would still be doing it full out. And she didn't miss performances. She worked when she was sick, she worked when she was exhausted . . ." He paused and looked at Carrie. "And she didn't stop working when her daughter came to live with her. Even though the kid had just lost her grandmother." He took a swallow of beer. "You can judge her for that, if you want. I know Rose did. I was there when Rose came to live with Lu after Lu's mother died. It was 1957."

CHAPTER 16

New York

1957

IT WAS WEDNESDAY, the matinee curtain had come down, and Lu was in her dressing room, wrapping her old cotton makeup robe around herself.. Her dresser, Lynne, had taken her costumes to the wardrobe room in the theater basement, where they would be ironed and spruced up for the evening show. Lu's supper—which she always ate as soon as she finished the matinee so she'd have a chance to digest before going back onstage—had been delivered from the '21' Club. She knew without looking what it would be: roasted chicken, steamed green beans, and a baked potato. She'd pull the skin off the chicken and she'd eat the potato without butter or salt. In addition to eating early, Lu ate lightly when she had a show to do. Dessert was out, since dairy and sweets were bad for the voice, although she did drink hot water with honey and lemon during the breaks in her performance. Lynne would keep the concoction warm on the hot plate that was always installed in Lu's dressing rooms for that purpose. Lu sat down with her dinner plate and began peeling the skin off her chicken.

Her dressing room—the star dressing room—was on the first floor of the theater, a short hike from the stage. Outside her door was the iron staircase leading to the second floor, where the rest of the principal actors had their dressing rooms. The third floor was where the chorus kids dressed in two communal rooms, one for the boys and one for the girls. Lu listened as the singers and dancers, most of them no older than she was, clattered down the stairs, laughing and calling out to friends who had dropped by to pick them up for a quick lunch at Sardi's, where the beloved Vincent Sardi would give them a percentage off their meal if they flashed their Equity cards. Lu listened wistfully to the commotion outside her door. She never went out of the theater between shows, although it sounded like everyone was having so much fun. She went back to skinning the chicken breast.

If her audience could see her now—their bouncy, free-spirited Lu. If they could see the carefully scheduled life she led when she was working: the nap before the performance, and the early dinner hour that killed her social life with anyone over the age of five. She skipped most social events except for those that had to be attended for the sake of the press, she missed luncheons with friends—in spite of her limited time she did have quite a few—and tried not to schedule professional appointments like interviews after two in the afternoon. Her entire day was geared to the moment when the assistant stage manager would stand outside her dressing room door in the theater and call out, "Half hour to curtain, Miss Lawson."

Mama gave up everything for her family, and I give up everything for my work, she thought. Then she shook off the idea fast. What she did was worth it. The stage was where she came alive in a way that she never could anywhere else.

The chicken was skinned, and Lu wiped her hands on the white linen napkin provided by '21' and started to eat. In a few minutes George would come back to her dressing room and they'd dissect the performance that had just ended, looking for any flaws that had cropped up. They did this after every show, because it was too easy to get sloppy during a long run. Lu's daily review with George kept her on her toes.

After George left, she would lie down on the cot in the corner of her dressing room and sleep for an hour, after which she would begin warming up her voice and doing some stretches to loosen up her muscles for the evening performance. She never really danced onstage, although she could move well enough to give the illusion of it, but she needed to be limber for the pratfalls, cartwheels, and splits that were the trademarks of a Lu Lawson performance.

The warm-up, the critique, the nap, and the carefully chosen meal were all part of her regular matinee-day ritual, which she followed religiously every Wednesday and Saturday. And this Wednesday was no different, she tried to tell herself. But that was a lie. Everything was different. Her whole life had been turned upside down.

The skinned chicken was too dry to swallow. Lu pushed her plate away. There was a new role she had to play now: it was called Mommy. And so far she was falling on her famous face.

Her mother had died and her daughter had come to live with her. And the child had decided to loathe her. Or maybe it wasn't a recent decision. Maybe Rose had always hated her.

Lu closed her eyes and remembered an incident that had happened a few years earlier. It was Rose's fifth birthday, and Lu had been in New Haven with a show, so she'd taken her daughter and her mother—Rose called Mifalda Nonna in the old-fashioned Italian way—shopping. They'd gone to Malley's, the best department store in town, and headed for the doll department, where

Rose was going to pick out her present. Rose was well known to all the Malley's saleswomen, which did not surprise Lu. The child and her beloved Nonna were regular customers at the store, and given the huge monthly bills Mifalda ran up for Rose's clothes and toys, Lu thought it was a wonder that the staff didn't genuflect when the little girl marched in. The saleslady in the doll department didn't go that far, but there was much carrying on about how much Rose had grown, and how pretty she was. It was clear that Lu's daughter loved being the center of attention.

She's as much of a ham as I am, Lu had thought with amusement. Maybe the apple didn't fall that far from the tree.

Of course it was at that moment that a customer recognized that Lu Lawson, who currently had a featured role in the show at the Shubert, was in their midst. Lu wasn't a star at that point, but New Haven was a theater town and the news spread throughout the store. For the next twenty minutes, Lu was surrounded by women demanding to know if the show's leading man really was that handsome in person and if the leading lady was a witch the way everyone said she was. Out of the corner of her eye Lu had seen her now forgotten daughter sulking. And after the ruckus died down, Rose had refused to choose a birthday doll.

Was that when it all started—the feeling that she hates me? Lu reached up to her face and felt a tear rolling down her cheek. *What the hell is wrong with me?* she thought. *I don't cry! Not over something that happened a long time ago that I can't fix. And not on a matinee day.* She got up and went to her makeup table to check her face in the mirror. There was no major damage, just a little smudge under one eye. She repaired it quickly; if she had to redo her makeup between shows, she wouldn't have time for her nap. She went back to her chair, took a forkful of dry chicken, and began to eat.

But the thoughts about her daughter wouldn't go away. Rose's animosity had come boiling to the surface during Mifalda's illness. Lu's mother's death three months earlier was still a raw spot that had not had time to heal—for Lu or Rose.

MIFALDA'S SICKNESS HAD started with stomach pains that she had ignored until she couldn't stand it anymore. There had been a trip to the doctor's office that everyone assumed would be routine. That was followed by a phone call from an incoherent Paulie, who was sobbing so hard, Lu could barely make out the dreaded word *cancer.*

The next morning she'd raced up to the hospital in New Haven to find her brothers crying in the hall outside her mother's hospital room. Inside, she found thirteen-year-old Rose putting a cold towel on Mifalda's forehead. Her daughter was saying in her clear, sweet voice, "You're going to get better, Nonna. I'll make you better."

Lu must have made a sound, because Rose whipped around to face her. As she straightened up, Lu thought wildly, *She's as tall as I am. When did that happen?* Then she said the first thing that came into her head. "It's Tuesday. Why aren't you in school?"

Her daughter's face turned red; her eyes were blazing. "I'm taking care of Nonna," she hissed. "Go back to New York; no one needs you."

The force of Rose's fury shocked Lu. "You're just a child. You can't . . ." she started to say, but her daughter cut her off.

"Yes, I can! You don't know what I can do. You don't know me!" She was terrified, that much was clear, and she was lashing out.

"Rose, you can't stay here," Lu said gently. "I'll get Paulie to take you home—"

"I won't leave. You can't make me."

The words *I'm your mother* hovered in the air. But Lu couldn't say them because that would be a lie.

"Go back to New York," Rose repeated, "and leave us alone."

They stood facing each other until the silence was broken by the sound of Mifalda trying to sit up in her bed. They both rushed to her side.

"Rose, go to the nurse and tell her I need another blanket," Mifalda said. Her voice was hoarse and so soft that Lu could barely hear it. Rose didn't want to leave, but Mifalda said, "I'm cold, sweetheart." With a glare at Lu, the girl left her mother and her grandmother alone.

Mifalda beckoned to Lu to come closer. "Don't send Rose away," she said.

She can stay today, Mama, but tomorrow . . ." A hand so hot it burned grabbed hers.

"Let her come every day. It won't be for long. When I'm gone, she's going to need to think she helped."

"Mama, she's too young to help, and she should face that . . ." Lu started to say, but the burning hot hand tightened its grip.

"You have to be gentle with her," Mifalda said. "Rose is not strong like you and me. She has our blood—the wildness—but she has the Gaspari pride. She can't bend the way we do. Let her have her fairy tales."

There was nothing Lu could do but nod. And her mother's hand finally relaxed.

For the next six weeks Lu lived in a nightmare of rushing to New Haven after the curtain came down each night in New York, catching a few hours' sleep in the house in which she'd grown up, going to the hospital at daybreak to sit at her mother's bedside, and then racing back to New York in time to go onstage. George had no notes for her during those grim weeks, and on her trips back and forth to New Haven she wondered if by some miracle she was actually managing to do a decent job each night or if he was just going easy on her. She didn't ask because she didn't want to know.

In New Haven, Lu became the one everyone else leaned on. Her brothers waited for her to show up to make the decisions about their mother's care. Even Eddie, who had dropped the search for his true self and was back practicing medicine in California, was too upset to discuss his mother's treatment with her doctors on the telephone. It was all up to Lu. And as she ran through her days, she was always aware of a pair of glowering green eyes following her.

Then came the afternoon when Mifalda motioned Lu to the bed and asked her in a voice that was now not even a whisper to sing the Panis Angelicus.

And so Lu began.

> *"Panis Angelicus*
> *Fit panis hominum;*
> *Dat panis coelicus*
> *Figuris terminum:*
> *O res mirabilis!"*

And, *o res mirabilis*, her voice, roughened by lack of sleep and years of belting on Broadway, still sounded as clear and pure as it had when she was studying with Maestro DiTullio. Mifalda drifted off to sleep with a smile on her face. And from the corner of her room, the green eyes were unreadable as they watched. The next morning Mifalda was gone.

THERE WAS A knock on Lu's dressing room door. Lu shook herself out of her reverie and checked her watch. George was right on time. They did their ritual air kiss, George stole the bread off her plate—also a ritual—and they got down to business.

"The string section in the opening number . . ." Lu said. They'd been doing this for so long, they had their own shorthand.

"Second violin was flat. Took care of it."

"In Act Two . . ."

"The tempo was too fast going into the duet. Fixed it." He paused. There was more—and worse—to come and they both knew it.

"I was off in the last act," Lu said.

"You were off for the whole show," George said brutally. "You have been for a week now. What's wrong?"

She'd told herself she wouldn't talk about it, but she heard herself saying, "It's my daughter."

Everyone knew Lu had a little girl; she'd never tried to keep it a secret. And like most people, George had swallowed the story of the husband who had been killed in the war. Or, at least, he pretended that he had.

"She's in boarding school, right?"

"That's where I wanted her to go." Lu rubbed her temples carefully so she wouldn't mess her makeup. "I found this place called Marlboro Hall, a Catholic girls' school right outside New Haven. I thought it would be easier for Rose to stay close to the place where she grew up, and she always liked the nuns at St. Mary's, so a parochial school would be more familiar for her. I really tried to think it all through." Lu paused. "She hated Marlboro Hall. First she stopped eating; then she ran away. The second time she did it, the Mother Superior sent her back to me."

"When was that?"

"Three weeks ago." Lu closed her eyes. "She didn't like the school I found for her here in Manhattan, even though it's supposed to be one of the best Catholic prep schools in the city, so I hired a grad student to tutor her. But Rose doesn't like Sonja Pearl any more than she liked the staff at Marlboro Hall. She doesn't like the way my cook makes lasagna because it's not like her nonna's, and she doesn't like it when the housekeeper tells her she has to be quiet because I'm taking a nap before the show. The truth is, she doesn't like me."

"The truth is, she's being a pain in the ass," said George.

For a second it felt good to hear him say it. But then Lu remembered her mother saying, *Rose isn't strong like me and you.*

"George, she's just lost the only mother she ever had."

"And she's taking it out on you. Which is none of my business—except that I'm seeing the results of it onstage."

"That bad?"

"You know it is. What are you going to do about it?"

"Damned if I know!"

At that moment, as if on cue, they heard voices coming from the hallway outside. The stage doorman was shouting, "I'm telling you, you can't go in there!" Then the dressing room door opened and Rose stood in the doorway.

As usual, Rose was scowling. Lu tried to remember if she'd seen her daughter do anything but scowl for the past three weeks, and drew a blank. There was a rolled-up copy of *Variety* clutched in Rose's hand. Behind her, the stage doorman was saying, "I'm sorry, Miss Lawson, I tried to tell her no one is allowed to disturb you when you're between shows—"

"It's okay, Henry," Lu cut through. "This is my daughter." Then she closed the door before he could launch into what promised to be a lengthy apology for not recognizing her offspring, and turned to Rose.

"What are you doing here?" she demanded.

"It says in this paper you're going to leave New York," Rose said. "This stupid show you're in will be traveling all around the country and you're going with it."

Lu had been holding back this bit of information until her child had had a chance to adjust to her new life. Or maybe, Lu thought in a nasty moment of truth, she hadn't told Rose because she wanted to avoid a scene. Either way, she had to face it now.

"Yes," she said. "I'm going on tour. We close here in the city and I'll be taking the show out—"

"And you won't be back until next September. That's what it says here in the paper."

"That's right. I thought you could come with me during your school vacation this summer—"

"But you're going to leave me alone in that ugly apartment all winter long."

Mama said to be gentle with her, Lu reminded herself.

"That's why I wanted you to go to Marlboro Hall."

"I'll never go back there! I don't care what you want!"

Mama said be gentle.

"I could try to find another boarding school for you—"

"No!"

"If you won't go to boarding school, then you have to live with me, and my schedule—"

"I hate living with you. You're selfish. You think you're the most important person in the world. You sleep in the morning when I'm having breakfast—"

"I work late, Rose."

"Nonna had breakfast with me every morning. She cooked it for me herself. She made all my favorite foods. She had applesauce cake for me when I came home from school, and she asked me how my day was, and she—"

"And she's dead."

The bluntness of the words stopped her daughter cold. From behind her, Lu heard George's sharp intake of breath.

Sorry, Mama.

Rose was blinking her eyes as if she'd been slapped. Out in the hall the chorus kids were coming back to get ready for the evening performance. Lu had missed her nap.

"Sit down," Lu said to her daughter. For a moment she thought Rose was going to cry. But the Gaspari pride held. Rose sat in the makeup chair.

"I'm sorry your nonna died," Lu said. "I'm sorry for myself, and I'm sorry for her, but most of all, I'm sorry for you. Because you've lost the most. Now all you have is me. I'll do my best for you. I'll care for you, and I'll hire people to look after you when I'm working—which is most of the time. You'll never need anything. But I won't be making applesauce cake and lasagna. The woman who did that for you is gone.

"I will go on tour and leave you in New York, because if I don't, the tour won't happen. And the people who work on this show—there are more than two hundred of them—will be out of a job. And the people around the country who bought their tickets a year ago because they wanted to see me will be disappointed. And I do my best not to disappoint people.

"You say I'm selfish. You're right. If I have a performance and I get sick, half of the audience will go to the box office and demand their money back. If I don't do a good job, the show won't be good, the audiences will stop coming, and the show will close. And if my shows start closing, there won't be an apartment, not even one you hate, for you to live in. And you won't have to worry about going to a private school like Marlboro Hall, because I won't be able to pay for it." Then she stopped herself.

Maybe I've gone far enough, she thought. *Mama says she needs her fairy tales.* But then she turned to her daughter. The look in Rose's eyes was knowing—it was almost cynical. *No, Mama, she needs the truth. And I need to tell it.* Lu drew in a deep breath.

"But it wouldn't be fair for me to tell you that I'm just trying to earn a living. I love what I do. I'm very good at it and I love that too. I won't give up my work because it makes me happy—even though that means that you have to be quiet in the mornings when you'd rather talk, and I'm not there at night when you have your dinner." She stopped for a second and then finished, "I won't give it up, not even if it means leaving you alone when you've just lost your nonna."

Rose's eyes were fixed on her, but the cynical look was gone.

"You may not like that about me," Lu said. "But it is who I am. The good part is, I won't be giving up my life for you, so you'll never have to feel guilty about me. And when your turn comes, I'll try to help you get what you want in any way that I can."

Once more the room was silent. Then Rose stood up, and for once she wasn't crying or whining. "I don't want to go to a boarding school. I'll live in New York. And I won't go to a Catholic school," she said resolutely. "I loved the nuns at St. Mary's and you're trying to replace them for me and you can't. There are plenty of good prep schools here. I'll go to one of them. And I'd like Miss Pearl to stay on so she can take care of me when you're gone."

"Good," Lu said, wondering when the hell this conversation had turned into a negotiation. Still, it could have been worse. "And maybe this summer after your school lets out, you can come with me—"

"Oh no," said the pretty child standing in front of her. "I don't want to go on your tour with you. I'll stay here."

Lu told herself it was totally unreasonable to feel hurt.

"Fine," she said briskly. "Now, I've got a show to get ready for, and we have to decide what to do with you. How did you get here?"

"I told the doorman at the apartment to hail a taxicab for me."

"I'll have to warn him not to let that happen again."

"You won't have to. I won't do it again."

There was something in the way she said it—a maturity Lu had never seen from her before. She said, "I believe you. Thank you."

Her daughter nodded.

Lu checked her watch—in ten minutes they were going to announce half hour. "On Wednesdays my driver's off duty until he has to pick me up at night, but the housekeeper may know where he is. If she can find him, he'll take you home." She turned to a fascinated George and said, "Tell them at the box office to call my apartment."

"Since she's here, maybe Rose would like to see the show tonight," George suggested.

Lu turned to her daughter. "Would you like that?" she asked. She could have killed herself for the eagerness in her voice. "The theater always keeps a few house seats in reserve for special guests."

"No, thank you," said her daughter. Her voice suggested she'd rather watch snakes copulate.

Well, what did you expect? Lu asked herself.

As it worked out, the driver wasn't needed. When Lynne came into the dressing room with Lu's costumes, Rose followed the dresser downstairs to the wardrobe room, where, the woman later informed her mother, she was very helpful. It seemed her nonna had taught her how to sew on buttons, and she was a whiz at fixing zippers. She was also very efficient when it came to washing dancers' tights.

CHAPTER 17

New York

2008

"DID MY MOTHER ever see Lu do her thing on the stage?" Carrie asked. They had finished the chili and she and George were washing up the dishes in his monster kitchen. The tiny, exquisitely behaved Yorkies were sitting in a row watching them.

"Rose didn't go to any of Lu's shows for a couple of years," George said. "She could really hold a grudge—even when she was a kid. But then she started attending the opening nights. And, baby, she stole the spotlight."

"Mother did?" Carrie asked, although it shouldn't have been a surprise. Her mother always had.

"She was what—fifteen, maybe?" George went on, "And she was beautiful. There was no awkward-teenager time for Rose—no puppy fat, no zits. She knew how to dress herself—pale colors and soft fabrics, nothing showy or stiff, even in the fifties, when everyone else was wearing those ghastly prom dresses. Where she got her sense of style I'll never know. Lu didn't have any. A lot of actresses don't—they always look like they're wearing a costume. But Rose was ravishing. So on opening nights, she got big attention in the press, and she learned to play the gentlemen of the Fourth Estate like an entire frigging string section."

Carrie thought about the three signature gowns her mother had had made for her public appearances and the white leather scrapbook hidden in the bottom of her bureau drawer.

"How did she do it?" Carrie asked.

"When a reporter tried to ask Rose a question, she had this cute little move she'd do where she'd duck her head and look at them from under those absolutely spectacular lashes—Rose had the shrinking violet thing locked up long before Princess Diana came up with her Shy Di routine—and she'd point to Lu and say, 'She's the one you want to talk to. I'm not interesting at all.' Then she'd run over and help Lu take off her coat or bring her a glass of champagne. And of course everyone ate it up. She was the humble little Cinderella who just happened to be drop-dead gorgeous." He stopped rinsing the dish he was holding. "I always wondered if those eyelashes were fake."

"Maybe it wasn't an act. Maybe she really was shy," Carrie said. George shrugged. "Maybe."

"It sounds like you didn't like my mother very much."

"I didn't know her. No one did. Certainly not Lu. After her grandmother died, I think Bobby Manning was the only person who ever really knew Rose. At least, he did in the beginning."

CHAPTER 18

New York

1962

AT TEN IN the morning, the skating rink at Rockefeller Center was pretty much deserted. Rose skated
onto the ice and did a few laps around the rink to warm
up, then headed to the empty space in the center. That was where
the advanced skaters went to free skate—which was the term for
spinning, jumping, and other fancy moves. The ordinary folks
skating casually went in circles around them. How this bit of etiquette had come into being, Rose had no idea. She just knew that
that was the way it was done on every rink—including the one in
the New Haven Arena, where she had learned to skate when she
was a kid.

Skating etiquette also decreed that when you were in the center
you staked out a patch of ice and did your best to stay on it. This
was a tricky proposition, because you had to give yourself enough
room to work but you didn't want to be piggy about taking too

much space. On this morning, Rose was the only skater in the privileged zone, so she could afford to spread out. She eyeballed a patch for herself, and then, as she had every Saturday morning of every winter when she was a child, she began working on her school figures—the training exercises that were the basis of figure skating technique. She always started with a figure eight. The goal was to make the two loops of the eight—which were skated on alternating legs—even in size, without any flat areas, wobbles, or bulges. It was tedious work, but it was the part of her skating routine Rose liked best.

When Rose was a child, Nonna had bundled up in a heavy coat every Saturday morning and come to the freezing cold rink to sit in the bleachers and watch her skate. Her grandmother had been mystified by Rose's obsession with school figures.

"The other children, they fly, *cara*," she would say through her chattering teeth when Rose had skated over the barricade for a break. Nonna would give her a cup of the hot chocolate she always packed in a thermos, and she would point to one of the other kids on the ice. "That girl over there in the yellow dress, she's not so good as you, but see how she spins around and jumps? It looks like she has fun." Then she would reach out her cold hand to stroke Rose under the chin. "I want my Rose to have fun," she would say wistfully. And Rose would assure her, quite truthfully, that she was having fun. Because she enjoyed trying to get things right. And she didn't want to fly, because if you flew, you could make a mistake and fall. Rose couldn't fall and laugh it off the way other kids did. Falling down was embarrassing and it made you look foolish, and Rose couldn't stand that. So she stuck to her safe school figures and threw big happy smiles at her nonna, who loved watching her skate so much.

But then the terrible winter had come when Nonna was too sick to come to the rink with her thermos of hot chocolate. Rose had gone by herself because she and Nonna were trying to pretend that Nonna was fine and everything was okay. Rose had learned about loneliness during those Saturday mornings she'd spent tracing her perfect figure eights and trying not to look up to the spot in the bleachers where her nonna used to sit. She had learned then that losing someone you loved opened up a big black hole inside you and you could never fill it up. She had promised herself that no one she loved would ever leave her again.

ROSE STRUCK OFF on her left foot on the outside edge, her right leg held behind her in a slightly turned-out position, her left arm curved in front of her body, the right held gracefully to the side. As she made her way around the circle, her right leg and arm would come forward slowly to help her rotate. She frowned slightly; her takeoff hadn't been strong enough, and she was going to have trouble when she reached the halfway point in the loop. She fought an urge to stop and start over. The problem was, she was out of shape.

When Rose had moved to New York she'd quit skating, because it brought back memories of Nonna, New Haven, and everything that had been taken from her. But in the last six months she'd started it again, coming to Rockefeller Center in the morning and putting in two hours of practice. At least it got her out of her mother's apartment.

She leaned into her edge, hoping that would give her the momentum to get around the circle. It was funny how the old memories came back when she was on the ice. The pain of losing Nonna was as sharp today as it had been five years ago, and the anger at her mother—would that ever stop?

In a way, the seeds for that anger had been planted when Rose was still in her stroller. Every afternoon Nonna would dress Rose

in one of her beautiful little dresses—hand smocked and embroidered by Nonna's seamstress—and take Rose for a walk around
the block. They soon developed a fan club of neighbors who
watched for the lovely little girl and her proud grandmother making their daily promenade. *"Che bellissima,"* Rose heard throughout her childhood. "God bless her, what a beautiful child, Mrs.
Leporello. You must be so proud." Hands would reach down to
pinch Rose's perfect little cheeks, or her sweet little fingers would
be kissed. She learned early not to pull back or cry. If she stayed
still and smiled just a little, she got even more praise. Little Rose
liked praise—a lot.

But when she was six, her life changed. Before that, her mother
had been an intruder in her world, but not a very important one.
Lu would show up to have Sunday dinner, fight with Nonna about
missing Mass, and in general take up Nonna's time and attention,
but then she'd go away again. There had been an incident in Malley's department store when people had rushed around Lu and ignored Rose, which Rose had resented, but for the first six years of
Rose's life, Lu was still relatively unknown. Then she became a
big Broadway star. Suddenly Rose's claim to fame wasn't her own
beauty, or her gracious way of handling admiration; now it was
that she was Lu Lawson's daughter. The little girl who had had her
own fan club while she was still in her stroller hadn't liked that one
bit. All these years later, Rose could still remember the night when
her mother's big break had happened. Rose had been in the audience to see it.

Lu had had a new show opening at the Shubert Theater. This
was nothing new—every year or so her mother was in a new show.
But this time Nonna had announced that they were going to see Lu
perform. Nonna had never approved of her daughter's profession,
but it seemed this play was special. For one thing, Lu had called
long distance to beg her mother to attend the opening night.

"I'm sending a check so you can buy whatever you want to wear," she'd said over the phone while Rose listened in. "And I had a hat made specially for you—it's from Hattie Carnegie, Mama!"

"You shouldn't throw your money around," Nonna had said, but Rose could tell she was pleased.

"I'm celebrating," Lu had said. "I want you and Rose to get all dolled up and come see me. I have the second lead, Mama, and I have a number in the second act that's going to be great."

"When is this show?" Nonna had asked, although Rose knew she had already circled the advertisement for it in the *New Haven Register.*

"In two weeks. You'll have tickets for Saturday night." There was a pause, and then Lu had said, "Please come, Mama. You're the one who made it possible for me."

Nonna had agreed, and what was worse from Rose's point of view, she was excited. When the hat arrived, it was an irresistible confection of pink tulle and roses, and Nonna had her seamstress make a dress to match it. She bought a white pinafore and blouse for Rose that made her look like an angel. Nonna and Rose loved to get dressed up, although Rose would have preferred it if her mother the interloper hadn't been the cause.

Before the show opened on Saturday there was a dress rehearsal at the Shubert on Friday night. During a break, Lu called to say that there was a problem with her number. She'd be staying in the Taft Hotel instead of coming home, so that she could go to the theater early in the morning and work on some new material.

"I don't understand what's wrong," Nonna fretted to Paulie. "They're changing Lu's dance."

"Mama, it's an out-of-town tryout," Paulie said. "This is when they fix the things that aren't working."

"But Lu said her number was good," Nonna worried. "Now they don't like it? What if they fire Lu?"

As far as Rose was concerned, Nonna was way too concerned. She started hoping that the Saturday-night performance would be canceled and they wouldn't have to go.

But the performance wasn't canceled, and Lu wasn't fired, and that night Rose and her nonna sat in the theater in all their finery, waiting for Lu's big moment.

Her number began the second act. Nonna sat up straight in her seat as the curtain went up, her hands clenched in her lap. Lu was on the stage. She was dressed for bed, wearing curlers in her hair, a big fluffy robe, and furry slippers. She had on a lot of makeup, which made her look prettier than she usually did, but the outfit was silly, and people were starting to laugh at her. Lu began singing and they laughed even more. Rose looked over at Nonna to see if she had noticed how embarrassing it was, but there was a small smile playing around Nonna's mouth.

Then Lu started pulling the curlers out of her hair and throwing them at the audience. There was a drumroll from the orchestra, and Lu did a funny little movement with her hips. Rose heard a sharp gasp from Nonna and turned to see that the smile was gone. But the rest of the audience kept on laughing. They laughed when Lu took off the furry slippers and did several barefooted high kicks. They were roaring by the time she peeled off her big fluffy bathrobe slowly, one sleeve at a time, and let it fall to the floor. She was wearing some ugly pajamas and she peeled those off too, slowly, in the rhythm set by the drum.

"*Madonn'a mi!*" Rose heard Nonna whisper at her side. That was as close as she ever came to cursing. Meanwhile, Lu stood on the stage dressed only in a flesh-colored silk teddy. The garment itself wasn't all that skimpy; Rose had seen actresses in the movies wearing bathing suits that were worse, but, of course, her prudish grandmother was scandalized.

The audience around them had started to clap for Lu. They

clapped harder when twenty men came onstage and danced with her. They stood up and cheered when she did three cartwheels off the stage at the end of her number. Only Nonna stayed in her seat.

For the rest of the act, every time Lu came out onstage, the audience laughed. Everyone except Nonna. When the curtain finally came down to huge applause, Nonna sat staring grimly at the stage. That was when Rose had an idea that would end the intrusion of Lu into her life forever. "Wasn't my mother wonderful, Nonna?" she said. "When I grow up I want to be just like her."

Nonna grabbed her by the hand and took her home right then and there. They didn't stay to see Act Three.

Later that night as she lay in bed, Rose couldn't believe her mother had been stupid enough to let Nonna see that dance. Lu had to have known how Nonna would react, so what was she thinking? The next day, Lu came to the house to explain what had happened.

"They changed my costume, Mama," she said. "You remember the name of my song? It was 'I'll Always Be the Girl Next Door.' The idea was, I was a dowdy girl who had a dream that she was a glamour-puss and all men adored her. It was really just an excuse to get a whole bunch of chorus boys onstage to toss me around like a whiffleball, and I'd mug and get laughs. So, like you saw, I started singing wearing a big fluffy bathrobe, and halfway through the number I took it off. The way we originally staged it, underneath I had on this fantastic gold sequined gown. But when we did the dress rehearsal on Friday night, the guys kept dropping me because the dress was cutting their hands and it weighed a ton. It was too late to build a new costume for me, so the next day, they decided I'd do the dance like a strip and they went out to Malley's and bought a silk teddy for me. I didn't know the number was going to be so racy until we started working yesterday morning, and I was rehearsing all afternoon, so I couldn't call and warn you."

Lu had paused in her explanation, and Rose thought she probably would have gotten off with nothing more than a lecture from Nonna if she'd just kept quiet and looked really remorseful. Instead Lu did what she always did when she got into a fight with Nonna. She said exactly what she was thinking. "And I'm not sure I would have warned you anyway. It wasn't like a real striptease, and this morning all the reviews said I walked away with the show. I'm glad you saw me."

That did it. "You're glad your mother and your daughter saw you wearing your underwear while you danced with men in front of everyone?" Nonna's voice was dangerously high. Rose could have told her mother that now was the time to shut up.

But Lu went on. "It was funny, Mama," she said. "It was a joke!"

"You acted cheap on that stage! Like a tramp!"

Her mother looked at Nonna for a long time. She stood up very straight and tall. "Just remember, when I act like a tramp on the stage every night, that's how I pay your bills," she said. She started to walk out the door when Nonna stopped her.

"You know what your daughter told me last night? She wants to be just like you when she grows up. Never, Lu! Never! I can't do anything about you, but I can make sure she never sees you on the stage again!"

And since Rose hadn't wanted to watch her mother onstage getting all the attention anyway, she felt things had worked out rather well.

ROSE FINISHED THE second loop of her figure eight and skated around the two circles to check the tracings she'd left on the ice. There was a little bobble on the tricky left side. She'd have to do it over. She skated back to her starting point and positioned herself to start again. But she couldn't stop thinking about the years when she was growing up under the curse of her mother's fame. Lu's stardom had made her life at school hell.

It might have been different if there had been boys in her class, but St. Mary's segregated the sexes after the second grade. As her mother got more and more famous, Rose's classmates punished her for it with the viciousness only prepubescent girls can manage. Rose was accused of being stuck up, and everything about her was subject to ridicule. Because she lived with Nonna and had heard broken English all of her life, she spoke with a slight accent herself. It was really more of a little lilt, and most adults found it charming, but Rose's schoolmates mimicked it mercilessly. They made fun of her smile, her walk, and the way she ate—Nonna had taught her to hold her knife and fork European-style. Her school uniform was usually covered with grass stains because someone had "accidentally" bumped into her during recess. She was probably the only girl in school who prayed every day that it would rain so they couldn't go outside.

She discovered quickly that prayer wasn't going to do the trick. And her winning ways that worked so well on adults weren't going to make a dent in the stony hearts of a clique of schoolyard females bent on torture.

The worst of her tormentors was a large girl named Patty O'Brien who had a loud laugh and could play just about any sport. In a class full of girls who were just starting to shed their addiction to horses and to notice boys, she was the most masculine figure around. Patty became a pack leader at St. Mary's, and she picked on Rose mercilessly.

In an act of desperation, Rose attempted to placate the girl with a gift. It was early in the school year—Rose was twelve at the time—and she asked Nonna to bake an applesauce cake so she could take it to school. Her grandmother happily obliged, not only with the cake but a dozen cookies. She woke up before dawn to bake goodies so they'd be fresh from her oven, lovingly packed them in a bread basket lined with one of her best white linen napkins, and handed the basket to Rose.

That next morning before the school bell rang, the girls congregated in the yard as they always did, but this time instead of waiting until the last possible second to slink into the building, Rose boldly walked up to her nemesis and, with her heart in her mouth, held out her offering. "Hi," she said, attempting to seem casual, "I thought you might like this."

There was instant silence among Patty's acolytes as the large girl drew herself up to her full height and stared at Rose. For a second Rose thought she was going to reject the basket without even looking at it. If she did, Rose's life at St. Mary's would be over, officially and permanently. But then, oh miracle of miracles, and thank you, Blessed Mother, Patty reached out, took the basket, and opened it.

The applesauce cake was still slightly warm and as Patty's meaty hand pushed back the napkin, a mouthwatering aroma of cinnamon and raisins rose into the early-morning air. The cookies—chocolate chip and walnut—nestled invitingly around the cake. Nonna was a terrific baker, and Rose thought she heard a couple of sighs of appreciation from the crowd. She held her breath, and for the first time she allowed herself to hope that her years of schoolyard purgatory were over.

Then it happened. "Ooh!" Patty screamed, dropping the basket to the ground. "Cooties! The star's daughter has cooties in her cookies!" She began stomping on the basket. It took only a moment for everyone else to start chanting Patty's words. "Cooties in her cookies! Cooties in her cookies!" they brayed, and in seconds the basket was squashed, the baked goods were a mass of crumbs, and Nonna's beautiful white napkin was ground into the dirt. Mercifully, at that moment the school bell rang and Patty and her mob ran off. Rose grabbed Nonna's napkin and stuffed it into her pocket.

She didn't go to her homeroom. She'd be late for morning religious instruction, but for once she didn't care. God hadn't helped her, so what did she owe Him? Swallowing back tears, she headed for the girls' room, where she began scrubbing Nonna's napkin.

"Here, try using this," said a voice behind her. She whirled around to see one of the nuns, Sister Philomena, holding a bar of soap. Sister Phil, as the girls called her behind her back, was well liked. She was strict but fair, and known for not having favorites. Rose took the soap.

"I saw what happened from the window," Sister Phil went on. "You know, the Patty O'Briens of the world are to be pitied. I'm afraid she'll never be very attractive, poor child, and she has neither the intelligence nor the personality to overcome that."

"I don't care!" Rose managed to choke out.

"But you should try to understand," the nun said softly. "You will never make friends with those girls. You're much too pretty, and much too . . ." She paused, searching for the right word. "Favored. There's something special about you, Rose. A girl like Patty feels she has no choice but to try to cut you down."

At that, the dam broke. Leaning against the sink, Rose sobbed until her tears mixed with the suds. "What am I going to do? I have to go to school here for the next six years!"

"Stop thinking about yourself," the answer came back, fast and firm. And it stung.

"That's not fair! I'm not—"

"I didn't mean that as a criticism," Sister Philomena interrupted. "I meant, quite literally, that you are now going into a period of your life that is going to be very difficult. You will not be able to bear it if you let yourself dwell on your unhappiness. If you had a great passion for one of the arts or some intellectual pursuit you could focus on, that would get you through. But I don't sense that in you. So my suggestion would be to find some cause outside yourself."

"I don't understand."

"Help others. It's not a goody-two-shoes religious notion, Rose. It's quite a practical solution. Nothing insulates us more from our own pain than recognizing the pain of someone else and working to alleviate it. That kind of selflessness is also a big boost to our self-esteem, because giving makes us feel like we can actually accomplish something. Most altruists are quite happy. Of course, one has to watch out for the sin of pride. But right now, Lord knows, that's not a problem for you. You need your cause. And I believe I know just the thing."

And that was how Rose became the youngest volunteer at St. Mary's Asylum for Orphans. Her duties were light; most of the time she read stories to the younger children, did puzzles with them, or played games. But the sad-eyed, lonely kids never left her thoughts. Patty O'Brien and her followers lost their ability to hurt Rose; she now had bigger concerns.

The primary thing on her mind that autumn was the St. Mary's rummage sale, an annual event held in the basement of St. Mary's Church on a weekend between Thanksgiving and Christmas. The proceeds were used to buy Christmas presents for the children at the orphanage, and for several weeks prior to the event St. Mary's students collected items from friends and neighbors to be sold at the sale. Previously, Rose's participation in this effort had been minimal since Nonna didn't approve of her granddaughter ringing doorbells and asking people for castoffs. "Like a beggar," she sniffed. She felt the same way about going trick-or-treating on Halloween and selling Girl Scout cookies. But this year Rose went to every house within a ten-block radius of her home, gathering piles of unwanted stuff . She then packed her loot into special cardboard boxes that had been issued by St. Mary's and were picked up every week by the school's handyman, who stored them in the gym.

"But I don't feel like I'm doing enough," Rose said to Sister Phil.

"What are you giving of your own?" the nun asked.

And Rose realized that she'd skipped the most important part. "Just some old dishtowels of Nonna's," she whispered, embarrassed.

"Real charity involves sacrifice," said her mentor.

So Rose went home to look through her belongings. She started small, choosing a doll and a puzzle, but toys had never been important to her, so that wasn't much of a sacrifice. Steeling herself, she took down her brand-new Christmas dress and the new winter coat Nonna had bought for her, and added them to the cardboard box. And then something happened to her. It was as if she'd gone into a blissful trance and she wasn't thinking anymore. In that state, she pulled clothes out of drawers and closets; shoes, bedroom slippers, and the pretty nightgowns and matching robes Nonna had hand-made for her. Everything but her school uniforms went into the rummage sale boxes. She pulled the Mickey Mouse watch—her pride and joy—off her wrist and put it in a box without a second thought. Then, in a final act of abandon, she took down her ice skates from their special hook on her closet wall. This action did give her pause. The skates were horribly expensive; even Nonna, who never talked about money, complained about the cost. Furthermore, they were custom made for her feet so no one else would ever skate as well on them as she would. But there was no real giving without sacrifice. She put the skates into the last box and closed it.

The handyman came for his pickup every Friday afternoon, so Nonna didn't discover what she'd done until the next day, when Rose was at the rink hobbling around in the pair of skates she'd worn the previous year. By then it was too late for more than recriminations and threats of punishments her grandmother would never follow through on. Nonna certainly wasn't going to lower herself to ask for the items back; Rose had counted on that. As for Rose, if a bit of remorse had started setting in, it vanished when the rummage sale made more money than it had any other year. Even though she knew she had to be careful of the sin of pride, she couldn't help feeling that it had been her efforts that had done it. And Sister Phil had been right; that feeling was wonderful.

Rose knew she couldn't give away everything she owned every year—even Nonna wouldn't stand for that. And besides, there had to be limits. But she also knew that for the rest of her life she would remember how wild and free she'd felt when she was throwing her possessions into the cartons. And as a side benefit, once Patty realized she couldn't hurt Rose anymore, she stopped her bullying.

Rose would never be popular with the girls, but she'd found she could survive them. And she was a big favorite with the faculty— several of the nuns were praying for a religious vocation for her. She thought she was settled in for the next six years. But by the following autumn, Nonna had died and Rose had to leave St. Mary's to start a new life with her mother.

ROSE STOPPED HER figure eight. Suddenly it was impossible to concentrate, and she had to move. She stroked her way out of the center of the rink and began skating fast around the rink.

What am I doing? she asked herself. *Why am I spending my days ice-skating and remembering things I want to forget? I need to get on with my life!*

But she didn't know how to do that. The year before she'd graduated from high school and had refused to go to college. The teachers at her school had been appalled. "You're such a good student, Rose," the headmistress had said. "I was hoping you'd get your Ph.D. and teach on a college level." But Rose didn't want that kind of daily grind. She'd wondered about getting a job, but she didn't need the money, and working just to keep busy seemed rather depressing. There were times when she thought about Sister Phil and the rummage sale for the orphans and she wished the nuns at St. Mary's had been successful when they prayed for a religious vocation for her. Maybe if she had stayed in Catholic school she would have felt the call. But she'd refused to go to the parochial schools her mother suggested—mostly to spite Lu, she now realized—and she'd been exposed to a much freer life. She might feel nostalgic for Sister Phil's world, but Rose knew she couldn't live in it. Not now. So when you summed it all up—and Rose believed in summing things up—she didn't need a job, didn't want to teach, and it was too late for her to become a nun. That left her with one option.

The most obvious choice for any girl was to get married. That was what Nonna had always wanted for her. And there had been plenty of men eager to date Lu Lawson's beautiful daughter. But they hadn't gotten much encouragement from Rose. She didn't want a man who wanted to date Lu Lawson's daughter. She wanted a man who didn't even know who her mother was—as impossible as it would be to find someone like that in Manhattan and the surrounding boroughs.

Besides, none of the men who took Rose dancing and sent her flowers was extraordinary. Rose wanted an extraordinary man.

THERE WAS A teenager up ahead who was tying up the flow of traffic by trying to skate backwards. Rose swerved toward the barricade to avoid him and stopped for a second to catch her breath. She was definitely out of shape.

"Wow!" said a voice behind her. "You're even more fantastic up close than you were out in the middle of the ice."

She turned to see a man grinning at her. His thick dark hair was unfashionably long, so it curled around his face. His mouth was full, and his eyes were large and dark, with thick lashes any woman would envy. If his nose hadn't been just a little too long, he'd have been movie-star handsome. He stuck out his hand. It was a big hand, and it looked strong, although the long fingers were slim. "Hi," the man said. "I'm Bobby Manning."

CHAPTER 19

New York

1962

ROSE IGNORED THE outstretched hand. "I don't believe I know you," she said in the frostiest tone she could muster.

"No, you don't," the man agreed cheerfully. "That's why I introduced myself." When he smiled his teeth were white and even. Bobby Manning was wearing a shabby suit that had been cheap to begin with, and he carried a briefcase. His dark eyes gleamed wickedly as he gave Rose an appreciative once-over. It was a look that saw past the surface of a person, deep inside her—Rose was willing to bet the look was reserved for women only—and it said, *I know who you are. And I like it!* But the wicked dark eyes were laughing at her too. Because she was trying to pretend she didn't notice how sexy he was. And he knew he was sexy as hell. She eyed his shabby suit and his not-quite-handsome face and wondered why. Was it the confidence? Or that all-knowing gaze?

"Blushing looks good on you," he said. "Although I'm sure you know that."

For once in her life, Rose was thrown. She didn't know where to look, or what to say, so she pushed off from the barricade and skated away. When she reached the opposite side of the rink, she snuck a quick look back at the spot where he had been standing. He was gone. Rose told herself she wasn't disappointed. Just to prove she wasn't, she circled the rink several times and then skated to the center and did a scratch spin. Her form was bad, she told herself, because she was so rusty. It had nothing to do with being nervous because someone might be watching her. She got into position to try again.

"Help!" a voice gasped behind her. *His* voice. She knew it as if she'd been hearing it all of her life. Relief—a completely ridiculous relief—flooded through her. She turned to see Bobby Manning lurching toward her. He was wearing ice skates—the cheap rink skates people rented, which had dull blades and gave the foot no support. He might as well have been trying to skate on butter knives, if you could call what he was doing skating. In addition to the cheap suit, Bobby Manning was wearing a loud yellow-and-red tie. She'd missed that before.

The lurching/skating continued in slow motion. Instinctively Rose reached out her hand to help him. He grabbed for it and missed. "I think I'm going to . . . fall." He collapsed on the ice. He was splayed out flat at her feet, and his awful tie was covered with white ice chips. There was no reason in the world for her heart to be pounding so happily.

"What the hell are you doing?" Rose blurted out. She blushed some more. She hated it when she slipped up and cursed out loud. It wasn't ladylike, and Nonna would have been ashamed of her. But in her mother's show business world everyone swore all the time, and the words got stuck in her brain.

"Trying to get your attention," Bobby Manning said. He attempted to pull himself to his feet, and slid back down. He looked up at her and grinned. "I'd say I did it."

He's way too confident, said a warning voice in her head. But the wicked smile was infectious.

"You're making a fool of yourself," she informed him.

"It wouldn't be the first time." He struggled to get upright for a few more seconds. "I think you're going to have to help me—unless you like having a man on his knees in front of you."

"Or I could just take off and leave you here."

He shook his head. "You're not that kind of girl."

She couldn't hold him up by herself, and Bobby was incapable of skating across to the barricade on his own. He'd barely made it the first time, he explained, and now his ankles seemed to have given out. Finally she commandeered one of the skating instructors who gave lessons at the rink and together they dragged him off the rink.

"Have you ever skated before?" she demanded when they were on dry land and Bobby was catching his breath.

"Once. When I was six. It didn't go very well."

"You do know you're crazy."

"But for a good cause. See, the way I figure it, now that I've ruined my best tie—"

"Are you kidding? That's your best?"

"Don't interrupt. The least you can do is have a cup of coffee with me."

She made a show of looking at her watch. "I guess I can manage it," she said.

"Of course you can." And she knew from the way he was grinning at her that he knew she had nowhere else to go.

He took her to a place on Forty-seventh Street between Fifth and Madison with cracked Formica on the tabletops and fake

paneling on the wall. She'd never been in a place like it before—
she and her mother usually ate at '21' when the cook had the
day off—but she decided that the Forty-seventh Street Coffee
Shop had its charms. Not the least of which was that it was not
the kind of place where a man who was out to impress Lu Lawson's daughter would take her, Rose thought as she watched the
waiter wipe off the table with a cloth that smelled of disinfectant.
Clearly, Bobby Manning didn't know who she was. Or who her
mother was.

"Think of the roaches as part of the ambience," he said as he
ordered a hot chocolate for her and coffee for himself.

She nodded and wondered why she felt so incredibly alive. It
was like all her senses were heightened; even her skin was tingling.

But suddenly there was something wrong on the other side of
the table. Bobby had stopped smiling, and he was looking uncomfortable—like a man who had to confess something. She had a
sixth sense about these things.

Please let it be my imagination.

"There's something I have to tell you," he said.

The tingling sensation stopped. She looked around and realized just how dirty the coffee shop really was.

"Running into you at the rink the way I did—that wasn't an accident," Bobby said. "I've been trying to meet you. I'd heard that
you like to ice-skate and I've been hanging around Rockefeller
Center and Wollman Rink in Central Park for about a month
now."

Oh, damn, she thought.

"Last week I saw you and I recognized you right away. I'd seen
your picture in the *Times*—the one they took of you at the closing-
night party for your mother's last show."

Damn, damn, damn.

"I'm a writer. A musical comedy writer."

I should have seen this coming. Why the hell didn't I see this coming?

"Two years ago, several of my sketches were in a revue that played down at the Village Vanguard. The show closed but I got good notices. I'm a composer too. I write songs—mostly special material for people's club acts. Two of my tunes have been recorded." He took a deep breath, and then he said what he'd been leading up to. "I've written a show that would be perfect for your mother."

What was surprising was how angry she was at him. Usually when this happened she was angry at Lu.

"I've tried to get it to her every way I could," Bobby went on. "I sent a copy to her agent, but he refused to look at it. I left a copy backstage at her theater, but she mailed it back to me without opening the envelope."

"She didn't mail it." Rose heard her voice strong and clear.

"Yes, she did. I got it back."

"But Mother didn't mail it," Rose explained. "George did that. He's her conductor—but he's also her friend. George protects Mother from all the two-bit, no-talent hustlers who try to take advantage of her." She stood up, took a ten-dollar bill out of her purse, and tossed it on the table. "This should cover my hot chocolate and the rental for your skates," she said, starting for the door.

"Wait!" Bobby called out, and she heard a chair scraping on the linoleum behind her, but she didn't turn back.

She had a head start on him, and she would have lost him for good if a guy on the street hadn't run into her, interrupting her stride. Bobby caught up with her and grabbed her arm.

"You didn't let me finish," he said.

"I didn't need to." She pulled her arm away and walked faster. So did he.

"I did want to use you—at first. I wanted to get to Lu Lawson any way I could. But then I saw you. You were skating, doing whatever the hell it is you do when you go around in circles for hours, and I watched you. And . . . you take a great picture, but in person you're unbelievable. I had to talk to you. Not because of your mother. Because you're the most beautiful woman I've ever seen." He was breathing hard. "I know I'm supposed to pretend that doesn't matter to me and I'm really interested in your mind, but I'm a guy. And we're shallow. Any girl who looks like you must know that." He was panting now. "Will you, for Christ's sweet sake, slow down before I pass out?"

He really did sound as if he might. She slowed down just a little. He grabbed her arm again and stopped her. This time she didn't pull away.

"Now that I've talked to you, I *am* interested in your mind. You're smart."

She'd always known she was, but most people didn't see it.

"There's something about you, something you keep hidden."

He'd seen that too.

"You don't know anything about me," she said.

"Not yet. But I'm going to. And I'm warning you, I know where you live. I'll be outside your building every morning and every evening until you give in." He was so close to her that he could have kissed her. Instead, he lifted her chin up so she was looking into his eyes. "And I promise I will never ask you to give my musical to your mother. I'll never bring it up."

Liar, she thought.

Then he grinned. "You'll have to ask me for it. When you've learned to trust me." Then he released her arm, and out of nowhere she was going to cry, and she couldn't let him see it. She turned and walked away. After a second, he called out, "One more thing," and ran after her. He pulled the ten-dollar bill out of his pocket and jammed it into her hand. "Don't ever, ever throw your money at me again," he said. He wasn't smiling. She nodded and swallowed back the tears. Then he kissed her—on the forehead.

"You don't have to stake out my building," she said. "I skate at Rockefeller Center every morning at ten." She could hardly believe the words were coming out of her mouth.

"Yeah," he said. "I know."

BOBBY CAME EVERY morning to watch Rose skate—the way Nonna used to, when Rose was little. Although, of course, this was totally different. The third morning, after Rose finished skating, she allowed herself to be talked into walking to the Theater District with him to drink coffee and talk.

Over the next few weeks she learned that Bobby had his special haunts in this neighborhood. One was the coffee shop at the Hotel Edison because a lot of shows rehearsed in the hotel ballroom upstairs and the actors, writers, and directors would come down to the coffee shop for a break. Another was a Greek cafeteria in Hell's Kitchen called Molfetta's, where unemployed actors hung out to exchange gossip between their classes and auditions.

But his favorite places were the restaurants on Broadway. When he was feeling flush, Bobby took Rose to Lindy's or Jack Dempsey's—both places served great cheesecake and they'd split a slice. As far as Bobby was concerned, Manhattan began and ended within three blocks of the Great White Way. He and Rose would walk past the Mark Hellinger Theater or the Winter Garden, and he'd stare at the cast list and the pictures of the actors encased in glass under the marquee with a hunger that Rose couldn't watch. It was hard to see how badly he wanted the life she'd always taken for granted. And, of course, they both knew she could have helped him get closer to that life. But Bobby kept his word and he never brought up the subject of her mother or his musical.

Instead, Rose asked him about himself. She learned that he was twelve years older than she was. Like her, he hadn't gone to college. For the past seven years he'd been working as a clerk in Hershemer's, a famous music store on Fifth Avenue. The place had been around since the days of vaudeville, and it sold sheet music and records for everything from pop to Beethoven. But the main emphasis at Hershemer's was musical comedy. There was a grand piano in the bay window of the opulent main floor, and the legend was that Richard Rodgers had walked in off the street one day and wowed the customers by playing the score from *South Pacific*.

"And last week Betty Comden bought three records from me," Bobby told Rose proudly. Like all the Hershemer's clerks, he was horribly underpaid, but the gig was prized by aspiring young theatrical types because their workday began at a theater-friendly eleven-thirty AM, and the management had an understanding attitude about time off for auditions and rehearsals. And there was always the chance that they'd get to wait on Betty Comden. Sometimes Rose wondered if Bobby and his fellow slaves thought the success of the great ones would rub off on them like Peter Pan's fairy dust. She couldn't imagine wanting anything as badly as he wanted to be in show business—or maybe she could. Because by now, she wanted him.

She asked herself why. She still didn't trust him and she knew somewhere deep down that he could hurt her more than anyone else ever had. Of course he never talked about the girls in his life, but every feminine instinct Rose had told her that there had been many of them—probably dozens. So the challenge was part of his allure. She wanted to be the one who finally got him. But that wasn't the only reason. And whatever else it was about him, the

combination of passion and hope, the dreams that drove him—
that had captivated her—she couldn't analyze it. She just knew he
was the man she'd been waiting for.

"Where do you live?" she asked him a few weeks after they'd
met. *Always keep a man talking about himself. Not only does it please
him, but you never know when the information you get will be useful.*

"In the Village, on Christopher Street," he said.

"Very arty."

"If you think a tub in the kitchen and a toilet down the hall is
artistic."

She waited for him to ask her to come see it, but he never did.
He'd never asked her to go out with him in the evening, either.
They seemed to have a standing date—if that was the right word—
for coffee every morning before he went to work. But he'd never
asked her to have dinner with him or to go to a movie or dancing.

He hadn't kissed her either, although she knew he wanted to.
And she knew why he hadn't. "You're for keeps, not for fun," he
said.

She told herself it was good that he understood that about her.
Men didn't marry women they didn't respect. She knew that from
watching her mother.

Lu's love life consisted of brief affairs that usually occurred
when she wasn't working or when she was on the road. For a few
weeks, the man would be underfoot all the time, with Lu laughing at his jokes, listening to his opinions, and going out every
evening on his arm. But once she started rehearsal for a new
show, she'd go back to her rigid schedule and the man would discover that coddling the star's ever-delicate throat was more important to everyone—including the star—than coddling him, and
he would disappear. Soon he'd be seen around town with a woman
who was more attentive, if less successful, than Lu.

Rose had watched this pattern and determined never to repeat it. She was going to save herself for marriage the way Nonna had told her to. Once she had a ring on her finger, she would dedicate her life to her husband. He would come first in all things; his needs would be her needs, his tastes would be her tastes. And he would never leave her the way men always left her mother.

I'd die if that happened, Rose thought.

But she wanted Bobby to kiss her. She wanted him to pull her close, press her to him, and kiss her. She fell asleep aching for his kisses. She daydreamed about his body underneath the shabby suit he always wore. She knew it would be lean and hard, because sometimes when they walked together he put his arm around her and she could feel his chest and the muscles in his arm. She imagined herself stroking his warm, smooth skin, and running her fingers through his curling hair, and then she'd be aware that her face was red and deep inside her there was a hot, fluttery feeling. At those moments Rose could almost convince herself that she really could trust him. Then she'd remember the hungry look in Bobby's eyes when he passed a theater marquee, and she'd remind herself that he had never asked her to go out for dinner. She still wasn't sure about him and how he felt about her. She needed to know more.

"Tell me about your family," she said one morning.

"I'm an only child," Bobby said. "My parents met in the twenties. My father was Fred Manning—he came out of northern California. I think I have a couple of uncles out there, but Dad lost touch with his family when he left home. He was a musician in a band at a summer camp for adults in the Catskills. Mother—her name was Caroline—was a guest at the camp.

"She was a stenographer. She lived in Queens with her parents, but she had a lot of class, so my dad thought she had money. By the time he realized she was as broke as he was, he was in love with her. So he married her anyway."

"That's very romantic," Rose said.

"Yeah." Bobby smiled a twisted little smile. "Then he cheated on her for the rest of his life."

Clearly he was bothered by that, and that pleased Rose. She thought it was a good sign for his future as a husband.

"My old man had plenty of opportunities to run around," Bobby went on. "After my folks were married, he got a job as a waiter during the week. But on the weekends, he and the band used to play weddings and bar mitzvahs around New Jersey, Connecticut, and New York State. There were always women who were willing to have a little roll in the hay with the hired help." Bobby stopped and finished off the last of their cheesecake—it was a Lindy's day—before continuing. "Dad died when I was six. He'd always had a bad heart, and it just gave out. My mother went back to work as a stenographer."

"She must have been a young woman—why didn't she get married again?"

"She said she couldn't count on God to save her twice, and she was going to quit while she was ahead." He poked around on the cheesecake plate for a couple of stray crumbs. Rose could tell he didn't want to look her in the eye. "Mom died three years ago. Before she got sick, I took her to see the revue at the Village Vanguard. She said my sketches were funny but she still wished I'd go to college and make something of myself." He smiled the twisted smile again. Rose wanted to do something, anything, to make him feel better.

"Do you have copies of your sketches? I'd love to read them," she said.

He shook his head. "That's against the rules. Remember?"

She wanted to tell him that the rules didn't matter. But she couldn't. Not yet.

*   *   *

ROSE STARTED ASKING around about Bobby Manning. Lu's agent had never heard of him, and neither had the producer who always mounted her mother's musicals, although George said he thought he remembered that someone named Manning had once sent Lu a script.

It was a different story with the chorus girls who were working on Lu's show. Rose had never spent much time backstage, but now she went every night to hang around the greenroom and chat. She discovered that Bobby was well known in the off-off-Broadway scene.

"He could have had a show done at the Café Larré," one of the dancers told Rose. "But he pulled it at the last second because he said the production was lousy. He can be an arrogant son of a bitch."

"It's not arrogance," a singer chimed in. "Bobby wants to work on Broadway. That's what he writes for. Off-off Broadway is too small for him. Bobby has a huge talent."

The first girl snickered. "In more ways than one," she said.

"I was talking about his writing," said the second girl, but then she started snickering too. Rose wanted to slap both of them— even though this bit of gossip was nothing more than what she'd already suspected.

"Bobby gets around, does he?" she asked as casually as she could.

"The way I hear it, he gives new meaning to the phrase 'can't keep it in his pants,'" said the singer.

"Marianne, you don't know that for a fact. It's just people talking."

"One of my best friends is the friend of his last girlfriend," said the singer, whom Rose was beginning to hate. "At least that's what she thought she was until she found him in their bed with her sister. The guy's a swordsman."

Fortunately, at that moment, the stage manager announced the second-act finale over the backstage loudspeaker and the girls had to go onstage.

He can change, Rose thought. *I can change him.* And then she thought, *I can win him.*

But what if she couldn't? What if he was unwinnable? There were people like that—her mother was one.

The last thing Rose needed in her life was another self-centered, workaholic egomaniac in her life. *But the right girl can change a man. And I'm the right girl for Bobby. I just have to find a way to make him see it.*

CHAPTER 20

New York City

1962

MEANWHILE, SOMETHING STRANGE was going on with Lu. For years her schedule had been the same. She'd open a musical, play it on Broadway for a year, take it on the road for a half a year, do a season in London, and then come back to New York for a couple of months of rest before going into rehearsal for her next show. It was a routine that everyone thought was etched in stone. But suddenly she'd announced that she wanted to take some time off.

Lu's last show had been a bit of fluff called *All the Boys*, in which she had played a girl who masqueraded as a cowboy to follow the man of her dreams on a cattle run. It was standard Lu Lawson fare, starring her as a wisecracking ugly duckling who tried to get the attention of the boneheaded leading man by engaging in a series of adorably tomboyish antics—until he finally noticed how fabulous she was in time for the third-act finale. There was nothing wrong with *All the Boys*. Yet for some reason Lu had refused to take it out on the road. She'd also announced that she wouldn't be going to London with the show. Lu's agent and her producer panicked. They asked if she was sick, and they ordered their secretaries to look up the names of doctors.

George said she was exhausted. "I told you not to let her ride that damn machine," he said to the agent and the producer over an emergency dinner at Sardi's. The first act of *All the Boys* had opened with a plucky Lu being thrown from a mechanical horse, and even with the special harness that was supposed to protect her when she fell, she'd spent most of the show's run swallowing aspirin and running to the chiropractor's office. "She's beat," George scolded.

But Rose knew the truth. *Mother's bored.*

And that was when Rose realized that she'd gotten to know Lu better than anyone else—even loyal, devoted George.

Rose hadn't wanted to get to know her mother, but when she started living under Lu's roof it had been unavoidable. Lu wasn't demanding or temperamental—not the way she could have been—but life in her home revolved around her, and the people who worked for her had learned to read her moods. If rehearsals were going badly or the first costume fittings had been a disaster, the cook would suspend Lu's spartan diet and her favorite baked ziti would appear on the menu. Lu's driver would make himself available for soothing late-night spins around Central Park. Miss Pearl—who had graduated from the role of Rose's babysitter to that of Lu's assistant—would order fresh flowers for the foyer. And Rose would call George and Davy to come over for a distracting game of Scrabble.

The truth was, over the years, Rose had developed a grudging respect for her mother, and not just because Lu was so good at what she did. Lu's honesty was uncompromising. She had never asked Rose for love or even for understanding. She rarely offered Rose advice, but when she did, it was sound. Rose quickly realized that her mother was smart about people. Lu had defanged a potentially mean English teacher at Rose's school by offering to give a speech to the woman's precious drama club about getting into show business, and Rose had scored points with her classmates throughout her teen years because Lu could scrounge up the tickets for any matinee on Broadway that the kids wanted to see—as long as they were accompanied by Miss Pearl. Rose was given a generous allowance, and she could use Lu's charge cards as long as she did not abuse the privilege. In return, Lu expected Rose to be polite, to stay out of trouble, and to get good grades. Rose had obliged her, but if you had asked her if she and her mother were close, she would have said her mother was too dedicated to her work—and too selfish—to be close to anyone.

But now, for the first time, her mother wasn't working. Lu still vocalized every day, singing the Panis Angelicus to warm up, and she still took her dance classes. But she hadn't signed on for a new show. Instead, she had started taking an interest in things she'd never seemed to notice before, like her apartment. Lu had always been a haphazard decorator, but one day she looked around her and said to her faithful retainers, "I'm living in some of the most expensive real estate on Fifth Avenue, and it looks like the No-Tell Motel in Boise."

An interior decorator was hired, and suddenly Lu was on a first-name basis with the owners of every antiques shop and furniture showroom in Manhattan. The same ferocious energy she poured into rehearsals and performances was now channeled into the feathering of her nest, and before she finished—six weeks later—two decorators would quit from exhaustion.

The home Lu had furnished for herself was elegant—full of

rich fabrics and delicate antiques. In the cabinets were crystal and bone china; the walls were painted a serene taupe. The conservatively classy choices Lu had made would have stunned her loyal fans, who knew her only as a charming hoyden with a brassy voice who leaped out of the orchestra pit and landed on the stage in a split—in her midthirties she was still famous for such horseplay—but Rose knew that the formal rooms expressed the character of the real Lu Lawson. Underneath the professional razzle-dazzle, her mother was a quiet woman who had an old-fashioned work ethic and old-world tastes. Her apartment full of antiques suited her perfectly.

"You should have a party," Rose said one morning, "to show off this place."

She'd said it in passing, but her mother had grabbed on to the idea. "I've never done that," she said. "I've lived here for ten years and I've had friends over for dinner but I've never had a real formal party . . ." She stopped. "I can pull it off, right?"

"Absolutely," Rose said as she headed out the door with her skates.

By the time she returned, Lu had already lined up a caterer, a florist, six waiters, and a bartender. She was waiting for Rose. "Good. You're home," she said. "What am I going to wear to this shindig?"

"You have closets full of clothes."

"We both know all my taste is in my tongue when it comes to my wardrobe."

"I'm sure you'll find something," Rose said reassuringly.

"Did you see me at the closing-night party for *All the Boys*? I looked like a Tyrolean schoolgirl." She thought for a second. "Make that Big Bo Peep."

Lu was right—her taste in clothes tended toward ruffles, bows, lace, and the color pink. Whether it was a reaction to all the boy-ish roles she played, or because, like a lot of small women, she thought she had to dress like an ingénue, she usually wound up looking like a pink meringue.

"I'll go shopping with you," said Rose. Jackie Kennedy was cur-rently wowing the country with her sleek Oleg Cassini A-line shifts and gowns, and Rose had taken the president's young wife as her own fashion role model. But remaking Lu into Jackie's mold wasn't as easy as she'd thought it was going to be. The trick to sim-ple little A-line frocks was, they had to fit perfectly or they looked like little A-line sacks. Lu's small body was very curvy: a dress that fitted her bust sagged at her waist, one that hugged her hips gapped at the top. And then there was the question of color; white made Lu look washed out, black made her look dead, and her beloved pink made her look like a pastry. Lu and Rose went from Best and Co., to Bergdorf Goodman's, to Saks Fifth Avenue, and to Lord and Taylor, with no luck. And it soon became clear that Lu's famous perseverance did not extend to clothes shopping.

"This is good enough," she moaned when she had tried on her fourteenth Jackie Kennedy–esque gown.

"It's about half an inch too big under the arms," Rose said.

"We'll bring it to the tailor."

Rose shook her head. "If you have it taken in, the seams won't be right."

"Does half an inch make such a big difference?"

"It's not a costume, Mother. It has to look good up close. And the color is wrong."

"How can beige be wrong?"

"It's making *you* look beige."

"How about pink? I like pink."

"Do you remember the Big Bo Peep dress?"

Lu moaned again. "This is such a waste of time!"

Rose, who could spend months finding just the right pair of shoes, shook her head.

They never did find a dress that met Rose's exacting standards, so they had it made. Rose pieced together a rough design from three *Vogue* patterns, they purchased a coppery brown satin that was the exact shade of Lu's hair, and then they took everything to a dressmaker known for her society clients. The finished gown had a narrow skirt, sleek lines, and no ruffles. Just lying in the box it exuded glamour and class. Lu was so pleased that she hugged Rose, who gave her a quick hug back. It wasn't exactly the kind of warm mother-and-daughter moment the women's magazines were always writing about, but for them it was a real step forward. "Thank you, Rose," Lu whispered, and they both knew she was talking about a lot more than an evening gown.

In a gesture of further goodwill, Rose offered to help Miss Pearl address the invitations for Lu's party. Her mother was inviting seventy people, among them her agent, her producer, and George. Rose decided she wanted to invite Bobby.

NOTHING HAD CHANGED for Rose and Bobby. They were still meeting at Rockefeller Center and having coffee on Broadway. He had kept his word about his musical; he'd said that he wouldn't bring it up until Rose trusted him and asked to see it. But she hadn't asked. There were times when she thought if she could, maybe other things would happen. Maybe he'd ask her to come to his apartment. Maybe he'd kiss her. He hadn't given her one single reason not to trust him—she knew she was being unfair. But something inside her just wouldn't give in.

She told herself that inviting him to her mother's party wasn't a test. Even though he would be meeting a laundry list of Broadway movers and shakers, she told herself that she was absolutely positive that he wouldn't try to hustle his musical to any of them. He'd promised her he wouldn't take advantage of her and her connections, and he'd keep that promise. She told herself she was absolutely positive about that too. So there was no test and it was perfectly okay when she asked Lu if they could add Bobby Manning to the party guest list.

"Who is he?" Lu asked.

Rose found herself spilling everything, telling Lu about Bobby's ambitions and the promise he'd made. "He says now that he knows me, he could never ever try to use me to get to you," Rose wound up her recitation. "And I believe him."

Almost.

"Oh, shit," her mother muttered.

"What's wrong?" she asked.

"You were just starting to like me, and now I've got to say something that you aren't going to want to hear."

"You think he *is* trying to use me."

"Do you really think he isn't?"

"If he was, why would he be so up front with me?"

"Obviously he's very smart."

"Or maybe what he said was the truth. Maybe he did want to meet me because of you, but now that he knows me, things are different."

"If you believe that, why are you making him prove himself?"

"That sounds ugly."

"It is. If this man is as desperate as you say he is—"

"I never said he was desperate."

"Rose, he's thirty years old and he's been knocking around trying to get a break since he got out of high school. Believe me, he's desperate. And putting him in a room with the people who could give him everything he's ever dreamed of is like putting a starving dog in front of a porterhouse and telling it not to eat."

"He's not trying to use me! He cares about me."

"He can care about you and use you at the same time, honey. People do that."

"You don't know him!"

Her mother sighed. "Oh yes I do, Rose. I know your Bobby Manning without ever saying hello."

It was the sadness in her eyes that got to Rose. "Why do you always try to hurt me?" she cried. "Why do you want to do that?"

"I want to *keep* you from being hurt. I'm not saying your Bobby Manning is bad. But people can do things to each other—"

"I know all about what people can do to each other. I know that a mother can dump her baby because she's got to have her own life and a kid would get in her way!"

"I gave you the best mother I could."

"You gave me a mother who died when I was thirteen!"

There was a long silence, and then Lu said, "You're angry at me. You have a right to be. But I hope someday you can get over it." She spoke so gently—as if she actually gave a damn.

"I bet you do," Rose spat.

"Not for me. For you."

They were in Lu's newly redecorated bedroom. On the bed was the coppery gown Rose had helped design. Lu picked it up. "It's going to look like a million bucks," she said. "Thank you."

"You already said that."

Lu nodded. She spread the gown on a boudoir chair and looked back at Rose. "I'm just so afraid you'll never let yourself be happy," she said.

"May I ask Bobby Manning to come to the party?" Rose demanded.

"Of course."

"Thanks." She started for the door.

"Rose," her mother called out. "Just remember, people can be cruel without meaning to."

"Bobby won't hurt me."

"I wasn't talking about him," said her mother.

CHAPTER 21

New York

2008

"I'M ASSUMING Bobby Manning did go to the party," Carrie said as she and George sipped coffee in his chorus gypsy/Belle Epoque living room. The dishes had been washed and dried after George had delivered a speech on his belief that anyone who insisted on owning a dishwasher in Manhattan should move to New Jersey. Now Carrie, George, and the Yorkies were all sitting on a couch that had been part of the set for a summer stock production of *My Fair Lady*.

"Oh yes, Bobby came to the party," George said. He paused to take a sip of coffee. "But it was a . . . weird night."

"Weird how?" Carrie asked

"The party was great. Lu swanned around with her chic new look, and the apartment was done up like frigging Versailles. And Rose was gorgeous, but that came under the heading of What Else Is New?"

"Okay, and the weird part?"

"Actually Davy and I kind of caused it—without meaning to." He looked off into space and chuckled. "In the sixties, there were a whole lot of clubs in the Village that showcased new acts—girl singers who wanted to be the next Barbra Streisand were real big down there—and I used to get invitations to them because of Lu and all the people I knew. A couple of weeks before Lu's party I got a flyer from a Barbra wannabe and Davy and I and some friends went downtown to catch her act, just for the fun of it. The girl's name was Antoinette Landovich—I'll never forget it. Davy and I tried to persuade her to change it to something a little more suitable for the biz—which meant white-bread WASP back then—but she kept on spouting all that sixties BS about not giving in to the bourgeois demands of commercial theater. That was before I'd told her I was the bourgeois conductor she'd invited to come see her do her thing. After that she got a lot less committed to her ideals. She did a whole number about how Lu Lawson was her heroine and she'd love to meet her.

"Antoinette seemed to know about Lu's soiree, which was a little strange because it was a private party, but I figured the grapevine was probably working overtime. Everything Lu did back in those days was news. Besides, by that point, Davy had gotten pretty stoned, and before I could stop him he was giving Antoinette Lu's address and inviting her to Lu's party as our guest. I tried to kill him on the way home in the cab, but it was too late. We both knew there was no way in hell that girl was going to miss a chance to get up close and personal with Lu Lawson and her friends." George took one of the little Yorkies onto his lap and started rubbing it behind the ears.

"Lu was fine with Antoinette coming," he continued. "And I didn't think anything more about it. Not then." George accidentally pulled one of the Yorkie's ears. It protested with a sharp yelp but he didn't seem to notice.

"You asked me if I knew what happened between Lu and Rose after Bobby died. I don't. Lu hasn't told me to this day. But she did say once that the whole thing started on the night of her party back in 'sixty-two when Antoinette Landovich showed up."

CHAPTER 22

New York

1962

ROSE WAS HAVING a mild attack of stage fright. Her mother's party had already started and she was still in her bedroom finding reasons not to emerge. She checked herself in the mirror for what had to be the twentieth time. She'd bought a new dress for the night; it draped over one shoulder, caught under the bust, and then fell to the floor. The fabric was a clingy crepe de chine that matched Rose's skin tone, and if she was standing in the wrong light—or the right light, depending on your point of view—it didn't leave a lot to the imagination. Rose intended to spend the night standing in the wrong/right light whenever Bobby was nearby. She'd tried piling her long red hair on top of her head in a fashionable beehive, but at the last second she'd pulled it down and let it fall freely around her back and shoulders. Given a clamshell, she could have passed for a modern-day version of the Botticelli's Venus. Now she just had to go out to the party, where all her efforts would do her some good.

Rose gave herself one last look in the mirror and thought about saying a quick prayer. But somehow it didn't seem appropriate. Not when she was doing her best to look naked. She left her bedroom and headed toward the sounds of the party.

The guests seemed to be distributed evenly throughout the living room, the dining room, and the foyer. Rose looked around. George had already arrived with Davy, and Lu's agent was there. Her producer hadn't shown up yet. Neither had Bobby.

Good, she thought as she smiled and nodded at an actor—he'd been the second banana in her mother's last show—who was waving at her from across the room. *If Bobby's not here then I didn't miss anything.*

Her mother had said she was making him prove himself, and Rose had said she wasn't. But what if she was? What if she was setting up one final test tonight? Was that such a sin?

It's like putting a starving dog in front of a porterhouse steak and asking it not to eat, Lu had said.

But what about me, damn it? Rose thought. *I have to know. I have to be sure.*

The second banana was heading her way, and she took off in the opposite direction, circling the rooms, nodding and smiling at people she wasn't seeing, always keeping the front door of the apartment in sight.

Bobby showed up five minutes later. He was wearing a new suit. It was cheap, but at least it wasn't the shabby one he wore to work every day. He was also wearing another loud tie. But that lapse in taste was something that could be easily fixed when she was the one picking his wardrobe. Rose made her way to the foyer.

"Hi," she said, and offered her cheek for him to kiss, but he was too busy taking in the Venus dress. "Very nice," he murmured, and then he added, "Thank you."

He knew she'd worn it for him. Well, of course he did. He knew women. For a second she felt like a fool—one who needed to put on some more clothes. But then she looked into his eyes and there was something there that made her feel as if she really were naked, and it wasn't an unpleasant sensation. Rose straightened up a little more, just in case he'd missed something, and took him by the arm.

"Your timing is perfect," she said. "Come mingle."

For the first ten minutes, he didn't leave her side. She introduced him to George, and Lu's agent and producer. She introduced him to Lu. He was charming, he was funny, he was delightful. He didn't even mention that he was a writer and a composer. When people asked him what he did, Bobby said he was a clerk at Hershemer's Music Store. Then Rose left him to circulate on his own. She didn't watch to see who he was talking to. She'd find out later.

The party was in full swing when a girl in a tacky yellow print dress appeared at the door. The dress—from the thirties or the forties—had probably been purchased in a vintage shop in the Village, and the girl had chosen to wear a slightly moth-eaten black fur jacket with it. It was that Lower East Side look that had been pioneered by some new singer—Rose didn't remember her name—but like most of those who tried to copy it, this girl couldn't carry it off. She looked like a waif, and not a particularly adorable one, as she stood in Lu's grand foyer scanning the living room, obviously looking for someone.

When George and Davy swooped down and rescued the girl, Rose figured that she was another one of the strays Davy was always befriending, and forgot about her. So she was surprised a few minutes later when Davy seemed to be leading the girl—sans the moth-eaten fur—in her direction.

"Antoinette is just dying to meet you," Davy said happily. Davy was always happy when he could do something nice for someone. That was why savvy, clever George stuck with him even though Davy wasn't exactly a genius. "Antoinette is one of Lu's biggest fans, and she—"

"Hey, Landovich," said a voice at Rose's side. She turned to see Bobby standing next to her. He was grinning, but there was something wrong. Something in the air between Bobby and the girl that Rose could feel. Above his smile, Bobby's eyes were glittering with an anger Rose had never seen before, and he was pale. There was defiance and a little fear in the look Antoinette shot back at him.

"I didn't expect to see you here, Antoinette," Bobby said. He sounded friendly enough—if she hadn't seen the look in his eyes Rose wouldn't have thought twice about it.

Obviously he's very smart, her mother had said.

"Just getting a look at the way the other half lives." Antoinette smiled bitterly at Bobby. Then she turned and looked at Rose. She looked like someone who was about to dive into a very cold body of water. She hesitated for a second, then took the plunge. "You see, Bobby and I . . ."

And Rose knew that whatever Antoinette Landovich was going to say next, it would be the end of all the dreams she'd had about herself and Bobby. Suddenly it was as if she were standing outside herself watching a scene in a play. She watched a character named Rose slip her arm through Bobby's arm and smile sweetly at Antoinette Landovich. She heard Rose say, "I'm sorry. Will you excuse us? There's a man I want Bobby to meet, and I think he's getting ready to leave." And she watched Rose lead Bobby away. Then, just as suddenly as she had stepped outside her body, she was back in it, and as she and Bobby crossed the room she could practically hear the gears cranking fast inside his head.

Don't lie to me, she urged him silently. But then she added, *Don't say something I can't live with.*

"I know Antoinette because I wrote some special material for her club act," Bobby said.

It wasn't a lie, but it didn't go far enough. He hadn't explained the looks he and Antoinette had exchanged, and the thick, hot tension in the air. And he knew he had to. As Lu had said, Bobby was very smart.

There was a little alcove at the side of the room. It wasn't totally private, but it was better than standing in the middle of the crowd. Bobby pulled her into it and turned her so she was looking at him. Then he picked his words very carefully. "Antoinette and I have had a thing. She knew from the beginning it wasn't going anywhere. I told her that."

Are you still having a thing? Rose wanted to ask. But she couldn't.

Bobby took a breath. "She knows . . . about you. And she found out I was coming to this party." He smiled the little twisted smile she'd gotten to know so well. "I bought a new suit and that made her suspicious."

That sounds like she's still your girlfriend.

"She came here tonight to . . . I don't know why she came," he went on. "To make a scene . . . to embarrass me . . ."

Is she still your girlfriend? Has she been your girlfriend all these months while you were having coffee with me and buying me cheesecake?

He wasn't going to tell her that; she was going to have to ask him. Rose drew in a deep breath. But then she saw her mother. Lu was at the opposite side of the room, watching them.

If I lose him I'll have nothing, Rose thought. She didn't ask her question.

"I haven't been a saint," Bobby said.

And what he was supposed to say next was *But that was in the past, Rose. Now I've met you. I'll never look at another woman again. I'll never leave you and I'll be yours forever.* In all of the plays her mother had starred in, that was what the leading man said to the leading lady.

What Bobby said to her instead was "I'd be crazy to try to tell you there haven't been girls in the past. You're too smart for that."

You got your lines wrong, Bobby! Rose thought. *And I need to hear the right ones. I deserve them.* But then she looked across the room. Lu was still watching them.

Rose shrugged. "Who'd want a saint?" she asked with what she hoped was a worldly smile.

But Bobby looked at her and asked, "Don't you?" And she knew he'd surprised himself; that was not what he'd intended to say.

She thought for a moment, then said slowly, "If anyone ever made a fool of me, I'd hate him for the rest of my life." And she knew that was the most honest she would ever be.

"I'd never want you to hate me." And she knew he was telling the truth too.

Antoinette Landovich left the party about twenty minutes later. Whatever she'd wanted to accomplish, she'd left undone. Bobby stayed at Rose's side for the rest of the night. He was charming and funny and everyone liked him. He never mentioned his musical once. But Rose didn't care about that anymore.

AFTER THE PARTY was over, Rose walked Bobby to the elevator. The hallway was empty and later on she would wonder if they had timed it that way without realizing it. Because that was when he kissed her. And Rose discovered that all the clichés were true; her knees really did wobble, the floor did fall away from under her feet, and if the elevator hadn't arrived when it did, she would have

stood there kissing him all night. But the elevator did arrive and
he got on it, looking as dazed as she felt.

If I lose him, I'll die, she thought as she watched the elevator
doors close. And she had to wait a few minutes until she was sure
her face wasn't going to give her away before she went back inside
the apartment.

Lu was sitting on the sofa with her feet up.

"I'm going to bed," Rose announced.

"Who was that girl?" her mother asked.

In Rose's present state of bliss the question was like a cold
shower. But there was no point in pretending she didn't know who
her mother meant.

"Her name is Antoinette Landovich and Davy invited her,"
Rose said. Then she added, "She's an old girlfriend of Bobby's."

" 'Old' as in she's not his girlfriend now?"

"Yes," Rose said. Although when she thought about it she realized she still didn't know for sure.

"Is he sleeping with you?" Lu asked.

"Of course not."

"If he isn't sleeping with you, he's having sex with someone
else."

"No he isn't," she said. But did she believe that?

"George asked around about him," Lu said. "Your Bobby Manning has quite a reputation."

"People can change," Rose said defiantly. But she couldn't look
at her mother. "Sometimes . . . all it takes is the right person . . ."

"Could you change?"

"What do you mean?"

"Could you become the kind of woman who wouldn't care if a
man cheated on you?"

"Bobby would never do that to me," Rose said. She left the
room before her mother could say another word.

*   *   *

THE NEXT DAY at Lindy's, before they had even ordered their cheesecake, Rose asked Bobby if she could read his musical, and if he'd play the songs for her. He opened the briefcase he always carried with him, handed her the manuscript, and told her he'd meet her at Hershemer's after the store closed for the day to play the score for her. And he didn't seem surprised.

CHAPTER 23

New York

1962

ROSE STARTED READING Bobby's musical in the taxicab on her way home, and by the time she reached her mother's apartment she already knew what she thought about his talent as a writer and the book of his show. She went to Hershemer's to hear him play the score so she'd know if he was a good composer. Then she could tell him what he had to do next. How or why Rose thought she was capable of judging a Broadway musical was something she never stopped to question. She didn't wonder if she should be giving Bobby advice. She just knew that whatever she said would be right because she loved him. She had no doubt about that now that he'd kissed her. Of course, he still hadn't said he loved her—but he would. Because now it was her turn to prove herself to him. And God wouldn't let her make a mistake.

So Rose sat in a chair in Hershemer's grand lobby and listened intently while Bobby played his score. When he was finished, she breathed a sigh of relief. She'd hoped his music would be as good as the book he'd written, and it was. She'd been spared having to tell him he'd have to find a composer, and she was grateful. What she was going to say to him was going to be rough enough.

Bobby was staring at her, waiting for her verdict. He looked so desperate that for a moment Rose hesitated. She gazed out the big bay window at Fifth Avenue. It was still partially light outside, and the workers who had stayed late at the office or to do a last-minute errand were still running for buses and hailing taxicabs. It would be another hour or two before the glamorous people would take over the city with their limousines, their evening gowns and tuxes. Bobby wanted to be one of the glamorous people. And if she wanted to win him she was going to have to see to it that he got what he wanted. She had to tell him the truth.

"You've written the wrong show," she said.

Bobby went on the defensive immediately. "What does that mean?"

"You've got the whole formula—sweet love story, breezy patter, plenty of spots for Mother to do her shtick, and she can belt those songs to the back of the house without ripping up her vocal cords. It's a terrific Lu Lawson musical."

"Then what the hell are you saying?"

"It's exactly like all the other musicals her agent has sent to her—I think there've been thirteen so far—and she's turned all of them down."

"That doesn't mean she'll turn down this one."

He was furious, and so, so disappointed. He hated her right now, and for a second she was scared.

I'll die if I lose him.

But she'd never win him if she didn't tell him the truth.

"Yes, it does," Rose said. "She'll turn it down cold."

"How do you know? When did you get to be an expert on theater?"

"I'm not. I'm an expert on Lu Lawson."

She told him about Lu redecorating the house and redoing her wardrobe. And she could see that she was getting through to him. Bobby waited until she finished, and then it was his turn to look out the bay window. When he turned back, he had swallowed his disappointment and was all business.

"You're saying Lu Lawson . . . your mother . . . wants to shake things up," he said.

Rose nodded. "She's been playing that same cute little clown for ten years, and it isn't her anymore. I don't think it ever was, but for a long time she made it work."

He thought for a moment. "What does she want now?"

"I'll tell you, but first you and I are going to have dinner. My treat, and don't give me any lip about the money. I'm going to buy you a porterhouse steak, because you're going to need it."

Bobby looked like he was about to balk, but then he smiled his big, boyish smile that showed up only when they were having cheesecake at Lindy's or Jack Dempsey's. "Okay, boss," he said. "Just let me turn off the lights."

So far so good, Rose thought.

She took him to the most expensive steakhouse she knew and waited until he had ordered. Then she said, "Here's what you need to know about Lu Lawson. She didn't grow up riding horses and climbing trees in the Midwest. She lived in a nice Queen Anne house in the Italian section of New Haven, Connecticut. There were a lot of antiques her father's people brought over from the old country, and her mother made the lace doilies that were scattered around with her own hands. Lu's family wasn't rich, and they hadn't come over on the *Mayflower* like the WASPs who lived up on the hill, but her parents had class in their own way, and they were proud the way only immigrants who have made it can be. Lu's father took her to New York City to see plays. Her mother made the best lasagna on the eastern seaboard. Trust me on that, because I know.

"It's time for Lu to get back to her roots. I'm not sure she knows that yet. But if you look at the way she redid her apartment, and if you knew her house in New Haven, you can see that's what she wants. She's an Italian American girl who made good, and if you tap into that history you'll write a show she won't turn down.

"She still does her voice exercises every day and she warms up by singing the Panis Angelicus—you might want to get a copy of it if you don't know it. When she was a kid she listened to the Metropolitan Opera on the radio on Saturday afternoons, and she sang Italian folk songs at people's weddings. You should play some recordings of Caruso singing "O Sole Mio," and arias from *La Bohéme* to get the flavor.

"Mother is in her midthirties, and she's tired of being a child onstage. She wants to be a lady," Rose wound up. Bobby was looking at her, fascinated.

He needs me and he knows it, she thought. She was making progress.

"What you're talking about is going to be tricky," Bobby said thoughtfully. "The audience loves Lu Lawson the way she is."

"You'll have to make them fall in love with the new incarnation."

"It's going to take time to come up with a new show."

"The way I see it, you have half a year."

"Are you crazy?"

"Mother has decided she wants to buy a place in the country— I suggested it. I'm going to help her find a house and then we're going to decorate it together. I think she's hoping it'll bring us closer together. I can keep her occupied for six months, but work is the only life she has, and she's already been away from it for a while. After six more months she's going to be crazy to get in front of an audience again. That's when I'm going to give her the new musical you're going to write for her. I think *The Lady* would be a great title."

He shook his head. "I can't do it that fast. I have a job and I write at night."

She had a checkbook in her purse. She'd debated long and hard about asking him if she could lend him the money he'd need to get him through six months. But now, looking at him, she knew she couldn't do it. He'd been too poor for too long to accept a hand-out without resenting it—and resenting the giver. She wanted him indebted to her but she didn't want him to dislike her. Besides, he was already starting to come up with a way out on his own.

"Hershemer's will let me have the time off," he thought out loud. "They'll hold my job for me. And there are a couple of people who owe me some money . . ." Rose could see him doing math in his head. "I'll make it work. I'll have to. I'm not going to blow this."

Rose knew he wouldn't blow it. After all, he was the extraordinary man she'd been waiting for. His show was going to be a smash and he was going to be the toast of Broadway—surely God would let all of that happen—and he would realize that she was the best thing that had ever happened to him. And then he would realize that he couldn't live without her.

"Thank you, Rose," he said.

Antoinette Landovich, eat your heart out! she thought. *I'll never lose him now.*

Six months later she almost did.

*   *   *

BOBBY WAS GOING to be under pressure; writing an entire musical in six months was almost impossible. Knowing that, Rose told him, "I don't expect to see you at Rockefeller Center anymore. And I know you're not going to have time to have coffee every morning."

The look he gave her was one of pure relief. "You're an angel!" he said, and he hugged her. She told herself she wasn't disappointed.

She gave Bobby her phone number written on a piece of her stationery. "So you can get in touch with me," she told him. "I realized that in all the time we've known each other, I've never done this." She waited for him to return the favor.

Instead he stared unhappily at the piece of paper in his hand. She realized she'd gone too fast.

"I don't want your phone number," she said quickly. "I don't want to call when you're working and interrupt the flow of creativity." She laughed to keep it light. "You call me when you want."

That seemed to relax Bobby again. "Thank you," he said as he carefully folded the creamy sheet of vellum. He stuck it in the back of his wallet. "If it's here, I won't lose it." Then he kissed her in a way that made up for a lot. "Thank you in advance for not making me feel guilty about going into hibernation," he whispered in her ear. Rose told herself again that she wasn't disappointed.

She wasn't disappointed at all that the coffee-after-skating meetings had come to an end. Now Bobby would call her when he wanted to see her and there would be no question that they were dating. And maybe—although she would never ask him to—he would share his work with her. She let herself daydream about Bobby asking her to read the scenes he was writing. Maybe he'd ask for her opinion—the idea for the musical had been hers, after all. And he'd finally invite her to his apartment. She wasn't sure why that was so important; she just knew it was. Of course, when she was in his apartment she would have to see to it that nothing happened between them—nothing more than kissing, no matter how tempted she was. She knew she was hopelessly old-fashioned, but the sexual revolution that was going on around her was not for her. Nonna and the nuns had trained her too well. And even though Bobby had played around, she knew that when he was ready to settle down he was going to want an old-fashioned girl. Like her.

But in the meantime, she thought she'd be spending at least some time with Bobby when she wasn't keeping her mother busy with house hunting and decorating and when he wasn't writing. She knew it would be less time than she wanted, but that was to be expected. What she hadn't expected him to do was disappear. She never dreamed that he wouldn't call her at all.

For the first week, she told herself that he was adjusting to his new work schedule. Then she told herself that he was having a hard time getting started on the show—writing was always tough-est in the beginning, she'd heard. She worked to keep words like *selfish* and *ungrateful* from coming into her head. She did that for ten long, frustrating days.

"Are you still seeing Bobby Manning?" Lu asked her one morning as the driver settled them in the backseat of the car. They were going to look at some property in Dutchess County. It was a long distance from the city, but the real estate agent said the area was very secluded and Miss Lawson would find it peaceful and quiet.

"Are you seeing Bobby?" her mother repeated.

"He's been working, and I've been busy, and I haven't been home a lot . . ." Rose hated herself for trying to explain, but she couldn't stop. "I'm probably missing his phone calls," she added.

"There are plenty of people at the apartment to take a message for you. The maid, the cook, Miss Pearl—"

"I know," Rose snapped. "He'll call me when he has the time!"

"Of course," her mother said. But the way she said it reminded Rose of the conversation they'd had the night of the party. Rose felt her fingernails dig into the plush upholstery of her mother's limousine. *If he sleeps with someone else after the help I've given him,* she thought, *I'll let him finish his goddamned musical and I'll tell him I gave it to my mother and she thought it was the worst thing she'd ever read. Then I'll burn it—page by page.*

But she knew she wouldn't do that.

THE NEXT DAY Rose let Lu go house hunting by herself. Rose took a taxi to Hershemer's Music Store, where she conned one of the clerks into giving her Bobby's phone number and address.

"I'm an old friend of his cousin," she said, hoping that was a distant enough relationship. "I want to get in touch with Bobby."

"Hey, anything for one of Bobby's cousins," the guy said as he wrote out the information.

"Actually I'm a *friend* of his cousin," she corrected him haughtily.

He handed her the invoice with a wink. "Usually it's a sister," he said.

On her way home, in the taxi, Rose reminded herself that people could mature. They could grow. Especially a man who had finally met the right girl.

That night she called Bobby's apartment. There was no answer. *He's working and he's ignoring the phone,* she told herself.

Rose called Bobby's number every day for the next week. She called him in the mornings before she and Lu drove off to whatever country manse they were inspecting. She called long distance from pay phones in Bucks County, the New Jersey shore, and Long Island. She called in the evenings after she and Lu had come home. Bobby never answered the phone. Rose went back to Hershemer's Music Store and humiliated herself in front of the winking salesclerk by asking if he was sure he'd given her the right phone number. He assured her with a look full of pity that he had.

Finally, she couldn't stand it anymore. For a second time she begged off on the house hunt with Lu. She stayed home and washed her hair, rinsing it in lemon juice to bring out the red-gold highlights. She thought about calling a beauty salon for a manicure and a pedicure, but she knew she couldn't sit still that long. She ordered a steak dinner with all the trimmings from the '21' Club, dressed in a skirt that showed off her long legs and a sweater that clung to all the right places, and applied an extra layer of mascara. She grabbed a bottle of her mother's best red Bordeaux, hailed a taxi, picked up the steak—nestled on a china plate with the famous '21' Club insignia—and told the cabbie to take her to Christopher Street.

Bobby's apartment building was a decrepit brick structure in serious need of paint and mortar. His apartment number was on the mailbox in the dirty little vestibule. Rose rang the buzzer under it, until she realized that the front door of the lobby was open and she could just walk in. The elevator wasn't working and she had to climb seven flights of stairs—none too clean—to get to his floor. Panting, she rehearsed what she was going to say when Bobby opened the door. *I'm not staying. I only have steak for one, see? I just thought you might need sustenance.*

Then, if he didn't seem too upset to see her, she'd make a crack about his not picking up the phone. She tried to ignore the voice inside her head that said she shouldn't have to go through all of this. That he should be on his knees to her.

I can't be angry. If he sees that I'm angry, I'll lose him.

When she found Bobby's apartment, she took a deep breath and made sure she was completely calm before she rang his bell. There was no answer. She knocked on the door. No answer. She tried the doorbell and knocked again. And again. And then she called his name, softly at first. Then louder. Before she knew it she was screaming, "Bobby! Bobby! Bobby!" and pounding on his door. Like a girl who had never learned that you got what you wanted in life by being sweet and smiling. Like a girl who wasn't beautiful and rich and the daughter of one of the most famous women in the city.

"What the hell is going on?" A loud harsh voice cut through her screams. Rose whirled around—and dropped the wine and the steak from '21' on the floor. China and glass shattered as creamed potatoes, peas, steak, and wine combined together in a mess at Rose's feet. That was when she started to cry. She cried for the weeks of waiting for a phone call that never came. She cried because she had humiliated herself in front of the clerk at Hershemer's. She cried because Bobby was probably sleeping with someone else. She cried because it looked like she wasn't the right girl after all.

Meanwhile, the owner of the loud harsh voice was eyeing her warily. The girl—although she was so flat-chested and her features were so large and craggy that at first it was hard to tell if she was a she—stood in the doorway of the apartment across the hall.

"You coming down from a trip? Dope or something?" the girl asked with minimal sympathy. " 'Cause if you are, you can't do it here."

Rose fought the tears and got them under control. She flashed the girl a look that was meant to mix dignity with disdain, but unfortunately she was still making little sobbing noises. "I'm not taking drugs," she finally managed to choke out. "I'm just . . . a bit upset."

This seemed to reassure the girl, and she ventured out into the hallway. It was hard to tell how old she was because she was so skinny, but Rose guessed she was about Bobby's age. She was wearing a black turtleneck sweater that was far from clean, and a pair of tight black pants that hugged her scrawny hips and jutting pelvic bones—the pants could have used a trip to the cleaners, too. Her blond hair fell below her shoulders in strings, and what seemed to be circles under her eyes were actually the remnants of blue eyeliner and mascara. She was holding an evil-smelling cigarette that Rose thought was French; either a Gaulois or a Gitane.

"I'm trying to find Bobby Manning," Rose said.

The woman was staring at her again. "You're the new one, aren't you?" she said. She picked her way through the slop on the floor and held out her hand. "I'm Tristesse—that's my stage name when I sing."

"I'm Rose." She decided there was no polite way to avoid the tobacco-stained fingers and shook hands with Tristesse.

"Bobby's right—you are gorgeous."

He had told this creature she was gorgeous. That was something . . . no, it was more than something. It was a lot. In spite of the two weeks of hell she'd just been through, Rose's heart started to beat a little faster. She decided to overlook the comment about being the new one. "Do you know where Bobby is?" she asked.

"You mean he didn't tell you he was leaving town?"

"What?"

"That son of a bitch! Well, that's what you get for falling for a writer, sister. All men are pigs, but they're the worst . . . When they want you, it's 'Oh baby, baby, I gotta have you now!' Then the fucking muse hits them and they don't know your name. I can't tell you how many times I've been through it."

Rose tried to picture the man who would want Tristesse. Then she tried to blot out the picture.

"Bobby sublet his pad for a couple of months—I think his tenant is coming in this week—and he took off for some place in Connecticut," Tristesse continued. "He said he's working on something big. And it's gotta be huge because he quit his job to write it and he's been borrowing money from everyone he knows to keep himself going. Hell, he hit me up for fifty—that's how desperate he is."

"You said Bobby went to Connecticut?" Rose tried to get her back on track.

"Yeah. Some crap about needing to be in the place where it all started. Whatever the hell that means." Tristesse drew heavily on her cigarette. "I don't know anything more than that."

"I do," Rose said. "He's gone to New Haven." And he had left her behind. Because he didn't need her. He didn't need to hear the family stories she had planned to tell him; he didn't need to hear her insights about Lu. When Bobby was working he didn't need anyone or anything. Rose was hit with a feeling that was so familiar it was like an old friend. She was a kid sitting at the dinner table, in her mother's apartment, watching her mother push back her plate and call for the car to take her to the theater a half hour early. There was a tricky piece of business in Act Two that needed work, Lu would explain, so she had to cut short their time together. Sorry. Then she'd rush off to the place where she really wanted to be and Rose was left to wander around the apartment all night with a hole inside her that could never be filled.

And now, as she stood in Bobby Manning's dirty hallway, she felt the hole again, bigger than ever. For the first time, she wondered if she really wanted to love him for the rest of her life. It was a rogue thought, and maybe even a dangerous one. Still she tried it on for size. What if she were to run right now? She could go someplace far away from the city, her mother, Bobby, and show business. She'd find a small town where she could get a job doing something

normal people did. She'd find a normal man who also had a normal
job, who would love her and who wouldn't leave her alone because
he was a damned creative genius who didn't want her around when
he was working. She would never have to be afraid of losing him.
Rose allowed herself a moment to savor the vision of herself as a
safe, secure housewife. But soon other visions crowded her brain.
She saw Lu holding court with a group of eager interviewers asking her opinion on everything from her favorite breakfast cereal to
peace in the world. Rose saw flashbulbs going off like fireworks
when Lu left a party, she heard the band strike up the hit song from
Lu's latest show whenever she entered a nightclub, and she saw the
adoration on the faces of those who stopped Lu in the street to ask
for an autograph. Most of all, she saw the triumphant smile on her
mother's face when she took her bow in front of a cheering audience. And that was when Rose realized just how much living with a
star had warped her. She was like a ballet dancer who had been
turning out at the hips every day at the barre for so many years that
she could never walk normally again. Rose wasn't talented
enough—or selfish enough, she thought—to be famous herself,
but she would never feel it was worth it to get up in the morning if
she was going to be plain old Mrs. Nobody. And besides, she loved
Bobby.

  If I lose him, I'll die.

  She looked down at the floor. "Do you have a mop I can use to
clean this up?" she asked Tristesse. The skinny girl nodded, went
back inside her apartment, and returned with two dirty rags, a
mop, and several brown paper bags. Rose bent over and began
picking up pieces of glass and china. Tristesse leaned against the
wall to watch, but something in the pile caught her eye. "Hang
on," she said, and bent down to inspect a shard of the broken dinner plate. "Is that from the '21' Club?"

"Yes," Rose said tersely. Her only goal in life now was to get out of this hallway.

"Bobby's coming up in the world. Usually the girls who come here bring a cheap Chianti and a pizza."

"Look," Rose broke in. "If it's all the same to you, I don't want to hear gossip about Bobby's personal life. Would you hand me that bag?"

Tristesse handed her the bag, and then she picked up the mop and started cleaning the floor where Rose had already cleared away the debris. After a second, she stopped. "I want to say something—but first you gotta know Bobby and I never got it on. We cool on that?"

Rose glanced at the caked makeup and the stringy hair. "I believe you," she said with total honesty.

"Bobby and me, we're like brother and sister. He tells me things." Tristesse went back to her floor mopping. She seemed to be very efficient at it. "What he likes about you is, you don't need him. That's what he tells me." She finished with the floor and straightened up. "You dig what I'm saying to you?"

Rose nodded. "He doesn't like clingy girls."

"Give that woman the blue ribbon!" Tristesse did a little gesture with her hand like the host on *Queen for a Day*. "And he doesn't want to . . . oh, shit!" She stopped midsentence and raced to the apartment next to hers. She began banging on the door. "Mrs. Forentino?" she yelled. "I know you're in there, you perverted old bitch." She banged again. "How long have you been listening at the door? I saw your eye in the peephole. I see it again, and I'll poke through the glass with an ice pick!"

"Screw you!" said the voice. But she must have removed the offending eye because after a second Tristesse came back to Rose. "The doors and walls in this dump are like cardboard; you can hear everything, and that old goat is nothing but trouble. She spends her life listening at that damn door. Two nights ago she called the cops on this guy I've been seeing just because we had a disagreement. Now he's pissed at me and I haven't seen him since he got out of jail." She took the bag of broken china and glass from Rose. "I'll get rid of that for you," she said.

"Thank you," said Rose. "I really should be going. It was nice meeting you," she added inanely, and held out her hand for another tobacco-stained shake.

Tristesse ignored the gesture. "About Bobby," she said. "You want him, I can tell. Why you do, beats the shit out of me. I'll admit he's sexy, but so are a million other guys, and a chick who looks like you, who can afford steaks from '21,' isn't exactly going to have a hard time meeting people of the masculine persuasion. But hey, each to her own poison is what I say. And if I were you . . ." She paused to reach into a pocket of her pants, pull out a crumpled pack of cigarettes, and extract one. "I wouldn't let him know that you showed up trying to feed him and went crazy when you couldn't find him." She lit the cigarette. "With Bobby, you want to play it mellow. You dig?"

And Rose did dig. Bobby must never know she missed him. Or—God forbid—that she needed him. It had been stupid to come to his apartment with her little steak dinner and her little-girl dreams. It had been worse than stupid.

"I understand," she said to Tristesse. "And when you see Bobby, please don't tell him—"

"Sister, my lips are sealed. We girls gotta stick together." She opened her arms and for a terrible moment Rose thought she wanted a hug. But then Tristesse stretched and started scratching the small of her back.

"Thank you," Rose said. "Thank you." Then she fled.

It wasn't until she was on her way home in the cab that Rose wondered how she was going to play it mellow when she still didn't know where he was in New Haven. Or if he was having sex with someone.

The next day, she went to the Catholic church in their neighborhood and prayed to St. Jude, the patron saint of lost causes, for help. She bought the saint's medal and put it on a chain around her neck. Desperate times called for desperate measures.

CHAPTER 24

New York

1962

WHETHER IT WAS an intervention from St. Jude or just Rose's reward for not going crazy, Bobby called two days later. And with her newfound wisdom she didn't even ask where he was. "Hello, stranger" was what she said. Her tone was light, and just a little amused—if you couldn't see her, you'd imagine that her tongue was planted firmly in her cheek.

There was a pause on the other end of the line. "You're not mad?" Bobby asked. Rose could hear how pleased he was; obviously tongue in cheek was the right choice.

"The thing is," he went on, "I started working and I got stuck and I knew I had to go back to the character's roots. Lu's roots. I got all wound up in subletting the apartment and trying to find a place to live in New Haven . . ."

"So that's where you landed." Was that light enough?

"I know I was wrong not to tell you," he said.

"You mean, because you vanished into the night without a trace and left poor little old me to pine? Why, Mr. Manning, I've just been crying into my pillow every night." It was dangerously close to the truth, but she got a laugh from him.

"You're amazing. Most women would be screaming so loud by now, my eardrum would be bursting."

"Talk about counterproductive for a man who writes music." She was just loaded with witty lines.

This time Bobby's laugh was as happy as a kid's. A rude, spoiled little boy who had just gotten away with murder.

"I know I can be a real jerk," he said, reading her mind, "but when I'm working, I'll do whatever I have to to get the job done. If that means taking bennies to stay awake all night and write, or going out of town to soak up local color, or getting drunk, or getting . . ." He stopped short, but she knew what had been next. "Nothing matters except the work, Rose. It's selfish, but that's the way I am. And anyone who wants to hang around with me has to know that."

For a rebellious second she thought about telling him he wasn't worth it. But she wanted to be the right girl. She wanted it so much.

"Is that a warning?" she asked. But hearing herself, she knew she'd lost the lightness.

"I just don't want to hurt anyone," he said. There was no lightness in his tone either. "I want to be sure you understand, and that you can take it, Rose." He was deadly serious now, and totally honest, and he'd know it if she wasn't honest back. But if she was, she'd scare him off. For the second time she thought about just telling him to get lost. But she'd staked everything on becoming Mrs. Bobby Manning. She searched frantically for the right thing to say. St. Jude—or maybe it was God Himself—sent an inspiration.

"You want to know if I understand how selfish people in show business can be?" she demanded. "Where do you think I've been living for the past seven years, on the set of *I Remember Mama*? I'm the daughter of the great Lu Lawson, and when it comes to self-centered, you aren't even in the same league with her. Don't worry about hurting me with your big bad ego, because I've been dealing with the biggest and the baddest ego there is for years." The best part of her speech was the ring of real anger that made it sound so honest.

Bobby was convinced. He laughed his happy-kid laugh again and started telling her about his life in New Haven—at least, the part he wanted her to know about. She bit her tongue to keep from suggesting that she could take a train ride up there to see him, and the conversation ended with him saying that she was magnificent and her basking in his admiration—even though she knew it was undeserved.

They talked to each other on the phone about once a week after that. Bobby was always the one who called, and since Rose never knew when the mood would strike him, she tried to stay home as much as she could. Not because it bothered him when she wasn't there to get his calls, but because she hated to hear how much it didn't bother him.

But Rose couldn't stay home all the time. Lu had finally settled on a house in the country, and it had to be furnished. Surprisingly, her choice for a second home wasn't a party mansion on Long Island or a pseudofarm in Bucks County; Lu had picked a genuine country cottage, hidden deep in the woods of upstate New York, miles away from the nearest train station or grocery store. She wanted to decorate it simply, she said, with furnishings from local stores and artisans. This meant Lu and Rose had to spend hours combing the Hudson River Valley for tiny antiques shops, and chasing after an elusive cabinetmaker who, all the locals agreed, turned out beautiful handmade chairs—when you could find him. Rose begrudged every second that took her away from the phone and Manhattan.

"You're probably doing your cause more good by being out of town," Lu said gently.

"What are you talking about? I don't have a cause," Rose said.

But she knew Lu was right. So when Bobby came back to town, she didn't suggest getting together. And when he finally did set up a coffee date, and when it was clear that on the date he was a million miles away, she didn't panic. At least, not so that it showed.

"Robert Manning, I hereby release you," she said.

"Huh?" He dragged himself back from wherever he'd been.

"Normal rules of decent human behavior say you don't get to treat me like a piece of furniture after not seeing me for two months. However, since you are a genius, I will absolve you of your responsibility to me. Go home and write, pal."

He laughed and hugged her, but he also left her to finish her cheesecake alone. After that they saw each other a couple of times, but he was increasingly edgy as his deadline approached.

"You look like hell," she told him. "Are you getting any sleep at all?"

"Not if I can help it."

"Well, do me a favor and instead of hanging around with me, go home and take a nap."

He took her up on it. Then for six weeks he disappeared again. At least this time she knew where he was—in his apartment working. *It's okay*, she told herself. *I have to be patient, that's all.*

THE GOOD NEWS was, Bobby finished his musical on schedule.

"The timing couldn't be better," Rose told him on the phone when he gave her the news. "Mother just finished decorating her getaway. She doesn't have anything to do."

"So she's ready for my show?" Bobby's voice sounded weary and hoarse.

"She hasn't worked in almost a year. And it's autumn, which is when she's usually going into rehearsal. In about another week, the way I figure it, she'll be getting antsy. In two weeks she'll be climbing the walls. By the time she's so desperate she'd be willing to read a script from her doorman, I will put your masterpiece in her hands."

There was only one thing that could go wrong with that scenario—if for some impossible, unforeseen reason Bobby's musical wasn't a masterpiece. Rose banished the idea from her mind as soon as it popped in. "I can't wait to read it," she added. "I could come over . . ."

"I need to do a couple of rewrites. Give me a day or two."

"Fine," she said. "Take all the time you need." She didn't even mention how long it had been since she'd seen him. Tristesse would have been proud of her.

BOBBY HAD SUGGESTED that they meet the next morning at Lindy's. Rose showed up ten minutes early, but he was already there, sitting at a table, with a slice of cherry cheesecake in front of him. Rose started toward him, but he turned and smiled at her and she stopped short. His smile was the old Bobby smile—boyish and vulnerable and just a little bit wicked, but . . .

"Are you all right?" she demanded. His face wasn't just pale; it was the kind of grayish white you saw in hospitals. Bobby's eyes were red rimmed and he hadn't shaved. She remembered what he'd said about using bennies—which, she'd since learned, were a form of speed—to keep himself awake.

"I'm fine," he said. He stood up and held out his arms to her, and she saw that he'd lost weight—enough to make a difference in the way his suit fit. How could that have happened in six short weeks? He must have seen the shock in her eyes, because he dropped his arms and said, "I'm sorry I'm such a mess."

Rose moved to him and hugged him hard, pulling his head to her shoulder so she could stroke his hair. It was an instinctive move, and if she'd thought about it, she never would have done it. But he looked so sick and weary, she couldn't help it. Surprisingly, he didn't back away.

"Bobby, what have you done to yourself?" she whispered.

"I finished the musical on time—like the lady told me to," he said.

"Nothing is worth making yourself sick."

He turned away from her. "Yeah," he said. "This is." He opened his battered suitcase and pulled out his manuscript—he'd had it bound in one of the fake leather covers that were always used for Broadway scripts. It was such a hopeful, childlike thing to do.

"You look half dead," she scolded.

"You don't screw around with the chance of a lifetime."

Rose read the entire script that afternoon. By night, she knew Bobby wasn't the only one to whom she'd given the chance of a lifetime—she'd just done the same thing for her mother. As soon as she finished reading, she walked into her mother's bedroom and thrust the script at Lu, who was sitting up in bed, absently flipping through the pages of a novel.

"Take a look at this," Rose said.

Her mother looked at the author's name on the front cover. "Your friend Bobby wrote this?" she asked.

"It's your new show," Rose said. "You can thank me later."

But Lu wasn't picking up the manuscript.

"I know what you're thinking," Rose said. "You've read so many turkeys and you don't want to have to tell me that this is another one. It's not. Believe me."

"You're very involved with Bobby Manning," Lu said. "That can cloud anyone's judgment."

"Not mine. I've been around your business long enough to know when a show is good and when it's not." Then Rose gave her mother a big grin. "You can trust me. I'm the girl who made you dress like Jackie Kennedy, remember? Look how well that turned out."

And so, reluctantly, Lu opened Bobby's manuscript and started to read. Rose stayed in the room and tried not to pace, chew her nails, or scream at Lu to read faster. Because there was always a horrible chance that her mother might not like the show, even though it was perfect for her. And Rose didn't know what she'd do then—or what she'd say to Bobby. She tried not to think that her life was hanging in the balance, but it was.

"Have you heard the music?" Lu's voice broke into Rose's bad dream.

"Bobby's going to play it for me tomorrow at Hershemer's. A friend of his is opening the store a half hour early. You can come with me."

"Uh-huh," said her mother, who had gone back to reading. Unable to stand the suspense, Rose fled to her own room.

*   *   *

THE NEXT MORNING when Rose woke up, Lu was already dressed and in the kitchen, making herself a cup of coffee. "Have Mr. Manning come here to the apartment this morning to play the score for George and me," she said. As Rose raced for the phone, she added, "And Rose? Thank you."

CHAPTER 25

New York

2008

"WHEN BOBBY CAME to Lu's apartment that morning and played the score for *The Lady*, I knew I was listening to history being made," George said. "I still get goose bumps thinking about it." He and Carrie were still sitting in his living room. By now the sun was setting. George stood up and lit a lamp that resembled a Victorian streetlight.

"It wasn't just that *The Lady* was a whole new direction for Lu," he went on. "Bobby was playing around with staging and orchestrations in a way no one had before." He smiled. "I put my own money in that show—the first and last time I ever did that. But I knew it was going to make a fortune. That's how I was able to buy the Taj Mahal here." He yawned. It was getting late and Carrie had kept him talking for the better part of the day. She knew she should offer to leave, but she still hadn't heard what she'd come for.

"So Bobby sold his musical, and Lu Lawson got the career boost she'd been needing," she said.

"What happened was a lot more intense than that. When Lu read *The Lady* one of those once-in-a-lifetime partnerships happened—that's the only way I know how to say it. She and Bobby had a kind of chemistry; they completed each other in some way that I don't think even they understood. Bobby had six hits, but his best shows were the two he wrote for Lu. And she did her best work in them."

"What about my mother? How did she fit into that partnership?"

"Bobby married her." George shrugged as if to say, *Wasn't that enough?* But of course it wasn't.

"Did he love her?"

"Sure." George shrugged again.

"Why wasn't the wedding written up in any of the newspapers? You'd think when Lu Lawson's daughter got married it would be big news, but there wasn't a word about it. I did some research."

"That was because they went down to City Hall to tie the knot."

"Mother didn't get married in a church?"

"Nope."

"No altar, no Mass?"

"Just quick and dirty.".

Rose tried to imagine her mother getting married without all the liturgical bells and whistles. "Why did they do it that way?"

"I don't think Rose wanted to make a big deal out of it. I don't think she dared." George got up and walked over to a sideboard to fix himself a drink. He offered her one, but Carrie shook her head. "Bobby wasn't exactly a white-picket-fence-and-pet-dog kind of guy."

"Then why did he get married?'

George took a deep breath. "Well, your mother was gorgeous. And she was smart and she was very well connected. And I think he did love her . . ."

"But?"

"Lu always thought Bobby got married because he was scared."

CHAPTER 26

New York

1962

LU AND GEORGE moved fast after they'd heard the score for *The Lady*. Contracts were signed, the investors who had begun to wonder if Lu would ever do another show breathed a sigh of relief, and money was raised, a theater was booked, and casting began. Bobby was walking around in a happy daze, and he told Rose he owed it all to her. And even though she said no, no, no, it was all because of his talent, they both knew he was right—partly, anyway.

She and Bobby were finally dating. At night, they went out to places where everyone could see that they were a couple. Bobby let Rose pick out new clothes for him. They were mentioned twice by the famous gossip columnist Walter Winchell in his newspaper column, and Bobby liked the notoriety. He seemed pleased that their relationship was out in the open and people knew Rose was his girl. And there were private times too—precious little moments—that she relived over and over in her mind after she'd gone to bed. There was the night when he'd held her so tightly that she thought she was going to pass out, and whispered, "How did I get so lucky?" There was the time when he had looked at her and said, "I'd be a fool to let you go." And there was the time when he had kissed her in a way that always made her knees melt and said, "Just give me a little time, Rose. I just need some time."

If there was a little voice in the back of her head whispering that maybe what he was feeling was gratitude more than anything else, she turned off that voice fast. Bobby loved her, she knew it. A proposal and an engagement ring would follow—she knew that too.

Of course, he still hadn't invited her to his apartment, but after her nervous breakdown in his hallway she was just as glad. She thanked heaven Tristesse was honoring her promise not to say anything, but she still didn't like remembering how close she'd come to destroying everything she'd worked for.

ROSE KNEW THAT with everything else Bobby had on his mind she couldn't expect him to focus on her. She would have to wait until after he'd gotten through the rehearsals, the out-of-town tryouts, and the opening night before he'd be able to concentrate on anything except *The Lady*. But she'd learned to be patient.

There was only one little dark spot in her shiny daydreams of life as Mrs. Bobby Manning. Whatever punishment Bobby had inflicted on himself—the coffee, the bennies, and whatever else had gotten him through his endless all-nighters when he was writing *The Lady*—he hadn't bounced back completely from the abuse. His color had improved, but he still looked exhausted too much of the time, and he was still too thin.

"I think you should see a doctor," Rose told him one day as they got into a cab.

"What for? I've never felt better in my life."

"If you're okay, then why are we taking a taxi?" she asked. "You used to walk all over the city."

"There were years when I couldn't afford taxis. Now I can. If you keep on nagging me, I'll hire a limousine to drive me everywhere." He smiled his wicked little-boy grin, but his eyes were weary.

"Bobby, I'm serious," she said, fear making her voice sharper than she intended.

"So am I." His voice was just as sharp, and there was a warning in it. "Don't hover, Rose. I won't put up with that."

He meant it. In spite of everything she'd done, she could still drive him away if she pushed—even if what she was pushing for was for his own good.

"Well, if you're going to have a private car, at the very least I expect a Rolls." She gave him a quick kiss on the lips to show him that the sharp-voiced harpy was gone and his understanding, undemanding Rose was back. But Bobby didn't respond. He sat silently in the backseat of the cab for such a long time that she was starting to get scared. Finally, he said, "Tomorrow night, I'd like it if you'd come to my place for dinner."

The way he was looking at her, she knew she'd been right: going to his apartment *was* a big deal. A very big deal.

"To see your etchings?" she said as lightly she could, although her heart had skipped a couple of beats and her breath was suddenly coming too fast.

"Maybe," Bobby said. But he wasn't smiling; he was looking at her as if he already knew what she'd be like when the room was dark and they were alone and hands and fingers were pulling at buttons and zippers.

"What time?" she managed to ask. And that was when she knew that whatever he wanted, she would do it—even without a ring on her finger. Because she wanted it too, no matter how well Nonna had trained her.

BOBBY DIDN'T GET out of the taxi to walk her into the lobby of her apartment building, and he didn't kiss her good night.

"Tomorrow night," she said softly as she closed the cab door.

"Tomorrow night," he said, and nodded.

But the next night her world fell apart.

ROSE SHOWED UP at Bobby's apartment dressed demurely in a skirt and blouse—on this night it would be overkill to go for a sexy look. That battle had already been fought and won. And she came emptyhanded—there was no food and fancy wine now. She didn't want to do anything to remind her of the last time she'd been desperate in his hallway, with her offering from '21.'

She felt Bobby was behaving a little strangely when he opened the door, but she told herself maybe he was nervous and that was a good thing, because it meant he cared. So when he gave her a quick peck on the cheek instead of a real kiss, she ignored it. She tried not to notice that he was staring at her as if he'd never met her before. And she tried not to notice how silent he was.

Fortunately, there was a topic for conversation.

"Your apartment is . . . very different from what I expected," she said as she toured his one room. Actually, she didn't know what she had expected—something shabby but charming, perhaps. Bobby's studio just looked . . . poor. It was smaller than her bedroom at home, and the only window overlooked the concrete wall of the building next door. The ceiling paint was peeling, the carpet was old and stained, and the lamps didn't give off nearly enough light. A daybed was crammed against one wall—there were pillows scattered over it to make it look like a sofa—and on the opposite wall was a small galley kitchen with ancient appliances. The bathtub was, as Bobby had told her, in front of the kitchen sink. A board had been placed over it—she remembered that he'd also said the tub doubled as his kitchen table—and a tablecloth, some silverware, plates, and two candles were piled on top. Bobby had been setting the table for their romantic dinner, but then for some reason he'd stopped. Had someone interrupted him? Who? And why was he staring at her with that strange look on his face? Warning bells started going off in her brain. She pushed them aside and made a show of sniffing the air.

"Do I smell dinner?" Rose asked brightly. Why the hell wasn't he at least trying to make this easier for her? He was the one with experience, for God's sake! "Would you like me to help? I can—"

"Rose, come sit down," he said, and he indicated the daybed. Without waiting for her to obey, he pulled out a wooden chair with several missing slats in the back, faced it toward the daybed, and sat in it himself. Rose might have been inexperienced, but even she knew sex wasn't on his mind.

"What's wrong?" she asked.

"Please sit."

"No." She was frightened now, and she needed to be able to move around. He stood up and came to her.

"My neighbor Mrs. Forentino came home last night," he said. His tone sounded accusatory. "She'd been in North Carolina visiting her daughter, and I hadn't seen her since I got back myself." He paused and Rose tried frantically to remember where she'd heard that name before and how it related to her—since it was obvious that it did.

"Mrs. Forentino told me about a girl who came to see me while I was gone," Bobby went on. "A girl who went crazy when she couldn't find me."

That was when Rose remembered the neighbor who had watched her in the hallway from behind her closed door. Tristesse had said she was a mean old goat who liked to spy on people and cause trouble . . .

Oh God.

"Mrs. Forentino said the girl was very pretty, with red hair and green eyes," Bobby said in his new prosecuting attorney's voice, "in case you were thinking of telling me that it wasn't you."

She tried to laugh. "Hey, I admit it. Guilty as charged, Your Honor. I hadn't heard from you in a couple of weeks so I came over to see you. I think I brought a very nice bottle of wine too—I don't remember."

He wasn't buying it. "The way I heard it, you were crying . . ."

"I got a little upset."

"You were hysterical. Tristesse had to come out and help you clean up some food you threw on the floor, and . . ."

"I didn't throw it, I dropped it," she protested stupidly. Then she hurried on, "I brought it because I thought you'd like something to eat. That's all it was. Just dinner and a bottle of wine."

"You were crying. You were banging on the door."

Suddenly Rose couldn't take the third degree anymore. "All right!" she shouted. "You win! I was crying and banging on the door! I made a fool of myself out there in your stinking hallway! What the hell did you expect, Bobby? You disappeared without a word!"

"You said you were okay with that."

"After everything I did for you? I had a right to know where you were going! I deserved a damn phone call—at least!"

"You said it didn't bother you."

"You took off! I didn't know where you were or when you were coming back or if you were coming back. That was a rotten, mean thing to do!"

"And you lied!" He was shouting now too.

"You left me alone!"

"I'm a son of a bitch. I warned you." Bobby stopped and closed his eyes. He was breathing hard and sweating. This was tough for him. Well, good! It wasn't exactly a walk in the park for her.

"I've never asked you for anything! I've kept my mouth shut. I did what you wanted—any way you wanted it!" She knew she shouldn't be saying all that, but it felt so good.

"I know." He wasn't shouting anymore. His voice was soft and sad. "And I don't want you to do that. I don't want you to be someone you're not. Not for me." Bobby wiped his face and tried to take a deep breath. "I don't want to hurt you, Rose. I don't want to hurt anyone."

"Then change!" For a second she was sure he'd say yes. Then he would kiss her and take her to bed and she would have her reward for all the bad things that had happened in her life.

"I don't want to change," he said. "I like working at what I love, and it'll always come first to me. Before anyone or anything else. And I don't want to feel guilty about it."

"Then how can you say you don't want to hurt me? If you know you do?"

He turned away from her, searching for words. "You said you could handle it. I thought you were different from other girls . . ." He finally came out with it. "We can't do this anymore."

And in a sickening flash Rose realized what she'd just done. For months she had bitten her tongue and kept her temper and smiled. And it had worked. She'd been so close to winning him. And then in a few short seconds . . .

I'll die if I lose him.

She swallowed her tears. "I am different, Bobby! I swear I am! This whole thing was a mistake. I made one tiny little mistake. It'll never happen again."

"It wasn't a mistake, it was you. It was what you want. And you have a right . . ." But he sounded as if he was having trouble getting the words out, so maybe she hadn't lost everything after all.

"Give me another chance, Bobby!"

He was still turned away from her and she couldn't see his face.

"Look at me, Bobby. Please!"

He turned to her. But something was terribly wrong. His mouth was twisted in pain, he was whiter than she'd ever seen him, and the sweat was pouring down his face. Then everything seemed to go in slow motion for a few seconds. He hunched over and he cried out, and in one terrifying movement, he collapsed.

Later, Rose would remember what happened next as if it were a dream. She called the operator for an ambulance, and then her mother for the number of their family doctor, who told her he would meet them at the hospital. She took Bobby's pulse, opened the one horrid little window so he would have more air, loosened his collar, and propped him up the way the doctor had told her so it would be easier for him to breathe. She got into the ambulance with him and went to the hospital. And all the time, none of it was real.

BOBBY HAD HAD a heart attack. A mild one. But if Rose hadn't been there and acted so quickly, Dr. Singleton said, it could have been much worse. As it was, when he heard what Bobby had done to himself for the past six months, he shook his head and said Bobby was just plain lucky. Bobby could never do anything like that again. He would have to be careful from now on, and he would have to take medicine at the first sign of chest pain. He certainly couldn't undertake anything as strenuous as a pre-Broadway tryout tour. Bobby didn't even try to argue with the doctor. That was when Rose realized how terrified he was.

Rose stayed in the hospital every day until Bobby was well enough to go home. She read to him and brought him food that Lu's cook had prepared according to Bobby's new salt-free diet.

When Bobby came home he didn't want to be alone. Rose stayed overnight with him, in a sleeping bag on the floor. During the day Bobby sat on the daybed and watched television. The casting sessions for *The Lady* had started, but he didn't even ask how they were going. He didn't talk much at all. After two weeks, Rose went to see Dr. Singleton. "Bobby can't go on like this," she said. "All he's doing is sitting around worrying about dying. He needs to get back to work; he needs to be a part of the decisions about the cast. He should go to rehearsals, and be with the show on the road before it comes into New York. Having a show produced is the only thing he's ever really wanted. I'll see to it that he takes care of himself."

After she persuaded Dr. Singleton, she had to persuade Bobby. "I'll be with you all the time," she told him. "I'll make sure you've always got your medicine, and I'll stick with you like glue. You're not dying on me, Manning. I've invested too much in you."

So Bobby went to the casting sessions for *The Lady* and Rose sat in the back of the theater in case he wanted her. And one night— she would always remember that it was after the cast was set but before the show went into rehearsal—he turned to her and said, "I don't have enough money for an engagement ring now, but I will someday. If you marry me, I promise the darn thing will be a knockout."

Of course, she said yes, yes, yes, she wanted to marry him! And she didn't even care about the ring! Bobby wanted to do it quickly, before he got too busy. So they decided to go to City Hall. Rose thought about Nonna, Sister Phil, and the nuns at St. Mary's High School. In the eyes of the Catholic Church she wouldn't really be married if she only had a civil ceremony. She and Bobby would be living in sin. But Bobby wasn't a Catholic, and the church would say she had to have a dispensation, which would take time, and Bobby was ready to marry her now. She closed her eyes and told herself God would understand. Her dreams were coming true. And nothing was going to get in her way.

ROSE DIDN'T TELL Lu what was happening until the night before the big event.

"Please don't do this right now," Lu begged. "Just wait a little while."

She and Rose were in Rose's bedroom, and Rose had just pulled an armful of dresses out of her closet. "I'm marrying Bobby tomorrow," she said firmly. "We've already made all the plans."

"Unmake them!"

Rose gritted her teeth. "Mother, I asked you to come in here to help me pick out something to wear to my wedding. I thought you'd want to be a part of the happiest day of my life. Don't spoil this for me."

"I just don't see why it has to happen so fast. Bobby's only been at work for a couple of weeks. He just got out of the hospital a month ago."

"I told you, he wants me to go with him on the road."

"Go with him! Sleep with him! Just don't marry him. Not yet. Give him a chance to think."

But Rose couldn't do that. She didn't want to give Bobby time to think. And if it occurred to her that the reason was that she didn't want him to get over being scared because then he might change his mind, she pushed that thought aside.

"Bobby knows what he wants," she said to her mother. "Do you think I should wear a hat?"

Lu tried another line of attack. "I think you should be married in a white wedding dress with a veil, and a bouquet, and a million bridesmaids. Don't you want a church wedding? Just wait until after *The Lady* is open, and if you and Bobby still want to get married, I'll pull strings and get St. Patrick's Cathedral for you."

It was tempting. Rose had always wanted a big wedding; she and Nonna had talked about it from the time she was a little girl. She knew exactly how she would look—her gown would have a full skirt with a tiny waist and a cathedral train, and her veil would be made of real lace, and . . . She shook her head. A big wedding would be too much—Bobby might have second thoughts.

"Bobby's not religious," she told her mother. "He wouldn't want to be married in St. Paddy's."

"Does he want to be married at all? Bobby's frightened out of his mind right now. He shouldn't be making a decision like this."

Rose threw the dresses down on the bed. "Will you listen to yourself? All you're worried about is Bobby. What about me? What about what I want?"

"You're the one I'm worried about! I don't want you tied to a man who is going to wake up in a few months, realize that he's not going to die, and then think he made a mistake."

"That won't happen."

"Do you really think he wants to settle down? To be a good husband?"

"He'll be a good husband because I'll make it easy for him."

"And what will you get out of that?"

"Him."

"Will that be enough? You deserve a man who cares about you. Bobby never will, not as much as he cares about himself."

Lu's words hurt. They hurt more than Rose would have thought possible. "You make him sound horrible," she cried.

"No, he's selfish. Because he has to be. Because what he uses for his work is every part of himself; his imagination, his feelings, his talent. And as he becomes more successful, he's going to get spoiled. Bobby has such a big gift, people will forgive him anything. He hasn't got the strength to resist all those people who will tell him he can have whatever he wants, do whatever he wants."

"You're saying he's going to be a monster."

"A gifted, charming one. Yes."

"Now you can predict the future? You know what Bobby's going to be ten or twenty years from now?"

"I think I have a pretty good idea. Do you?"

"Maybe there was a time when Bobby was the way you say he is, but then he got sick and that changed him. He's more serious now. He understands what's important."

"What if he doesn't?" Her mother's voice was scraping away all the pretty pictures Rose had painted over her own doubts.

"He loves me! He says he does," she shouted, to drown out the voice.

But Lu went on. "And maybe he means it. As far as he can. But he'll never love you as much as he loves his work. He can't help it, Rose. It's just the way he is."

Images of Bobby's face when he talked about show business flashed through Rose's mind. She saw the eagerness in his smile, the hunger in his eyes. Then she saw other images—she saw Lu coming to the house in New Haven for a hurried visit and leaving before Nonna could serve the baked ziti because she had to go back to the theater, or Lu canceling another date to see her daughter ice-skate because there was an emergency rehearsal. And in a sudden clear-sighted moment Rose thought, *I never had you, Mother. I'm going to have him.*

"I'm going to marry Bobby Manning tomorrow at City Hall," she said.

"Why him, Rose?" Her mother was almost crying now. "You could have any man you want."

"I am going to wear a street dress, and there won't be a Mass, or a wedding party, or a veil and a gown. And it won't matter. Bobby and I love each other. And we are going to be happy for the rest of our lives."

CHAPTER 27

New York

2008

DARKNESS DESCENDED OUTSIDE George's living room, now that it was lit only by the Victorian street-light. George polished off his drink and said, "So Bobby and Rose got married. They moved into a huge apartment on Fifth Avenue, and thanks to Rose they became the high-glam New York power couple of the sixties and early seventies. Anyone who was doing anything important in New York knew them. I remember one party Rose threw when the guest list included Walter Cronkite, Richard Burton and Elizabeth Taylor, Norman Mailer, Lennie Bernstein, Kitty Carlisle Hart, and Gloria Steinem. Hell, the mayor came to their house."

"But was my mother happy? Because that wasn't the message I got when I was a kid."

"That I don't know about." George shrugged. "I wasn't close to

Rose; no one really was. Whatever she felt she kept to herself during those years."

"And my father?"

George's face lit up. "Ah, Bobby. I wish you'd known your father."

"You liked him."

"I admired the hell out of him. He was a giant, but he never acted like it. The man had nothing but hits, back to back, but he'd always say, 'Ain't I a lucky guy? I'm working on Broadway!' like he just couldn't believe it." George paused, and Carrie could tell he was being careful. "Rose was a great woman—everyone says so. But your dad wasn't exactly chopped liver, baby."

"But was he happy being married to mother?"

"Bobby was happy when he was working, and he worked most of the time." George stood up. "I need to take the girls out for a potty break." He pointed to the three dogs now lined up in front of the door. "Want to come with?" Carrie nodded and the next few minutes were spent putting tiny leashes—all heavily decorated with rhinestones—on the Yorkies, and walking them to the elevator.

"Do you know why my mother and Lu stopped speaking to each other?" Carrie asked when they were down on Fifty-seventh Street.

George shook his head. "It was weird. And I always thought whatever went on between them was the reason why Lu retired."

"Did you ask her about it?"

"Dozens of times, especially after she told me she was quitting the business. She was only forty-seven, for God's sake, and she could have—" he broke off. "Maxine, leave it!" he commanded one of the little Yorkies, who had found something that looked decidedly unpleasant in the gutter. "Nasty!" he added to the dog, and scooped her up.

"What did Lu tell you?"

"Just some crap about how she'd been around for a long time and there's nothing more pathetic than an over-the-hill diva who doesn't know when it's time to go."

"I meant, what did she say about my mother?"

"Nothing. That was family. Lu's very Italian about family—you don't talk about the secrets." He looked at Carrie. "Of course, she'd probably talk to you . . ."

"I'm not sure she'd think I'm family," Carrie said hastily. "We don't really know each other."

George and the Yorkies accompanied Carrie to the corner. She'd refused his offer to hail a cab for her because she wanted to walk and clear her head. She kissed George on the cheek. "Thank you," she said, and started down Sixth Avenue.

"Carrie," George called out. She turned. "Lu thinks of you as family. She may not have the answers to all of your questions, but she'll tell you everything she can. I know she will."

CARRIE'S APARTMENT SEEMED even more claustrophobic than usual when she walked inside. The furniture loomed out of the darkness at her and there was an overpowering scent in the air of flowers past their prime. It was time to get rid of Uncle Paulie's roses. She'd been avoiding doing it, but saving a basket of dead flowers wasn't going to make her feeling of loss go away. But when she leaned down to pick up the basket, a light suddenly went on behind her. Carrie whirled around, scattering dead rose petals on the floor.

"Howie, what the hell are you doing here?" she demanded as soon as she'd made out the figure in her ugly oversize chair. "How did you get in?"

"Sometimes, a cigar is not a house key," he said. He seemed to be having trouble saying words that began and ended with *s*.

"Are you drunk?" Howie wasn't a drinker; two glasses of wine with dinner was his limit.

"Don't change the subject," he slurred. He heaved himself out of her chair and swayed in place for a couple of seconds.

"You are. You're wasted—"

Howie waved his hand dismissively. "The point under discussion is this." He held up a house key. "When we didn't get married, I had the key for your apartment . . . I never gave you it back . . ." He stopped to consider the syntax of what he'd just said. "Or whatever. You never asked me for it to be given back." He stopped again, then seemed to decide to plow on. "Thing is, I still have it."

"And you used it to break in here."

"I did not break in. I used my key. And I am going to sit down now. Because I had a few drinks in Grand Central Terminal before I came over and I don't feel so good."

"Howie, are you going to be sick?"

"Probably, but not yet. First we are going to talk about the cigar."

"What cigar? You don't smoke."

"Freud said sometimes when something happens that looks like an accident it isn't, and sometimes a cigar is just a cigar. Are you following me?"

"Sort of."

He held up the key again. "This is not a cigar." He was speaking very clearly and distinctly now—too distinctly. "It is not an accident that you never asked me for your key. I will bet you a skillion dollars you still have the key for my place."

"You moved to the country after we split up." But it was true; Carrie still did have the key to his old apartment.

"Doesn't count," Howie said. "We are talking about accidents.

Which it is not when you call me at three in the morning because you miss me and you are lonely."

"If this is about the other night—"

"Shush," he said somewhat dramatically. "It is not an accident that every time I meet a woman—like the woman with whom I was in bed with the last time you called me—"

"I said I was sorry about that—"

"I'm not, because it would have ended anyway. It always does. I meet a woman. She's nice and smart, and pretty and she likes me, and everyone I know likes her, but she's not you. I love *you*." He belched dangerously. "I tried to be your friend because you wanted it. But I can't do it anymore."

Carrie's heart sank. "I thought you were okay with—"

"I'm not. I wanted to marry you—you don't befriend the woman you want to marry." At that, for no reason at all, Carrie's heart stopped sinking and started to float. Meanwhile Howie squinted at the key, working to focus on it. "I think you love me. If you don't, stop calling me every time you think of something funny or sad or you can't sleep. Take your goddamned key back. It will kill me not to hear from you anymore, but that's the way it has to be." He belched again. "And now, if you will excuse me, I'm going to go throw up."

Howie made it to the bathroom in time, and afterward Carrie managed to roll him onto her bed before he passed out. Then she went back into her living room. The rose petals were still on the floor. Carrie picked them up, along with the pretty little basket, and started to take all of it down the hall to the trash. But she stopped. She pulled the dead flowers out of the basket, put the basket in the center of her coffee table, then went back out to the hall.

When she came back there were tears stinging at her eyes, but she didn't let herself cry. She had to think. Howie had gotten drunk because he needed more than the fake friendship she'd been telling herself they had. If she couldn't tell him she loved him, he would be out of her life for good. And he'd be right.

Carrie took out her phone and started to punch in Zoe's number. Then she put the phone away. She wasn't going to cry, and she wasn't going to lean on her best friend yet again. She went back to the couch and looked at the basket on the coffee table.

Why do I always feel like I'm settling for an empty basket when I want one that's full? Why can't I let myself be happy? What would life be like without Howie?

Carrie picked up the basket. Maybe she'd buy a plant to put in it. She'd never tried to grow a plant before. She put the basket down and walked into her bedroom, Howie had stopped snoring and he was sprawled out on top of the covers. She watched him for a moment. She'd stuck to her decision about not marrying him. Would she have changed her mind if Rose hadn't gotten sick? She'd wondered about that. Not that it mattered. Rose had gotten sick, and Carrie couldn't have betrayed her.

And that's how Mother would have seen it. She would have thought I was abandoning everything she believed in. So I didn't.

But Carrie had asked Howie to be her friend. That was the only way she could stay with her decision. And now he was saying he couldn't do that anymore. She lay down next to him on the bed. He didn't move.

"I said I wouldn't marry you because I didn't want to hurt you," she whispered. "But that was bullshit." She stroked his cheek with her finger, but Howie still didn't move. He was going to have one hell of a hangover when he woke up. "I couldn't let my mother down." Carrie hoisted herself up on her elbow. "In spite of every-thing—all the awards she got and the good things she did—I al-ways knew there was something broken inside her. I thought I had to fix it. That was bullshit too, but I believed it. Now I need to know what went wrong for her. I know more than I did—but there's still a big piece missing." She got up off the bed and stood next to it. "I hate sounding like a mental health manual, but Zoe says I need closure and she's right. There's just one thing I have to do. Please wait for me."

She started out of the room, but when she reached the door a voice came at her from the darkness. "About the waiting thing—how long did you have in mind?" Howie asked. "I have to get back to work by Monday."

CHAPTER 28

New York

2008

"ZOE, ARE YOU dipping or can you talk?"

"I'm up to my ass in lemongrass ganache, but I can talk—fast. Where are you?"

"Home, but not for long, I have something to tell you."

"Finally!"

"What 'finally'? I haven't said anything."

"You're going to see your grandmother."

"You're not supposed to kill my moment like that. You're supposed to be shocked, and in awe of my growth as a person, and then you're supposed to be supportive."

"I'm shocked, I'm awed, I'm supportive, and I'm dipping ganache. Before I lose four dozen truffles, where are you meeting the old girl?"

"She lives in Mount Kisco and I'm taking the train out there today. I said I'd rent a car but she said no, the train was easier and her driver would pick me up at the station. She has a driver. She probably has a whole staff. George said—George was her conductor—I told you about him—"

"Carrie—"

"George told me she sold her apartment in the city and her country place—that was where my father died—and moved to Mount Kisco after she retired, and she—"

"Carrie, you're rambling."

"I've never met her. She's my grandmother and all I know about her is she was famous and my mother was angry at her for thirty-five years."

"And now you're going to Mount Kisco to find out why. The sound you hear is me clapping—figuratively speaking."

"I'm going to be picked up by a chauffeur. She probably has a big stupid car and she makes the poor man wear livery. The whole staff probably wears uniforms. Who has a staff of servants in Mount Kisco, for God's sake?"

"You're regressing."

"She's going to be pretentious and pushy . . ."

"Or not."

"Mother would hate it if she knew I was doing this."

"Carrie, this is a good thing."

"Easy for you to say."

LU LAWSON'S CAR wasn't big and stupid. To non-car-savvy Carrie it looked like every other vehicle on the road, except maybe even a little smaller. And Lu's driver wasn't in uniform; he was wearing jeans that were a little muddy, and a sweatshirt. He confided that in addition to his driving duties, he also took care of Ms. Lawson's lawns and gardens. His wife did the cooking and the daily cleaning, but they didn't live in. They had been with Ms.

Lawson since she moved to Mount Kisco thirty-five years ago. His name was Dan and his wife was Cecile.

Carrie's grandmother's house was a big two-story affair—possibly a colonial?—that sat on the top of a hill. There were four pillars holding up the roof of the front porch, which was flanked by two huge bay windows, and more large windows dotted the front of the first and second floors at regular intervals. Painted white with black trim, the house had red and black striped awnings jutting out from all the windows. The touch of red gave the place a slightly rakish air, which Carrie would have liked if she hadn't felt obligated to disapprove. The driveway leading to the house was a gravel semicircle that swept around the expanse of lush green front lawn. "Looks like your average greensward," Carrie said. "Or a golf course." In the rearview mirror she saw Dan pick up on her sneer.

"Wait'll you see Ms. Lawson's tomato garden in the back," he said defensively. "She's got four different kinds of heirlooms and takes care of them herself. She won't let me go near them."

They pulled up to the front door of the house and stopped. Carrie sat rooted to her seat.

I can't go through with this, she thought. *Screw closure.*

But then Dan got out of the car and came around to her side to open the door, and it felt too late to say that she'd changed her mind.

I knew I should have driven myself, she thought.

The big front door of the house opened and a woman stood framed in the middle of the doorway, waiting.

If she does anything phony I'm out of here, Carrie thought. *Any big actressy hugs, any reunion scenes, and we're done.*

The woman didn't move. Her hands were jammed into her pockets. Was she nervous too? There were three wide curved steps leading up to the porch. Carrie climbed up them and then she was standing in front of her grandmother. The woman whose facial features, legs, and cleavage Carrie shared.

Lu Lawson had aged well—she looked closer to seventy than eighty. Her hair was still thick and curly, and whoever did her color was a master; it was a soft brown with light golden highlights—no harsh old-lady dye job for her. Her face was surprisingly youthful; had she had some work done? If so, it had been very discreet. Lu was taller than Carrie thanks to high-heeled pumps, and she was wearing a pink wraparound silk dress that showcased a curvy figure with a small waist, and legs that were still world class. She wore glasses, chic and slightly oversize, with frames that were the same flattering shade as her hair. The big brown eyes behind them were studying Carrie as hard as Carrie was studying her.

"My God," Lu said softly. For a second neither of them moved. They didn't know what to do next. Then her grandmother did a defiant little shrug, leaned over, and kissed Carrie on the cheek. "I don't care," she said. "I've been hoping for this moment for a long time." And she led the way inside.

Her house was bright, done mostly in light colors; butter yellow, delicate peach, and pale, mossy green. The furniture—upholstered in the same light colors—was large and comfortable-looking. There was a lot of cream-colored wainscoting and wood trim, and huge pastel rugs scattered over gleaming hardwood floors. The effect was cozy and warm.

Why didn't I ever see this place when I was growing up? Carrie thought. *I should have at least known it existed.*

Lu took Carrie to the back of the house, where the living room opened onto a lawn surrounded by gardens, and they walked outside.

"I grow the vegetables and Dan takes care of everything else," Lu said as she started down a flagstone path. "Over there, those are the rosebushes, and the peonies." She pointed in the direction of one patch. "My herbs are in that little bed over there, and . . ."—she pointed again, this time with a flourish—"this is where I have my tomatoes!"

In addition to her tomatoes—which were indeed heirlooms— Carrie's grandmother's backyard boasted three apple trees, a cherry tree, and a grape arbor. There was a picnic table under the arbor that had been set up with a linen tablecloth—dazzling white in the early spring sunshine—silverware, china, and sparkling crystal glasses. "I thought we'd have baked ziti for lunch," Lu said. "Do you like it?"

She should know what I like, Carrie thought. *I should know what she likes. We shouldn't have to ask each other.*

Meanwhile, the big eyes behind the chic glasses were getting anxious. "I didn't know if you usually eat a big meal in the middle of the day, you see. If you'd rather have a sandwich, I can ask Cecile to make one for you. Ham and cheese, or I think there's some eggplant parmigiana." Her grandmother was rambling.

Because she's nervous, Carrie thought. *This is so wrong. We shouldn't be nervous with each other.*

"Or soup," her grandmother was saying. "I'm sure there's some soup . . ."

"What the hell happened?" Carrie burst out. She added more softly, "What I mean is—"

"I know what you mean. You want to know what happened between me and your mother. You want to know what happened when Bobby died." Lu took Carrie's hands. "Come," she said. And they walked over to the picnic table to sit under her grape arbor.

"BEFORE YOU CAN understand what I'm about to tell you, you need to know where we all were in our lives in the early seventies," Lu said. "Bobby and Rose had been married for about ten years."

She paused, picking her words carefully. "It wasn't a bad marriage, not totally—"

"George Standish said they were a power couple."

"They were a good team. He had the talent—huge talent—but he had a lot of rough edges. I think in his heart he was still one of the kids hanging around the dives on Forty-second Street, hoping for a break. Rose was the one who made him fashionable—and really famous."

"Did he resent that?"

"He loved it! Writers and composers didn't get that kind of public attention back then—not the way the actors did. They were the ones behind the scenes. But Rose always knew how to play the press. After she finished decorating their apartment, three magazines wrote stories on it. She redid Bobby's wardrobe and they were considered the best-dressed couple in New York. They showed up on the society pages of the *Times* all the time—not just in the theater section like the rest of us. And everywhere they went, Bobby was the star."

"What was she?"

"Mrs. Bobby Manning."

Carrie tried to imagine her larger-than-life mother as a woman who was dependent on her husband for her identity. "And was she happy with that?"

Lu looked out at the gardens that were so neatly laid out in front of them. There was some kind of purple flower blooming in one of the beds. "Bobby was a workaholic. If he was in rehearsal he'd forget everything—including Rose—existed. He had an office near Shubert Alley and some nights he'd sleep there, and he wouldn't remember to call her to say he wouldn't be home. If he was writing a show, he'd hole up in his office or a hotel room for weeks."

"I can't see Mother accepting that."

"That wasn't the worst of it." Lu stared at the purple flowers. "Bobby was . . . well, in my day we would have said he was a cad. He cheated on Rose, from the beginning. It wasn't unusual in our world; a lot of men in Bobby's position played around. They had money and power, and they were surrounded by beautiful girls who wanted to make it in the business."

"And making it with my father was a stepping-stone?"

"Bobby was too smart for that. He'd never let his fun interfere with his work. He always cast the best woman for the part—always. But, he was just one of those men . . ." Lu sighed, but her voice was affectionate.

"You liked him," Carrie said, realizing it was the second time she'd said this to someone in the last two days.

"I loved Bobby. He was one of the most talented people I've ever met. He was charming and funny." Lu smiled and shrugged. "And when I worked with him, I won two Tonys."

"He ran around on your daughter!" Carrie said indignantly. Her mother would have been so humiliated by that. Protective feelings Carrie hadn't known she had rose up.

Lu's smile faded. "I never said he was the man I would have picked for a son-in-law. No woman in her right mind would want Bobby Manning to marry her daughter—especially if that daughter was Rose. But that didn't change how I felt about him as a person. Do you understand?"

Carrie sighed and nodded, her indignation melting away. She *could* understand her grandmother. Lu Lawson was a realist who accepted people as they were. Rose Lawson Manning had never learned to do that.

"Did Mother know Bobby was cheating?"

"I don't know. Rose was so proud, she never would have admitted it. Especially not to me."

"Why not? You were her mother."

"I had tried to warn her about Bobby before she married him. My relationship with Rose had always been . . . rocky. But after that . . . I was the last person she'd tell if she was having a problem. You know?"

Carrie nodded again. She knew what could happen when you said something her mother hadn't wanted to hear.

"Rose knew what Bobby was like before they got married; he told her himself. But she wanted to believe her love could make him into a different person." Suddenly there were tears in Lu's eyes. "She had everything going for her. She was beautiful and bright—she could have done anything. But all she wanted was a man who couldn't give her what she needed. I'd hear the gossip about him at the theater and I'd pray she didn't know. And then I'd pray that he *would* change, even though I knew people don't." Lu blinked back the tears.

"It sounds like things were pretty bad for them," Carrie said. And then she had to ask. "Did I make it worse? When I came along? George Standish said Bobby wasn't the white-picket-fence-and-pet-dog kind of guy. He couldn't have been happy about having a baby."

"You are so wrong!" Lu shook her head. "The way that man fell for you—it was typical Bobby. Rose had been wanting a child for years and he'd been saying no. Then she finally got pregnant—I never believed it was an accident even though she said it was—and after you were born, Bobby took one look at you and it was like he'd invented fatherhood. He went straight from the hospital to FAO Schwarz and bought out the doll department. He insisted that he and Rose had to move to that huge apartment on Park Avenue because their old place only had one room for your nursery. He wanted you to have your own suite. I don't know if you remember it; it was all done in pink, and—"

"I've seen pictures."

"He said it had to be as beautiful as you were."

Then Carrie felt her eyes fill up, which was totally insane because she'd never known her father. "He said I was beautiful?" she breathed.

"You were his princess. He would have spoiled you rotten if he had lived." Lu paused. "Sweetheart, by the time you were three years old, Rose and Bobby had gone through a lot of ups and downs—their marriage was like a roller coaster. But you were always the up—for both of them."

CHAPTER 29

New York

1974

ROSE WALKED INTO the pink bedroom that her husband had created for their baby daughter when they moved to Park Avenue. Normally the home decorating was Rose's job, but Bobby had insisted on doing over the baby's two rooms himself. Instead of hiring the chic decorator Rose always used, he had asked his favorite set designer to come up with a "palace for a princess." So there was an overdone child's bed with a silly silk-and-lace canopy. The swagged curtains—also overdone and silly—were pink silk too. The furniture, covered with fussy ruffles, looked like mounds of pink whipped cream. In Rose's opinion the whole thing was a pink cliché, but Bobby loved it. And little Carrie was only three years old, so she wasn't expressing opinions on the décor.

Rose looked over at the bed, where her daughter was taking a nap. She liked to come into Carrie's nursery and watch her sleep.

It was a time when Rose could think. She'd been doing a lot of that lately. She'd been doing a lot of remembering too—and it was all because of the small person with the head of dark curly hair sleeping in the ridiculously canopied bed. Rose moved quietly to a rocking chair and sat, carefully, so she wouldn't make any noise and wake the child. She leaned back and closed her eyes. And began remembering.

FROM THE BEGINNING of her marriage there had been the Girls. That was Rose's name for the pretty predators who stalked her husband. The Girls didn't care if they wrecked a home or broke another woman's heart if they thought they could further their careers or have a shot at being the next Mrs. Bobby Manning. The first Girl had shown up about six months after Bobby and Rose were married. Bobby hadn't even waited until their first wedding anniversary to start playing around. However, he had waited until his show, *The Lady*, had opened and became a smash hit. First things first.

Bobby never flaunted his affairs; Rose knew he didn't want to hurt her—or rock the boat—as long as he could do what he wanted. So Rose pretended she didn't know about his Girls. What other choice did she have? There was nothing a wife in her circumstances could do except smile when she wanted to scream, swallow her pride, ignore the pitying looks from her husband's friends who thought she was too stupid to know what was going on, and pack her husband's bags when he went out of town to work on his new show, even though she knew he'd probably have a Girl with him. The bag packing might have seemed humiliating to an outsider, but it actually made the wife feel safe. As long as her husband needed her to do things like that for him, she could convince herself that he wouldn't leave. So she folded his shirts carefully in

tissue so they wouldn't wrinkle, and made sure his favorite toi-
letries were tucked into his monogrammed shaving kit, and she
waited until the Girl of the moment finally went away. Then a
couple of months later it would start all over again. And always in
the pit of the wife's stomach was the fear that this new Girl might
be the one who would not go away. That the marriage the wife had
fought so hard for would end. That she would be alone. That her
mother had been right.

NIGHT AFTER NIGHT as she lay in her bed, Rose would remind
herself that she had won. *Everyone said Bobby Manning would never
settle down. But he did—with me. I won Bobby Manning.* But then the
unwanted, unbidden question would come. *What the hell did I win?
Forget that he can't stay faithful for fifteen minutes. Forget that he's so
insecure he has to buy every kid in the chorus a thousand-dollar Christmas present, and he overtips so much it's a joke. What about his talent?
Everyone says he's a genius, but is he? It's not like he's ever written something uplifting and meaningful that will stand the test of time, like the
Panis Angelicus. He writes Broadway musicals, for God's sake.*

She'd think about leaving him, but what would she have without him? Who would she be? Lu's world was still Rose's world. In
their world, Bobby was fast becoming a god—and incidentally, Lu
might be a star, but a god trumped a star. Rose couldn't walk away
from all of that. Besides, she still loved Bobby. And she still believed that someday he'd realize that she was the best thing that
had ever happened to him. He'd dump the Girls and he'd be hers.
And she'd win for real. So she kept on smiling and pretending.

The thing about smiling and pretending—and tongue biting—
year after year is that eventually it takes its toll. So Rose shouldn't
have been surprised when she found, as she and Bobby were ap-
proaching their sixth wedding anniversary, that she was having

trouble sleeping. One night, as she was roaming around the apartment, she found herself standing in the middle of her closet—the space was actually a separate bedroom that had been converted to accommodate her wardrobe. She looked at the floor-to-ceiling clothes racks jammed with evening gowns, hostess gowns, cocktail gowns, day dresses, afternoon dresses, pantsuits, leisure suits, slacks, skirts, sweaters, and tops. There was a wall of shelves on which her shoes and boots—did she really have four hundred and seventeen pairs, as the maid claimed?—were stored. There was another wall for her furs; the calf-length sable vest that had been such a hit when she'd worn it to the opening of Bobby's third show, the floor-length marabou cape that had made all the fashion pages when she'd worn it on closing night. And in the corner was the safe in which all her jewelry was locked away, all those glittering tributes to his own success that Bobby had given her. It was all there—the sum total of what she had achieved in her life.

As Rose stood there, trying not to weep, she remembered St. Mary's and the rummage sale. And she remembered Sister Phil saying that there were times when you couldn't think about yourself because you wouldn't be able to bear your life.

There was a soup kitchen connected to the Catholic church in her neighborhood. Rose had been a sporadic attendant at Mass in the last few years, but she'd gone often enough to be on a first-name basis with Father Xavier, the parish priest. The next day, the good father seemed a little shocked when she said she wanted to wake up at the crack of dawn to feed the homeless—who, he warned her, didn't always bathe—but she was adamant. Rose began going to the church in the morning to make sandwiches and coffee for the soup kitchen regulars to eat while sitting on the church steps. The best part was, none of Father Xavier's hungry little flock knew who Rose was; even more important, none of them knew about Bobby Manning. They didn't know Rose was the wife of a man who cheated on her and then gave her expensive gifts as if that would make up for it. They didn't know that in the snake pit called show business everyone pitied her. The men and women who showed up to eat on the church steps were just grateful that the coffee was hot and the sandwiches were freshly made. As the weeks and months passed, Rose spent more and more time in the church basement helping Father Xavier and listening to him talk about the homeless shelter he wanted to open if he could raise the funds.

Now Rose winced when Bobby picked up the tab for the entire bar at Sardi's, knowing that the money could have done so much good in the right hands. Her jewels seemed too gaudy and too flashy when she put them on. At the same time, she was feeling something she'd never thought she'd feel again. She realized what it was—she was rediscovering the joy she'd felt so long ago at the St. Mary's rummage sale.

Then, suddenly, she found out she was pregnant. It was an accident, and at first Rose was distraught. She'd wanted to have a baby for years, but Bobby had always said a kid would slow them down, and she'd never had the courage to do anything he didn't want—not with all the Girls lurking around. But then the accident had turned out to be the best thing that had ever happened.

BOBBY HAD BEEN in Toronto in tryouts for his sixth show when Rose had gone into labor. By the time he'd managed to finish up the rewrites on the second act and catch a flight to New York, the baby was already a day and a half old. When he arrived in Rose's hospital room, he hadn't shaved or slept, and he was still worried about the second act finale.

Please don't let him hate me for doing this to him, Rose thought as they walked together to the nursery to look at their little girl. *Let him see how beautiful the baby is, with her perfect little nose and her big eyes and her soft sweet skin.*

Then she and Bobby were in front of the nursery window. Even though Rose had already seen the baby, and held and nursed her, the same words that had come into her mind the first time came back now. *She's mine!* For a moment Rose forgot the man at her side and watched Carrie sleep. *I'll never be alone again*, she thought.

At the same time she heard Bobby draw in a deep breath. "My God, she's a blank slate," she heard him whisper. "She can be anything she wants."

Rose hadn't thought of that. "We have to be careful raising her," she said. "We have to do it right."

Bobby laughed. "There is no 'right.' She's my daughter! Bobby Manning's kid! She's going to be a princess! She's going to have whatever the hell she wants!" He kissed Rose. It was a kiss like the ones he used to give her when he was still grateful to her for handing him his career on a silver platter—and for taking care of him. "Thank you, " he said softly. "Thank you for having her no matter what I said I wanted."

And when she'd tried to protest that it had been an accident, he'd said, "I don't care how it happened." Then he'd turned back to the baby. "Things are going to be good from now on, Rose," he'd said. "I promise."

It was the closest Bobby had ever come to admitting to the cheating. Rose had looked at little Carrie in the nursery and known that she finally had an ally in the battle against the Girls. But she also knew she had an obligation to the child.

I can't let her grow up thinking the way we live is right, Rose thought. *We have to set a good example for her, give her a good sense of values. Everything we do is self-indulgent and trivial. We have to change.*

But she didn't want to spring that on Bobby. Not right away. Because he was already changing. At least, that was what she thought.

Rose and Bobby brought the baby home from the hospital and set up her crib next to the window in their bedroom. Carrie's pink extravaganza suite wasn't finished yet, and besides, the new parents wanted to keep her close to them. One night when Carrie had been home for about six weeks, Rose woke up to hear a noise coming from Carrie's crib. The baby was cooing and gurgling, and the sound was so musical that if you wanted to stretch the point just a tad, you could say she was humming. Carefully, so she wouldn't wake Bobby, Rose got out of bed and tiptoed to the window. Carrie was lying on her back, her baby pretzel spine curled up so her feet were in her hands, and she was staring out the window at the moon, which was—for once—clearly visible in the Manhattan sky as she cooed. Or hummed.

"She's singing to the moon," Bobby whispered in Rose's ear. He'd gotten out of bed and was standing next to her. He looked down at his little daughter with shining eyes. "My kid sings to the moon," he whispered again.

The two of them had stayed there watching their brilliant baby until she turned to look at them. She let go of her feet and favored them with a little wave of her fingers, and then drifted off to sleep. Her parents went back to bed. But when Rose woke up a couple of hours later to nurse Carrie, Bobby was gone. She went into the living room and found him sitting at the piano, working.

"I'll come to bed in a little while," he said. But he'd stayed up for the rest of the night. In the morning, he was still there.

"Listen to this," Bobby said when Rose walked in, and he started to play the song he'd been working on through the night. The melody was sweet and simple and so light that the notes seemed to melt into the air after he touched the piano keys.

"It's the prettiest thing you've ever written," she said.

"It's called 'Carrie's Moon Song.' "

Even though she knew he wouldn't, Rose hoped he was going to keep the song as his gift to the baby, that it would be something private that would stay between the three of them. But of course it was going into the score of his new musical. "It's the first thing I've written for it," he said.

IT HAD TAKEN Rose a while to believe in the new Bobby, who spent his weekends with his wife and his baby, who now worked at home instead of going to his office near Shubert Alley. This last change was a huge one for a man whose previous routine had been carved in stone. Once Bobby's latest show had opened and he wasn't needed in the theater anymore, he'd go back to his office. He'd show up every morning at nine and stay until six. "Even if I'm dry as a bone and I haven't got an idea in my head," he said once, "I can't sit home waiting for the muse to hit. I'm like a plumber. I've got to go to the job."

But now Bobby said he didn't have to go to the office. Because he said the muse *had* hit him, and it had happened at home. His new show, the one that had been inspired by "Carrie's Moon Song," was going to be called *Family*.

"It's going to blow everyone away," he told Rose. He was pacing with excitement, the baby in his arms. Sometimes it seemed to Rose that he carried the little girl everywhere.

"Bobby, maybe you could take a little time off before you start the new show. Spend more time with Carrie. Think about the future a little," Rose said tentatively.

He looked at her like she'd just suggested he spit on God. "My future is what it's always been. I'm in show business."

"But you can't keep up this kind of pace forever. Maybe you could try writing a novel, or . . ."

"I work on Broadway. End of story." And Rose knew if she pushed, she'd get nowhere.

"Well then, tell me about *Family*," she said quickly.

"It's going to scare the shit—excuse me, Princess," he added to Carrie. "It's going to scare the life out of the money people. I may have to back this one myself."

But of course there was no danger of that. In twelve years Bobby had had six Broadway hits and no misses; investors lined up to put their money in a Bobby Manning musical.

Still, the new offering was going to be risky. There was no chorus, no big Broadway orchestra, no turntables or huge sets or elaborate costumes, and no love story—at least, not in the conventional sense. There would just be three actresses on the bare stage backed by a five-piece band. They would play a mother, a daughter, and a grandmother.

"Carrie is going to help me write it," announced the besotted Bobby. He put Carrie's playpen near the piano while he was working, and he even stopped in the middle of the day and took her to the park with her nanny, Sandy.

Rose hadn't wanted to hire a nanny at first, but Bobby insisted that she needed one. She had spent weeks interviewing candidates and was about to give up the search when Bobby stepped in.

"You're looking for Mary Poppins, Rose, and she doesn't exist. I'll find someone." And in no time he'd settled on Sandy. "She's not much to look at," he said. "But the princess loves her and she makes us both laugh."

When Sandy had started the job, she'd been a little overawed to be working in the household of the famous Bobby Manning, but she'd quickly learned to relax around all of them, and she proved to be a terrific nanny—smart, warm, and nurturing. Rose felt secure leaving her precious daughter in Sandy's capable hands. Not that Carrie was alone with Sandy very much; Bobby kept his baby daughter with him most of the time. Once a week he and Sandy and the baby had lunch with Lu at Lindy's or the Edison Hotel Coffee Shop.

"We've got a club going," Bobby told Rose. "The princess is our Head High Honcho, Lu and I are the Lowly Peons, and Sandy is the Head Peon. We call ourselves the Gang of Four. If you'd like to come along it'll be the Gang of Five. We've got room."

But somehow Rose always seemed to be busy working with Father Xavier when the Gang of Four met. The truth was, she wasn't sure she wanted to watch her mother and Bobby—the two Broadway giants—work their magic on her baby daughter. Carrie already had way too much show business in her life as far as Rose was concerned.

Yet things with Bobby were so much better than they had been—it was almost like a miracle. He decided he wanted to stay home more in the evenings, so they cut back on the frantic social life Rose had grown to dislike. Now she and Carrie had him all to themselves several nights a week. When Carrie was a year old, Rose realized that it had been that long since there had been a Girl. So even when Bobby gave her a diamond pendant to commemorate Carrie's first birthday, Rose didn't say anything. She felt guilty about the waste of money, but she didn't want to do anything to derail their new life.

IT USUALLY TOOK Bobby a year and a half to write a musical. For the first six months he'd "cook." That was his word for the many false starts he had to go through to get himself on the right track. Scenes would be considered, sketched out, and discarded; songs would be started and abandoned. "I'm clearing away the underbrush," he'd say. Rose thought she'd be screaming in frustration if she had to try and fail so many times, but Bobby would cheerfully throw away pages that represented weeks of effort, and say, "You don't know what'll work until you find out what doesn't."

And sure enough, after about six months, he'd have a detailed outline of the book and know what and where every number was going to be. Then it would take him another year to actually write the show. Once his outline was set he never deviated from it. "That's why I wait until I know I've got it before I start. So I don't have to waste time."

But now, with his new, looser work schedule, it took almost twice as long as usual for Bobby to come up with a first draft of *Family* before he was ready to start writing. And he still didn't have his last scene sketched out. All he knew was, at the very end of the play, someone—he didn't know who—was going to sing "Carrie's Moon Song."

He told Rose the ending would come to him, which was a very misty statement from a man who normally set his outline in concrete. But Bobby wasn't worried. He looked at Carrie, who was now almost three. "It's her show and we'll do it together," he said.

It was also Lu's show. Bobby had asked Lu to play the grandmother and Lu had jumped at the chance, even though the musical didn't have a starring role for her and for the first time in her career, she'd be sharing billing with two other women. The truth was, Lu needed a new Bobby Manning musical even more than the investors did. Lu's career was circling the drain; she'd done three shows that hadn't made it and she was looking for a comeback.

CHAPTER 30

New York

2008

"BY THE EARLY seventies, I was washed up," Lu said. She and Carrie were still sitting at the picnic table under the grape arbor. The baked ziti was in front of them, but neither of them had eaten much. Carrie was dying to ask her grandmother what had happened to the song she'd inspired, but she didn't want to break Lu's flow.

"When I realized I was on my way to being the first question in a 'Where Are They Now?' quiz, it stunned me," Lu went on. "I'd done *The Lady* with Bobby in 1962, and that show had given me a new rep as a serious actress—up till then I was just a cute ingénue. Then Bobby wrote another show for me called *Soldiers*. It was an antiwar piece—everyone was angry about Vietnam in those days— and it was totally different from *The Lady*. I won my second Tony for *Soldiers*, and after that I thought I was golden." Lu chuckled sadly. "That was really stupid."

"With two Tonys, I think most people would think they were golden."

"First rule of the biz, sweetie: they can always find someone new to fill your tap shoes while they're still warm from your feet. No one is golden. You can't ever forget that." Lu did her sad chuckle again. "Anyway, after *Soldiers*, Bobby had an idea for a new show, but he didn't have a part for me."

"That must have been rough."

"I'd always known that he'd have to move on; he couldn't write for one actress for his entire career. But no one else knew what to do with me. I couldn't go back to the kind of shows I'd done before *Soldiers* and *The Lady*. I was past playing the cutie-pie parts. Maybe I could have gotten away with it, age-wise—if the lighting was really good—but that kind of thing just wasn't me anymore. Besides, those musicals were considered old-fashioned by the midsixties. Then *Hair* came along and all of a sudden everything was rock music and kids getting naked onstage." She laughed—a big, hearty laugh this time. "Mama thought I was lewd when I stripped down to a silk teddy in the fifties. If she could have seen what the girls were doing in 1968 . . . Don't get me wrong, I liked *Hair*. I saw it twice. But after it came on the scene, there were only two kinds of shows being done: rock musicals with at least half the cast in the buff, or what we used to call the 'big lady musicals,' like *Hello, Dolly!* and *Mame*. I was too old to wander around without my clothes on, and I never felt right playing the diva. I needed someone brilliant like Bobby to come up with a part that was good for me and good for the time. Unfortunately there weren't a lot of Bobby Mannings running around. I had three bombs back to back." Lu looked up at the grape arbor above their heads. "I was scared; I thought my career was over. I didn't need the money, but I didn't know how I'd live if I couldn't work." She brought her gaze down to Carrie. "I learned," she said drily. "I haven't worked in thirty-three years."

"George says that was your choice."

"George never understood that I was brought up Catholic."

"What does that have to do with anything?"

"Catholics do penance for their sins."

"I know that. But what did you do that was so bad that you had to give up your career?"

"My daughter was such an unhappy woman—I had to take responsibility for that. As the kids used to say, I blew it."

"I thought you said her life was good after I was born." Carrie was confused.

"For a while. But then things between Bobby and Rose went sour again. It was around the time when you were three years old."

"Right before he died."

"Yes. That was when everything went to hell."

CHAPTER 31

New York

1974

ROSE LEANED BACK in the pink rocker. She owed Sandy a thank-you; the nanny had called in sick, so Rose had cleared the decks to take care of Carrie herself. And she was glad she'd taken the time, because her days of watching her child sleep like this in the middle of the day were numbered; soon Carrie would be too old for naps. But for the moment Rose could still sit in Bobby's stupid pink rocking chair and remember what it had felt like to be happy. Before the new nightmare had set in. Before things had changed again. She could practically pinpoint the day it had happened.

BOBBY HAD ALMOST finished the final draft of *Family*. His producer had already scheduled a series of backers' auditions for the angels who were waiting for the privilege of putting their money into another surefire Bobby Manning hit. Lu had signed on the dotted line. George would be doing the orchestrations and the conducting. The team was in place, and all was right in Bobby's world.

Then he had his second heart attack.

Rose hadn't been at home at the time. Sandy was the one who realized what was happening, found his medicine—he always forgot to carry it—and gave him the pills that the doctor said had probably saved his life. Sandy had called the ambulance, ridden with him to the hospital, and had the presence of mind to insist the hospital use a false name for him when he was admitted, because Bobby was paranoid about word getting around that he was sick.

"That's not the image I want out in public," he said from his hospital bed. "No one needs to know I'm not healthy as a horse. Because I will be again. I'll be good as new."

But the doctors had a new diagnosis for him. Now they said the angina that had plagued him for so many years was to be categorized as unstable which was a far more serious form of the problem. The chest pains Bobby had always tried to dismiss were dangerous now—another heart attack could follow. Bobby was ill in a way that he hadn't been before. Rose knew she couldn't keep quiet any longer.

"I think you've just had a sign that you need to slow down," she told him. He was home from the hospital and she'd overheard him talking on the phone with George about the backers' auditions. "You've been pushing yourself too hard for too long." When she looked back, she would realize that her timing couldn't have been worse. Bobby was scared about being sick, and he wanted to hear that everything was going back to normal.

"That's what you'd like me to do, isn't it?" he snapped. "But you don't just want me to slow down—you'd like me to quit altogether. What am I supposed to do all day, Rose? Go hand out sandwiches at your church? Try to convince myself that I'm doing good when I'm only there because I'm bored out of my mind?"

"At least it's better than adding to the mountain of forgettable theater that's produced every year!" The words just seemed to pop out of Rose's mouth. If he hadn't attacked her work at the soup kitchen she never would have said them—even if it was what she felt. But now it was out, and in a way she was glad. Bobby looked stunned. "Bobby," she added, more reasonably, "you've proven you can write—"

"Forgettable theater," he broke in. His voice was cold as ice. But now that she'd started, she knew she had to be honest.

"Not forgettable; that was too harsh. But it's not earth-shattering either. It's certainly not worth risking your health for. Listen to me," she went on eagerly. "We don't need the money. We can live on your royalties, if we just cut back. We don't need this huge apartment and the servants . . ."

He was staring at her with such a strange expression. She let herself hope that he was actually listening to what he had to say.

"I've been thinking about this for a long time, Bobby. We don't need things, all the glitzy jewelry, and the clothes, and the cars—that's just stuff. And doing anything to get our names in the papers all the time. I know I was the one who started that, but I didn't realize what a trap it was . . ." She was so eager to say it all, she was practically tripping over her words. "We can walk away from all of that. Do something meaningful, something really useful!"

There was a long pause. When Bobby finally spoke, he used his new icy voice. She hadn't gotten through to him at all. "I like the huge apartment. I just wish it were bigger. I like having a maid and a cook, and I get a rush when I walk into Tiffany's and blow what would be three years' salary for anyone else on a necklace for you. I want that necklace to be glitzy. I want pictures of you wearing it in every newspaper in town! I want my life to be over the top! Because all of that says, 'Bobby Manning is in the room, ladies and gentlemen. Move over because he's coming through.' And now you want to take that away from me."

"I want you to have a better kind of life . . ."

"You want to take away who I am. You want to take away what I do."

"You're more than your work. You're a father and a husband."

"The world is full of fathers and husbands! Do you realize how lucky I am? Do you realize what I get to do every day of my life? How many people get to be Bobby Manning, Rose? Even if my stuff is forgettable—"

"I've already said that I'm sorry about that."

"I've had six hits back to back!"

"It was a stupid thing to say. I didn't mean it. I'm your biggest fan, you know that." But she wasn't—not anymore. Now they both knew it. And he would never forgive her for it.

THE DOCTORS SAID Bobby could resume normal activities within reason, and so he picked up his old routine of working in his office overlooking Shubert Alley. Now he said the apartment felt like a prison; he seemed to have forgotten how much he had enjoyed being at home. The quiet evenings ended too, as he and Rose went back to their old social life. Rose knew Bobby was trying to prove to himself that he was fine. He wanted to erase the past few months and act as if the heart attack had never happened. He finished the final draft of *Family*—except for the last scene. He still hadn't decided which character was going to sing "Carrie's Moon Song." He was even more careless about his medicine than he had been before, resenting Rose when she reminded him to take it with him when they went out. Finally, she just started carrying it herself.

Bobby continued with the Gang of Four lunches. Only now he never asked Rose to join in. He was still angry at her, but she couldn't stop trying to make him see reason. Especially since the angina attacks were becoming more frequent. And now they knew that one could be a precursor to a heart attack.

"Thank God your wife had your pills in her purse," the emergency room doctor said after one particularly scary and painful bout.

"Bobby, you've got to slow down," Rose sobbed after the doctor left them alone. "You have to accept it. You're acting like a child."

"But that's what I am. Didn't you know?"

"Then grow up."

"Leave me alone, Rose. I am who I am."

And then the day came when Rose knew there was a new Girl. It had been three years, but she always knew when Bobby had a new one. She couldn't have said how. She just knew.

ROSE LOOKED OVER at her sleeping child. All she had to do was get out of her chair, walk over to the bed, reach down, and touch one round little cheek. Then Carrie would wake up and Rose wouldn't be alone. The hole inside her wouldn't feel so deep if Carrie were awake. Rose started to stand but then she sank back. Let the baby sleep. There was nothing she could do to help Rose's pain. Not really.

He's punishing me, Rose told herself. *This new Girl is my punishment for telling him to slow down . . . and for saying his work is forgettable.* But she knew that was only a part of it. Bobby was just being Bobby, and she'd been a fool to think he'd change.

I don't know if I can do it again, she thought. *I'm not sure I can smile and pretend. I've gotten out of the habit.* But of course she had to do it again. For herself and for Carrie. *She's his daughter, I'm his wife. We can't lose him.*

She listened to the silence in the apartment. Everything was so quiet now that Bobby wasn't working at home anymore. But she wasn't going to dwell on that—or the ache in her heart. She stood up and started for the door. The soup kitchen was chronically in need of cash and she'd promised Father Xavier she'd call a few of her friends for donations. *Sometimes you can't afford to think about yourself, because you won't be able to bear your life. Sometimes you have to do things for others.*

At the doorway she looked around Carrie's ruffled pink domain. Bobby really did have lousy taste. She closed the door behind her and headed for her office, where she would try to raise some money for the soup kitchen. And wait for the new Girl to go away.

CHAPTER 32

New York

2008

THE PLATES OF ziti had been cleared away and replaced by bowls of fruit and nuts. Lu cracked a walnut,
took out the meat, and stuffed it into a dried fig. "This
is the way my pop used to fix them for us when we were kids,"
she said as she handed the fig to Carrie. They both chewed for a
moment—the figs were really good—before Lu picked up her
story again. "Bobby told me he needed to get away to work on
the last scene of his musical. He still hadn't written it."

"That was the scene with my song?"

Lu nodded. "He asked if he could go to my place in the country. 'Just for a couple of days, Lu,' he said. 'That's all.' I told him
he could have the place with my blessing. Hell, I wanted that show
so badly, I would have offered him a kidney if he'd said he needed
it." She took another nut out of the bowl, cracked it, and stuffed
another fig. "I'll never understand what was going through his

mind that weekend, why he did what he did. Bobby was careless, but he wasn't cruel. He'd never deliberately hurt Rose before. Although I had the feeling in those last few months that he was angry with her about something . . ." She trailed off and looked down at her hands. After a second she looked up again. "I'll always wonder if I should have seen it coming. If I hadn't wanted the role in his show so badly, I think I might have."

CHAPTER 33

New York

1974

ROSE SAT AT her desk, trying to compose a letter that would beg for money without sounding like begging.

"Rose," said Bobby's voice behind her. But he couldn't be home this early. He was supposed to go to her mother's house in the country to work over the weekend, but he wasn't leaving until five. She hadn't even packed his bag yet. So unless he wasn't feeling well . . . She whirled around.

"Are you all right?" she demanded. "Are you having pains? Do you have your pills?"

"Forget the damn pills!" he said. "I need to . . ." He stopped and started again. "We have to talk."

And of course she should have known what was coming. But after all the years of fearing this moment, and anticipating it, when it actually arrived, she didn't see it. "Are you leaving early?" she asked him. "I'll go get your suitcase." And she started for the door.

"Rose!" he called her back. "I have to tell you . . . I want to . . . Oh, Christ, there's no good way to do this. I'm in love, Rose. I'm in love with Sandy."

There was a wind roaring in Rose's ears. For a second she couldn't imagine who he was talking about. Then she forced herself to focus. Sandy. Carrie's nanny. Bobby was saying he was in love with a quiet little girl with mousy brown hair that was usually pulled back in a ponytail. Her eyes were . . . blue? Or were they brown? She'd worked for them for two years and Rose couldn't remember the color of her eyes.

"I'm in love with Sandy," Bobby repeated stupidly.

It was stupid because he couldn't be in love with a girl whose eyes you couldn't remember. "She isn't even pretty!" Rose blurted out.

It was the wrong thing to say—not that there was any right thing to say at this moment. Bobby looked like she'd just defiled a loved one's grave. "Sandy is sweet and good and loyal—"

"So is a golden retriever."

The look he gave her was full of pity.

"She's a child. She's twenty years younger than you," Rose went on.

"She's mature for her age."

"She's not funny, she's not charming . . . She talks with a Bronx accent, for Christ's sake."

"So did my mother."

"Is that what this is about? The great man returning to his humble roots? Save it for one of your musicals, Bobby."

"I didn't mean to fall in love with her. I didn't want to. But I've never felt like this before . . ." There was something in his voice, a tenderness—or was it joy?—that she hadn't heard for years. If Rose had ever heard it. Had that tone ever been there for her?

"Sandy makes me happy."

"Fine! Go shack up with her and fuck her brains out until you're bored with her. That should be a week from now. Then come home and we'll forget we ever had this conversation." She had shocked herself with the obscenity, but she wasn't going to back off. Not this time.

"I need Sandy. And Carrie loves her."

"If you think that little slut is going to be near my daughter again, you're crazy! Tell her never to come back to this apartment." She started out of the room, but Bobby blocked her way.

"I want a divorce," he said.

He'd never used that word before. She had never used it. Not that unthinkable, unbearable word. The room spun, and there was a good chance that she was going to be sick. She grabbed the back of a chair and hung on.

"Rose, we have to talk about this."

"No, we don't. We're married. I'm your wife." The room seemed to have settled down a bit and the nausea was slowly passing. "I put up with the cheating and the lying and your friends laughing at me behind my back. I stay home while you go out of town and screw whatever cheap little bitch you've picked up on the road. I go to bed and wait for you to come to me when you're smelling of that little bitch. I smile. And I pretend I don't know what you're doing. That's the way it's always been and that's the way it's going to stay."

"Not anymore," he said gently. The gentleness was worse than anything.

"Bobby, don't do this," Rose heard herself start to beg. "I've always been a good wife. I've backed you, and—"

"It's not about you. It's her. She makes me feel alive."

"And I gave you everything!" she screamed. "Could she hand you your career all tied up in a nice red bow? Could she turn you into the golden boy of Broadway? I made you!"

"I know. Why the hell do you think I've stuck around this long? Because I know how much I owe you."

And there it was. He had stayed with her out of guilt. She had not won him after all.

"You never loved me." She said it softly, trying to make the words stick in her brain.

"Oh, Rose." His voice was soft now too, and it was sad. Not for himself, for her. Well, he'd said he didn't want to hurt her all those years ago. He didn't want to hurt her, but he didn't want to be inconvenienced either. "You haven't been happy with me for years," he said. "Maybe not from the very beginning. We were always wrong for each other—you have to admit that."

But she didn't have to. She shook her head.

"You're still young," he went on, kindly. So very kindly. "You're lovely. You can find someone."

"The way you have." And then the age-old pathetic cry burst out of her. "What does she have that I don't?"

"She's not gorgeous like you, she's not even as smart as you are. She just . . . accepts me. She doesn't want to change me."

I don't want to change you! Rose wanted to shout. But she couldn't. Because it wouldn't be true.

"I'm miserable when I'm not with her," Bobby went on. "I can't think. I can't work . . ."

"Screw your goddamned work!"

She hadn't meant to say that, would have given anything not to have said it. Because that was when she saw him decide that this was a waste of his precious time. "I'm moving out," he said briskly. "I'm leaving now for your mother's place in the country to finish the play. When I get back, I'll come pick up my things." And now he was the one walking to the door and she was the one trying to block his way.

"Bobby, we can work this out. We have a history, we have—" She stopped short. Because he had leaned down to pick up his suitcase.

"Who packed that?" Rose demanded.

"I did."

He had packed for himself, for the first time since they'd been married. He had taken her job. Her insurance. She watched in mute horror as he picked up the suitcase and walked to the door.

"I'm sorry," he said, as if somehow saying it would keep her from falling apart. "I'm so sorry." And he was gone. From somewhere deep inside, she started to cry—a wail that hurt as it came up through her throat.

I've lost him.

CHAPTER 34

New York

2008

"AFTER BOBBY WALKED out on her, Rose came to my apartment," Lu said. She was looking off into space. "I wasn't there, and the way I understand it, she ran all over the city trying to find me. She went to George's place, but George and Davy were in the Hamptons for the weekend. She went to the dance studio where I took class, and every store I'd ever shopped in, and all my favorite restaurants." Lu sighed. "I was out celebrating because Bobby was going to finish his musical at last and I was going to have my comeback. I'd gone to a movie and I'd taken myself to Rumpelmayer's for a hot fudge sundae. When I got home, Rose was sitting on the floor in front of my door. All she had to do was knock and someone would have let her in, but she was sitting there, like a stray puppy."

"Why did she want to see you?" Carrie asked. "No offense, but after everything you've told me, it doesn't sound like you were the person she'd go to for comfort."

"No." Lu brushed a few nut crumbs off the table onto the grass. Whatever she was about to say next was something she wished she could avoid. Finally she took the plunge. "Rose thought I knew about Bobby and Sandy. She thought I'd given him the keys to my house so he could stay there and sleep with her replacement."

Carrie waited for Lu to follow up that statement with an emphatic denial.

Instead, Lu was silent. She was sitting up very straight, as if her spine were made of steel. Clearly, she was bracing herself for something.

"Was Mother right? Did you know?" Carrie asked.

Lu's spine got even straighter. "After all these years, I still can't answer that. If you mean, did Bobby or Sandy tell me? No, they didn't."

"But you had lunch with them twice a week for a year. You were a part of the Gang of Four."

"Yes. And I watched Sandy coax Bobby out of his bad moods and make him laugh. I watched her build his confidence back after he got sick."

"She was good for him."

"Yes."

"Better than Mother was?"

"Rose loved Bobby—in a way, she loved him too much. But she wanted him to be a better man than he could be. Sandy thought he was perfect the way he was."

"So his choice was mindless adoration or a woman making demands. And he went with mindless," Carrie said scornfully. Her mother might have been difficult, but she was the one who had been wronged. It seemed to Carrie as if everyone who'd known them had been willing to cut her father way too much slack.

"He needed Sandy—then," Lu said. "I don't know how long she would have lasted. And whatever Bobby needed, Bobby got. Everyone saw to it."

"Including his mother-in-law?" It was a rude question. And it was certainly one you didn't ask a virtual stranger. But Carrie didn't care. She needed to know.

"I didn't know he was planning to leave Rose," Lu said. "And I definitely didn't know he was taking his new girlfriend to my house that weekend."

"Would you have let him go there if you had?"

"No. And I told Rose that. I tried to."

Carrie could imagine the scene. "But she didn't believe you."

"It was like she'd lost her mind. She screamed that I was lying. She said I'd be his pimp if I thought that would help him finish his show. I'd go out and find the girls myself. All I could do was tell her she was wrong." Lu paused. "So she told me to prove it."

And Carrie knew that whatever was coming next was the big betrayal. This was what had sent Lu into early retirement.

"What did she want you to do?" Carrie asked.

Lu closed her eyes. When she spoke, her voice was ragged. "She wanted me to call Bobby on the phone and tell him I was turning down the show. She wanted me to promise that I'd never work with him because of what he'd done to her."

Carrie didn't have to ask what Lu had answered. Her grandmother's straight spine was sagging now; she didn't look ten years younger anymore. Carrie got up and put her arms around her, holding her. She thought she heard a sob, but she wasn't sure. "It's okay," she whispered. "It's okay."

But after a second, Lu pulled away and straightened up again. "I told her no," she said.

"You had to—that's who you are. And it's okay."

"Your mother didn't see it that way."

"She couldn't. Because that's who she was."

"Rose told me she never wanted to see me again and she ran out the door." Lu leaned against Carrie, and they sat together silently in the waning sunshine.

"I thought it would pass over," Lu went on after a moment. "I knew she'd be better off with Bobby gone, and I thought if she could just have time to find out that she was happier without him, she wouldn't be so angry . . . But when she got back to her apartment, there was a message from Sandy. Bobby had had a heart attack out in the country. He'd forgotten his medicine back at the apartment, and by the time Sandy got him to a hospital up there in the middle of nowhere, he was in bad shape.

"Sandy left as soon as Rose got to the hospital—Sandy really was a good person. And all of Bobby's friends raced up to Poughkeepsie as soon as they heard. The only time Rose left his side was when I came in—she didn't want to be in the same room with me. But once, when she didn't know I was listening, I overheard her saying to him that she was sorry because it was all her fault. Back then I thought she felt guilty because they'd been fighting and that had brought on his heart attack.

"It took Bobby two weeks to die. I went to the funeral, but after it was over, Rose said that she never wanted to see me again. She said if I wanted to have any contact with you, I'd have to take her to court." Lu closed her eyes. "She was in so much pain. There was no way I was going to hurt her any further."

"And you had all that Catholic guilt going on," Carrie said. Lu looked at her. "Because you probably did see what was going on with Bobby and Sandy but you blocked it out because you didn't want to know. You'll always feel guilty about it."

Lu allowed herself a little smile. "How do you know that?"

"It's a DNA thing. I'm familiar with guilt." They both smiled. "So that was why you quit working."

"It wasn't the only reason. Bobby hadn't finished writing his show, and Rose wouldn't let anyone else touch it, so that was the end of my comeback. And after he died, and after all the fights with Rose, I wanted to get away. I spent a year traveling—Europe, Canada, Mexico—all the places I'd never had time to see before.

"By the time I came back, Rose was doing her philanthropy gig and people were starting to notice her. For the first time she was her own person, not my daughter or Bobby's wife. I think that was what she had always needed." Lu shrugged. "What she didn't need was me."

"So you retired for her sake."

"I wish I was that good. The truth is, there wasn't any work for me; nothing I wanted. And being a performer is a funny thing— it's like exercising. It's hard to get back into it once you stop."

"And you didn't want to rain on Mother's parade."

"No, I didn't. Of course, if a terrific role had come along . . ."

"Right." They sat silently. Then Carrie said, "So what's the part of the story you left out?"

Lu straightened up. "What do you mean?"

"When Bobby was dying, Mother told him it was her fault. You said *back then* you *thought* she felt guilty because she'd had a fight with him, but you were very careful with your words and you didn't say that was the real reason. So what was the reason?"

There was another long silence, then Lu stood up. "Can we go inside?" she asked. "It's getting cold out."

It was still warm, but Carrie said, "Sure."

They walked into the house. Lu led the way into her bedroom— a choice that seemed odd until Carrie thought about it and realized that there was something safe about being in your own bedroom. Her grandmother needed to feel safe for what was coming next.

The bedroom itself was a remarkably spartan affair decorated in shades of white; the only colorful thing in it was a fussy rocking chair with faded pink padding. Lu closed the door and sat on her bed, collecting her thoughts. Finally she was ready.

"A few weeks ago, when you finally took Rose to the hospital, I wanted to see her," Lu said. "I wasn't sure how you'd react if I asked you for permission—you didn't know me. So I went to the hospital one night after visiting hours. I thought I'd have a hard time getting in, but the guard at the front desk recognized me from the old days—he was a fan. He let me in and the nurses let me sit with Rose. She was asleep, so I figured I wasn't bothering her. Then she started to wake up and I headed for the door. But Rose asked me to stay. She thanked me for coming." Lu took a deep breath. "I came back every night. Usually I just sat in the dark while she slept, and she seemed to like to know I was there. Then one night she started to talk. She told me what really happened the day Bobby died." Lu paused. She was looking old and tired again. "Rose didn't leave the apartment right after Bobby walked out on her. She went into their bedroom first."

CHAPTER 35

New York City

1974

BOBBY HAD GONE. He'd walked out the door with the suitcase he'd packed himself. At least, that was what he'd said. Rose ran to their bedroom. There was a crazy idea in her head that maybe the suitcase was empty. Maybe he actually hadn't packed, maybe all of this was just a whim. Or a cruel joke. Or . . . She ripped through his closet, checking off items in a ˙rdrobe she knew as well as her own. The green short-sleeved ˙he'd bought for him at Saks was gone, and so was the blue Turnbull and Asser—why the hell was he taking a dress ˙untry? Maybe he hadn't seen what he was grabbing ˙n in such a hurry to get away—away from her. ˙om Bloomingdale's weren't on their hanger, ˙y ones. He *had* packed. Still, Rose pawed ˙underwear drawer, gathering evidence ˙he rushed into the bathroom. He'd taken his toothbrush, his toothpaste, the electric razor she'd given him for Christmas, and the citrusy cologne she'd had made up especially for him at Floris.

I've lost him.

Rose walked back out to the bedroom and sat on the bed. And that was when she saw it. Bobby's pill bottle was on the floor on his side of the bed. Either he'd meant to pack it and he'd dropped it or he'd been carrying it in his pocket and it had fallen out. Or maybe it had fallen off the nightstand where he kept it in case he had an attack during the night. No matter how it had happened, the medicine was here in the apartment and Bobby was leaving without it. Rose picked up the bottle and raced for the foyer, where there was an intercom phone that connected their apartment with the doorman's desk in the lobby below. She knew the doorman could still catch Bobby because it always took forever for the concierge to retrieve the car from the garage underneath their apartment building. Bobby would be in the lobby or outside waiting. He had to be. Rose lifted the phone and waited for the doorman to come on the line. As she waited, she looked out the foyer window to the street below.

It seemed that this one time it hadn't taken forever to get Bobby's car from the garage. His distinctive black convertible was parked in front of the building—in plain view of the building staff and every neighbor who might be in the lobby. So everyone would know that he was in it, and there was someone in the front seat with him. A passenger they'd know because she showed up every morning at seven o'clock to start her day as Carrie's nanny. And not only was she sitting in the front seat, but Bobby was kissing her as if she were the last woman on earth and he didn't give a damn who saw them. Rose put down the phone. She turned and walked back through the apartment to her bedroom with Bobby's pill bottle in her hand. She walked past the four-poster bed she had shared with her husband for the past twelve years, and she dropped the bottle on the floor where she'd found it.

He must have those pills with him at all times, his doctor had said. She looked down at the little bottle, barely visible in the deep carpet. *Those pills probably saved his life,* the emergency room doctor had said. All she had to do was bend over and pick up the bottle. She started to reach for it. Maybe she could get it to Bobby if he hadn't driven off yet . . . If he was still too busy kissing Sandy to start the car . . . At that thought, Rose straightened up and left the bottle on the floor.

Then she ran. She ran to the front entrance of the apartment, called out over her shoulder to the maid to take care of Carrie when she woke up, and ran for the elevator. She ran across the lobby, not giving the doorman a chance to ask if she wanted a cab. She ran through the streets to her mother's apartment. People stared at her as she passed them; an elegantly dressed showstopper of a woman with red hair and beautiful green eyes, running as fast as she could.

CHAPTER 36

New York

2008

"MOTHER LIVED WITH that secret for thirty-four years," Carrie said softly.

Lu nodded. "She told me that in that moment when she decided to leave the bottle where it was, it was like she was turning back the clock. The pills were back where they'd fallen, and she'd never seen them. Then later, when she was a little more rational, she thought Bobby would realize he didn't have his medicine and he'd come back to the city. She said she wanted him to know that he still needed her to pack for him."

"But my father had a heart attack, and died."

"The truth was, there was no guarantee that the medicine would have saved him. It took too long to get him to the hospital. My house was out in the woods, miles away from the nearest town . . . a man in Bobby's condition never should have gone there."

"But the medicine *might* have kept him going until he got to the hospital."

"Yes."

"And Mother knew it."

"Yes. And she was horrified—not just because of what she'd done, but because she'd become someone who could do something like that. She decided she'd been corrupted by ego and pride and had been too invested in possessions and position."

Carrie could hear her mother saying this. And suddenly, she started to laugh. After a shocked second, Lu joined in. They laughed and laughed for a long time until the tears started running, and then they were crying and holding each other. They did that for a long time too, until Carrie felt empty, but kind of clean. Lu got them each a wad of tissues from her dressing table and patted her own makeup expertly. Carrie wasn't wearing any, so she just blew her nose.

"So Mother dumped her whole life, everything that had mattered to her," she said.

"Penance," answered Lu.

Images of her mother's radiant smile when she was working at the shelter ran through Carrie's mind. She thought about the three signature beige gowns Rose had had made for her public appearances, and the white leather scrapbook she'd kept. "I think the penance worked out for her," she said. Then she remembered sitting with her mother at Mass when Rose bowed her head and didn't go to receive Communion. "Part of the time," she amended.

"I hope so." Lu's voice shook a little. "I want to believe she was happy—at least part of the time."

"It's funny—she tried to get rid of Mrs. Bobby Manning and start over. But she couldn't escape his legend."

"Bobby had nothing to do with it. Your mother couldn't escape her own star power. All the women in our family have it." Carrie looked at her grandmother sitting next to her on the bed, but Lu wasn't bragging; she was simply stating a fact.

I wish I could have seen her on the stage, Carrie thought. *She must have been magical.*

"I'm afraid that star power skipped my generation," she said.

Her grandmother reached over to stroke her face. "Oh, the jury's still out on you, sweetie." She smiled. "I loved your chocolate truffles, by the way. When I smelled the lavender one I was afraid it would taste like soap, but it was delicious."

"I ducked out of that business."

"I'm sure you did. It wasn't showy enough for you. Come with me." She got off the bed and beckoned to Carrie to follow her into a walk-in closet. On the back wall was a safe. She opened it and pulled out what looked a manuscript bound in fake red leather. *Family* was stamped on the cover in gold ink.

"This is my copy of Bobby's musical," Lu said. "It's all finished except for that last scene. But 'Carrie's Moon Song' is there." She handed the script to Carrie. "I think it belongs to you now."

"Thank you. But what do I do with it?"

"Whatever you want."

IT WAS TIME for Carrie to go back to Manhattan. She and Lu walked to the front door. They agreed that they didn't want to lose each other. Kisses were exchanged and Carrie started down the steps of the portico. At the bottom she turned back to see her grandmother standing in the doorway, framed the way she had been when Carrie first saw her. Carrie ran back up the steps.

"I'm glad you were the one Mother told about the pills," Carrie said. "After all the years, when she was ready, you were the one."

"Yes," Lu said. "I was glad about that too."

CHAPTER 37

New York

2009

"ZOE, I WANT you to be my maid of honor," Carrie said as soon as her friend answered the phone. "Howie wants to do the whole wedding-with-a-gazillion-family-and-friends-at-the-ceremony thing, and I said yes, because I really want a big party, and I'm hoping people will be talking about this one for years, and besides, the man sold his place in Katonah for me even though he says he did it because the roses had blight and that was enough country life for him, but I know better. And I'm going to wear a white dress and a veil, which wouldn't be my first choice because I'm not exactly twenty-two, but Howie says it'll really make his mother happy, and she was so understanding about my not having an engagement ring after I explained about the diamond mining, and she was the one who found the organic farm in New Jersey where the flowers are coming from, so we don't have to worry about kids in Guatemala picking them, and—"

"Carrie, breathe!" Zoe's voice cut in.

Carrie shifted the phone to the other ear and took a breath.

"Now, about being maid of honor," Zoe said after she was satisfied that Carrie was getting enough oxygen. "Will there be any of Howie's little nieces and nephews running around dumping rose petals on the ground or carrying the wedding rings on fancy cushions?"

"What do you take us for?"

"I will not wear black; I think that's creepy at a wedding."

"You and Lu can color coordinate—she'll be walking me down the aisle."

"Okay, I accept."

"Thank you," Carrie said. A lump had suddenly risen in her throat. That seemed to be happening a lot lately. "I'm really happy, Zoe."

"I know." It sounded as if Zoe had the same lump. "When is this bash?"

"We're thinking this fall." Carrie paused, to add to the drama. "Right after I produce *Family*."

"Excuse me?"

"That's my father's musical."

"I know what it is. It's the 'I produce' part I didn't get."

"Well, I've kind of been keeping that a secret until I got everything lined up, because I've screwed up so many times before, although Lu says I shouldn't look at it that way, and . . ."

"Carrie, focus. Your dad's musical?"

"I'm going to produce it. I've never produced anything before, but I think I have a feel for it. George Standish says I do, but maybe that's because I asked him to finish that last scene Bobby never wrote. We've turned it into an epilogue and we're bringing in a new character—the great-grandmother. We wrote her as an eighty-year-old for Lu, although she could play a lot younger.

She's going to be the one who sings 'Carrie's Moon Song.' We only had to lower the key one step, and she was able to hit all the notes. It's amazing how she's kept her voice in shape all these years."

"You're going to put on a play? You?"

"Yeah. Every producer in town wants to be my partner—I mean, I've got Bobby Manning's last musical, and Lu Lawson's going to be in it, so it's a no-brainer—but I decided to go with a little theater in Georgia I heard about called the Venable Opera House. It's run by two young women; one's married to a lawyer and one is a single mother. They've been very successful with new material, and I think it will be the perfect place for us—not too big, but they are starting to get a bit of a national reputation. We'll come into New York after the Georgia run."

"Howie knows about this new career of yours?"

"He was the one who thought I should do it. I kept saying, what if the play bombs, or what if it doesn't and I bail on the producing thing like I have with everything else, and he said to stop worrying, because the world needs dilettantes. And then I said what happens if I become a big power producer, and he said he'll stay home and take care of the kids. He wants kids."

"He should have them—and that is something I almost never say about friends of mine."

"He's good for me, Zoe."

"Yes. I know."

"Mother wouldn't approve of any of this. She'd hate what I'm doing."

"Maybe."

"But it's my life now."

"Yes, Carrie. It is."

New York City

2009

THE TRAFFIC ON Eighty-third Street was heavy. Carrie paid the cabdriver at the corner and walked to her mother's apartment building. It had taken eight months to sell Rose's co-op, but it had finally happened. The new owners would take possession of the keys that afternoon, and by the end of the week they'd probably be changing the locks. Carrie had come over to check on the old place one last time. "I want to make sure I didn't leave anything when I cleaned up," she'd told Zoe.

"You're going to say good-bye," Zoe said.

"Thank you, Oprah," Carrie said.

The climb up to the apartment—according to the real estate agent the five flights of stairs had been a deal breaker for at least three prospective buyers—didn't seem to take as long as it used to. Zoe would say it was because Carrie was doing it for the last time. She opened the door and went in.

After she'd cleared the apartment out, Carrie had vacuumed the place and scrubbed everything until it gleamed; now she wandered through the empty rooms admiring her handiwork. In the kitchen she stopped in front of the spot where Rose's famous refrigerator had stood. The new owners said they were going to toss it, so Carrie had had it hauled off to the homeless shelter. It was the right place for it. She sat on the windowsill and closed her eyes.

So, this is it, Mother, she thought. *I'm not sure you'd like the new owners, but I got top dollar for this place and all of it is going to the Rose Manning House. That's what Father Xavier is calling the shelter now. I know you said you didn't want that—to have your name on it—but I persuaded him. And as soon as people heard about it, the money started pouring in. You're still the best fund-raiser they've got. The shelter is going to need every dime, because they're building a garden and a playground for the kids on the roof.*

I've done some other things you might not like, but I have to play it my way now. Bobby's trust will continue to support the Rose Manning House. I don't know if it's what he would have wanted. I don't know if it's what you would want. But I'd like to think it would make you both happy.

I started this . . . I guess you could call it a quest . . . because I wanted to know who you were. I've learned a lot about where you came from— and who you came from—but I still don't understand you. And that's okay. I'm not sure what I would have done if I were the one holding those pills while my husband was kissing another woman. I'm pretty sure I wouldn't have reacted the way you did after he died, but who knows? Lu says you were always a little operatic, no matter how hard you tried not to be. Well, what the hell, we're Italian. And you did a lot of good in your life.

If you still need forgiveness wherever you are, you've got it from me.

I hope you're at peace. The one thing I do know is, I love you, Mother. I always have, and I always will.

Carrie went back out into the living room and looked around one more time. Then she walked out the door and closed it behind her.

Acknowledgments

Always on my list is Eric Simonoff, my friend and my agent. There's no way to truly thank him for the faith and support he's given me all these years—but this is my best chance. So, thank you, Eric—for everything. And thank you to Laura Ford, who gave this book such a great edit, and who is always there for me no matter what I ask for. We've been together in one way or another since I started writing and I am so lucky that she is now my editor. Thank you to Eadie Klemm who listens and reassures, and, when all else fails, commiserates in a way that always makes things better. Thank you to Libby McGuire for support that is rare in this business, and to Jane von Mehren, who is now taking me and my books on a whole new journey. Thank you to Robbin Schiff for the gorgeous cover, and to Dennis Ambrose, who takes care of the things I miss that make such a huge difference—and for managing to be the most patient man on the planet. Thank you to Brian McLendon, Lisa Barnes, Kim Hovey, and Katie O'Callaghan for working their magic in getting out the word about *Serendipity*.

Thank you to Cynthia Burkett, who is the kind of rock-solid

friend you hope for but so seldom find, and Charlie Masson, who is always there no matter what, and Gerry Waggett, who manages to say the right thing every time. Thank you to Margaret and Barbara Long, whose generosity hits a surreal level, to amazing Betsy Gilbert, and to Ellie Quester, and Emma Jayne Kretlow, whose enduring friendship makes life worthwhile. Thank you to a special new friend, Rachel Pollak, who won my recipe contest and then went on to become a kind and caring email buddy and a one-woman band for my books. Thank you to Kathy Patrick, who is a one woman band for writers everywhere. Thank you to Jane Ryan, who listens endlessly to the stories and to the staff of the East Fishkill Library, especially Cindy Dubinsky and Kathy Swierat. And thank you to Ellen Tanenbaum of the Dover Plains Library, who provides chocolates and sunflowers as well as great talk.

Thank you to the women who continue to inspire me and make me proud to be one of them: Mary Minnella, Phyllis Piccolo, Virginia Piccolo, and Jessie O'Neil. And thank you to Albert Piccolo for reminding me always of the power of faith. You are all my heroes and have been throughout my life. Thank you to Carolyn Rogers, who is a new hero—someday someone needs to tell the story of your smarts and strength. Thank you to my stepsons Colin and Christopher, who are the incredible perk I never expected and couldn't live without, and to Annalisa—if I ever grow up I want to be you—and Bee and Iris, who are safety nets in more ways than I can count. And, as always, thank you to my sisters, Lucy and Marie, and my brother, Brad.

And I'd like to end by remembering my cousin Claudia Glassman, who left such glorious footprints in the sand.

Serendipity

a novel

LOUISE SHAFFER

A Reader's Guide

A Conversation with
Louise Shaffer

RANDOM HOUSE READER'S CIRCLE: Your background is unusual in comparison to most authors'—you were a soap opera actress and then a TV writer. What made you want to start writing novels?

LOUISE SHAFFER: The smart-aleck answer is, I was over forty and I wasn't about to have knee surgery. That's what we call it in show biz when an actress's PR person announces that she's taking off for six weeks to fix an old dance injury, and when she comes back those lines on her face have disappeared. Sometimes her knee works better too. Anyway, I wasn't about to do that, and landing jobs was getting harder and harder—okay, it was impossible—and I still had to make the mortgage.

But that's not the whole story about my switch. I'd always loved writing and telling stories. When I was a kid they worried about my grasp on reality—in fact, some of my nearest and dearest still do, because I love the imaginary worlds and people I get to create when I write. It's probably the closest I'm ever going to get to playing . . . well, not God, but a really powerful person. In many ways, I like writing better than acting because these are my stories and my characters and I get to say what I want to say. And no one in publishing has ever, ever suggested that I should have knee surgery.

RHRC: Which character in *Serendipity* felt most natural to create? Whom do you identify with most?

LS: Oh, Lord, that's such a good question. And the answer is, all of the characters were natural for me. But then, my characters always are. As an actress, I was trained to find something I could identify with in every character I played, and believe me, it was fun trying to find, say, your inner Lady Macbeth. So when I started writing, I realized that every one of my characters is me—sometimes in ways that I don't even recognize. And then, one of the perks of the whole writing thing is that some of my characters are also the person I'd like to be. Lu, for instance, is a huge musical comedy star, which is what I always dreamed of being when I was a teenager. Other kids of my generation listened to . . . well I don't know who they were listening to, since rock and roll left me cold, but I was swooning over Ezio Pinza singing "Some Enchanted Evening."

RHRC: *Serendipity* is a different novel from your others. What made you shift settings? And you so vividly capture a New York City that no longer exists. What is your relationship to the City?

LS: Thank you for saying that about my vision of New York City! I come from the tri-state area, and when I was a kid the only place I wanted to live was Manhattan. When I was growing up I visited it all the time with my folks to see theater and opera. When I was in my teens I studied acting in New York, and when I moved there in the seventies I couldn't believe my luck that I was actually living in what I thought was God's country. I floated around for years just feeling privileged to be in a place with so much diversity and energy. I still feel that way. To me, New York is a magical place where something wonderful can happen to you anytime just because you are there. And if the miracle doesn't come along on a given day, you can still get some fabulous dim sum for dinner. I love New York City. I want to go back there—but not while I have so many dogs and cats.

RHRC: You've now written four novels. What is your writing process like? Do you have a set routine? What inspires you, and what do you do when you get stuck?

LS: I guess I do have a process—it's evolving, so I don't really notice it, but it's there. I always have a story I want to tell, which is usually some sort of spin on my own life. Then I create characters who are believable doing whatever it is that happens in the story. At least, I have to believe they'd do it. Then I play out the consequences of what they did.

As to specific routines for writing, I wish I were that well organized. Basically, I kind of wander around the house talking to myself until I feel like I've got the plot worked out, then I spend a lot of time emailing to ease myself into my writing head, and then eventually I get scared about my deadline and I just start doing it. The first few days are the worst. I tend to fall asleep a lot at the computer. The weird part is, I love to write. So I don't know why I dance around it so much. When I'm stuck, which happens a lot, I stop trying to figure out what I want to do next and go clean the kitty litter. Most of my big breakthroughs come to me that way. I think it's because it's an activity that gets me away from my desk, so I can't keep on beating my brains out, and yet it's not the kind of activity I really want to focus on, so my right brain gets a lot of latitude to play around. When I'm working—especially on revisions—I have happy cats with exquisitely clean litter.

RHRC: Complicated relationships between mothers and daughters have come up in a few of your novels. What interests you about the dynamics between the generations?

LS: That's a great question because I was about to say that I don't write about complicated mother-daughter relationships and then I realized that, yeah, I do. Talk about not recognizing a piece of yourself in what you write. I just think mothers and daughters are so important to each other: Your mom is your role model as well as your parent. You learn how to be a person from both of your parents but you learn how to be a woman from your mother. For so many of us, the dreams and the hopes came from our mothers—the ones she told us about, and the ones we inherited from her without her knowing she was passing them down. In my case, that setup was heightened by the fact that my father died when I was young so my mother was an even stronger influence on me. And I'm fascinated by the question of how much of what we are is in our genes. I guess I find it very romantic to believe that certain traits are handed down in families. It sort of puts us and all our attempts to control things in perspective. And I like that.

RHRC: Do you plan out your story lines before you sit down and write them, or do you see what happens as you go along?

LS: I plan, to an extent. I need to know before I start writing how it's all going to end. And I need to know what I hope the reader will get from the book—beyond a good read. That's a sneaky little trick of mine; I always have a message I want to get across—but

since I don't believe it's my job to preach, I try to slip in my opinions in a way that you can ignore if you want. And I usually have a
plot twist in the middle that everything hinges on and I need to
know what that's going to be and how it's going to work. But I
don't always know how I'm going to connect all the dots and get
from point A to point B. And I will never write it all down because
if I did that, then I'd feel locked in. And I want to pretend that I'm
this free spirit. Although actually I'm probably pretty well struc-
tured when I work.

RHRC: Which authors have influenced your work, and who are
your favorites?

LS: For so many years I read southern authors because I was writing southern books, so that does color this list a little. I love *To Kill
a Mockingbird*, *Cold Sassy Tree*, and anything by Pat Conroy, Rick
Bragg, Maya Angelou, or Russell Baker. Every once in a while, I
still take a trip back to Louisa May Alcott. Then I have the authors
I love for light reading and escape: Georgette Heyer, Philippa
Gregory, Harlan Coben, Janet Evanovich, Sue Grafton, Sara
Paretsky, Dave Barry, Carl Hiaasen, and P. G. Wodehouse. I
started reading Wodehouse when I was a kid because I saw my
father—who was not a very demonstrative man—laugh out loud
when he read Wodehouse, and I figured any writer who could get
that kind of a response from Dad had to be really funny.

I'm not sure how any of these authors have influenced my writing except that I like to have a mystery at the heart of my books
and I love books with some kind of historical context. And humor.
I really hope readers get a laugh or two when they read my books.

RHRC: What are you working on now?

LS: The next book is going to be back in Vaudeville again. I love that genre because as far as I can tell it really was the entertainment of the American melting pot. You had all these kids from all these different ethnic backgrounds doing their thing. And I'm going to be writing more about a favorite theme of mine, which is second chances. And strong women. Also, this time I want to explore a love story more fully—romance always pops up in my books but it usually isn't the engine driving the story.

Questions for Discussion

1. How has Carrie's past affected her decisions and ability to choose a life path? Which characteristics does Carrie share with Rose, and how are they different from each other?

2. Shaffer is known for creating well-developed, convincing female characters. Which of these women did you most identify with? Sympathize with? Disagree with?

3. Carrie's best friend, Zoe, states that Carrie has "mommy issues." Why do you think mother-daughter relationships are often so complicated? How do you feel about the way Rose raised her daughter?

4. Why does Rose hold back so much family history from her daughter? How does Carrie's eventual discovery of what happened affect how she perceives her mother?

5. Rose is a complicated, dualistic character with a love-hate relationship with wealth and fame; she is constantly telling Carrie to be wary of one's ego. What, in your opinion, made Rose shun her

lifestyle after Bobbie's death? Do you think her choices made her happy?

6. What do you make of Rose's multiple copies of the same dress? What was her reasoning behind this?

7. How does Mifalda change over the course of the novel? How do you think she came to her decision regarding Lu and her new baby, and could you imagine doing the same thing in her position?

8. How do you feel about Lu's picking career over family? What other sacrifices do the women in *Serendipity* make in their lives? What betrayals do they make?

9. What attracts Rose so deeply to Bobbie Manning? How would you characterize their relationship, and in which ways does it change over time? Why does she go to such great lengths for him? On a similar note, what attracts Carrie to Howie?

10. How does Shaffer use ice skating as a symbol, for both Mifalda and Rose?

11. Carrie asks herself "Why do I always feel like I'm settling for an empty basket when I want one that's full? Why can't I let myself be happy?" What do you think the answers to these questions are, and how do you envision her future at the end of the book?

12. "Mama, Lu, and Rose," Carrie's uncle Paulie states, "standing in a line. Three young girls, handing down all the good and bad from one generation to the next. They couldn't get away from each other." What did each woman pass down to her daughter?

What role does family legacy play in this novel, and is it portrayed positively or negatively?

13. One of this novel's themes is that women can't do it all—career, family, love—successfully. Today, many women seem to be revisiting this idea. Do women have to choose their priorities? What about men?

14. If you were casting the movie *Serendipity*, whom would you pick for actors?